JONATHAN LEVI

A Guide for the Perplexed

Jonathan Levi graduated from Yale College in
1977. He received a Mellon Fellowship to Clare
College, Cambridge, where he was a cofounder
and subsequently U.S. editor of *Granta*. He lives on
the Upper West Side of Manhattan with his wife
and three children.

A
GUIDE
FOR THE
PERPLEXED

A NOVEL BY

JONATHAN LEVI

VINTAGE CONTEMPORARIES

VINTAGE BOOKS

A DIVISION OF RANDOM HOUSE, INC.

NEW YORK

FIRST VINTAGE CONTEMPORARIES EDITION, JULY 1993

Copyright © 1992 by Jonathan Levi

All rights reserved under International and Pan-American Copyright
Conventions. Published in the United States by Vintage Books, a
division of Random House, Inc., New York, and simultaneously in
Canada by Random House of Canada Limited, Toronto. Originally
published in hardcover by Turtle Bay Books, a division of Random
House, Inc., New York, in 1992.

Library of Congress Cataloging-in-Publication Data
Levi, Jonathan, 1955–
A guide for the perplexed: a novel / by Jonathan Levi.—1st Vintage
Contemporaries ed.
p.   cm.—(Vintage contemporaries)
ISBN 0-679-73969-6 (pbk.)
I. Title.
[PS3562.E8878G8   1993]
813'.54—dc20   92-50606
CIP

Manufactured in the United States of America
10 9 8 7 6 5 4 3 2

For Stephanie

CONTENTS

A GUIDE
FOR THE PERPLEXED

. . . in most treatises on the violin, a great deal of attention is paid to the manufacture of the Perfect Sound. The author strains to pass on to the student his own experience of Technique which, in combination with that indeterminate quality called Taste—and the proper instrument, of course—will infallibly produce the Perfect Sound.

These teachers are putting the bow before the horsehair, holding the fiddle with their teeth! The proper concern of both teacher and student, before bow ever touches string, must be the Origin of the Perfect Sound itself. For how will we recognize our Sons if we don't know our Fathers?

—Sandor, *In Search of the Lost Chord, A Brief Guide*, p. 3

PREFACE TO THE NEW EDITION

Dear Reader,

You are traveling. You are perplexed. You want to know.

Not just which restaurant serves the strongest margarita, the freshest *chirimoya*, the tenderest tenderloin, the most incendiary vindaloo; not just which hotel room cradled Napoleon, Babe Ruth, JFK, Liz Taylor, and Jim Morrison; not just which beach boasts the softest sand; which island the most perfumed breeze; which city the most lyrical opera, the tallest women, the broadest burlesque, the most compelling philosophers, the lowest average humidity and incidence of pickpocketing.

You've come to the right place.

I am the one who comes up with two on the aisle, a box for the seventh game on the first-base line, a mosque in Provo, a fifth of Jack in Jedda, a last-minute ticket (upgraded to first class) on the sold-out plane to your mother's funeral. I am the one who moves your great-aunt's porcelain without breakage, your miniature schnauzer without suffocation, your cares without delay. I know the schedules. I write the schedules.

But be warned. There are no itineraries in this *Guide*. No three-hour signposted walks, no *routes touristiques*. No train schedules. No seasonal weather maps. No stars, bars, rosettes, toques, forget-me-nots, forks, or chopsticks. There are letters from readers, occasional opinions, bits of history. Subjective, subjective—I'm the first to admit.

The current *Guide* contains a series of letters from three

women facing a common dilemma in the south of Spain. I introduce this latest edition, however, with a note from an old friend, an old traveler, a puzzle that has introduced so many editions past.

Dear Ben,

I grew up in a country at war. I learned in school and at home to love my land, its trees, its flowers, its flag. When I was old enough, I fought alongside my brothers and cousins to protect the borders from our Enemy to the North. Later, as both sides tired of endless fighting, I was asked to negotiate a peace. I traveled to the North, and was treated most luxuriously and with the greatest deference. In the course of my mission, I had occasion to taste rare meats, bathe in the ocean, and fall in love several times.

When I returned home with a treaty, I was hailed by some as a hero. But others, to my surprise, greeted me with a certain scorn, as if my interests were no longer theirs, as if I loved my country less for having been abroad.

Shortly thereafter I was sent by my government to negotiate a peace with our Enemy to the South. Once again I received a splendid welcome. I dined on fruits that rid the body of fatigue, on nuts that rid the mind of care. I drank wines full of fabulous histories and wisdom, and lost my heart more times than I can count.

When I returned home, with a settlement far better than my countrymen had dreamed of, I barely recognized my neighbors, so ill did they treat me. Without unpacking my bags, I set off on private business to the West.

I have been traveling so long now that no land is new, no ocean fresh. I have seen every flower, every bird, every side of every issue, and no longer have a heart to lose. I returned to my country once to find that our old enemies to the North and South had moved south and north. Strangers were living in my town, in my house. They greeted me with open arms.

I no longer have enemies. I no longer have friends. I set

down roots, but the sun drives me away. I wander, but the
moon laughs at my back. Where shall I go? How shall I go?

To this traveler, to those of you who have been traveling for
five days, five hundred, five thousand years, I dedicate *A Guide
for the Perplexed*.

Ben

ITINERARY ONE

AEROPUERTO

PLAZA LA RÁBIDA

MERCADO

VILLA GABIROL

HOLLAND—DUTY FREE

8.00 P.M.

Ben Darling,

To see Cristóbal Colón is to see the dim future of travel. Everything about it is new, newer than new—an airport designed by teenagers, illuminated by dental surgeons, accessorized and fragranced by antivivisectionists, and musicked by reliable descendants of the Grand Inquisitors. Halogen, zirconium, french curves. Everything shines, everything reflects, everything flows.

Iberia, BA, and the rest of the Majors have yet to stick their big toes into the hottest tarmac on the Costa del Sol. Only the Torremolinos packages and the Marbella-bound super-specials like Air Flamenco and British Armadan have cut their Mylar ribbons and chamois-milk brie. Which is all very much what it is, seeing that my flight is an hour late. Nonetheless, sculpted chairs, adjustable table tops, and Conchita's coffee almost write my last review for me.

But before the review, the real discovery—Sandor is In The Can.

Not just the interview—Histon and Duxford flew that back to London yesterday. Eight hours of evasions and half-truths, the kind of doddering, pedantic, overwhelmingly charming nonsense you'd expect from a seventy-nine-year-old hermit. On his Youth in Peru: "A tune on my fiddle bought a packet of cigarettes, a packet of cigarettes bought an hour with a girl, and an hour with a girl bought a measure of Paganini." On his Departure to Europe: "The last time I saw Lima was from the back of a tramp steamer hauling jute from Conchin through the Panamá Canal." On Why He No Longer Plays the Violin: "Ask my fiddle."

In my can lies the real Sandor, the unheard Sandor, thirty-one minutes of Sandor playing the Bach D Minor Partita, his first performance *for anyone* in seventeen years, played for me and the Spinoza Portacam, its PanaTrac lens drawing every bit of light from half a dozen candles and the moon, a barely touched stuffed pheasant, courtesy Sandor's remarkable María, an empty bottle of Marqués de Riscal, and two over-sized snifters of the Grand Duke on the fountain behind Sandor, both backdrop and sudden inspiration for the signal event, too precious a reel to entrust to any airport, thank God some clever soul invented telescopic wheels.

Sandor and Bach. And what Bach! Perhaps, as in the bad days of the early nineteenth century, Bach unplayed, Bach that had been lying dormant, ruminating at a barely viable temperature in its fugal sac. A German Bach and a Spanish Bach. A Brandenburg Bach and a post-Holocaust Bach. The Mathematical Bach of the Six-Part Fugue, the Acrobatical Bach of the sixteen children. The dark poetry of the Allemande, the insistent tussle of the Courante, the stately striptease of the Sarabande, the breathless Gigue around the four-poster, and finally 272 relentless bars of Chaconne—a theme repeated and a theme repeated, sometimes solitary and self-satisfied, sometimes layered in an orgy of quadruple stops, the melody soaring on top, pounding below, squeezed by the staff, tickled by arpeggios into lacy underthings, throbbing, gasping, squeaking, mewling, a brief pause in D major for a smoke, and then six more variations in search of a climax.

Hungry?

LA ROSA NÁUTICA

La Rosa Náutica is properly approached on foot by a narrow pier leading from the parking lot on the beach of El Palo, approximately 4 km (2.5 miles) east of town. (There is also a small landing for private boats on the seaward side.) The building is constructed in the octagonal shape of its namesake, the Compass Rose, with the pier providing the traditional extra length of the Due North leg. A circular bar, reputed to feature the widest selection of Spanish brandies in the country, fills the middle of the restaurant. A spiral staircase at the bull's-eye leads down to the subterranean kitchen, a structure that dates from at least the end of 1491, when, legend reports, Columbus huddled with ten advisers to plan his final assault on the purse of Ferdinand and Isabella.

Sixteen tables ring the restaurant. Ask Abbas, the Moorish maître d', for West-Southwest with its mixed view of the Mediterranean, the port, and the gardens of the Gibalfaro above the city. The decor is early nautical slum, designed to bring nostalgic tears to the heavy-lidded eyes of the Piraean shipbuilders and Saudi arms dealers who are the restaurant's most dedicated patrons. Planked tables (white linen optional), pewter flatware, leaded glassware. Nets, antique spyglasses, and astrolabes hang from the conical ceiling next to worm-eaten chandeliers ripped timely from some galleon graveyard. And everywhere snailshells and musselshells, bits of lobster and saffroned rice, swept up every half hour or so by a posse of flamenco-playing gypsies.

My companion had a five o'clock plane to New York, and my appetite suggested only a light lunch before my own flight a few hours later. We ordered the Zambra de Mariscos, a fresh assortment of lightly fried shellfish. A basket arrived that must have held two kilos of cockles and mussels, starfish and winkles, squid, octopus, sea urchin, crayfish, crab, lobster, scallops, and giant sardines the size of bread knives, all fried in an olive oil that smelled of wood smoke and sherry. With time to waste on a bright December afternoon, Mediterranean finger food can be masticated at leisure. The basket faded slowly, as did two bottles of brightly chilled Campo Viejo.

Expect to stay at least two hours and to pay what you would a high-class masseur. Cash only, credit cards not accepted.

Submitted by H.

A little note—don't include this, Ben—but Sandor introduced me to the owner, Santángel, a tall, soft-eyed greybeard (couldn't possibly be Spanish!). He intimated there was a documentary in the history of the Rosa Náutica, but with a certain forceful nonchalance (is that really possible or am I just a sucker for soft eyes?) that reined in my Ugh-Reflex—something about Columbus and the Expulsion of the Jews. I told him, ever so politely, that we had all the footage we needed on that particular subject, care of a Sephardic filmmaker in Kentucky. Of course, he said. He himself was an amateur historian, and was preparing "something modest" for the Sephardic Pavilion at the '92 World's Fair in Sevilla. If only I had more time, I said, demurring like a bitch. But Santángel was all manners, and sent over Abbas with a bottomless plate of *alas de mariposas,* butterfly wings—exquisite crescent-shaped hazelnut biscuits.

Superb restaurants, Ben, throughout Andalusia. But, of course, you know. Why do you value my retelling? Which one of us is preacher, which one convert? What's in it for you?

Three hours later, Ben Darling.
A Question: Why do I always buy Carlos III when in Spain?
An Answer: Because all other Spanish brandies are named after useless battles and royal shits.
· "Cardenal Mendoza"—Yenta of Spain. Hooked Isabella with Ferdinand, Columbus with his boats, the Church with the Inquisition. *¡Muchas gracias, Mendy!*

- "Gran Duque d'Alba"—Cut off every towhead in the Netherlands. *¡Qué tal macho!*
- "Lepanto"—Picture it. October 7, 1571. A fine, cloudless, mezzotinto Thursday of a morning. Philip II of Spain (and half the longitudes of the known World) and Pius V, Pope of the Catholics (and the Jews and the Lutherans and the bloody Jehovah's Witnesses for all I know), send the floating, leaking Christian might of Europe to drive the Ottoman fleet from Cyprus. Cyprus, for bloody-sake! They sit around bobbing on the Med like Bush and Gorbachev in a Maltese bathtub, hundreds of men drown, thousands are maimed, including the author of *Don Quixote*—although not badly enough to keep the lifts of the twentieth century from playing endless nasal oboe passacaglias of "The Impossible Dream"—collectors of Titian, Tintoretto, and Veronese make a mint on oil and canvas Lepantos, and then two years later the Venetians give the greasy little olive grove back to the Turk!

That's why I stick to my Carlos—Carlos Tres of Spain. Son of Philip V and Isabella of Parma. A truly enlightened despot. A man of Faith within Reason. Swapped Florida for Havana, put the Inquisition in its place, helped negotiate American independence from Mad George. All that and less than ten quid a litre, Duty Free.

My flight is late, Ben. Very, very, late.

I could have stayed in Mariposa. Sandor offered me the run of his villa. But all those years at the BBC trained me to view every story as having a beginning, middle, and end in that order. It would have broken every rule to return to the set for a retake.

While I've enjoyed making friends with Conchita, who has kept coffee in my cup and roving businessmen from my table, the steady stream of happy travellers shop clerks to Tangier, secretaries to Palma, curious girls on convent trips to Tenerife, none of them quite the right age—has dwindled to a trickle. I have finished my Fay Weldon. I have finished the Fay Weldon I was saving for the plane.

Step Four of my System for Dealing with Delays is to locate the Ladies', which is normally adjacent to Duty Free, as if the architects who specialize in the mechanical design of Waiting have practised the sport with greater concentration than we mere commercial travellerettes—and thank God for the cosmopole who created the universal symbols for peeing, the only successful use of Esperanto south of Finland.

Of course, the Spanish *Señoras* is only this side of two footprints and a hole, even in the freshly unwrapped Aeropuerto Cristóbal Colón, so brand-spanking new that when I saw two sinks were stopped up and a third bled brown water, I attributed it more to the surprise of opening than to sabotage— the five seats in a state of wide-mouthed astonishment that their doors had not yet arrived. I generally don't care whether my habits are witnessed, but I still have enough of a social conscience that I prefer to transfer Carlos III from flask to thermos in the private confines of a stall.

It must have been well on to 8.00 P.M.—I was in the Ladies' for the third or fourth time, adjusting my lipstick in preparation for boarding—when the Tannoy crackled on. Three flights were called to board, two charter and another regularly scheduled British Armadan direct to Stanstead, all leaving after my 8.45 departure.

Out in the corridor, the video screens were no more helpful. British Armadan Flight 802 had disappeared. I wasn't immediately concerned, veteran of the infamous Stanstead–Isle of Wight connection that I am. But I felt one of those five-cup-o'- coffee sweats coming on, until an immensely cheerful modern Spanish woman—no doubt rewarded with a job at Colón after eight years of refuelling Piper Cubs in the Estremadura— popped up from behind an unlit Information sign. She plugged my question into her chic little Minitik terminal and ten seconds later handed me a chic little printout.

" 'Flight 802—Weather Delay at Destination'?" I asked her. "Then why is Flight 41 scheduled to depart on time to Heathrow?" Another slip of paper—"Flight 41—On Time."

"You are now going to ask me, Señora, when Flight 802 is scheduled to depart," she said to me in prettily accented English. "I am afraid I have to tell you I do not know. But do not fear, when it is known, it will be announced." I trudged back to the coffee shop. Efficiency is disarming.

At 10.00 P.M., when I should have been gazing down at the lights of Bristol, Conchita brought me a note with a cup of coffee: "Flight 802 delayed until 11.00 P.M. Intermittent weather. Apologies. Srta. Alicia Zacuto."

"Intermittent weather," Conchita asked me, "is it very bad?" At 10.45 I returned to the counter. Duty Free was deserted. The shop hawking Seiko watches and Hermès scarves was shuttered and dark. A pair of businessmen took the final dive of the day into the Encyclopedia of Booze. The whiskey clerk flicked off the lights in her stall. Señorita Zacuto had disappeared. In her place, a man in a military uniform.

"Are you Information?" I asked him.

"What do you need to know?" He sighed, looking around my shoulder with the nonchalance of a Spaniard who is not attracted to the woman he is attending.

"British Armadan, Flight 802. Can you please tell me its rescheduled time of departure?" He pecked at the keyboard, all the time his eyes on some distant point. The Minitik terminal beeped. He sighed.

"Flight 802?" he asked. I nodded. "Perhaps the Señora has made a mistake. Please check your ticket." I did. I had not. He punched Minitik again, another beep, another little white slip. "British Armadan Flight 802—No Such Flight."

I looked up sharply. There was something about this military man that looked familiar and out of place—Spanish but not quite, military but in uniform alone—like Rod Steiger playing the Mexican bandito in *A Fistful of Dynamite*.

"Where is Señorita Zacuto?"

"I do not give out such information."

"She told me an hour ago that Flight 802 not only existed but was delayed by weather conditions."

"Then you are certainly better informed than I." He smiled, all oil and no more questions.

"Please." I smiled back, with no need to win, only to fly home to the gas fire of Kensington Gore. "Could you check Flight 41?"

"Whatever you wish, Señora." He pushed. It spat. I took the slip. The flight was leaving in ten minutes.

"Please"—I smiled again—"can you change my ticket, give me credit, whatever, and get me on Flight 41?"

"But, Señora . . . Holland?"

"Holland, *sí*," I answered, with the all-purpose matter-of-factness I employ when I have no wish to defend my singularity of name.

"Señora Holland," he apologized with the merest whiff of sincerity, "how could I possibly change a ticket for a flight that does not exist?"

"Fine." I pulled out my wallet in defeat. "Give me a seat on Flight 41. First Class." There is a rule I learned in my assistant days called the Law of Jammed Film. If there is anything wrong when you sign out a camera, Do Not Attempt to Fix It. Get a new camera. Get a new cameraman. Leave the country.

"Ah, Señora, it is our fault," he said with his Rod Steiger smile, "but the airport is not yet equipped to handle credit cards. Perhaps you have traveller's cheques?" I looked at my watch, turned around, and ran to Duty Free.

Armed with another demi of Carlos—paid for with my unravelling ball of toy money—I wandered in search of unjammed Information. Fifteen minutes later, and none the wiser, I was back at the Ladies' doing my flask.

I was puzzled, not cursing you, not yet. I have relied on your travel suggestions for what, almost fifteen years, and have always been pleasantly surprised by the small serendipities, the upgrades, the complimentary champagne and caviar, the side trip to the diamond merchant, the room with the best view of the old Moorish Quarter. But this delay was out of character, perfectly understandable with any other travel agent, but for you, as rare as a decent cup of airport coffee. I took an unladylike, uncoffeed swig in front of the painted tile. I wondered whether the man in the military uniform was correct, that Flight 802 was No Such Flight. I apologize, Ben. I doubted.

"¿*Qué lindo, no?*" Conchita was standing at my shoulder, appreciating the mural across from the mirrors.

"*Sí,*" I said, for want of any better response to the surprise.

"I am very proud of this picture, Señora Holland," she said. "The artist copied it from a painting in my home."

"Really?" Again, I was at a loss. There was, in fact, a mural painted on the tile, reflected in the long lipstick mirror. I hadn't noticed it before, but then, the picture was not particularly beautiful. A seascape, three boats, three women on the shore waving handkerchiefs, a few shacks. The blue was dull, the red crosses on the sails garish, and the focal point of the mural a smouldering ruin on a hill, charred and frankly hideous.

"It is Colón, who you call Columbus, the discoverer of your country, no?"

"No," I said, "I am from England." But now, at least, the picture made a certain amount of sense. "What is the ruin, Conchita?"

"I am sorry, Señora, but I do not know. That part was not in my picture." She picked up her bag. She had changed out of her waitress uniform into a rather striking black sheath, with a reasonable slit up the outside of one thigh. Her hair had fallen out of the elastic waitress net and been caught up by a palm-sized emerald comb. Otherwise, she was all black and red. I hadn't realized how truly attractive.

"Your work is finished, Conchita?"

"*Sí*, I must hurry to meet my *novio*. We have a meeting, and then a concert. Would you like to join us?"

"That is very kind of you, Conchita," I said, "but you forget. I am here to catch a flight."

"Oh no, Señora, there are no more flights tonight. Everything is closed." Conchita looked at me and my flask.

"You must be mistaken," I said, and then the Tannoy crackled on.

"We regret to announce that British Armadan Flight 802 has been unavoidably delayed due to weather at the destination. The new departure time is seven o'clock tomorrow morning, December 31."

"You come with me. You like flamenco?"

"Thank you, Conchita," I said, "but I think I will try to get some sleep. You never know with these flights. Sometimes they take off as soon as the weather lifts."

"As you wish, Señora." Conchita shrugged. "But there are no sofas in this section of the airport. You must return through Passport Control. Good night." An attractive girl, I thought, as she turned and her skirt rode up to show a bit of Iberian peninsula.

The trickle of remaining passengers shuffling through Passport Control bore out Conchita's message. All seemed hassled, tired, confused. One older woman struck me as less perturbed. I followed her towards an unmarked door.

"Excuse me," I called, "Flight 802?"

"Yes?" Luminous blue eyes, round, whites as bright as the halogen lighting, a face as wrinkled and soft as a chamois cloth, surrounded by wayward strands of stone-white hair. "If you want to claim your baggage," she said, without waiting for any further questions, "come with me." It was a rough voice, brusque, impatient, filled with the gravel of unfiltered cigarettes and travel. It was an American voice with a hint of something else behind it—more than the stray foreignness that many solitary travellers cultivate. The hurry, the strangeness, the familiarity, the luminosity—of course, Alice's White Rabbit!

"Do you know what happened to Flight 802?" I asked her.

"No!" she said, and I expected some mollifying hypothesis instead of the minute investigation of my hair, my ears, my scarf, my blouse.

"Then what makes you think . . ." I began, adjusting this and that about my person. But just at that moment, a flicker of light shot behind the scraggle of the woman's hair, from the second level of terrorproof glass on the Spanish side of the balcony overhanging the Duty Free Lounge.

It was the silver tip of a violin bow, a Torte perhaps—although I never acquired the same ability to identify instruments as I did music—attached to a slender hand, attached to a solitary violin player. She was not a tall girl, but had a full-arm vibrato, very Russian school, and laid her cheek on the chin rest, one eye peering over the bridge up the strings to her left hand, down through the glass to my gaze, only twenty feet away. With the slope of her cheek just disappearing around the dark side of the fiddle, with her brown hair long, the way we all wish we could wear it, dipping below the floor from my vantage point, with her picador nose and single eye, she was the reason Picasso was born in this quarter of Andalusian gypsy country.

My own violin studies never survived adolescence. But in preparation for the film on Sandor, I watched so many hours, so many weeks of footage of Heifetz, Milstein, Elman, and, of course, Sandor, that I developed, at first, a kind of perfect pitch, where I could hear a note on the violin merely by seeing the position of the left hand on the neck and the angle of the bow on the string. Later, as my knowledge of the repertoire expanded, given fifteen seconds of videotape with the sound turned off I could beat all but the greatest fiddlephiles at Name That Tune. There were exceptions, of course. Itzhak Perlman, with a mitt as big as Muhammad Ali's, reaching and stretching and groping for every note like a wolf spider from an eternal third position in the middle of his web. And then the prodigies, the five-year-olds with the full-size Amatis, playing impossible stratospheric exercises because their tiny arms couldn't reach past the f-holes.

But the girl on the bulletproof balcony, sixteen, perhaps seventeen years old, was in perfect proportion. She began with an F, an octave and a fourth above middle C. A long note, even though I had missed the upbeat of preparation, the swing forward of the elbow, the contact of the downbow. As the F stepped carefully and deliberately down the carpeted stairs of E and D to a long C, the White Rabbit's voice melted into the familiar tones of the continuo, the regular ebb and swell of the second movement of the Bach Double Violin Concerto in D Minor as played by, say, the Academy of St. Martin-in-the-Fields under the direction of Neville Marriner. Turning away from the girl, away from her fingers, looking out the far window to the light of the moon on the Mediterranean, I could still hear the B-flat, A, pass to the drawn-out mordent around the lower F, back to B-flat, the roll of the harpsichord glancing off the crests of the waves, the thrum of the double bass tugging on the lights of the runway, the elegant modulation like a raising of the spirits, lifting the chin, the eyes, up to a higher vantage point, the scale down, the G, F, E, D, leading with such hope and necessity that, turning back to the girl on the balcony, I expected to see the first violin appear at its famous entrance, expected the holy note, the exquisite high C, expected Sandor.

No Sandor, of course. I had driven him to the airport from La Rosa Náutica. I had seen him strut across the tarmac with his precious Guarneri, climb the stair to the Tristar, watched the plane taxi, take off to the south, and turn into the sunset towards Gibraltar and Carnegie Hall. No other violinist either. Why would some young beggarita choose to play the second violin part alone? Why not a solo sonata, a partita, a local folk tune, a *malagueña*? What brief and tragic partnership ended when the first violinist's plane lifted its wheels off these Spanish shores, leaving the young girl alone with her descending scale, her G, F, E, D, leading with hope and necessity to an inevitable silence?

"Last chance," the old woman snapped.

"But the flight will be leaving," I said, half an eye still on the girl. "Aren't the bags on the plane?"

"Suit yourself." She pushed through the door. Up on the balcony, the girl was gone. I voted against Rabbits and trickled back through Sheep Control.

The pandemonium of Flight 802 barely touched the empty hangar of the departure lounge. I had my pick of telephones. I rang through first to Sandor's villa. No luck, María probably asleep. I doubted, after our behaviour in the last ten days, disrupting her routine with cables and cameras and endless pots of Spanish roast, whether she would welcome me back in Sandor's absence. The concierge at the Hotel Mayor apologized graciously over the phone. My suite had been given up, and he doubted whether any other hotel room "of a reasonable class" could be found, as a shoe convention had just occupied the Plaza de Toros.

So I dialled the number of your Mariposa office. Your machine, your machine, *encore* your machine. I left a message, in the vain hope that you'd ring in and find me, wherever I'd kip down tonight. I wish we'd hooked up, Ben. At least for a drink.

Other passengers, mostly families, were queuing for vouchers and boarding a coach to the Youth Hostel, 10 km west on the coast road. A few businessmen were jockeying for an international line out to Jolly Olde E. Four couples, the men in designer windbreakers, the women, Benetton cardigans draped over their shoulders, local Socialist millionaires on their way to the Harrods sales, had settled down for a few dozen hands of hearts, an aluminium shaker in the middle of the table and a pile of plastic airport martini glasses. Half a dozen Spanish students in Union Jack T-shirts were drinking wine from a *bota* and playing reggae music from a buzzbox at the foot of a giant plastic Orangina. No girl, no violin.

I arranged the right combination of armless benches with decent cushioning in a deserted aisle near the seaward window where the radiation was least harsh. Shoes, handbag, wheels collapsed, precious Sandor on the bench, Issey Miyake jacket folded above, head weighing all down, I clutched my handbag to my chest, took one last look at the moon over the sea, voiced one last profanity at the customs officer who had separated me from my beloved Charlie Three, closed my eyes, and began to think myself to sleep.

I saw myself watching Sandor in the Moorish courtyard, hundreds of years older than the rest of the house, arcades finished by delicately arched cypress transoms, low olive trivets topped with hammered copper trays, thick carpets and pillows everywhere embroidered with episodes of the Moorish occupation, from the retreat of Charlemagne at the battle of Roncesvalles to the tears of Boabdil mourning the surrender of Granada. In the center, a simple fountain weeping into a pink granite pool.

And Sandor, like an Arabian knight in his ever-present caftan, all sixty-four bantam inches, dark, compact, wispy grey hair blowing away from his head in the windless sanctuary, eyes closed, lashes resting on unwrinkled cheeks, violin parallel to the ground, bowtip balanced, well-rosined horsehair flat on the G string, wrist firm, little finger raised in balance, index tensed, all in anticipation of the first upbow.

As I drifted, Sandor grew, the years falling into the pool at the base of the fountain. The woman watching Sandor became the beggar girl on the balcony, more child than woman, perched on the Siege of Granada, legs gracefully tucked beneath her, long hair curving behind a shoulder, under one armpit and around into her lap, back so grenadier straight, eyes so wide open you'd think she'd never seen a man play the violin. And I tried, in my dream, to lift her chin in one hand, to peer under her eyelids, ask her a question, to be sure, to be sure.

A voice crackled, "Ladies and gentlemen . . ." I blinked and stared at the ceiling. No Moorish stars, only pre-stressed concrete. "Ladies and gentlemen. We regret to inform you that the United Andalusian Workers of the Air have announced a strike at the Aeropuerto Cristóbal Colón. We are sorry to have . . ." and then another sound of banging metal and heavy chanting. I sat up. Thirty feet away, a phalanx of cleaning ladies and pilots, visa stampers and dishwashers, Duty Free clerks and tile scrubbers, were marching on my position. Conchita in her black sheath led the way like Victory, wing in wing with—God forbid, could he be her *novio?*—the anti-helpful military man, banging on dustbins, overturning benches, armed with broom handles and hoover hoses, chanting vaguely heard slogans. I grabbed my bag, my jacket, jumped into my pumps, telescoped my wheels, and blinked desperately to locate the outside door. A strong hand grabbed my arm.

"Help me and follow . . ." It was my White Rabbit, the lady of the grey hair and the chamois skin, with an oversized steamer trunk of Marx Brothers vintage. One hand on my wheels, the other on a strap of her trunk, I stumbled over the abandoned buzzbox and kicked the overturned martini shaker across the lounge, the roar getting louder, the workers tripping us with their mops, throwing cartons of Duty Free Gitanes at our backs, picadors goading us past Bureaux de Change and Bikini Stands, around giant Fundadors, me trying to keep Issey Miyake between my teeth, and thirty-one minutes of Sandor upright. My shoulder, tortured by the weight of the Rabbit's trunk, shouted to be heard above the roar. We ran. We ran from sheer sound, from the union Concorde taking off at our heels, past the desks of Air Flamenco, Air Oporto, Air Divine, searching for any exit from the noise. Finally swinging the trunk through a double door, up into the fetid, jet-fuelled, real night air, only for the dying roar of the workers to crossfade into the unbearable attack of a dozen unseen aircraft, camouflaged underbellies, otherworld silhouettes, shrieking down at us from the hills, until the blast, the explosion into the pit of my stomach and then out the same way, punching me down behind the trunk with a forecast of hail and shrapnel and airport refuse, but only the fallout of motion-becoming-sound as the sonic boom of the fighters—cryptic hieroglyphs close enough, but too fast, to read—erupted overhead and flowed over the airport, down the beach, into the Mediterranean. And me, peering up, somewhat abashed, on scraped knees, as my White Rabbit hurled the trunk single-handedly into the boot of the last taxi, as Conchita rammed a broom between the handles of the outer doors, shrugging her shoulders as if sympathy would pick me off the ground, as the Aeropuerto Cristóbal Colón on the Costa del Sol—with easy access to all major European destinations—went suddenly, totally, black.

HANNI—CHOOS AND CHURROS

Dear Benjamin,

In 1935, my parents, both direct descendants of Moses Maimonides, received an engraved invitation from the Alcalde de Córdoba to an eight hundredth birthday party. I was a skinny nine in Mrs. Benning's fourth-grade class at P.S. 145, and too young, in Spanish eyes, to skip school or stay up for a party. But to my mother, it beat lunch with Eleanor Roosevelt.

"Look, Papa," she said, "an apology."

Poor Mama. She always believed there would be an apology. In 1290, Edward I expelled the Jews from England. Cromwell apologized, and the Jews returned. In 1306, Philip the Fair expelled the Jews from France. It took the Revolution, but the French invited them back.

"Fourteen ninety-two was a mistake," Mama explained, "a failure of imagination. Isabella had to pay for Columbus's expedition. She couldn't think of a better way than to expel the Jews and confiscate their property." From a framed watercolor above my bed, Columbus's three boats sailed out of Palos de la Frontera, leading a flotilla of other less-seaworthy craft filled to the rails with sad-eyed Jews. Although the centuries following the Expulsion were pockmarked with the occasional efforts of needy politicians to bring wealthy Jews back onto the peninsula, the bishops prevailed over the bankrupts, and the Jews were kept out.

"Columbus Schlamumbus," Papa said, and I tended to

agree with him. "If the Spanish really wanted to apologize, they'd have sent the boat fare."

Mama never returned.

I did. In '44, eighteen years old and geographically naïve, I was seduced over the border by a musician. Even then, I spent under twelve hours on the peninsula, and was back in Vichy by noon. Afterward, firm resolve, never again! They told me that after Franco died life returned—a rabbi was invited to lecture in Barcelona, a synagogue reopened in Córdoba. I should care, who never went to college, who never set foot in a synagogue? As Papa said—forget the apology, send cash.

Until the business of the Esau Letter. After Leo died—how wonderful to write that word, "passed" being the required term in the condo, as if you moved out of South Glades Drive and into the North Miami Beach Funeral Parlor in gown and mortarboard—I was worried that some of my wiring upstairs might start to crumble. But it wasn't for another fourteen years, until 1989, when I left London and moved back to the Home of the Brave, that I began to forget, and worse, to remember that I had forgotten. Memory—the black lung of Miami Beach. Twenty-seven percent of my condo has Alzheimer's. Don't tell me it isn't contagious.

It was barely six weeks ago, a quiet pre-Thanksgiving morning. I was up in 9H, drinking Sanka and talking about this and that with Gershon Mundel while his wife was out shoplifting at Burdine's, when we got onto the subject of Miami zoning restrictions. I told him that since my parents were second cousins—in-breeding being one of the few foibles the Jews share with racehorses and Spanish nobility—they had a common ancestor, the first European settler of Miami. Gershon politely inquired when that might have been. I told him, and went on to describe the cross-fertilization with the Indians and the conversions. I was well into the story of how, by 1495, my great-great-ancestor Esau had filled enough swamp and taught enough Hebrew to hold the first minyan on the North American continent when I noticed Gershon's eyes searching for the telephone.

I told him, no, no, don't call the white jackets yet, I have written proof, and took the stairs two at a time down the fire exit to my apartment. When Gershon knocked an hour later— my bank books, my journals, my junior high school diploma, all my paper possessions laid out in a grid on the living-room rug—the Esau Letter was still unfound. He suggested that we eat a little something. I opened a can of mushroom soup but insisted that he sit down with a pad and pencil and help me work out when I had last seen the Letter.

When I moved from London to Miami? No, I'd only assumed it was in the brown satchel with Papa's other papers.

When I married Leo? Definitely not. We married out of such desperate need—in 1950 I was still searching for something far more important—that by the time it occurred to me that we had never had a courtship of late-night schnapps and autobiographical recitation, the moment had passed, and Leo was dead.

The fall of 1977, when Sonny rented my front parlor? It seemed likely he would have been interested. But I could not picture the two of us in the green room with the bay window and Leo's pianola, me sitting next to Sonny on the fold-out sofa, Letter in hand.

"Zoltan!"

In a single breath I told Gershon of that suicide, forty-six, forty-seven years ago, in Port Bou on the Spanish border, high above the Mediterranean. How Zoltan had undoubtedly died with the Letter among the other forged papers I had given him. How the Letter, wrapped in a purple ribbon, stuffed in Papa's portfolio, must have bounced on the stretcher alongside the lifeless body of my virtuoso lover, down a rocky goat path toward the hospital in Figueras. Gershon fed me a spoonful of cold soup.

Sonny called the next night, as he does once or twice a year,

from Ft. Lauderdale, Orlando, an airport phone somewhere.
My old brain was still full of the Letter, and Sonny was very
comforting, assuring me that a document as valuable as the
Letter would certainly have been saved, even by Franco's
stone-stupid border police. Fascists and the Catholic Church,
he said. They burn copies, but they file the originals away for
a rainy day. The Letter must be around, he said. And probably
in Spain. A note arrived a week later, with a list of a dozen
names of priests, scholars, and collectors throughout the country, and a suggestion that I write to you, dear Benjamin, and
book a trip immediately.

Your arrangements were faultless. Irún to Burgos: the train
was punctual and comfortable—the conductor moved me to
First Class, thank you very much. Burgos to Salamanca: shared
a compartment with a woman my age and her grandchildren,
aged seven (the boy) and five (the girl). Sweet, I suppose, though
I've lost all patience with anything under sixteen—they turned
up their noses at my orange; I still dream about fruit, fresh,
canned, rotten, bruised, or artificial. Fell asleep to their voices,
a song I remember hearing in '44, on the rainy night we tried
to sleep in an olive grove outside a tiny refugee camp. The girl
sang:

> *"El sol se llama Lorenzo,*
> *Boom da da, boom da da, boom,*
> *El sol se llama Lorenzo,*
> *Y la luna, Catalina,*
> *Boom da da, boom da da, boom."*

Then the boy:

> *"Cuando Lorenzo se acuesta,*
> *Boom da da, boom da da, boom.*
> *Cuando Lorenzo se acuesta*

Catalina se levanta,
Boom da da, boom da da, boom."

The old days, when Lorenzo never set on the Spanish Empire, are thankfully *vorbei*. They tell me Lorenzo has been rehabilitated, that in the latest climate of tourism he has passed from devil incarnate to patron saint of the dustbowls of Castile. You can't drive into a travel agency in Florida without getting mugged by that neo-Miró of a Spanish travel poster—the kindergarten letters, the ESPAÑA scrawled haphazardly across Lorenzo's grinning face.

Why Lorenzo, why Catalina? Why not Abraham and Sarah? There's a question for the readers of your *Guide*.

I don't know which is worse—leaving Spain after two weeks without the Letter, or being kept from leaving five hundred years after being expelled. Still, no complaints—I don't suppose you have any control over wildcat strikes by Spanish airport workers. I can't blame Sonny for his list of recommendations. Maybe Don Lucho did have it in Burgos, or it was sitting all the time in Salamanca in the safe of Dr. de Salas, or the mattress of Doña Carreres, the great-great-grandsomething of Ferdinand the Catholic. Maybe none of them liked my looks, despite the color of my traveler's checks. Maybe I need a better map. Maybe I need to bury my obsessions. Is there room in your steamer trunk?

I am, in fact, relieved to move from a quest of my own to a task for you. Although, Benjamin, when you wrote suggesting I carry a package to the Dominican Republic in return for my airfare, I didn't expect a package the size of the Ritz. Even the attendant at Baggage Claim was shocked that any man would give a woman such as myself a ticket to a trunk such as this.

Still, I will follow your orders to the letter. I am a woman of great, severe independence. But I have always known that I am happiest, that I am at my best, my most successful, when my independence is strictly, knowledgeably, faithfully guided. It's about time, with the rest of my traveling, that I see a bit of the Caribbean. It might as well be in the company of your steamer trunk.

Our super Roberto is a Dominican and guarantees that I will adore Sosua. He used to play professional baseball, for Cleveland or Pittsburgh or one of those other godforsaken Ukrainian capitals. I caught him one day swatting aluminum Metrecal cans with a mop handle into the dumpster outside the Activities Room. He gave me a demonstration of the batting postures of the great Dominican ballplayers—Manny and Jesús, a pitcher named Walking Underwear.

"Ancient Dominican game," Roberto confided. "Baseball before Columbus, way, way, before." Everyone around the condo has his own personal time bomb. I promised to keep his secret.

He told me New Year's Eve in Sosua ought to be festive. The town is so small that there are only two parties, one for the people who are willing to march through the cane fields to dance at the Town Hall, and one for those who aren't. As a foreigner, I will be invited to both, claims Roberto, and I will undoubtedly meet your contact. I can just see myself wandering down a muddy goat path from the Town Hall to the other party, with your trunk on the back of a burro.

My burro at the airport tonight was one particularly flighty model—one of those New Women who started taking over England in the early eighties when gender was denationalized. This one had Unmarried Journalist tattooed all over her exposed parts—camera on a trolley, Palestinian scarf (100 percent raw silk) wrapped a little too Amelia Earhartily around a too-long neck, soft corduroy jumpsuit (another memento from Qaddafi's bunker), and a self-enclosed look of naïve confusion when I passed her my best MittelEuropa baggage tip before Colón went on strike. Luckily, at six feet she had enough

Anglo-jump and Saxon-bicep to lug one end of your trunk out of the airport and into a taxi.

I left her lying flat on her shoulder bag outside Colón. A squadron of fighter planes—ours? theirs?—overflew us (that's the condo term) as soon as the airport workers ran us out of the departure lounge. I'm from the generation to whom the sound of planes overhead is the sound of rescue. My poor lady journalist must have had a Southeast Asia assignment somewhere in her past, filming Hanoi Jane for David Frost—who knows what horrifying matinee shot into her retina at that moment. I felt bad leaving her on the pavement, but it was late, and the last taxi, and rain was threatening, and by the time the driver could hear me over the roar of the fighters, it was too late to stop. Besides, I hate journalists.

I asked the taxi driver to head for the Casa Curro, where I was sure the manager would give me back my old room. The driver told me there was a choo choo convention in town, and that the Curro was undoubtedly full. He dropped me at the Huéspedes La Rábida instead and suggested I talk with the night maid, Maraquita, and mention his name.

Maraquita was no maid. The Huéspedes La Rábida, as you well know, is a bordello, pure and simple, and the taxi driver, long gone, is another Iberian imbecile. No matter, I told Maraquita, if you have a room to spare I will take it and reimburse you for the lost business.

"Impossible, Señora." She smiled. "There is a chew convention in town. Even if you could afford the cost, you would get no sleep, and worse, I would feel guilty." Indeed, the line of well-dressed men with shiny shoes, stretching past her desk, through the inner courtyard and up a flight of wooden stairs in the dim distance, was neither patient nor quiet. The moment called for dramatic gesture. I sank down on the trunk and pulled out your *Guide*. The effect was instantaneous.

"Señora," she said, moving me away from the comments of

the customers into the office behind the desk, "you are welcome to stay here. You will not sleep, but I have television and coffee, and the boy has just run out for *churros*."

An office! The couch was a lightly upholstered remnant from the sixties with the Ilums Bolighus tag still on the arm. Two Louis XIV–repro side tables held a pair of Chinese lamps. Maraquita drew me coffee from a stainless steel samovar and tuned the TV—every bit as big as Mr. Samson's in 12E, who made his fortune in cable—to a remarkably clear rerun of *Roots* dubbed into screechy Castilian. Everything in beige and chrome, not a flake of whorehouse red.

"A furniture convention last spring." Maraquita beamed at my approval. "I took payment in trade."

Two of the customers lugged your trunk into the office. I tried to tip them, but they raised their hats and handed me their cards: S. Jaime Carranque, BigFoot, Lima; Ryszard Koksacki, Shoe Coup, Krakow. I offered coffee, but they begged off with more-pressing business. A couple of real gents. I almost forgot I was in Spain.

"About that book." Maraquita closed the door on Messrs. Carranque and Koksacki.

"Do you know it?" I asked, handing your *Guide* up to her. She backed away.

"Of course, I know it. Everybody knows it," and her accent on "know" seemed a comment on how few appropriate words there are in English to convey what the Spaniards think of your *Guide*.

"You aren't by any chance . . ."

"Of course I am, page 34." And sure enough, there she, or rather her establishment, lay.

HUÉSPEDES LA RÁBIDA

In the Old Spain of long engagements and formidable duennas, serenades to unseen señoritas and sex supervised by sextons, establishments like the Huéspedes La Rábida carried out a noble and necessary function. Much as the picador initiates the bull in the art of the game, sapping the beast of his vital spirits before his encounter with the inevitable matador, so have the ladies of La Rábida prepared scores of Mariposan men for the Spartan hardships of the Spanish connubial bed.

One legend has it that La Rábida reclines on the site of a tenth-century Moorish bordello, the first established in Spain after the landing of Tariq at Gibraltar in 711. Another popular story dates from 1498. That was the year in which Cardinal Ximenes, Queen Isabella's confessor and later Grand Inquisitor, ordered all Spanish clergy to refrain from the common practice of concubinage. Despite appeals to Rome and Isabella, the better part of the ecclesiastics obeyed. Four hundred monks from Andalusia, however, fled to North Africa with their "wives" and turned Muslim. And a small group of disgruntled friars from the monastery of La Rábida—which had sheltered Christopher Columbus only six years earlier, before his first Voyage of Discovery left the Church and carted their concubines across the marshes of the Coto Doñana to the site of the current establishment in the center of Mariposa Antigua.

Among the patrons reputedly registered in the guest book, carefully locked away daily by the proprietress, are Ernest Hemingway, Pablo Picasso, Miguel de Unamuno, Francisco Goya, Pope Alexander IV, and Ferdinand V, the Catholic, King of Aragón and Castile.

In the New Spain, the house has become infested with Germans and Japanese on well-financed Sexspielen and Labu-Tripu. To the extent that Mariposa can boast a red-light district, Huéspedes La Rábida is at its scarlet heart. This may explain its popularity with conventioneers, although the house discourages British clientele, especially coach tours. The girls are generally well maintained, with most hailing from the region, suffering neither from the severity nor the wit of the Big City.

You will also pay less at La Rábida than you will in Madrid or even Granada. The difference in price is reflected in the decor. The rooms are functionally appointed, lacking both the picturesque antiquity of the novels of García Márquez and the big-hearted Catholicism of Graham Greene. This may come as a disappointment to the non-Spaniard, who equates the function of a bordello with fantasy and adventure, who requires the Chinoiserie of one room, the rawhide of another, the chalkboard and ruler, the lace, the ribbons, the fresh-baked smell of buttermilk biscuits.

This is a Spanish whorehouse! Enough with form, enough with ceremony, enough with ritual and dignity! Those are for courtship, marriage, and widowhood! The function here is Aristotelian: pure, complete, cathartic.

Tel: (39) 492 291. 33 Plaza La Rábida. Reservations not accepted. From 1,500 pesetas upward, safety equipment provided. AE, MC, Visa, Diners Club, Traveler's Checks.

Submitted by S.Z. (with additional comments from P.P., E.H., and B.H.)

"Not a bad recommendation," I said, with the slight conviction that had more to do with my ignorance of these places than my judgment of your critique.

"Ben doesn't recommend," Maraquita said. "He comments."

"Isn't the fact you are listed a recommendation?" I asked. She smiled.

"How do you find Ben, my dear Hanni?" I hadn't remembered introducing myself to Maraquita, but it was late and perhaps I had. I said a few nice things, of course, Benjamin, more curious to hear the sound of her voice.

"I've never had the privilege." If a three-hundred-pound middle-aged madam could look coy, Maraquita would have been stuffed there and then, with eyes full of the question, "Have you, dear Hanni, met the boy?"

"Never," I said, and I saw her relax immediately. "But I owe him."

"Even though he's left you stranded in the middle of the night in a Mediterranean whorehouse?" Maraquita rested back against a teak veneer doorjamb. I closed the *Guide*. "Why not call him? His office is right here in Mariposa. Ask him how he plans to get you out of Spain."

"Certainly there will be a flight tomorrow," I said, and stood, feeling I had worn out my welcome with either argument or gullibility.

"Certainly?" she said. "There was a strike, no?"

I sat down. I stood. I sat down. I opened your book and looked for your phone number in Mariposa.

"Forty-six, sixty-five, thirteen," Maraquita said. "Dial nine to get an outside line." And she left me alone.

I'm always reluctant to phone travel agents when I'm in a jam, when it's less a question of planning and more a question of screaming for help. But I phoned you. For all the good it did. That synthesized message of yours with all its preplanned options—press "1" if you need transportation information, "2" if you need hotel reservations, "3" for daytime entertainment, "4" for nighttime. I tried "1," and then "1" again for airplane, "D" for departure, "8" for Aeropuerto Cristóbal Colón, "12" for the month of departure, "30" for the original date, "H-A-L-E" for the first four letters of my last name, "H" for the first initial of my first, "M-I-A" for the city I called from to buy my ticket, but by mistake I pressed "M-1-A" and the recorded voice, more obsequious and scratchy than that of the worst day nurse on the Beach, apologized that the code I had dialed was incorrect, and hung up. My own fault. Never should have screamed.

I flipped the channels on the TV   only one other station broadcasting after midnight, a talk show, with what seemed to be either two transvestites and a magician or three local politicians. I understand Spanish through French, and Andalusian through hand signals and grimaces.

I took out my map and found the Plaza La Rábida.

My comedian of a cabby had driven me around the statue at the center several suggestive times—what a beacon for the red-light district, a fifty-foot column topped by Columbus. But we had somehow bypassed the Teatro La Rábida. How thoughtful of you, Benjamin, to include a flier with a translation of this month's schedule in my copy of the *Guide*.

TEATRO LA RÁBIDA

"Because All Men Desire Happiness"

Shows at: 20.00, 22.15, 00.30, 02.45. Program changes daily.
Closed Fridays

December 1991

1. Morocco Bound
2. I Am Curious—Basque
3. Inside Isabella
4. Autoerotic-da-Fé
5. Inside Lola Falange
6. CLOSED
7. The Golden Rain in Spain
8. Tilting at Windmills
9. Rocky of Gibraltar
10. Extrema Dura
11. The Lewd of Kima
12. Venus in Monteras
13. CLOSED
14. Lez Is Moor
15. Cris and Izzy
16. Carmen Whore

Is this what pornography has come to, Benjamin? Not that I am an authority. (I have, in fact, gone once, or should I say *only* once, on a date with a Gestapo officer in '42, *Heisse Hebräische Huren*—how could I forget?) But the titles in the old days used to be literal, bare of irony and illusion—Corn Flakes was Corn Flakes.

I'd seen *¡Adiós, Colón!* at the Hampstead Everyman back in the sixties (although that isn't pornography, is it?), and I wish I'd been here on the 18th to see *Naughty Anarcho-Syndicalists*. Nevertheless, I was intrigued that this being the night of the 30th, although several minutes already into the new day, the Teatro La Rábida had planned a rare program of *echt Kunst*. And *Flamenco Halevy* no less, not that I knew the company, but what a name!

So I breathed in heavily through my nostrils, the way Gershon Mundel's yoga instructor—he's fighting Parkinson's—has instructed him, and, with my measured exhalation, decided not to worry that my flight had been delayed, not to spend all night on the phone to your office, on the phone to the airport in the

hope that the strikers had gone back to work, not, in short, to
kvetch. I walked out. Maraquita shrugged—the trunk would be
perfectly safe. I passed the boy on the stairs and relieved him
of a *churro*. Halevy Ho!

Under the sconce above the outer door I took my bearings.
Lorenzo was long set. I was glad to have my cardigan and a
warm piece of dough to munch—although *churro* can't hold a
candle to kipferln. A trio of American sailors chatted on the low
seawall across the street. Below the column, Columbus presumably secure on top, a violinist played through the sound of the
distant waves. Across the plaza, six golden lanterns lit up an
arcade below the gilded sign of the Teatro La Rábida. My
watch read 12:45. I was slightly late. Not at all, I reminded
myself. I am off my itinerary.

I had almost passed the violinist when I was ambushed by
sound and memory. The song she was playing—for it was a
she, a very young she with thick dark hair, a seductive pout to
the lips, and just the tiniest fold of baby fat where the chin met
the violin—flashed a sudden, vivid image of Zoltan, Zoltan the
violinist, Zoltan on the train. I had heard a great deal of violin
music since—Leo was a particular fan of Henryk Szeryng—
but not this, and not played as if I were still in my private
boxcar recital hall, rocking gently through the green-veiled
innocence of the Auvergne, with Zoltan standing above me,
rolling quietly through his entire repertoire. Forty-seven years
ago, this piece of music had rescued my mind from politics,
distracted me, for a few golden moments, from the danger of
our journey. It was a slow movement, a handful of notes, each
one simple, together weighty with a fully lived youth. I remember thinking that this piece was written for me, about me,
eighteen years old, my own long hair long since bobbed, my
own short life already well beyond experience.

But to find the composer, the title to fit the sound?—my
Alzheimer's again. I was sure I hadn't heard the piece since my
marriage to Leo. So it couldn't have been Mendelssohn or

Bruch—Leo had a thing for Jewish composers. Bach was the strongest candidate. Leo hated Bach with an irrational but immovable passion. Play Leo the most obscure cantata, the organ snatch that hadn't seen daylight since Bach wrote it for a bygone Sunday, and Leo would snort that guttural name from the least attractive *barrio* of his throat.

So Bach, in all likelihood, but which Bach? Bach of the partitas, Bach of the concerti? Zoltan didn't mind playing without accompaniment, the clicking of the train wheels over the splices of the rails was orchestra enough. The incessant, obsessional Bach, that was for sure, although the girl played with a depth and a concern for each note that painted Zoltan's own profile down to the fine droop of the eyelashes and the concentration of the lips. Or maybe not obsession, but confession— Zoltan playing out his own failure, measure by measure, through the repertoire, coaxing his sins out the narrow f-hole that was his talent.

He had failed. I could see that the moment Frau Wetzler led him into our flat on Iranische Strasse. My duty was to escort this failure to the Pyrenees, where he might find the safety to try again. But each click of the train wheels made it more and more difficult to hang failure around the neck of this wonder. Here was Success itself, every note proof of Man's triumph over God. By the time we jumped from the boxcar at Port Bou, I believed to the depth of my eardrums that as long as Zoltan continued to play the violin, we would win the war.

I was right, of course—that stretcher disappearing down the goat path to Figueras. I had lost Zoltan. We had lost the war. All that remained was the clicking of wheels to the east.

The music stopped. The girl stood shyly, the violin tucked under an arm, the bow dangling from long fingers toward the ground, her eyes lowered. I groped for my purse, struggling to cross the tracks to 1991, wondering if this was the proper response, or whether I was interrupting some fantasy of the house of La Rábida. Then I heard the click.

I turned, expecting a stiletto, or, worse still, the re-enactment of a nightmare of half a century ago in godforsaken southern Spain. It was My Lady Journalist. My Lady Journalist with her clicking trolley and her Palestinian scarf, crossing the cobble-stones to the arcade of the Teatro La Rábida. I watched her disappear through the double doors and took my second deep breath of the night. I turned back to the girl with my hundred pesetas. She had vanished.

I looked up at Columbus, vaguely searching for what? A violin, a Zoltan? The Explorer stood, peering out to sea, to the west, holding a robe, a toga, a map. The moon, a cold winter Catalina, floated naked above him. Out where he looked, even the sailors had gone, all was darkness. I held my *Guide* closer, and turned to the lights of the arcade.

HOLLAND—PHARAOH'S DAUGHTER

FAT MAN

Ay, ay, ayaaaaaayyyyyyyyy . . .

(throat squeezed through a buttoned-up size 0, no
collar, jacket too tight for shirt, sleeves for arms,
trousers for thighs, socks for ankles, words for heart,
so squatting just milli-inches above a terrified chair
in the narrow tunnel between the burning dust of
the theatre's footlights and the golem of the singer's
own shadow, drawn like the monstrous cave paintings of La Pileta on the half-curtain of burlap bags
and clothesline)

> *Cada vez,*
> *Cada vez que considero,*
> *Cada vez que considero*
> *Que me tengo que mori* . . .

STIFF MAN

(stately, cool, flamenco, nothing moving but his
fingers on the guitar, three dignified beats alternat-
ing with two, the Spanish signature—alone with
your lover for a single measure, then watched, then
left, watched, left, always denied—until the Fat
Man remembers that one day he must die)

Bum beelee um-bum dung,
D-e-e-e-e, d-e-e-e-e, d-e-e-e-e,
D-e-e-e-e, d-e-e-e-e, d-e-e-e-e,
Bum beelee um-bum dung.

FAT MAN
¡Tiendo la capa!

(and his hand seizes the back rail of the guitarist's chair)

¡Tiendo la capa en el suelo!

(and gives it such a shake that, when the guitarist, firmly nailed to the planks of the stage, moves not an inch, the ripple reverses itself back up the Fat Man's arm, igniting face, neck, voice, rage)

¡Y me jarto,
Y me jarto de dormi!

AUDIENCE
(short men, tall men, men in tan safari jackets, men in once-tweed work caps, men with golden teeth, men with sunken cheeks, men with yesterday's, today's, tomorrow's beard, men of twenty, thirty, forty, seventy plus, men half-asleep, comatose, dying, coughing, crossing, uncrossing their legs, arms, removing caps, replacing caps, scratching, all the time scratching. All men)

Shout, grunt, stomp,
spit, bang the seats
built more for leering
vagrants than flamenco
aficionados, cough, clap,
cough again, encouraging

the damage, the scar
tissue breeding like rot
on the larynx of the
singer, in order to
communicate that, when he
remembers that one day he
must die, he spreads his
cloak on the ground and
flings himself, flings
himself, with the weight
of songs past and future,
on the hard ground of the
sierra, the pavement of
Mariposa, the vinyl sofas
of the Aeropuerto
Cristóbal Colón.

STIFF MAN

(still stately—*one*-two-three, *one*-two, *two*-two, *three*-
two—still dignified—*one*-two, *two*-two, *three*-two,
one-two-three—a man I could love)

Bum beelee um-bum dung,
D-e-e-e-e, d-e-e-e-e-e, d-e-e-e-e-e,
D-e-e-e-e, d-e-e-e-e-e, d-e-e-e-e-e,
Bum beelee um-bum dung.

AUDIENCE

¡Ándale, ándale!

(Men pushing, men forcing. All men. Except for my
White Rabbit, how did she get in? Standing at the
back of the stalls, the light from the lobby making a
halo of that wisp of hair, men standing back, men
pointing, whispering. Sans steamer—I hope she was
mugged until her voice box bled)

TRANSLATION
You'll sing it till you sing it right.

Ben Darling,

When I directed "Flamenco: Gypsy Rip-off or Jewish Rite?" for WGBH's thirteen-part *Wide World of Ethnomusicology*, I collected enough audiotape for thirty-five CDs and never once thought of Sammy L. and my first time in Granada.

But this town at midnight, this odd, crumbling La Rábida, spawns odd, crumbling memories.

Granada, fourteen years ago, running away from the strangest, half-imagined love affair of my life. I ran to Liaden, my sister, my well-upholstered, super-capable, ultra-fertile lifesaver of a sister. Normally, it would have been a five-minute hop from my nest in Hampstead to her hive in Temple Fortune. But Liaden was in the midst of an uncharacteristic loss of nerve, and had fled too much husband and too many children for the sunshine and solitude of Andalusia. So I had to express-coach the width of western Europe in search of sisterly wisdom and a cup of tea.

I arrived in Granada with an overnight bag and a scribbled address on the inside cover of an Iris Murdoch. After an hour's search, I located the house and rang the bell, listening hopefully for the jolly-hockey-sticks hello of my sister. What I found instead was a lanky, bearded, forty-year-old hippie, in torn cutoffs and sleeveless vest, pouring watered-down sangría for half a dozen middle-aged American women on tour from Council Bluffs, Iowa. He hadn't the slightest idea where my sister was. But he found me a chair, poured me a glass, and told a story.

Sammy L.—so he called himself, not Sam, not Mr. L., and certainly never Samuel—had been, among many other things, a long-distance lorry driver. He had been cruising along, popping pills and listening to Wishbonc Ash at something in excess of eighty-five per, when Liaden left six semicongealed yolks on a frying pan and ran onto the North Circular Road just south of Henly's Corner. Although he was three days late on a run from Aberdeen to Ouagadougou, with a full load of something too common in Scotland and too rare in Burkina Faso, Sammy L. pulled over and made room for my sister, who, full-breasted and wild-haired, bits of jam and cellotape clinging to her cardigan, was irresistible. In under thirty-six hours, Sammy L. forded the Channel, drove the length of France and Spain, sold the trailer to a wholesaler in Madrid, the lorry to a gypsy collective in Santa Fé, and put down a three-month deposit on a courtyard with three rooms and a cypress in the Moorish Albaicín of Granada.

The good women of Council Bluffs applauded enthusiastically. I crawled off to a bedroom and collapsed.

Liaden finally rang, two days later, from a public telephone in Temple Fortune, her voice conspiratorial and exhausted. After two weeks of glorious inactivity, Sammy L. had committed some crime aboard some boat in some port. Only a bribe, posted by Liaden's husband, had saved Sammy L. from the unspeakable horror of Spanish prison. There had been a quid, of course, for the quo. Liaden returned home to children, Cheerios, and chicken pox. She was sorry she couldn't help. She would ring again when she could. I decided not to tell her I was fifteen weeks pregnant.

Gradually, we made accommodations, Sammy L. and I.

He spent his days out, working "the tourist trade," as he called it. I spent my days on the patio working Elizabeth Bowen and sunning my growing tummy. I hadn't shared a house with a man or any other living thing since my divorce. Our occasional intersections—cups of coffee, World Service broadcasts—suited me fine. Granada suited me fine. I would wait.

One night, it must have been May, close toward eleven P.M.,

Sammy L. brought my shawl to where I was sitting, legs tucked under me, very comfortable with *The Little Girls* or *The Hotel*, and announced that we were going out.

I had walked the streets with Sammy L. before. There were rules, accommodations. He never forced me somewhere I would rather not, or away from curiosity. My feelings were short of Trust. But his business was navigation, after all. I let him guide.

Our house was only steps up from the *río* Darro, lazy and quiet even in the spring rains that fill the Genil. There was a late bourgeois crowd at the tables on the Plaza S. Pedro, eating Serrano ham and drinking wine, but so enclosed by the hill of the Albaicín and the hill of the Alhambra across the river that we lost the sound of voices only steps down the road towards the Plaza Nueva. A few of the Bib-Rambla longhairs were camped out with their guitars against the newspaper kiosk. But the street up the hill to the steps of the Calle Negros shone only in the stillness of the puddles.

La Bulería stood in a zigzag, where two bends of the alley opened out into a tiny plaza. Not a historical structure, not one to draw the attention of even the intrepid tourist—mud-caked door, wall free of all decoration, even graffiti. A charcoaled number 9 became visible only as Sammy L. drew me closer. His touch that night, hand on my elbow, was both more acquiescent and more insistent than on the other occasions when he had touched me. Encouraging. Attractive ergo frightening. Sammy L. already had four inches on my six feet, and seemed to grow another four in the dark of the Granada alley.

The door swung. Inside, a small patio, square, paved with bricks, surrounded by a low arcade. A long table stood to our right, a few bottles, a few glasses. All lit by fire—candles on the tables, oil lanterns hanging from the apices of the honey-combed ceiling of the arcade. The skinny boy at the door lisped a greeting to Sammy L. through missing teeth. Sammy L.

scanned the room and chose a table to the left. The boy poured
from a bottle without a label. Sammy L. scanned on.

Only one other table was occupied, three men and two girls.
The oldest man wore a cape and a cocked hat above white hair
swept back to his shoulders, a Stephane Grappelli costume
from central casting. The other two, his sons perhaps, hair
receding, shirts open, designer jeans, could have been partners
in an architectural firm, lawyers out for an evening, aficionados
out for a *juerga*.

The younger girl tried to cover nine years of baby fat with
a pair of cheap designer jeans and a peasant blouse. An exposed bit of flesh above the tummy-button pinched and
cramped, as her feet swung a good few inches above the paving
stones. Her doughy hands toyed with a yellow-haired stick doll,
but her lips sang to a far, dark corner of the patio.

The older girl was too young to be her mother, too dark to
be her sister, too still to be her cousin. I was busy taking in the
candles, the waiter, the wine, Sammy L., so didn't notice just
how quiet and dark she was until she moved. What it was that
made her jump and dash to that far, dark corner I couldn't tell.
I suspected it was a private word whispered by one of the men,
though it could have been Sammy L. and me, the sight of me
with Sammy L., or merely random gypsy motion, the unsensed
bolting of a feral pony.

"Here you have it, Holland," Sammy L. said to my unasked
question. "The final convulsions of the twentieth century. Russians, Romanians, Argentines, Anglicans . . . the whole bloody
world is making up, wigging down, yanking together the last
bits of Velcro on their new costumes. Why should the *gitanos* be
any different?"

"These architects are gypsies?"

"You didn't expect bandannas and stilettos, did you?"

"I didn't expect anything," I answered. "You suggested a
walk, I brought my shawl."

"And they brought theirs."

"I didn't think they lived in houses," I whispered to him. "I thought they were nomads, caravans, you know, the Travellers."

"Isn't much in it these days, the old Romany thing," Sammy L. said, "fixing pots and whatnot. Not much in travelling neither, what with anyone with two weeks' vacation and the phone number of a bucket shop drinking their way off to some petroleum-drenched Mediterranean sandbar. The *gitanos* are diversifying, retail clothing, long-distance transport, arbitrage . . ."

"Arbitrage?"

"Bit of a gamble, isn't it, betting on the direction of the breeze?" Sammy L. smiled. "That hasn't changed."

The girl appeared, the older one. I hadn't seen her approach, but suddenly, a plate, a fork, a knife, a steak in front of Sammy L. His left hand rose to catch the girl's wrist, but she stopped short of the touch, half-bent, leaving but returning, and looked full at me. Dark, everything dark, black hair, black eyes, cat eyes, black turtleneck, black trousers, black look, anger, resentment, nature? A moment—and then Sammy L.'s fingers snaked around the fork. The girl was back at her chair toying with the stick doll, sister pouting.

What had I missed? Everything. I poured myself another glass of wine, though I knew I shouldn't, stroked my belly, and vowed to pay closer attention.

The old man moved to the bar. The toothless waiter poured him an *aguardiente*. A shot down, the cape pulled closer, he left.

As the door slammed shut, the younger girl grabbed her doll and ran to the dark corner. The older girl didn't move. Her elbows stayed on her thighs, her hair pulled back around her far shoulder, her eyes on her empty hands.

The architects stood and walked to the center of the courtyard. A low platform set between four tables. Two chairs, back legs set at the edge. The taller of the two reached behind a table for a guitar. They sat. The shorter gripped the back of the guitarist's chair.

Sammy L. finished the last of his steak, spit the last piece of gristle onto the bricks. He set his fork and knife back on either side of the plate, wiped his mouth with the back of his sleeve. The invisible upbeat.

The first attack, bright, sharp, dissonant, the strings of the guitar, the sound brightening the candles from all four arcades. The first shout from the singer, the dark *O* of the mouth, then lips pulled back from teeth, the painful *"Ay . . . ,"* the cry of San Jerónimo against an El Greco sky, the wounded Goya peasant, the bleeding Picasso bull, glowering skies, black murals, bloody Christs.

My wineglass was empty. I couldn't call for another drink.

Then clapping, rhythmic, three to a bar, the older girl, still bent forward, palms sharply together, moving only from the elbows, then faster, the sound of sap popping in a pine fire, of Sten guns in old newsreels, and back to three.

The singer looked straight at me.

Words, only sounds in the bad Spanish of my ears, empty of meaning but full of dark imaginings—narrow alleys, stalled trains, uniforms, priests, pickpockets, knives, the screams of women, the smell of roasting flesh.

A figure moved in the shadow. A mantilla, a comb, the head of the nine-year-old girl. She stepped onto the stage. Below the neck, a full flamenco dress. Below the dress, two women's shoes, held on by elastic.

The girl looked straight at me.

Her arms moved, slowly, all dignity and age. Then her feet, in those shoes, six sizes too large. She was a *menina* from a painting by Velázquez. She was the dwarf-in-waiting from an oil by Picasso. She was a *homuncula* from a play by Goethe, from a movie by Ridley Scott. She was the six-month-old fetus inside me. She was me myself in the days not long past, when my body was galaxies away from my mind, my self, my sex.

Movements, felt, not understood, too much sex, too enticing. Pudgy fingers inviting gnarled and hairy paws, naked children on marble slabs, hairless, odourless vaginas. Horrible, grotesque, horrible.

I closed my eyes. When I opened them again, the music had shifted, less painful, more coquettish. The young girl had disappeared. The older one had taken the stage. I caught my breath. She looked straight at Sammy L.

Later, I would learn the word *duende*. But there, on the platform of La Bulería, the girl gave a look in a language I had yet to understand. It was a look no less perverse than that of her younger sister. But with the curves of her body drawing her over to the acceptable side of adolescence, the dark girl's demon was dangerously attractive, confusingly provocative, deceptively approachable. She held Sammy L. with the demon of flamenco, with a look, with *duende*, with the spirit of the music. She danced.

If her claps were gunshots, her feet were bombs threatening to immolate the singer, the guitarist, all in the tiny patio. Her legs pounded in her tight, dark trousers, her hands flew, her shoulders, her arching back, her dark, dark breasts pulled, stretched, whipped her hair in dark, wet streaks through the candlelight.

"*¡Faraona!*" the guitarist shouted at her, filling the time with more notes, more accents. "*¡Faraona del río!*"

The faster she danced, the deeper she drove me into the mud of that riverbank, the pharaoh's daughter dancing me down beneath the bulrushes, waiting desperately to steal the swaddled manchild from me. The mud, the frogs, the locusts, the death of the firstborn. The far, dark corner moving at me, sucking me under, dragging me down. Look at me, I wanted to shout. Burn your eyes into me and mine. I had come to Granada, I had brought my baby to Granada to die.

It was over. I looked around. Sammy L. had disappeared. The gypsies, gone.

I stood. The cobblestone steps of the Calle Negros brought some comfort with their silence. Otherwise, groping, much as I did tonight from the airport, not understanding how, but only that I have moved.

Back home alone, naked on my bed, belly large, the light from my courtyard seducing familiar shadows onto my ceiling. The shadows moving into breasts, legs, dark, musky hair, a slit of light up the side, like Conchita's dress tonight in the Ladies' of Colón, all dressed up and ready for a strike, a meeting, flamenco? Lying, twisted in the sheets, as unsatisfied as the fisherman's wife, calling for the flounder to bring me the new, the impossible. I wanted to be rid of the weight that dragged me down to Spain. I wanted to be Sammy L. I wanted to be a man. I wanted to take, ravish, climb, I wanted to plunge, time and time and time, into the darkness of the dark girl of La Bulería.

Granada, fourteen years ago. Tonight, emptiness, no dancers in La Rábida, no architects, no gyppies, no yupsies. Only two chairs in front of a half-curtain, a fat man,

FAT MAN

Si la Inquisición supiera
Lo mucho que t'he querio,
Y er mai pago que m'has dao
Te quemaban por judío.

a stiff man,

STIFF MAN

Bum beelee um-bum dung,
D-e-e-e-e, d-e-e-e-e, d-e-e-e-e,
D-e-e-e-e, d-e-e-e-e, d-e-e-e-e,
Bum beelee um-bum dung.

a theatreful of unwashed linen and stale semen, an endless sea of rheumy satyrs reading me, deconstructing me, queuing up to rub their baggy flies against my arse every time I stop to watch the show. Raw, dirty flamenco, empty of romance,

> *If the Inquisition only knew!*

of *duende,*

> *How much I loved you!*

of the demonic.

> *And the brass farthing you paid me for my love!*

The merest, unnatural, denatured spirit

> *They would have burned you!*

of music.

> *Like a Jew!*

Exit Holland through Stage Door in search of a working telephone.

HANNI—RAMBAM'S DAUGHTER

Dear Benjamin,

The lobby of the Cine La Rábida smells of tobacco, urine, male shoes, and reused cooking oil. False granite columns, fungal-green walls, a faded adagio of classical debutantes above the moldings, a single flickering fluorescent lighting up the ceiling, honeycombed by Moorish termites. The ticket seller is a horse-toothed gypsy with a stableful of noiseless brats. Above her cage, as on the program, the motto of La Rábida: "All men by nature desire happiness."

"Aristotle," said a voice at my shoulder. Señor Carranque, the Peruvian shoe-man, tipped his hat, bowed slightly. "He also said, 'All men desire to know.' You figure it out."

"Figure what out?" I asked. "Aristotle or architect?"

"Men," he said. "Or Man. Capital *M*, small *a*."

"Wouldn't that Man feel more at home across the plaza?"

"There is happiness and there is happiness." He smiled, looking up at the inscription.

"I was thinking of the desire to know."

"Are you a curious woman?" He turned and faced me, both hands in his trouser pockets, his fedora—its shiny ribbon and nylon feathers not quite Lubavitcher but unusual in a man young enough to be my son—pushed back to reveal a strong widow's peak of blue, bear-oiled hair. A portly, smiling rogue, with just enough of the unobvious in his question, more snake than shark, more newt than snake.

"Señor Carranque, I am a sixty-five-year-old woman out on a strange town for an evening of flamenco at a porno theater. If that doesn't qualify me as a curious woman with a capital *M*, small *a* . . ."

One of the ticket seller's brats tugged at Carranque's jacket pocket. Carranque's smile vanished, his hat found itself quickly tightened on his head. Carranque barked something at the child in something other than Spanish. She ran back to her mother. The ticket seller gathered the herd under her skirts and spit in our general direction.

"Come." Carranque guided me by the elbow toward the double doors.

"What was that?"

"Ach, we have our beggars in Peru, much worse than Spain."

"But what did you say to her?" I allowed myself to be pulled away from the drama into the theater.

"Nothing significant. I stepped on her foot. Hard. It's a universal language."

Inside the theater proper, a few red bulbs defined the corridor behind the orchestra while respecting the anonymity of the audience. A voice and a guitar groped vaguely toward us from a narrow slit of light past the overhang of the balcony. From the front of the orchestra, shouts. In the back, shadows of dark wool jackets, a few turned faces, the smell of men, mumbling, shuffling. Señor Carranque moved me sideways, behind the backs of the standees, dark in the dark. We reached the last aisle. I squinted for a seat.

Instead, Carranque opened a door. A long corridor, fluorescent tubes—hissing, crackling fandangos. I disengaged.

"Come," he said. "I have something to show you."

"I came for the flamenco," I said, "if you will excuse me," and I turned back to the door to the auditorium.

"But you are a descendant of the Rambam, are you not?" I

stopped. "The Rambam," he repeated, "Rabbi Moses ben Maimon, known as Maimonides."

A tube flickered, popped back to life. This was odd. Odder than being out and about with a shoe salesman at midnight. I remembered odd times past, other cold nights, cold corridors, cold lights. I remembered how to keep my mouth shut.

"Come. It's better if we don't talk here." He didn't take my elbow. I followed. Women, indeed, desire to know.

The corridor opened into a lounge, carpeted in Astroturf, wallpapered with newspaper and magazine nudes. At the far end, My Lady Journalist, bescarved back to us, talked into a pay phone. The stage manager kept one hand on the phone box and both eyes on her breasts. Acknowledging us with his other hand he pressed a buzzer on his desk. Carranque opened the door.

"The proprietor is an associate of mine," he whispered over his shoulder. We climbed a staircase to an office. A desk, a few chairs, a speaker delivering occasional flamenco sounds from the stage, a table with bottles. Carranque picked up a glass, wiped it once with his handkerchief, thought better of it, and switched off the speaker.

"Señora Maraquita, you must know, is my informant," Carranque said, removing his jacket and draping it neatly over a filthy stool. He was a heavier man without his jacket, I thought, conspiratorial only in the mode, say, of Alec Guinness in *The Ladykillers*. Sweat stains matched his yellow suspenders, hair oil beaded on his forehead. He gave off an odor of burlesque.

"I barely spoke with Señora Maraquita," I said carefully. I am never certain these days.

"She mentioned the book." Carranque nodded at your *Guide* tucked under my arm.

"And?" I faced him, fighting a sudden urge to giggle.

"Well . . . ," he said, and I couldn't tell whether he paused because of my manner or from embarrassment at having to say what he believed obvious.

"The *Guide*," he began. *"A Guide for the Perplexed.* You know, it is the title of a book by Maimonides."

"And the title of a guide written by my travel agent as well, Señor Carranque." I turned to the double doors. "Now, I would like to hear the Flamenco Halevy."

"Señora Hanni," he said, and I wondered when I had told anyone my name. "You and I—we are not tourists. I know of your interest in Maimonides. I know you came to Spain in search of some letters."

Aha, I thought, here's the shell game, the bait and switch, the three-card monte.

"Señor Carranque," I asked, "exactly what kind of a shoe salesman are you?" I, of course, already had an answer, a pocket-bio of this fortyish traveling peddler—a tiny, undemonstrative wife, two quiet teenage daughters just barely keeping the floors above the dust of urban Lima, and Papa moving around the potted highways of the country in a thirty-year-old American tank, one hundred different left shoes in the trunk, one hundred other novelties from swizzle sticks to girlie pictures when the shoes didn't sell, one hundred packets of Bromo when nothing else did. Three steps up from a salesclerk, two steps from a coronary, one step from jail.

"Salesman?" He looked perplexed.

"Aren't you a delegate or whatever they send from Latin America?"

"Perhaps," he answered, "but I have nothing to do with shoes. It is you who must have heard wrong."

Choo convention, shoe convention—Carranque smiled and waited until the second you-know-what dropped. "You mean you are here for a Jew convention?"

"Partially," he answered, "and partially on private business."

"Private business meaning Maimonides?"

"I am no expert on the Rambam, not like your friend the travel agent," and he nodded toward your *Guide*. It wasn't that he was heavier without his jacket, it was that he was *heavier*, Claude Rainsier, more cinematic, more noir.

"Señor Carranque," I began, reading from a once-familiar script. "Since you seem to know so much about my reasons for being in Spain, it is useless for me to deny that I am indeed looking for some letters." It was a delivery full of rust and fifty-year-old phrasing. I was embarrassed the moment it played back, and grateful that Carranque was examining his fingernails.

"Señor Carranque," I began again, trying to sound less coached. "I am looking for transcripts of a letter written by a Spanish ancestor of mine who sailed with Columbus in 1492. Maimonides must have died . . ."

"Nearly seven hundred and eighty-seven years ago," Carranque said. I smiled. "An invitation was sent to your mother some time back, I believe," he continued, "to attend the eight hundredth birthday celebration in Córdoba."

"She never went."

"There was the question of funds."

"I give up, Señor Carranque," I said. "What are you? A cousin, an attorney, a rabbi, a con man?"

"I am certain that at some level we are related, Señora. At another level, I simply desire to know."

"What have you heard about the letter I came to find, the Esau Letter?"

"Only that it is not yet in your possession."

"Yet?" I asked.

"Please sit down, Señora." He pointed to a vinyl sofa, and perched himself on a bare corner of desk. "Your mother, *alehah ha-shalom*, used to boast about her descent from Maimonides, through his daughter."

"To everybody and everything." I sat down. Why not?

"Have you ever read a biography of Maimonides?"

Carranque stood up from the desk, lifted his hat, ran a comb through his hair, replaced his hat, sat down again.

"I told you, Señor Carranque, my interest in my family has only gone back five hundred years. Perhaps if I live a little longer . . ."

"But you are certain that Maimonides had a daughter?"

Certain? She was my Jewish Cinderella, Louisa May Alcott of the Hebrews, my Esther, my Judith, my Ruth. One of my earliest memories was the voice of Mama telling the story of Kima. It was a New Year's afternoon, it must have been 1931, '32, a black-tie buffet in our building on Riverside Drive. Although the luxury travel business took on water for a year or so after the Crash, my father's nose for budget excursions and cut-rate train travel for those who had to leave town in a hurry put us in an airy corner apartment near Columbia University, with a view of the Hudson and the brand-new George Washington Bridge. Mischa Elman lived upstairs, Pola Negri on the twelfth floor—it was with great satisfaction and a six-year-old's pride that, when the jazz band took a break, I watched a small crowd gather around my gentle Mama as she quietly gave out the story of our illustrious heritage . . .

Shortly before dawn, on the ninth day of the Hebrew month of Av, in the Hebrew year 4925, corresponding to 1165 of the Common Era, in the grandest bedroom of the grandest house of the al-Funduk al-Yahudi, the Jewish quarter of the royal Moroccan city of Fez, a woman named Judith died in child-birth. Within a week, her father, the *dayyan* Rabbi Judah ha-Kohen ibn-Shushan, was also dead, burned alive at the stake by the Almohades, the fierce Berber warriors, who had embraced violence as fiercely as they had embraced Islam.

When the month of mourning was over, Judith's husband, Moses ben Maimon, known to many of you as Maimonides, the greatest Jewish philosopher of the Middle Ages and perhaps of all time, fled the city for the Mediterranean coast, and packed his father, his brother, his sister, and his infant daughter onto a ship bound for the Holy Land. After thirty days of stormy seas and predatory sailors, the family landed, exhausted but safe, in the port of Acco. Sixty-five days after the death of his wife, Maimonides walked into the synagogue of Acco and solemnly named his daughter Kima.

Kima—the Hebrew name for the constellation Pleiades, the seven sisters of the sky, the stars of the east that lit her father's path away from the Spain of his birth and the Morocco of his persecution toward the promise, the hope, of the Holy Land.

But Kima also signifies Wisdom. And it was Maimonides' quest for wisdom that moved the family to the shores of Egypt, to the Academy of the Aristotelians outside Alexandria. There Moses studied, while his brother, David, sailed around the Mediterranean dealing in precious stones, providing the family with the wherewithal to build a comfortable home. As the years passed, the girl Kima grew in both beauty and wisdom, with a fine head of thick blond hair and a finer command of Arabic calligraphy than her father's. By the age of eight she was fluent in Hebrew, Arabic, Aramaic, and Spanish, and had transcribed the whole of Maimonides' celebrated commentary to the Mishnah.

By seventeen, Kima was the most revered woman in the Jewish community of Fostat. Her father was sought after as a physician and authority on the stars and the Talmud. But it was to Kima that the ordinary Jew came with questions about the earth—why does the Nile flood, why are there tides, why does my husband beat my children, why am I so unhappy?

Eventually Maimonides took a second wife—a sister of Abu'l-Ma'ali, private secretary to the mother of the heir-apparent. Within a short time, Kima's father began to share his love with a new child, a son named Abraham. Kima sought comfort in the company of a slender, dark-haired young man, Joseph ibn-Shimon, a prize pupil of Maimonides'. Joseph's love of poetry, of the outdoors, his hunger for the physical world, drew him on long walks with Kima. K'sil, Maimonides called him, the Hebrew name for Orion the Hunter, always searching for Wisdom, betrothed to the Pleiades.

K'sil indeed became the husband of Kima, and, on her nineteenth birthday, moved her to Aleppo in Syria. There Joseph became a wealthy businessman and a respected physician in the community. Kima dispensed her brand of advice to men and women alike. A year passed, then another. Kima was happy with Aleppo, happy with her husband. But people were talking. Joseph and Kima were childless. Perhaps it was not proper for Kima to counsel men behind closed doors.

Joseph wrote to Maimonides, a letter of complaint. He had married Kima in good faith and love, done everything proper, the way a good Jewish husband ought. And yet she had not borne him a child. It's your fault, Joseph complained to his mentor. All this learning, this free-thinking, I wouldn't be surprised if she were damaged goods. Come, take her back!

Maimonides, of course, was upset by this letter. He made private inquiries through intermediaries in the Aleppo community and discovered that, as he thought, Kima was the model of discretion and propriety. His son-in-law, his disciple, was the problem. A man capable of deep thought, he was struggling to integrate his studies in the natural world into a life of faith with a loving wife.

So Maimonides, in the bumbling way of all devoted fathers-in-law, sat down to write a letter and stood up, having written a book—the *Dalālat al-Hāirīn,* known by its Hebrew title as the *Moreh Nebuchim,* or *Guide for the Perplexed.*

An Arabic copy arrived in Aleppo in 1190, on Kima's twenty-fifth birthday. Nine months later, she put down her pen, the Hebrew version completed, and went into labor. For three days, Kima struggled with the child inside her. Joseph stood at her side wiping her brow, holding the damp cloth between her teeth when the contractions became too hard to bear. On the afternoon of the fourth day, it did not seem that Kima could survive another night. To save his wife, Joseph sharpened his scalpels, and performed a cesarean section. In those days, it was not so simple. By morning, Joseph's son was nursing at a foreign breast.

After six months, the friends of Joseph took it upon themselves to send the news to Maimonides. Joseph himself was incapable of motion, incapable of speech. He could bring himself neither to look at the child nor give it a name. It was left to the grieving grandfather to name the son of his lost daughter.

"Eudaimon" was the answer that came back.

"What about a Hebrew name?" Joseph's friends asked with some consternation.

"Eudaimon is enough," Maimonides replied, "the Greek word for happiness. Our teacher Aristotle said, 'All men by nature desire happiness.' My daughter died desiring happiness. She was enough of a linguist to understand."

Joseph later named the child Benjamin, "son of my right hand," the name Jacob gave to the child his beloved Rachel bore for him before she, too, died in childbirth. But for Maimonides, the boy was Eudaimon. And it is out of Happiness that our family has descended.

"So you see, Señor Carranque," I said, "I'm as friendly with Aristotle as I am with Kima."

"Ah, Señora Hanni." Carranque looked at his left shoe for a long time, a half-smile, a memory. "You are a lucky woman. I would give up my beach house in Totoritas and half a year's income to hear Mischa Elman play the violin." He stood up, took my hand and, with the delicacy of a fat man, danced me around the tiny office while humming the second theme from Saint-Saëns's "Rondo Capriccioso." For the first time that evening I gave in to the urge to giggle. I took one edge of my skirt between two fingers and danced and laughed. There was something of the European Leo in Carranque's exuberance, something of Sonny in his ability to surprise me. It had been a long time since I had been surprised.

"Señora . . ." Carranque stopped, still smiling, one hand still holding mine, the other wiping sweat and oil from his forehead onto a handkerchief. "I don't mean to keep you away from the flamenco with my poor excuse for dancing. I brought you here to give you something. A pair of letters."

"The Esau Letter?" I tried not to sound too excited, but he'd caught me wrong-footed.

"Ah no, Señora, not yet. I am still thinking of Kima, your golden-haired ancestor. You mentioned two letters in your Mama's story—the letter of complaint Joseph wrote to Maimonides from Aleppo, and Maimonides' reply." Carranque opened a drawer in the desk and removed an oversized leather portfolio bound crosswise with leather straps. It too shook a memory out of my head, the shape, large enough to hold sheet music—the click of wheels, the shouts of soldiers, the orchards of the Auvergne.

The telephone rang. Carranque put the portfolio down on the desk and spoke briefly into the receiver. "You will have to excuse me," he said. And, with a short bow, he picked up his jacket, replaced the hat on his shining head, and was gone.

Thinking back on the scene, I can't help but believe that Carranque somehow buzzed himself on the phone to give the semblance of a natural exit, presuming that my native curiosity would lead me to peek at the letters of Joseph and Maimonides and arrive at an instant understanding. It didn't. The sight of Zoltan's portfolio of music lying on Carranque's desk, the memory of the one piece of luggage Zoltan carried with his violin from Berlin, had not completely condensed into a recognizable image. I sat for a minute, stood, touched the portfolio, wandered around the room, a room without a face, without a plaque, an award, a book—only dirty glasses and a taste for the sweeter wines and brandies of Andalusia. I flipped on the speaker Carranque had turned off as we had entered, hoping to hear at least a snatch of the Flamenco Halevy.

What sounded at first like static separated into the calls of human voices, no longer singing but shouting. I thought I had tuned in the wrong channel, but a twist of the knob only altered the volume. My Spanish is almost nonexistent—what little haggling I did among the booksellers of Sevilla was through the borrowed mouths of interpreters. But I recognized the husky mezzo in the foreground, a woman's voice, a veteran of debates and microphones. A moment later I heard Carranque. He must have gone down to the stage, I thought. Gypsy problems, no doubt. I turned the volume up again, and found that the knob was also a latch, that the speaker was hinged. I pulled, and a panel of the wall opened onto a confessional bit of latticework. I looked through the screen, out from above what would have been the Royal Box had Juan Carlos a taste for *Barbara of Seville*.

From my acute angle I saw more berets and bald spots than faces. But onstage, it appeared, the Flamenco Halevy were no longer in control. The floor was in the hands of a gang of men and women, a dazzling dark girl in a slit skirt at the fore. She was in constant motion, trying to rouse the political passions of the assembled aficionados. But the comments from the back and the barely suppressed guffaws from the front implied that the men in the audience were suggesting something deeper than oratory.

"*¡Periodista!*" I heard her cry, "*¡Periodista!*" and it was then that I recognized the mezzo as the woman from the airport, my Rosita Luxemburg, the strikers' moll, the slit-skirted Fury who had chased me from the waiting lounge. A cadre of her male comrades unfurled a banner onstage—"*¡Colón a Bajo!*"—as she signaled for someone, something offstage. A figure moved, a shout went up from the audience. There, in the dusty spotlight of center stage, stood—who else?—My Lady Journalist.

Imagine, Benjamin, my frustration. There I was, with my

superroyal's-eye view of, perhaps, the explanation to the mystery of why I was passing a cold December night at the skin flicks in the godforsaken city of Mariposa and unable to understand a word of the dénouement. Nightmare, pure and simple—textbook definition.

Two things made themselves clear, however, in the universal language of emotion and pantomime. The first was Rosita's insistence that MLJ take a picture of the strikers. The second was the impression that MLJ made upon the audience. I hadn't realized before, hurried and hassled as I was by your steamer trunk, that the woman was six feet tall if an inch, and built like a pornographer's dream. Where before I had focused on Palestinian scarf and jumpsuit, too-long neck and imperious innocence, now I saw, and not without a certain sympathy for her stage fright, the possessed, confident representative of northern European womanhood.

Rosita saw this too. And though MLJ was hardly in front of the footlights through the booking of her own manager, it was clear that Rosita viewed her as more than a handy photographer—as an ally, a leader, a mover, a friend.

My Lady Journalist squatted down on her magnificent haunches—and I remember thinking "magnificent" even from my perch behind the screen—and unstrapped the bungee cords from her infernal wheels. So that was it, I thought, a video camera. How long had Rosita known her, I wondered? Had she invited her to the meeting at La Rábida? If so, why did she bounce MLJ from the airport as thoroughly as she did me?

The theater fell silent as her thighs flexed and she stood, camera perched on shoulder, and began to film Rosita. But the next sound was not the opening of a party political speech but the bass string of a guitar. And the one after was not a call to arms but an arpeggio, followed by a beaten-out, a struck, a stricken rhythm, pounded into the stage by the heels of the dancing Rosita. The Halevy guitarist, the Halevy singer, I imagine, had moved forward from within the onstage crowd of stewards and waitresses, duty-free clerks and pilots, to accompany the flamenco pronouncements of slit-skirted Rosita.

For the first time, I was given a language to understand the strike. Or rather, I understood the surface sense of her message, the questioning of her arms, the despair in the turn of her wrists. She was searching for something, with her fingers, with her eyes, for what? Not a lost reservation, a pineapple Danish, a fog-bound runway. But backward, forward, in and around, up through the sleeves and out the buttonholes of the Halevy singers. Through the pockets, rifling the hair, searching under armpits, between shoulderblades, casting net after net over the blue-capped waves of the auditorium, asking the camera with her mouth, the workers with her hips, the audience with the unanticipatable staccatos of her heels—why travel? Why travel? What is the purpose of a motion-filled life? Why take off when there's no point in landing?

I picked up Carranque's, Zoltan's, portfolio, wondering if Kima, dying miles and miles from her father, ever asked herself that question. Whether Joseph, whether Maimonides, would have traveled unless they had been pressed by others, from the outside. Would they have been better off if they had converted? If they had stayed put, if they had chosen to live out their lives in Córdoba, in Fez, in Alexandria, as Muslims? Would we all have been better—be better? Had I ever, in my years in the business, ever sold a ticket to a client who was traveling unpressed, unforced, who was traveling on pure, unguided whim?

As if in answer, My Lady Journalist handed the camera to Carranque and joined Rosita in the circle of light. I held the portfolio tight to my chest and swallowed with the crowd, roared my approval with theirs. *"Ándale,"* they shouted. *"¡Ándale, Faraona!"*

The tempo caught fire. The singer jumped with a painful, charcoal-coated *"Ay . . . ,"* a sound that carried with it tragic memories, carnal longings, the agony of too much too many times. Rosita danced back to the edge of the spotlight, giving way to this towering beauty. *"¡Faraona del río!"* went up the shout, and two pilots picked up the clapping, moving in on MLJ. *"¡Faraona del río!"* That much I understood. *Faraona.* The pharaoh's daughter. *Del río.* Of the river. Perhaps the one, the pharaoh's daughter, who plucked Moses from the bulrushes by the river, and raised him as her own son. Out of what? Pity? Loss? Pure, unguided whim?

Faraona del río, the *shiksa* godmother, not a Botticelli but an incandescent high-wattage Vermeer beauty, face upraised, the hair, now loosened, shining, maternal, a helmet and a comforter. And I saw, as she looked to the heavens for inspiration, or rather, as she looked to the beam of light above the Royal Box that glowed from behind my head, how beautiful, how truly, purely beautiful she was. And my heart, really, Benjamin, is it possible, for the first time in years and years, softened at the torment, the utter foolishness. Because, the poor girl, My Lady Journalist of the too-long neck and the Palestinian scarf, didn't know how to dance.

MARIPOSA—A BRIEF HISTORY

Once upon a time, a river of twine, a river of offal and fish skins, of chicken heads and rotten fruit, flowed through the broad southern door of the Mercado. Its headwaters were the hooks and racks, the shining carcasses of beer-fed cattle and curly-haired sheep, the open mouths of thick-muscled hares and half-plucked geese, the oversaturated sawdust beneath chickens, partridges, quails, pheasants, the melting snows beneath the hakes, the flounders, the baskets of *pulpitos, calamaritos, langostinos,* and *boquerones,* the psychedelic pulps, the severed stalks of the dozens of edible flora that began their journeys in the hopeless predawn black, on the shoulders of half-back carts pulled by mules harnessed with twine, on the open chassis of farm-converted *deux-chevaux* with fan belts made from doubled, tripled, lengths of twine, from farms far up the Guadalaljama, held together by a history of bits and knots of borrowed, stolen, reclaimed twine.

The river gushed out the broad southern door onto the cobblestones, unobstructed, save for the occasional dam of a horse hoof or urchin foot, the nightly beaver lodges of the suppurating forearms and bloated torsos of careless drunks who had stumbled safely across the footbridge of Sto. Domingo from the bars of La Rábida, only to slip in the fecundity of the Mercado. Six days a week, the river wound around the open cobblestoned gutters, stampeded down the length of the Calle de la Nación, leapt blindly into the muddy waters of the

Guadalaljama, for a final cathartic embrace with the wine-dark, blood-dark, shit-dark, Francophilic plutonium-luminescent Mediterranean.

On the seventh day, the river rested, and the poorest of the poor, the *más gitanos* of the *gitanos,* cleansed the riverbank of its organic silt, making rags, soap, and breakfast of the remains.

Progress, in the form of a hydroelectric dam fifty miles above Mariposa, has turned the Guadalaljama itself into a dry gutter. A bridge-jumper will encounter nothing damper than spit-moistened grass and tin cans, except during an infrequent lunar bender when the moon spews a garbage-strewn tide a mile or so upriver.

The Junta Andalucía, in the foreknowledge that 1992 would bring tourism in the form of curious, womb-obsessed Americans to the shores of Spain, indentured the itinerant *gitano* knife sharpeners, musicians, pickpockets, and other vagrants serving time in the regional prisons, and pressed them into digging three-foot ditches in patterns decipherable only by students of the Rosetta Stone. These trenches were then cobbled over thoroughly enough to protect the sensibilities of the out-of-towner, but with a grating giving access, every twenty feet or so, to the familiar sewer, so the freedom-loving Mariposan gentry could continue to liberate itself of whatever liquid or semisolid matter happened to inconvenience it at the time.

So fundamental are the rights of the individual that, since the days when their harbor serviced the Phoenician ships of Tarshish, Mariposanos have clung proudly to their reputation of being at odds with whatever authority presumed to establish itself. While the bulk of Andalusia fell to the Fascist insurgents within the first few days of the Civil War, Mariposa hung on for a few more months—not for love of the Republic, but merely to show a difference. So it was with Ferdinand the Catholic in 1487, with the Moor Tariq in 711, with the Romans and the Carthaginians before them. Walk the streets today, sixteen years after the death of Franco, and you will still see the occasional obstinate Guardia Civil, refusing to exchange his snub-front hat and machine gun for the more sophisticated cap and pistol of his comrades.

The only truly successful conquest of Mariposa has been by the tourist trade, and by the tourist trade I do not mean the Hilton, Club Med, American Express, or Thos. Cook *zaibatsus*. In Mariposa, individuals slip a tip to other individuals, small operators match clients to desires that only Mariposa can fulfill. In Mariposa, renegade sons, unmarried daughters, owners of decrepit, fictitious buildings, sell out to wildcat real-estate developers, unencumbered by zoning laws or European standards of taste and tradition—a twenty-story condo here, a ranch house there, an elementary school next door to a Palm Beach-based haberdashery displaying dyed summer furs, all surrounding a gaudy nineteenth-century customs house that stands resolutely, defiantly useless. In this climate of un-regulated, uncontrollable movement, the tourist expects nothing and is surprised by everything. She moves about the city and believes not that this world was created for her eyes alone—as she might, wandering into an exquisite begonia-choked patio in the Barrio Santa Cruz of Sevilla—but that she herself is doing the work of architects and time, creating a city in a way she thought possible only in her sleep. As in the days of the Phoenician sailors from Tyre, Mariposa is the headquarters of the unplanned, unlooked-for vacation, the birthplace of Anarcho-Hedonism.

Although the Mercado closes shortly after noon every day except Sunday, a few bars and restaurants remain open until late at night, primarily to serve the unexpected diner the unanticipated adventure. Recommended are the Pinta and the Santa María. The latter serves nothing but wine and beer, the former nothing but fried fish. One orders the fish by weight, choosing a fleshy piece of *merluza*, a whole baby flounder from the salt marshes of Cádiz, a dozen pieces of squid, or a couple of hundred thumbnail *chanquetes*, which are then coated in batter, deep-fried in soybean and olive oils, and delivered in a paper cone at a temperature designed to be edible by the time a drink has been bought across the street.

At the Santa María, all wine is drawn from double hogsheads propped up on sawhorses around the perimeter of the shadowy hall. Although beer and a variety of sherries can be ordered, the rule of the establishment is to drink the wines of Málaga, throttled from the rich, overripened muscat grape, then mixed in permutations to please the driest to even the sweetest of tastes. From Seco Añejo, the color of straw, to Lágrima Añejo, Seco Trasañejo, Lágrima Trasañejo, and the vintage Pedro Ximenes 1908, as impenetrable as Guinness with a smoothness to coat a full set of teeth, all can be ordered and folded into the sherries to spawn yet another generation. At sixty pesetas for a three-ounce glass, three or four samplings are the least politely possible, and several more are often required.

Ben

HOLLAND—THE WANDERING JEW

Ben Darling,

I waited, hid for fifteen minutes behind a refuse bin, behind a buttress of a pedestrian bridge, behind the burned-out hulk of a church, behind a sign reading "JUNTA ANDALUCÍA: RE-STAURACIÓN DE LA IGLESIA STO. DOMINGO—TERMINADA 1989." Which one of us was most foolish?

Someday, Ben, when I rank my embarrassments in descending order, you will find my night on the stage of the Teatro La Rábida in Mariposa well above First Date and First Kiss. But for now—silence. There are Things That Happen that are too terrible to reveal even to one's travel agent.

Once I was confident that no one had followed me from the flamenco hall, I stepped out onto the bridge. Call it nerves, call it atmosphere—I hadn't taken a dozen steps when I was shang-haied by a memory of Paris that flushed the heat back into my face and gripped my feet like magnets. The bridge, short as it was, spanning a dry riverbed of dead winter grass and Spanish garbage, was nevertheless a wrought-iron wonder, a worthy southern cousin to whichever Parisian *pont* it was that played Waterloo in the disastrous Affaire Maimonides.

Nineteen eighty-five   only weeks after Lina Philosopoulos had returned to active duty as my executive producer. Paris—UNESCO's international conference in honor of the 850th birthday of Maimonides. By the opening of the first session, the Senegalese director general, Amadou Mahtar M'Bow, had so antagonized the Western World that both the U.S. and the U.K. had withdrawn from the organization and the staff of UNESCO had gone on strike to protest salary cuts imposed after the loss of funding. Only a handful of scholars showed, from Pakistan, India, Cuba, Spain, the Soviet Union, Algeria, Morocco, Senegal, Nigeria, Saudi Arabia, Kuwait, and Iran— hardly countries one would expect to provide Maimonidean enlightenment.

The evening before the conference, while the plenary session was planning its own salvation, I was dining with the ambassador of New Zealand—who kept a top-notch Vietnamese staff—when Newby, my A.D., rang to announce two slight obstructions. Our co-producers had withdrawn their financing, and our French crew refused to cross the UNESCO picket line. I handed the phone, ever so gently, to Ambassador Braithwaite, who happened to be not only ambassador to Belgium, Luxembourg, Spain, Monaco, Italy, San Marino, and the Vatican, but Kiwi's representative to UNESCO as well. By the time we had finished our Sweetbreads Da Nang, my documentary had a fix.

Newby rang the doorbell at half past ten. The cameraman stood just streetside of the iron gate of the embassy. The girl with the boom perched on the shoulders of the boy with the tape recorder. Three Middle Eastern-looking scholars in Italian suits watched with unsophisticated amazement from the far gutter as Ambassador Braithwaite and I sauntered down the steps of the embassy to greet them under the tender gaze of lens, mike, and Parisian moonlight. We chose Raymond Poincaré, an avenue of foreign boutiques and discreet boîtes for the diplomats and dignitaries of the 16ième, chatting at a leisurely pace about the strike, M'Bow, U.S. imperialism, making small talk.

I had instructed Newby not to begin filming in earnest until we'd reached the Trocadéro, but merely to go through the motions, allow my ivory-mosque media-naïfs a good twenty minutes of nervous rehearsal time before delivering them of their theses on Maimonides. But as we crossed the rue de Longchamps, I noticed the little red Record light on the Frenchman's camera blinking furiously. I shifted into high gear with my first serious lead-in.

Abderrahmane, the Kuwaiti, began with a discourse on the Missing Period of Maimonides' life, the twelve years of wandering, from the flight from Córdoba in 1148 to the reemergence of the family in Morocco in 1160, when Maimonides was twenty-five. He detailed the common explanations and the uncommon—visits to relatives in Granada, trips as far north as Provence, a secret life under assumed names in the port of Mariposa.

Hassan, the Palestinian, clocked in with the phrase of all adoptive cousins—Maimonides and his family must have converted from Judaism to Islam during the Missing Period. "It is inconceivable," he argued, "that they could have survived in a Spain ruled by the insistent Almohades without having converted."

"But it was not just a conversion of necessity," Abderrahmane replied, in equally precise French. "Have you not noticed that in all the millions of words that Maimonides wrote, there is not a single slur on either the teachings or the person of the Prophet?"

"The reason is Aristotle." Gebelawi, the Egyptian, was a good twelve inches shorter than I and spoke in a high-pitched, ungrammatical dog-yip. We were crossing the broad, sharply lit plaza of the Trocadéro, dodging skateboarders with boomboxes, as Newby guided the crew backwards toward the Eiffel Tower across the Seine. A glass-roofed tourist boat was blaring statistics over its speakers. But as near as I could make out, Gebelawi argued that twelfth-century Muslims, Jews, and Christians all drank their philosophy from the same Greek coffeepot. "They were all People of the Book," Gebelawi piped excitedly. "But the Book wasn't the Old Testament or the Koran, it was the Ethics, the Physics, and the Metaphysics of Aristotle."

So far so good, I remember thinking. I hadn't really done my homework, but I was pleased that these three were able to engage without any prodding from me. Ambassador Braithwaite, a not unattractive widower, was impressed by the high tone of the discourse, the stylishness of our Aristotelian stroll through the 16ième. I had never been to New Zealand, and my mind was half-clicking through a project file.

Then I tuned in to trouble. Somehow I had allowed Hassan, the Palestinian, to make a political speech. "Mankind," he was saying, "must be unified through universalism, not sectarianism, parochialism, ethnocentrism, or chauvinism. The United States has failed, the Soviet Union has failed, Africa, India, Cuba, the nonaligned states have all failed. It is universalism, long defended by the prophets since Noah, Abraham, and Moses, reaffirmed by Christ in the name of the new covenant, and realized in Islam, in the Andalusian model of Spain. Universalism is the answer. Universalism is the centrepiece, the guiding light of a new Palestinian State, in which Jews, Christians, and Muslims can live in peace, freedom, and harmony."

"Bullshit!" came the sound, in clear, Frankish tones. To this day I don't know who said it, whether the cameraman, the soundman, or the girl with the boom. But in a moment, the girl was reading out loud from a copy of Maimonides' "Epistle to Yemen," picking out, phrase by phrase, all of the philosopher's attacks on Mohammed—"The Madman and his notorious religion!"—on Jesus the Nazarene—"May his bones be ground to dust!"—and suddenly the camera was down, the red light still blinking, as it recorded sidewalk, feet, and ultimately the brownish scum of the Seine, as fists, feet, words flew. I don't think specific racial insults were hurled—Arab, Jew, Christian—but somehow the crowd on that Parisian bridge heard enough to pick sides, and within seconds, the sirens of the *gendarmerie* were wailing towards the pitched battle of universalism that my documentary had become.

Newby and I ran Leftwards, for the uncertain cover of the Eiffel Tower, while poor Braithwaite, who I imagine had hoped that his sophisticated planning and Vietnamese cuisine would lure me into the ambassador's suite, was stranded on the far side of the battle, fleeing for the Right Bank and the bright lights of the Trocadéro.

Late at night, over the dry Guadalaljama of Mariposa, camera and clothing were intact. I wheeled across the bridge towards the lights on the far side of the riverless river, stopping in the first pool of the first streetlamp to open my *Guide* and locate myself on the map of Mariposa. Six minutes later, I was sipping Lágrima Trasañejo in the Santa María and wondering whether a second meal of fried fish would help keep me awake.

Because her table was hidden by the row of wine casks behind the bartender, I didn't see the girl at first. It was only as the perspiration cooled from my eyes that I recognized the violin case propped up against a cask, the fingers of her left hand tapping a rhythm on the scroll end, the third movement, possibly, of the Bach Double, although rhythms are more difficult to decode than fingers on strings.

Perhaps it was the backdrop of the wine casks, perhaps it was the way she sat—straight-backed against the chair, eyes lowered, motionless except for the fingers of the left hand—that made her look both smaller and younger than when I'd spotted her on the bulletproof balcony above the Duty Free Lounge. The dozen or so tables were peopled with a family tree of candles melted into the backs of their ancestors. In the upcast light, the girl's face glowed with the luminescence of a china doll, a piece of delft pottery. The whole, the wood behind, the girl before, the candle in front, had a clear, precise restorative effect on my mind, as if I knew every pore of the face, every joint of the hand, every long, brown, girlish hair. Yet the mystery of this second meeting, with a girl who looked all of fourteen, bathed the scene in a halo of unease and confusion— an effect tempered somewhat by her attendants, who appeared to be, at a distance, a pair of nondescript local seamstresses and three out of four members of a rock band.

"The Lost Tribes." The fourth member blindsided me with his approach from the bar. "Our band, The Lost Tribes." I said nothing, pretending not to understand the language, generally the safest course when alone in a strange bar in a strange town at two-thirty of a December morning.

"Maybe you caught our gig tonight at the Plaza de Toros?" I looked at my girl, still thrumming her fingers on the top of her violin case. "We record for Warner Brothers," he continued. "We're big, BIG!" he stressed. "We're the Julio Fucking Iglesias of Clapham Junction!" I must have smiled. He sat down. I stopped smiling.

"I don't mean to be rude," I began.

"You're Holland," he said. Statement, not question. I thought of Hook, how many years ago, standing at the kerb while I tried to flee to the safety of Hampstead Heath, stopping me with the same surprise declaration.

"Don't worry." He leaned forward. "Your secret's safe with me." I looked at him, not an unattractive rocker, spiked black hair on a rising forehead, wearing, I'd guess, about forty years fairly lightly.

"I've taped everything you've done," he went on, "carry a full set on the bus when we do the States. 'Cromwell,' 'Marlowe,' 'The Mighty Mississippi,' 'Heterosexual Poets,' 'The Samurai of Ethiopia,' 'Sosua: Dominican Kibbutz,' 'Flamenco: Gypsy Rip-off, Et Cetera, Et Cetera . . .' " He paused. "Do I have to go on?" I looked over to the bartender, trying not to seem too helpless but to give an impression—some impression.

"Listen," he continued in a dangerously soothing baritone, "you are much safer talking to me than sitting by yourself, late at night, in a Spanish bar in full view of the front door." I could see through the glass to the chippie across the street, where a trio of high school types were counting their pesetas.

"My Angelica's at school with your ex's Arielle. What more do you want, my National Health Card?" I looked back at him.

"I didn't know Foss had a child."

"So much for investigative journalism," he said. "My name's Roger." He held out his hand. I couldn't very well refuse. I apologized. He smiled, really quite a beguiling smile. I reckon that's what separates the men from the rock stars.

"I'm sorry I've never heard of your band," I said.

"The Lost Tribes?" He laughed. "It's a new name we're stretching for this tour. Used to be Roger and the Rogers, but Ivy over there, the guitar player, got tired of being called Roger."

"Now, that I've heard of!" I said with some pleasure, never very au courant with rock and roll. The one he'd called Ivy had started plucking a rhythm on an acoustic guitar. Across from him, the darkest of the bunch, shorter and mustachioed, in leather boots and corduroys, began singing:

"Listen to the jingool, the rrrumbool and the rrraw . . ."

"I know that," I said. "Is that yours?"

"Roy Acuff used to sing it," Roger answered. "A Yank. All the good ones are. But we're trying something new with it."

*". . . Heah the mighty rroosh of the enjawn,
Heah the loneson hobo's squaw . . ."*

"Sounds like I've always heard it, with a Spanish accent, perhaps."

". . . on the Wabash Cannonbaw . . ."

"That's Fredo," Roger said. "Acoustic and electric bass, timbales, guerreros, congas, and all the Orff instruments. We rescued him from a Club Med off the coast of Tunisia just before the tour. Colombian Piano Bar cartel was holding him for ransom."

"Thoz Easton Estates are dandee,
So the peepaw always esay . . ."

"We open the show with 'Wabash Cannonball,' " Roger explained. "Move on to 'She'll Be Comin' Round the Mountain When She Comes,' Vim's favourite. He only started playing drums up in Cambridge, whilst writing his doctoral thesis on music therapy and early child development."

"Not under Jock Bismuth?"

"Of course." Roger grinned. "Vim couldn't take his eyes off you the whole time you were up at Pembroke. There's a bit of him in that film you did of Bismuth, 'Rock 'n' Rollabye, Baby.' " I looked over at Vim. A tall, skinny boy, like many another, shag haircut, pleasant Norman nose. "You know the shot? The shaved mouse on the marble pastry table dancing the Watusi? Vim's the slack-jawed bloke running the amps."

"I'm afraid I don't recognize him at all," I said.

"Oh, but he will you, I'm afraid," Roger said. "He keeps your pinup above his bunk in the bus."

"My pinup?" I must have said it too loud. The whole band turned and looked my way. Only the girl kept her eyes turned down to the table.

"Oh, my dear, you've been documentarized in more ways than you could possibly imagine," Roger whispered, and raised me gently by the elbow for the inevitable introductions.

Ivy, the guitar player, was a small-eared King's College grad, wearing a T-shirt and a padded plaid suit that I had once coveted at John Lewis. Poor Vim was so flummoxed by my arrival that he departed immediately to retrieve more drink, serenaded by Fredo's Spanish obscenities and a chorus of giggles from the two local girls, whom no one attempted to name.

I was hoping for an introduction to the little violinist, or at least an explanation of what such a young girl was doing in this crowd at so late an hour. But Ivy insisted on an impromptu audition.

"Roger must have clued you in on the Grand Concept," Ivy began, retuning his guitar.

"Ivy," I tried to say gently but firmly. "I'm afraid I'm not in my best form to judge anything right now."

"That's a Spinoza Portacam, isn't it?" he carried on without looking up. "Vim can tape me and Roger, and Fredo can beat out the drum part while humming the bass line." Vim set the glasses on the table and looked down at me with big doey eyes. I could refuse? Any better than I could refuse Conchita at the Teatro La Rábida?

"Worse comes to worse"—Roger winked—"you can sell the tape to MTV."

Ivy hit a loud open-string chord. Fredo upended an overflow bucket off the tap of a Seco Añejo for a conga drum. The bartender's head shot around the wall of casks. Ivy vamped on, a fast, pounding choo-choo train in some minor, maybe G. Fredo shrieked with pleasure. It was going on towards three in the morning. There were no other customers. The bartender shrugged.

"The Grand Concept," Roger announced, as Vim crouched and the red Record light flashed into action. "About thirteen thousand five hundred miles into our last tour, we realized that we Famous Rock Musicians, Roger and the Rogers, knew more about travelling, more about the ins and the outs of the ons and the offs, than we did about musicology, more about Upgrade than Retrograde." The English sophistication, I thought, trying to freeze a certain look of interest into my jaw.

Every English boy over the age of forty-five tries to impersonate Clive James on camera, and every boy younger aims at Jools Holland. I recognized this familiar banter. They all wanted into my knickers. But I was safe. They were British.

"Accordingly, we transformed Roger and the Rogers into The Lost Tribes, named after those famous sons of Jacob who sometime around 722 B.C. were exiled well over the rainbow, somewhere past the arm of long-distance telephone and American Express traveller's cheques. We took as our repertoire 'Charlie and the MTA,' 'The Midnight Special,' 'Leavin' on a Jet Plane,' 'Route 66,' 'Highway 61'—part of our Grand Concept: Travel. Travelling Music. Music About Travel. Music to Travel To. Music About Famous Travellers.

"And who . . ." This must have been a prearranged cue, for Vim swivelled to shoot Roger from a position just above my left shoulder. "Who was, who is, the greatest traveller of all time? Called Cartaphilus by Roger of Wendover, Ahasuerus by the seventeenth-century Germans, Juan Grazia al Dei by the Spaniards, Giovanni Buttadeo by the Italians. Damned for shoving the Man with the Cross from his door on the way to Calvary. Condemned for his pains to wander the earth until Judgement Day. Who is he? None other than that long-bearded Frequent Flier, the Wandering Jew!"

And with that, Ivy modulated into an angry string-breaking mixture of Bob Dylan and Richie Havens—angry, you must understand, in the British sense of the word.

THE BALLAD OF THE WANDERING JEW

(as performed by The Lost Tribes at
the Bar Santa María in Mariposa)

When I was just a young man,
And looking for my Soul,
I travelled to Jerusalem,

And stood by the Wailing Wall.
An Arab in kefiyah,
Called me by my name.
He didn't look familiar,
So I began to walk away.

He said, "Don't be unfriendly,
I won't keep you for long,
I know your folks and family,
I mowed your uncle's lawn."
He described my cousins Sofie,
Mona, and the twins,
The curly hair on all their heads,
And the one on Mona's chin.

I smiled and said, "I'm sorry."
He said, "Don't apologize.
Since I returned I cut my hair,
Bought contacts for my eyes.
You see, while I was doin' spadework,
For the landscape company,
I was studyin' down in New York town
To get my Ph.D.

"I was up all night with Conrad,
In commune with Mr. Kurtz,
While watching I Love Lucy,
And digging Ethel Mertz.
My chief supervisor
Was a homeboy from big J,
A brainy Joe for the PLO,
Speechwriter for Y.A.

"He talked of Susan Sontag,
He talked of Derrida,
Of Sir William Jones, and what kind of stones
Pave the streets of Ramallah."

CHORUS
Oh, I've been wandering so long.

"I tried to integrate it,
Thought he'd be proud of me,
If I incorporated
His guerrill-philosophy,
How Hemingway and F. M. Ford
Taught Conrad how to shoot,
How it's one big heart of darkness
From Gaza to Beirut.

"Five hundred pages double-spaced,
Five-oh-one with the epigram:
A rifle shot from the Rubáiyát,
Of my man, Omar Khayyám.
Seven short days later,
His secretary phoned,
'Seven at The Marlin,'
And then the dial tone.

"When I arrived, he was sitting down
With a shot of Johnnie Black,
And a ticket-of-leave to Tel Aviv
With my name writ on the back.
I asked him if he'd got me,
A Fulbright Grant or two,
The tenure track in Haifa,
A gig at Hebrew U.?

"I saw he wasn't smiling,
So I took another tack,
I asked him when I would defend
In the face of the English Fac.
'Defend?' He laughed, and raised an eye.
I thought he looked impressed,
And wondered if he'd sent my script

To the University Press.

"He offered me a cigarette
And advice to go with it:
'You'd best defend your homeland, boy,
Cause your thesis is for shit.' "

CHORUS
Oh, I've been wandering so long.

"Ten weeks on the West Bank,
In training, living rough,
I finally got my sheepskin,
And a new Kalashnikov.
I'm a Graduate in Plastiques,
I'm a prof of Sturm und Drang,
I'm a Ph.D. in TNT,
I'm the Dean of Datsun Bombs."

"Just wait a minute, Abdul,
I don't want to hear no more,
I came here as a tourist,
I don't countenance no war.
I don't know why you trust me,
Don't know why you take such pains."

"Cause your Uncle T., he trusted me
With his lawn up in White Plains."

CHORUS
Oh, I've been wandering so long.

I have to admit that they weren't the awful collegiate string band I'd expected when I first sat down, and it was a tremendous relief to hear real English, even if real English required that "Sturm und Drang" rhyme with "Datsun Bombs." Ivy and Fredo were, to give them credit, setting up a rather sophisticated polyrhythmic counterpoint behind Roger's declamation, throwing expectation slightly off balance, a five-cylinder polka, a one-legged reggae, a dance impossible to dance to, impossible to ignore. I had heard them before, I was certain of it. But was it Wembley or the White House? Opening for Kate Bush or George?

I was on the verge of a recognizable picture when I noticed that the girl was halfway out the door. It was Fredo's move that pushed me out of the current, the way he cradled the wine bucket between elbow and thigh, and slid between the girl and the exit. The girl, for her part, was grasping the violin case to her body, her face still bent towards the floor, so her hair hung in a protective curtain around the fiddle. Fredo was talking to her as he drummed, something Spanish, but too low and fast for me to understand. The girl had stiffened, terrified, refusing to move back towards us, incapable of moving forwards.

I stood. Roger was thrown back in mid-chorus, as were the two local girls draping his shoulders. I moved to the door, taking Fredo by the elbow, and urged him to the public telephone at the far end of the bar.

"Fredo," I asked him, "I need to call a friend, but I can't make heads nor tails of these Spanish telephones. Please," and I twisted the drum from his arm, "please, talk to the operator for me."

"Señora Holland," he protested, and it took all my strength to maintain seduction against that declaration of my forty-six years. But it worked. When I turned around, the girl was safely gone.

With Fredo's help, I tried calling your Mariposa office again, Ben. This time, I followed all your instructions, pushing this button and that, waiting five seconds, speaking slowly, leaving a message to reach me at the Santa María, where I hoped "The Ballad of the Wandering Jew" would last me until daybreak and Hertz, if not the end of Conchita's airline strike.

Three steps into the procedure, Fredo deserted me to follow the local girls out the front door. I hung up the phone and

retrieved my unused pesetas from the slot above the dial. The
waves of Ivy's guitar swept around the casks to the bar. Without
the girl with the violin, my only reason to return to the table
was to retrieve Spinoza and Sandor.

"Señora!" the bartender whispered to me as I walked past.
I stopped, looked down. He must have lacked five feet by more
than three inches. But he made sure that I waited by the
counter for his message while he turned to the spout and drew
me a fresh Lágrima Trasañejo. "Señora," he said, and I bent
down to catch his raspy English, "that song they are singing,
the boys. They are making a joke out of something we Spaniards take seriously, very seriously." He walked out from
around the narrow wooden trestle and pulled a chair over for
me.

"Once upon a time," he began. But at that moment Fredo
punched open the double glass doors, and his grin looked, if
anything, twice as diabolical.

"*Hombre,*" he said to the bartender, "are you bothering the
lady? Can't you see she is with our party?"

"*Nada, nada.*" The bartender returned behind the counter,
outnumbered and outranked.

"Please, Fredo," I said, "the gentleman wanted to tell me a
story. You sang your song. I think equal time is only proper."

"Then let's get it on film." Roger stood at the wall of casks,
Vim over his shoulder, Spinoza over Vim's.

"Turn that thing off," I said, and Vim jumped to the command. But the bartender stuck out his chin, walked back
around the bar, locked the front door, and poured a round of
drinks for the assembly.

"I would be honoured, Señora, to tell my story to your
camera. Then the television can decide who tells the truth." He
lifted the tray up on one palm and led us back to the far side
of the bar. There, to my utter amazement, sitting back in her
original position, was my girl with the violin. In the clearing of
half-full glasses and the wiping of the table, no one else seemed

to find her presence astonishing. I tried to sit in the seat next to hers, but the bartender took firm control of stage movement and corralled me into my original chair. Vim began to film.

"The story, Señora," he began, "that the English boys were singing is based on a four-hundred-year-old fiction by an Italian who made a pilgrimage to the Holy Land, smoked hashish for three months, and found the need to create a fabulous tale to impress the father of his wife, who had financed the excursion. This is the story the Italian told the assembled guests":

I was walking one day in the piazza of Jerusalem, the piazza that surrounds the Church of the Holy Sepulcher above the Western Wall, when I was confronted by a Turk who asked, in perfect Italian, "Do you know me?" I had my hand on my dagger, half ready for an adventure, half ready for a fight. But aside from his turban the man looked so harmless and transparent that I felt compelled to answer his question and admit that I had never seen him before in my life.

The Turk smiled and said, "But I know you! For I was a slave in your uncle's house in Turin and I received many favours from you and from your parents." He gave their names correctly and also those of many prominent people in Turin. "When I was released," the stranger continued, "I went to Venice and soon gained the friendship of some Turkish merchants. They brought me in their ship to Constantinople. There I sought out my old master, whom I had served in the naval forces in 1571. He had recently been appointed governor of Jerusalem, and, upon the death of his police captain four months later, he did me the honour of selecting me for the post."

"Congratulations," I said to him, "that is quite a step up from scrubbing floors in my uncle's house."

"Service is service," the Turk replied with a casual twitch of his moustache. "But kindness must be repaid, so I trust that you will do me the favour of dining with me tonight. We shall be alone." He described his house and advised me to come at four in the evening, so as not to be seen. But if I was seen by any police, I was not to worry, for he was their chief.

I accepted the invitation and was received at his house with much display of friendship. After a splendid meal, he told me he would show me something which no other living man had seen, save his master, the governor of Jerusalem.

"But please," he said firmly but without a trace of begging, "reveal this secret to no one. Should I be discovered, the penalty is impalement."

The Turk took a ring of keys from an iron box, prepared a piece of wood for a torch, and lit a lantern, which he then carefully covered. He led me out of the room, shut the door, and gave me his hand to walk with him a good distance in the darkness of a narrow passage. In a short time we came to a large drawbridge, which led to another room. He shut the door from the inside and uncovered the lantern. Then he trudged an equally good distance to an iron door. It opened to reveal a corridor all worked in mosaic. Near the end we passed ten iron doors and entered a large hall ornamented with very fine marble and mosaic work in the vault.

At the left end of the hall there was a man, well armed in the antique style, with a halberd on his shoulder and a sword at his side. The man was continually marching from one side of the hall to the other without rest. The Turk said to me: "See if you can stop him." I tried two or three times with all my strength, but it was impossible for me to hold him. He lighted the torch and gave it to me so I could see the man more clearly. I observed that he was of middle stature, thin and emaciated, with hollow eyes, black beard, and black hair. I asked the Turk who this man was and he answered, "I will tell you only if you swear by your Christ not to reveal it for three years." This, I knew, was the extreme limit of office for a chief of police. Curious to know, I gave my solemn pledge.

"This man," he said to me, "is the servant who struck your Christ before the high priest Annas. For punishment of his terrible crime, he was condemned by your Christ to remain here. We too believe in the old traditions. In this place he stays, never eating nor drinking, never sleeping nor taking rest, but always walking as you see him, and always—look, my friend— always the arm that struck, twitches!"

We left and returned to the room where we had dined. At my departure he tactfully reminded me of my oath. He trusted me to remember him to his friends in Turin and offered me money if I had need. I told him I lacked nothing and thanked him warmly for his kindness and, following his instructions, found my way to the inn. I returned to my native country, spent the past three years in Candia, Corfu, and Zara, and now I can tell what I saw without scruple, having observed the oath.

"Amazing," Vim said, lowering the camera from his shoulder.

"Not bad," Ivy allowed, picking a half-hearted tune on the guitar.

"Far fawking out, man! That's the story!" shouted Fredo and let out a Turkish battle cry of his own composition.

"I am not finished," said the bartender. Ivy stopped pluck-ing. Fredo sat down. The bartender waited until Vim began to record. "What is the point of this story?" he asked, but like all storytellers I've ever interviewed, he sped on without reply. "The answer, of course, is that there is no point. The young Italian macho merely wants to impress his friends back home by displaying the ultimate trophy of the tourist, the unique. He tells a story that is unbelievable, yet bears the appearance of authenticity because his uncle himself is present and can attest to the character and bearing of the Turk, can assert that it is very probable that this man was made chief of police. Given one likelihood, it is only a short leap for the gullible listener to believe the most preposterous stories of endless dungeons and marching Jews armed with swords, halberds, and superhuman strength.

"Here in Spain, this Christ, who is just a minor character in the Italian's story, is a very real, very central creature. There are those who believe He is God and those who are not afraid to fire rifles at His image and shit on His name. But everyone, every Spaniard, treats Him very, very seriously." The bartender took a sip of his drink, let it roll around the inside of his mouth and trickle down the back of his throat.

"The true story"—he looked straight at me—"has a very real point, and that point is not about the Wandering Jew, but about God." I tried to say something encouraging, but I was too dry to speak, and the moment too quiet to reach for my glass.

"This Wandering Jew," said the bartender, "was a shoemaker who lived in Jerusalem in the Street of Bitterness. When the Saviour passed by bearing His cross, He was in so desperate a state, so exhausted, when He came to the door of the house, that He wished to rest and said to the owner: 'Juan, I am suffering much.' And Juan answered: 'Go, go! I am suffering even more, I who labour here like a galley slave bound to his oar.'

"Then the Saviour, seeing Himself so cruelly rejected, said to the shoemaker, 'Very well! Go yourself, walk. Until the end of Time!'

"Immediately this man felt his feet moving. He began to walk. He walked from dawn to dusk, from dusk to dawn. He walked through towns and out, through deserts and over mountains. The man recognized this endless walking as a punishment from Heaven for his hard-heartedness and his cruel words 'Go! Go!' which he had hurled in the face of the unfortunate one who had asked to rest. As he walked, he repented with all his soul for what he had done, and he fell to weeping his offense and to despairing.

"Thus he walked until, at the end of a year, on Good Friday, at three o'clock in the afternoon, he saw appearing on the distant horizon, mingled with the clouds of Heaven, three crosses. At the foot of the highest of these—the one in the middle—there was a Lady, as beautiful as she was sad, as sad as she was sweet. This Lady turned her face towards him and said to him, her face pale and tearstained, '¡*Juan, espera en Dios!*' Juan, believe in God!

"And that is why we Spaniards call him Juan Espera en Dios, the man who has been walking ever since without ever stopping, who will walk until the consummation of Time, that the curse of God, which he drew upon himself, may be fulfilled!"

"I don't understand," I said when the bartender paused to empty his glass. "If the Jew repented, why must he continue to walk?"

"Because"—the bartender smiled calmly—"after our Civil War, we Spaniards discovered that none of us were right and that all of us were right. We discovered that Christ exists and that Christ is God. But we also discovered that we are doomed to worship the biggest two-timing, lying son-of-a-shit that ever lived, may his bones be ground to dust!"

"Madonna!" Fredo said. Ivy and Vim remained silent. A light bulb flickered at the far end of the room. I was never a churchgoer, even in my brief childhood. But early images—the blasted yew outside our deserted vicarage, the half smile on the face of my half-sleeping mother, the shadows of lace on the ceiling of my aunt's bedroom—were enough religion to make me shiver at the ferocity behind the bartender's blasphemy.

When I turned, I noticed that my girl with the violin had raised her eyes, perhaps out of appreciation for, or general interest in, the bartender's story, but with a look of curiosity directed at Roger, waiting for, perhaps urging him on to, rebuttal. He, too, was looking at her, half smiling, sharing a joke, more likely just refuelling for the next lap.

"Gimme," he said, taking the guitar from Ivy. In one stroke, he picked up the stumbling rhythm of the Ballad, but with a fiercer, less indulgent feel for the instrument, snapping string against wood, slapping palm against soundboard, more to shock an argument from the guitar.

"While you were phoning your travel agent," he said—and I did wonder at the time how he knew whom I was phoning— "you missed the organic difference between the song 'The Wandering Jew' as written by Yours Truly of The Lost Tribes and the primitive Renaissance tale of Pablo over here." The bartender jerked up his chin sharply, whether offended by the attack on his story or the presumption of his name, I couldn't tell.

"In my version," Roger continued, punctuating his words with attacks on the guitar, "the tourist does indeed go to Jerusalem and meet the Turk, in this case a young Palestinian Freedom Fighter named Abdul. But," and his left hand slid up the neck in a dramatic glissando, "in my song, in the verses you missed, we discover that the Wandering Jew is not some old bearded codger buried beneath the walls of the city, marching a gutter into the earth, but he's the young Palestinian himself!

"You see," Roger continued, as Fredo supported him with a fresh tattoo on the bottom of his pail, "the bartender hasn't taken his weak Iberian argument far enough. Cartaphilus, Ahasuerus, Malchus, Isaac Laquedem, Juan Espera en Dios, whatever you want to call him, the Wandering Jew was no dummy. Sure, he converted to Christianity. Maybe not at first, maybe he liked travelling, wanted to see the world, once, maybe twice. No planes, no trains, only ships, carts, horses, elephants, and camels, and all those most likely prohibited by the curse. Say he's in Casablanca and has a yearning for Cádiz, he's got to tramp across North Africa, up the Middle East, march around the Black Sea and then back west, around— never across rivers, and over the Pyrenees:

> I asked him for his favourite spot,
> He smiled and answered: "Spain.

I was there before the Inquisitor,
And I'll be back once again."

"He's in Jerusalem and hankers for a glimpse of the pyramids of the Mayans? He's doomed to the polar route. Doesn't matter how cold, he can't freeze to death. Worse luck, since after a couple, three hundred years he wants to die, dreams of dying, tries it countless numbers of times.

"It's after one of these heroic attempts, somersaulting down Everest, sunbathing in the Sahara, donating free periodontic service to the lions of Lake Manyara, that he sees the Lady and the Crosses, or thinks to himself maybe there's something to all this Christ business. So he talks to the pope, tells him he's sorry he told the Lord to fuck off, promises to build a shelter, a whole block of flats for homeless riffraff, gets himself sprinkled, immersed, whatever, gets himself a brand-new Christian-sounding name like Paul or Thomas, starts eating pork and shellfish, and waits to die.

"No dice. Maybe it's the water, he thinks, not holy enough. Maybe it's the pope, one of those Dark Age types who stole from the poor and buggered anything that couldn't run. But after another few hundred years of walking and meditating, he thinks, maybe it's the religion what's worn down—the curse is still potent, but the antidote's way past the expiration date.

"Along about this time, our friend happens to bump into a caravan of hapless souls in the middle of the Arabian desert. They're all hot about this new prophet Mohammed, and though it sounds like the same old Adam, Noah, Moses, Jesus promise, the Wandering Jew wanders off to meet him. He finds Mohammed on the road to Medina and, over a cup of chicory, spells out his dilemma.

" 'I will tell you three things,' Mohammed says straightaway. 'First, there is no God but Allah,' and he smiles as the Jew raises his eyebrows. 'Second, I, Mohammed, am his prophet, which is why you must both believe everything I tell you and fundamentally doubt it. Third, and most important, you as a man have responsibility over your own actions. You are capable of distinguishing good from evil, free to choose and to act. Perhaps you need me to explain, to point, to guide you from time to time. There may be things beyond your control—the creation of worlds, the power over death, wind, rain, and the stars. But this wandering—you have the power to stop it, you have always had the power to stop it at any time.' "

"Like Glinda in *The Wizard of Oz,*" added Ivy, "telling Dorothy she could have clicked her heels together whenever she wanted and left Technicolor forever."

" 'There's no place like home, there's no place like home,' " Vim whispered from behind the viewfinder.

"Well, the Jew sits and thinks about this for a while after Mohammed buggers off and founds Islam and gives good and wicked men alike the power to interpret his Koran any way they choose. And after one hundred years or so, he realizes that Mohammed was only half right. He does have power over his wandering. Hasn't he been sitting and resting, after all, while his seven-hundred-year-old blisters peel off and turn to sand? But no matter how many times he clicks his tender, pink heels together, he cannot die. The morning of his eightieth birthday dawns, as it has ten times before, only to find him a young man of twenty once again. To Hell with this laying about, he thinks, and he trudges south to Yemen, where he catches a boat—because he can—and spends his next thousand years on the sea.

"In my song," Roger said, "The Wandering Jew has become a Palestinian Freedom Fighter, just another manifestation of his wishy-washy weltanschauung—one century he likes to wander, another century he wants a homeland, somewhere he can put his feet up, pop a cold one, and everyone on the block looks just like him. Most of all, he wants the power over creation and destruction, the one thing God or Jehovah or Allah won't give him. So what does he do? He becomes a tourist, a critic, comparing this tower and that burger joint with this campanile and that sushi bar, home in no tradition, sans native land, sans native tongue, sans good homecooking.

"After all," Roger said with a great Pete Townshend sweep of his arm, scattering the glasses from the table with a dominant seventh chord, "when you're immortal, it's just one mid-life crisis after another."

> *The last time I saw Abdul,*
> *His head was bended low,*
> *He was shuffling away down the Great White Way,*
> *With a sackful of Foucault.*
>
> *The next time you pick up stone,*
> *Or heft a piece of sod,*
> *May your aim be keen, cause the guy you bean*
> *Might turn out to be God.*
>
> *He may make you immortal,*
> *As he looks into your eyes.*
> *But like Abdul, you'll find that you'll*
> *Be doomed to criticize.*
>
> *CHORUS*
> *Oh, I've been wandering so long.*

And that's when I heard it, far off at first, a single bowed violin note, consonant with Roger's key, then two, three, an inverted major triad, like a train whistle far off in the night. I looked at the girl, still smiling shyly at Roger, but her fiddle was well cased, and no one else was in the restaurant. It couldn't have been a sympathetic ghost tone from Roger's guitar, since, as the chord grew louder and nearer, Roger stopped strumming and we all, looking upwards, downwards, to the walls and windows, listened to its approach in amazement. Or not so much its approach because it was in the room with us all the time, but listened as some invisible hand turned up the volume to three, four, seven, an exquisite, perfect, disembodied violin pumped past the bursting point into our bodies.

The bartender was the brightest physicist. He was first under the table, followed by Fredo and the others, as the front windows exploded inward, smashing into the barrier of wine casks, raining glass over our heads to the back wall, as the triad turned into the roar of the jet fighters, the phantoms that had terrified me at the airport, coming, this time, in from the sea, this time only sparking my curiosity, introduced as they were by that heavenly chord that could only have come from Sandor.

I grabbed my wheels and my camera and ran out into the street, where the moon was blinking like a strobe light behind the shutter of hundreds of planes. A taxi screeched to a halt, a door flew open. It was only after I'd thrown Spinoza and wheels into the empty back seat with one hand, that I felt the young girl with the violin holding my other. I pushed her in, closed the door, shouting Sandor's address to the driver, knowing that this is what I wanted all along, then looked up and saw, in the front seat next to the driver, the wild-haired White Rabbit.

The taxi shot through the narrow streets of the market, curved under the eternal scaffolding of the Catedral, climbed up the Calle Victoria around the Roman ruins, higher into the darkness, past the Gibalfaro, cut into the unpaved turning, and suddenly broke into the open blue-black of the sea, sky, and moon that signalled the height of the town and the massive gate to Sandor's villa. I climbed out and ran to the gate, pulled at it, pushed at it, all locked and dark, as the sound began again and I had to run for the road, my camera out, to somehow film, record, just bear witness to the phenomenon of the music of the plane, as the last, solitary fighter flew so close that its belly lights lit up the taxi as it sped away down the mountain, and showed, as clearly as if it were daylight, the young girl with the violin, prying loose a bit of brick from a stanchion, and, with the iron key beneath, calmly, as if she did this every week, unlocking the gate to Sandor's villa.

I didn't need to be told. I picked up one end of the White Rabbit's trunk, flung it inside the gate, the metal clanged shut, and except for the distant continuo of the planes—which could as easily have been the sea or the concentrated breathing of three women—all was quiet.

ITINERARY TWO

VILLA GABIROL

The true criminal is the aficionado. He has a terrible addiction to faces—a dark, soulful Eastern European to play Tchaikovsky and Dvořák, a complex Oriental, preferably a woman dressed in red with shoulders bare, to tackle Bartók and Stravinsky, a broad-backed Swede, male or female, to pull and jerk Beethoven. Those who find the face of Heifetz in a Wieniawski polonaise are as profoundly simpleminded as the pilgrims who worship the shroud of Turin.

To free the note from the nose, the rhythm from the arch of the eyebrow, the twitch of the lip. To free the downbow from the wrist, the pizzicato from the finger. To find the heart of the music, and hear it pure, disembodied, ungeographied, de-raced, un-sexed, with all trace of the Human removed except that initial shove called Composition—that is the goal of the true musician.

—Sandor, *In Search of the Lost Chord, A Brief Guide,* p. 101

THE VILLA GABIROL—A BRIEF HISTORY

The Villa Gabirol was designed at the end of the last century by the Spanish industrialist and architect Marrano in the Mudejar style, and built on the ruins of the ancient fortress of the Almoravides. Four sets of apartments on two levels, not including the renovated and re-plumbed baths dug into the hillside, surround a squarish courtyard.

Before the Civil War, the Villa served as the centerpiece of the Mariposan social season. The Picasso exhibition of 1924, the famous Heifetz/Rubinstein/Casals recital of '32, the Lorca/de Falla Concours de Flamenco, all provided occasions for the unlocking of the massive gates to the garden. Citizen and tourist alike were treated to a view of the open Mediterranean, a view that once made Jews, Christians, and Muslims bury their enmity in a common worship of salt and water, sun and wind.

Shortly after moving into the Villa in 1950, the Russian violinist Sandor established a master class for half a dozen promising students. The final week of the July session was given over to recitals. Every evening, one of the young violinists held court by the fountain for an audience of fifty of Mariposa's worthy. Only at the end of the week, after each of his students had laid his offering on the altar, did the maestro take the stage. Sunday-night tickets were harder to come by than a box behind the president of the Corrida. They were given as wedding presents, bequeathed in last testaments. A pair of front-row seats served as collateral on any number of loans and gambling debts. The crush of the great unwashed outside the gates was matched only by the reverential silence with which every Mariposan ear strained for a single drop of Sandor's matchless tone. It was a tone that was said to sweeten the most bitter humor, to soothe the most profound despair. Five minutes of Sandor could change a senator's vote, ten could move an entire parliament. At one famous recital, a woman claimed she sat down barren and stood up three months pregnant.

Sandor last played in public in 1966. The gates closed on his master classes ten years later. Although Sandor has continued to teach, the numbers have dwindled in recent years to perhaps a single student. The view from the road outside the gate is also spectacular, and pilgrims climb the hill as much for the sight as in the hope of hearing the master at practice.

Best chance: 6:00 A.M.

Ben

HANNI—HOLLAND'S TALE

Dear Benjamin,

I have a few answers.

My Lady Journalist has a name. A single name. Holland. Explanation follows, although perhaps you've already heard the story, as I have discovered that you are also her travel agent.

The young violinist does not. Or perhaps she does, and it is just my Spanish, or my and Holland's Spanish, as she worked on the girl while I heated the milk. Even nameless, she is an exquisite thing, and I am not accustomed to finding myself moved by young girls. I grew up in an age of bobbed, rational hair, and the sight of a long, virginal mane is enough to make me weep for an innocence I never had. Her eyes, Benjamin— undoubtedly you are her travel agent too.

The owner, the owner of the villa, has a name (Sandor), a hobby (violins), a profession (hermit), and apparently a hotel bed (Carlyle) and a recital (Carnegie) in New York tomorrow night (New Year's Eve).

The young girl may be his student. Then again, she may not. All I know for certain is that she is familiar not only with the location of all gates, doors, keys, locks, combinations and per- mutations of the villa, but with the whereabouts of milk, coffee, and chocolate. Despite the language barrier, she is a cinch to direct. Within a few minutes I had her carrying a tray out to the courtyard, where Holland had plumped several cushions around your massive steamer trunk.

Balmy and clear, an odd, welcome December night. Quiet now that the planes have gone. The fountain at the center of the courtyard quiet too, rippleless. The warm stones underfoot—heat pipes, Holland claims—the shelter of the arcade, the hot drinks, and my bottomless jar of kipferln make for a cozy, late-night tea party. The slice of winter garden I have seen, the bit of copper-potted and clay-dished kitchen, unlit Moorish lanterns, pitted marble columns, fragmented capitals—all is familiar and inviting in a way that nothing has been in Spain. I am glad our host is away. A man—I suspect even you, Benjamin—would disrupt the peace and balance of women's voices in such a comforting place.

With her scarf off and in a seated position, My Lady Journalist is a good deal more *gemütlich* than I'd supposed. Perhaps her ordeal on the stage of La Rábida softened her corduroy. Perhaps it softened mine. Holland, it seems, is an expert—although she, in a lovely self-deprecating way (am I becoming that soft?), never spoke the word—has been spending the past year producing a documentary on the subject of our absent host. Of course I know of Sandor, of his reputation. Leo refused to have his records in the house—bad for the arteries—and, having my own sentimental favorites, I never complained. But Holland is enthusiastic about her film, especially proud of the tape she made of Sandor playing Bach—ergo, the box on wheels. The film, she said, will be part of a series on the five hundredth anniversary of Columbus's discovery of America.

You'd be proud of me, Benjamin. I didn't rise to the worm—not a single insult to Columbus, not a word about Esau or Maimonides. I slipped out of my shoes and rolled my stockings from my feet, bit down on a stray fragment of hazelnut, and let the sound of my crunching carry a neutral message for Holland's interpretation. I think the subject would have melted with the kipferln if the girl hadn't spoken up for the first time all evening.

"Tell me a story," she said, lifting her eyes first to me, then to Holland. The voice was deep, the language was English, or at least the phrase, learned like some seafaring parrot—a surprise, but not a shock at 3:30, hours till dawn, till you would release your answering machine and give us some answers.

I had never told a bedtime story. But something about traveling alone, about being a woman alone, about a month of simple foreign explanations to simple foreign strangers, had left me—both of us perhaps—eager for more complicated conversation, even at such an hour, the conversation of women, for the chance to pour my history down a willing set of feminine ears.

"Shall I?" I wondered. Holland looked at the girl with openmouthed interest. "Shall we?" I felt the same question floating unspoken between our minds. Purely rhetorical. It was a decision made, made when I first saw the girl under the statue of Columbus in the Plaza La Rábida, made while listening to Zoltan forty-seven years before. And I, for one—perhaps it was the fountains, the violins, Spain—knew exactly which story I would tell.

"Oncé upon a time," Holland began—and I was grateful that she spoke first, the decision to confess being much easier than the act—"there was a young girl. A young girl not too different from you . . ."

"Isabella." She might as well have said Beelzebub. But it made no difference. I was in love.

"From you, Isabella," Holland continued. "Her name does not matter, because shortly after my story begins, she changed her name. What is important is that this girl had a name, and she had a life, and she had a husband, and she was relatively content with all three."

"Tell me a story," Isabella said again.

I poured Holland another cup of coffee. It was only later, halfway through Holland's tale, that I realized she was speaking to a girl who understood no English, that I wondered who was listening.

The morning after my divorce I began to grow. It took me a full day to recognize the symptoms—it is not one of the more common signposts of turning thirty-two. Weariness in the joints and a hard swelling in the glands behind the ears led me to a preliminary diagnosis of summer flu, the low-grade fever of relief I contract as soon as any project is in the can. The usual cure, which could hardly be grudged by the BBC, is a day's lie-in, supplemented by duty-free bath oils, a fresh nightie, squid with black bean sauce from the local take-away, and pots and pots of tea with a well-congealed half pint of Devonshire cream. But as it was a Sunday, and my neighbours were off tramping around the Fens, I could indulge in a little nude sunbathing in the late-summer afternoon, order an early supper, take two pages of Margaret Drabble, and fall asleep.

The dark limbo of Monday morning stirred me to the peculiar truth. Not a flu but a liquid weight between my chest and the bed—a rubber cushion, a floating bolster that could not be heaved off, a new attachment to my unattached body, a well-upholstered something keeping me from total communion with the mattress. There was nothing E. A. Poe-ish about the awakening, no sudden panic, flailing about in an unfamiliar language against straps or rusty springs, no premonition of CANCEROUS LUMPS set in twelve-point type. It was a cozy weight, a familiar weight, a weight I hadn't dreamed in fifteen years, since the teenage nights when I hoped to tears that the double islands of Atlantis would rise from the subterranean floor of my boyish breast. I rolled onto my back and massaged myself into dream.

I saw my sister standing next to Adolescent Envy. I dreamed

of her body at ten, already fully hipped and bra-cd, of her armpit hair and the thick growth between her legs that neither nightgown nor bikini could hide, while I, even four years later, could still swim in knickers without a vest with nary a glance from the sixteen-year-old public. I dreamed of her body at twenty, I dreamed of our wedding dresses—mine, a functional Bauhaus of lace up to the throat; hers, a baroque pulpit of whalebone and mystery.

And Liaden proceeded to have children, dozens of them, at least one a year, five, or was it six at last census? While *we*, Foss would repeat afterwards in his Jonathan Miller TV surgeon's voice, *we*—and by that he meant *me*—remained barren, despite the thermometers and the ovulation tests, despite the sonograms and the sperm counts, despite *in vitro, ex nihilo,* and *sub rosa,* despite—and this from his favourite obstetrician—a veritable Amazon of the fastest, strongest sperm since Man O' War.

And yet, for all her rococo charms, how staid and wall-papered Liaden had turned out, while the smell of unwashed sex dripped like fresh paint from my marriage. Even at the end, months after Foss had moved out, when Lingfield, my solicitor, told me he would drop the case if I didn't stop sleeping with my husband, we would meet under assumed names in chintz-smothered Russell Square B&Bs for frantic, groping, always loud and unconscious lovemaking.

I jumped at the alarm, fully *dreamus interruptus.* My hand reached at its automatic length for the clock, but toppled a lamp before retreating and finding the button. There it stayed for a heart-thumping minute. I returned slowly from my dream, my senses as alive as in any hot encounter with Foss. It was less the rising blood and damp, less the bedclothes gone and my nightie bunched up below my chin. It was the elbow against the headboard, bent, where I had always needed a straight-armed lunge for the alarm; it was the hand that could grasp the clock like a Spanish plum; it was the vertigo of my head on the pillow and my heels dangling like bananas off the foot of the bed. And yes, as I ventured with my un-alarmed hand below the bunch of the nightie, the no-longer-palm-sized tomatoes, but full-flowing, wobbly, hanging-slightly-off-the-side-to-kiss-the-sheets, womanly breasts.

The sun burst around my curtains—my hand had not lied—shining on England's green and pleasant land in full Jerusalem strength, striking my new body in new, largely vulnerable places. I had been flung full-blown, smack into the middle of an ancient Greek soap opera. I had been pumped up—doubtless by the bellows of an overly imaginative Hephaestus, under the supervision of an equally ditto Venus in Sunglasses—into the perfect Helen, with the legs of Cyd Charisse and the breasts of Sophia Loren. And somewhere this side of the next commercial break, the Sun God, Apollo—played with grim wit by Arnold Schwarzenegger—was hurtling down from Olympus, across the North Circular and Hampstead Heath at the speed of a television signal, only seconds away from smashing through the double glazing onto my new John Lewis down-filled duvet.

A passing cloud took pity and covered my distress. I guided my legs over the side of the bed. I attempted a stand—one foot, one leg, and then the companions. There was no pain, no acrophobia. There was my chair—O Comforting Chair! There was my bed—Soft Friend of My Happiness! There my books, there my paintings, there the mantel, slightly dusty, above my fire—O, O, O, clear and brilliant and new and of course! I hopped on my long toes across the carpet to the bathroom, bouncing and jiggling, my nightgown no more than an ill-fitting chemise. I felt, well, of course, this is how I've always felt. *This* is the body I was born in—the other a flat-chested five-foot fiction. I am only now getting independent visual verification. And what I am getting is far more than the two stone and twelve inches that my scales tell me have drifted onto my soul in the last twenty-four hours. I have found the physique to match my libido, the words to match the thought.

I have become the bombshell to case the bomb. Mount St. Venus has erupted. I have solved the Mind/Body Problem.

That morning, I discovered I had twenty-seven portable mirrors in the house, not including the two full-length on the doors of the master bathroom. That morning, I discovered that I had nothing to wear. And that morning, the voice that answered my phone at work belonged to an American affiliate named Hook.

"Congratulations!" the voice said, by way of introduction. "I heard about your weekend." Ah yes, my divorce. "We figured you'd probably take a couple of days off to celebrate. Don't worry, everything's under control." From the beginning he knew how to pull my chain. Control, indeed!

"You've settled in, I take it?" I asked, trying out my new expanded voice, which, comfortingly enough, sounded recognizable.

"I thought I'd drop by around six," he continued. "We can have a drink and run through this week's schedule."

"Let me speak to Monica," I said, suddenly impatient at being bull-phoned by a strange American man while totally starkers.

"She gave birth last night," Hook said, "didn't you hear? See you at six." He rang off.

I sat by the phone for a minute, suddenly less concerned about the chaos in my department than about my utter lack of wardrobe. With my sister and her herd on holiday and Monica in hospital, there was no one I could trust to shop for me, to measure me, to teach me, for Christ's sake, how to hook a bra! And what about Monica's baby?

"A girl," Hook said, picking up my call on the first ring. "Seven pounds five and a half ounces. Alison Patricia."

I tired of the mirrors. I drank coffee, tried to read, watched a video of *The Women*, dusted the mantel. I retrieved a pair of Foss's overalls from the garden shed and weeded around the *acer*. I dialled three digits of Foss's phone number, four of

Lingfield's. I thought for a moment about calling my last gyne-cologist. But after her encomium to Foss's testicles—I moved her name to the bottom of the list, and when I reached it, crossed it off.

At five minutes to six, I squeezed into a pair of sunglasses, zipped up the front of the overalls, stepped into two undersized zoris, turned the key in the lock, and limped across the street to the Heath to avoid the confrontation and, by the by, see what the world made of me.

"Holland," a voice called. I stopped. Holland, you see, was my maiden name, a name I hadn't used in exactly ten years. And with my parents long dead, not even Monica knew it. Three boys kicked a football in the meadow. An elderly groundsman pedalled an ancient black bicycle down a footpath into the trees.

"Six o'clock." The voice was deep and soothing, a strong presence, insistent but not urgent, and above all, in control. A man appeared at my shoulder. "I'm Hook."

Perhaps my heightened state still expected an Apollonian Schwarzenegger. What I got, and you'll forgive me for being so direct, was a Jew. Not an unattractive one, mind, but someone tall and dark, with a little more nose and a little less hair than the perfection I felt my new self deserved. American, without a doubt—jeaned and booted, blow-dried and corduroy-jack-eted. But something about his face, less the nose and the mouth than the eyes, definitely the eyes, suggested something more than American, more than Jewish, something wise and pre-Columbian.

"Shall we go in?" He led more than asked, and guided me back across the drive. "Nice house," he said, turning the knob and opening the door I was certain I had locked. "Cost a million in the States."

"I'm sorry, Hook," I finally said, still bewildered by the initial "Holland" and feeling very much like bolting out the front door and climbing the nearest horse chestnut, "I don't

know if I'm up to it this evening." The whole story followed—
the divorce, the growth, the confusion—the two of us standing
there in the foyer, Hook in his boots, me in my zoris, the front
door wide open, the boys kicking goals in the evening light.
Hook shut the door gently and led me to the kitchen table.

"I know all about it," he said. He drew a bottle of Margaux
from his leather shoulder bag and coaxed several glasses down
my throat while from secret depths he pulled radicchio and
endive, veal and spring rice, and a golden rhum baba that had
"Eat Me" written all over the top.

Alice, I thought, that's who I am. I'm Alice. It's perfectly
natural in Wonderland to wake up in the morning and find
you're six feet tall and 38-D. I'm Alice. But who is he, this
American Jew with the magical mystery meal and the over-
priced wine? Too tall to be the Mad Hatter, too visible to be
the Cheshire Cat. Neither Caterpillar nor Butterfly. Who
baked the Eat Me cake? Who distilled the Drink Me hooch?

"I want you to hear something remarkable." The dishes
were rinsed, the bottle was empty, I was drinking Sambuca,
and Hook was guiding me into my own parlour. He found the
stereo, took a cassette from his pocket, and pushed Play.

There we stood, me looking at the carpet, Hook watching for
my reaction, while the most extraordinary music surrounded
us. A note, a low note, a red-wine note, full of resin and peel,
a violin note, although that not apparent until a full thirty
seconds had passed, and still the same note for another thirty.
Then another, higher, but only by inches; lighter, but only by
grams. Each note vibrating for a count of sixty—eight minutes
for the first octave, eight minutes of undisputed beauty, but an
eternity for any polite party trick.

By the second octave, it was clear there was no stopping the
tape. Hook had invited himself to my house, had cooked me
three courses and half a bottle, for no other reason than to
make me listen to a G-major scale played on the violin. And the
miracle of it: I bought into the show with the same ease I'd

accepted my bonus twelve inches. It all seemed right, appropriate, *comme il faut.* I hadn't offered Hook a seat. But this was music to stand by.

On and up the scale, well into the third octave, each note setting the stage for the next, each note making sense of the one preceding. Each note carrying movements, resonances, definitions, suggesting beginnings, directions, variations, unravelling diversions, melodies, sonatas, cantatas, concerti, meanings—none played, all possible. Up, up, nearly half an hour, four alarming octaves to an impossible anti-feline G, and then down, down just as slowly, down, with a knee-wrenching, thigh-flexing deliberation, down another twenty-eight minutes to the hollow bottom, beyond which nothing—relief, apprehension, terror.

This was the New Vocabulary, the New Language that Hook had brought me. This was the Berlitz course, total immersion. This was *Larousse* and Laura Ashley, *O.E.D.* and Footnotes to *Alice,* Pith Helmet and Puttees for my safari into the New World of my New Body.

That was the first time I heard Sandor play the violin, although Hook wouldn't identify the violinist until he'd played me the entire oeuvre, which took the better part of the evenings of the next three weeks. The schedule was invariable. Hook arrived at six with the latest goss from the office, I cooked dinner. Then three hours of violin. The four-octave scale led quickly to Corelli, Vivaldi, and Bach. So effective was the drug that it took me until the next morning to wonder why I was allowing this, if I was allowing this. And by the time I'd determined to retake command of my evenings, it was six o'clock and too late to flee to the Heath.

Hook assumed merciful charge of those early daytimes. The Beeb was led to believe that I was laid up with a post-divorce depression that was contagious to any who had known me married. Hook was entrusted with all communication, which relieved the sympathetic hordes no small amount. He read my

mail, he wrote my replies. He materialized a catalogue from
Spiegel's of Chicago, and from that a new wardrobe, not too
expensive, but foreign enough that no Englishwoman could tell
how cheap.

He taught me how to hook a bra. By midnight he was gone.

You would have thought in those three weeks, we'd have
slept together. There wasn't time in the plan. Not that I wasn't
dying of the itch. There I was, legally divorced and literally
Lollobrigidized, without the time in the evenings or the will in
the daytime to get it off. The first week, Foss called with urgent
lunchtime importunings. I tried to explain the change, what
had happened the morning after the divorce. He took the
whole story as a metaphoric kiss-off. He wanted to try one more
time, to talk, actually talk with me. But I couldn't see confront-
ing his sixty-four inches with my seventy-two in some seedy
haunt near the British Museum, and risking having him faint
away and hit his head against a rusty shilling-a-toss gas fire.
And as he couldn't take the time to travel up the Northern Line
during the day, the phone calls ceased.

Instead, I drew the curtains, laid my chin music on the
turntable, and touched myself shamelessly. The first movement
of the Beethoven Concerto was the best, left and right hands
working on my approximations of ebony fingerboard and
horsehair bow. Or Mischa Elman's recording of Saint-Saëns's
"Rondo Capriccioso" with its timely grace notes.

But nothing could match the unbearable heat, the physical
agony of the Sandor tapes. I sat, I stood, across from Hook,
next to Hook, on the carpet, leaning against the mantel, but
always away from the speakers that liquefied my very being. I
had no vision of Sandor, no picture of face or physique, and
never once was drawn to anthropomorphize the torturous
sound. But I itched, itched in torment, to wrap my legs around
the JBL's, take woofer and tweeter, crossover and horn deep,
deep inside me, to have the sound itself, free of body and
psyche, harmonizing with my own perfection. And every mid-

night, I gazed in silent longing at the bag of X-rated cassettes bouncing away on Hook's departing bum.

I returned to work at the beginning of November—Hook eased that transition too, guiding me around the stares and the whispers of men who had once known me eyeball-to-eyeball and now had to deal with a retinaful of breast.

I pestered Hook for details about Sandor. All I could glean was a vague story of a child prodigy who had given up performing and recording years before. Hook had attended Sandor's final master class the previous summer, and by his own account had been the star pupil, though my efforts to provoke a performance from him were as fruitless as my requests for tapes. Something about Sandor's Method, diktats against stunts, against playing for an audience of even one, against copying his image—something medieval, superstitious.

All other Sandor info—whereabouts, phone numbers, country of residence—were, *bien sûr*, Top Secret. After a few months, when the itch had scratched itself dry with its own lack of success, my interest became purely documentary. My new body had given me new powers. I had carte blanche at the Beeb—top camera crews, prime programming time, and the slavering tongues of the Publicity Department. I offered Hook a tithe of my projects, but no bribe was sufficient. He was vaguely uninterested in the business of documentary filmmaking, and was using whatever journalism grant had brought him to the U.K. for entirely private purposes. I suggested he was an agent of the CIA one evening over dinner at Bianchi's. He laughed. His project was mysterious, he confessed, but far more so than anything the U.S. government could cook up.

One day in February he was gone—desk cleared, no forwarding address, no phone number, poof.

By then, I was used to surprises. Maggie became PM. The City opened up. Lina and Tina Philosopoulos, a pair of kittenish teenage twins, made a middle-size fortune trading olive oil and diverted a large chunk to form a TV production company with myself as creative director. I sold Hampstead. I bought a ninety-nine-year lease on a corner house in a gate off Hyde Park. I bought my production company when Lina and Tina were extradited to Athens for wire fraud. Award followed award, until I made so much sterling that I couldn't afford to go anywhere near a camera. Morning was spent in First Class, lunch with distributors and accountants, dinner with bankers and ambassadors, drinks, if I was lucky, with the occasional director. Chastity and Cash were inevitable. My films couldn't lose.

But every night, entirely alone, whether between silk at the Okura or satin at L'Hôtel, I dreamed of the sound of Sandor's violin, four octaves of rising excitement, four octaves of descending recovery, fifty-seven minutes to fall asleep. And every time I flew to the States, I searched for Hook, in the papers, in the phone book, in casual conversation.

Then one December morning two years ago, one of those brilliant, crisp blue—I had a suite at the Carlyle, fourteenth floor, view of the park—un-London, New York mornings, coffee arrived with *The New York Times* opened to the Arts page. In the top right corner, unmissable—Hook—same eyes, same nose, a little more flesh, a little less hair. Below—a time and an address, beneath the bowels of Manhattan, in the genitalia of the Lower East Side, well past my bedtime. But rearranged, unbooked, dereserved, and enlimoed, I travelled *toute seule* to the steam-spitting cobblestones of Downtown.

I queued behind a cordon of downtown types—black shoes, black socks, blond hair, a few nuns. The Plaza de Toros was more of a sandpit than a club. At five minutes to midnight, two or three hundred people were already seated in the circular bleacher. I glanced at faces, searched laps for any other ready-folded editions of *The New York Times*.

At midnight sharp the lights went out. No dimming, no announcement, no accommodation for conversation. With the lights, all sound. I shifted on my bench, but the acoustics of the club muffled the rustle of my skirt to silence. For five minutes we sat, then a dim light, a bull's-eye in the middle of the sandpit, a violin and a bow, suspended six feet off the ground. I shifted again, wondering, is this what twelve years has accomplished for Hook, returned him to a prepubescent avant-garde? Is it for this the mystery? I sat for half an hour, impatience on the rise, waiting, if for nothing else, for a glimpse of Hook.

Then I heard it. Starting on the low G, settling there for a count of thirty and for thirty seconds more. Up to the G-sharp, the A, the A-sharp, the B. The violin all the time motionless, the bow hanging parallel to the instrument, all sound impossible, but still—Sound—not from speakers, but from violin, bow, joined in dim light, six feet above sand—Sandor. After twelve years of imagining, here was the sound again, not in my head, but vivid, public, the others around me moving, itching, groping, mumbles, gurgles in the backs of their throats, giving way to screams as the third octave gave way to the fourth and the insupportable scratchless shriek of the high-high-high G.

To this day, I have not seen a loudspeaker small enough to hide in a violin, faithful enough to reproduce the tone I heard in the Plaza de Toros that late night. Conceivably Hook had perfected a form of ventriloquism, so concentrating our attentions on the dangling violin that if the voice of Elvis had spoken to us, we would have been convinced it had drawled out the f-holes.

But this was the voice of Sandor, with a tradition behind it as long and torturous as the Memphis Blues. And now, no longer just the G-major scale that Hook had played me twelve years before in my parlour, but the full range of Western chromatics, all the notes to all the scales, all the modes, from Aeolian to Babylonian, the Full Vocabulary, the Entire Language. Twelve notes to an octave, four octaves up, four octaves down, eight octaves and the final G, one minute per note, ninety-seven minutes to hear every note in the repertoire.

No Sandor. No Hook. Not out front. Not backstage.

It was well past two when I fell down onto the business end of my Carlyle suite, hot and unsatisfied as ever, more angry than aroused. I had grown used to having orders followed, expectations fulfilled—to getting satisfaction. A strategically opened morning newspaper, as innocent as half a grapefruit, had provoked me into the kind of frenzy I had buried long before on the Heath. The phone rang.

"Did you like the concert?" The same cheek. The same Hook.

"I've got to see you." Joan Crawford at her least beguiling grimaced back at me from the mirror across the room, hair askew, telephone like a Dorian Gray goiter.

"That's impossible," Hook said, "but look"—before I could hurl twelve years of invective back at him—"I've got something for you."

"Yes?"

"Sandor. It's time."

"You know where he is?" I found a Carlyle biro and pad in one unconscious move.

"Nineteen ninety-two," Hook said.

"In the Carlyle!" Just five floors above me?

"The year," Hook continued. "Not far off. I want you to do the picture." I put down my biro.

"Hook," I said, "what in the world are you talking about?"

"You wanted to meet Sandor?" he asked. "I'm giving you the chance to make a documentary—in time for ninety-two." Ninety-two, I thought, the United Europe, big deal, what's that got to do with Sandor?

"Columbus," Hook said. "Five hundred years. Sandor and Columbus. It's a helluva story." I felt like throwing the phone into Madison Avenue airspace.

"Hook"—I put on my cajoling voice—"can't we have breakfast? It's two-thirty in the A.M. and, frankly, I am having great difficulty following what I suspect is an interesting and provocative, and, need I remind you, the first, conversation we have had in thirteen years."

"Listen, Holland," Hook said. "Go to sleep. We'll talk, but not tomorrow. There'll be something for you to read with your coffee—the Carlyle dug up some Devonshire cream. Fax Ben, he'll sort out the details. Sleep tight."

"Ben?" Isabella had ridden the waves of Holland's story with an intensity that gave nothing away, neither comprehension nor bewilderment. "Ben?" she asked again.

"Yes, Ben," Holland said, standing for a stretch of those long legs and a walk around the fountain. "That was the first I ever heard of Ben."

"And so, Holland," I said, "did you live happily ever after?" She stopped and looked down at me, the same bewildered look I saw in the airport when I asked her to help lift your trunk. I offered the girl another kipferln.

"With every other film," Holland began, "every other documentary I've ever made, I've known, with absolute certainty, after the last frame has been shot, whether it's a prize-winner or a dog best left in the kennel. Last night, here in this courtyard, Sandor played for me thirty-one minutes of Bach. That's it, over there, in the camera, on the wheels, the child of a fourteen-year-old obsession. Last night, I thought that's it, that's the ace, the closer, the finish, the coup, the winner. Tonight, I'm not so sure."

"Ben?"

"That's it." Holland smiled at the girl. "Ben."

HOLLAND—HANNI'S TALE

Ben Darling,

> *"S'i' credesse che mia risposta fosse*
> *a persona che mai tornasse al mondo,*
> *questa fiamma staria senza più scosse;*
> *Ma però che già mai di questo fondo*
> *non tornò vivo alcun, s'i' odo il vero,*
> *senza tema d'infamia ti rispondo."*

Ah.

When Guido spilled his guts to Dante, when J. Alfred told all to T.S., they were convinced that the travelling poets were down in Hell to stay, not out to gather dirt for the unauthorized hardcover, bio-doc, or Studs Terkel oral history.

> *If I ever thought I were telling my tale*
> *to writers holding return tix,*
> *I'd freeze right up and turn my tail;*
> *But since I know there are no round trips,*
> *if the stories I have heard are true,*
> *open your ears and read my lips.*

Poor Guido. Dying for a good natter, dying to tell his dirty secret to someone. How was he to know that Dante would publish, that his story would be studied and ignored by millions of adolescents? How can you tell someone to go to Hell when they're already eight rings down?

The rest of us tell our tales to uncomprehending girls and immovable old women.

And you. You I tell more.

Still, I wish I had my Carlos.

Why do I think of you now, Ben, with my jumpsuit down around my ankles, on the very loo where I found Sandor peacefully asleep just twenty-four hours ago?

What are you like, Ben?

Strange, how I know you only from your writing, and then, mostly for "BR342 J 10DEC LGWMRP HK1 1000 1235." Are you tall, slim, ruddy like Histon, receding like Duxford, olive-complected like my Hook? Do you have an age, a history, a favourite colour, a sexual preference? Are you attracted to forty-six-year-old women?

Whatever—tall, short, slim, plump, young, mature, dark, or fair—you'd be different, a man in a different image. I couldn't tell them, Isabella, Hanni, could I? About the fourteen years, the fourteen years since Hook. The fourteen years and hundreds of penises, great and small, thick and thin, knobbed and veined, circumcised and un-, consistent only in their inability to—*s'i' credesse,* Ben—to sustain an erection.

The first four or five times you think, oops, a spot of bad luck, girl. These men are working too hard, drinking too hard, making love too recently to their wives, donating blood at lunchtime. Then the suspicion begins to creep up your thigh that you attract only impotent men. And there you are, just one frustrating truth away from the recognition that your spanking-new, ultra-fantastic, super-sexy body is just Too Much. Men are overwhelmed by it, can't see past the curves how they could possibly please it, fill it, excite it, satisfy it, stand up to it. So they don't.

Word gets around. For a while, you become a challenge, and, itchy as you are, you revel in it. The airline pilots, the muscle-builders, the construction workers, the entire trombone section of the Berlin Philharmonic have a go at you. Blind men, men wearing gloves, it doesn't matter. No sensory deprivation is total enough for you to find a man who can make love to you the way Man ought. I have it on film—one doctor insisted. It's like a Looney Tunes cartoon, the potted plant wilting as soon as the watering can comes near. Then the challenges dry up. It's hardly reasonable to expect an entire species to play sexual Sisyphus.

But you'd be different, Ben—*s'i' credesse*! You would take me here, jumpsuit down, unclasp my bra. You'd bend and cup my breast around your bearded, bristled, smooth-shaven cheek, take its fullness into the wide *O* of your mouth, tease my nipple with your tongue. You'd lift me up and off—whatever your size, your strength would be infinite. You'd take me in your hairy, muscled, tattooed, slender, balletic arms, and float me into the garden like Good King Sol with the Hashemite woman, lay me beneath the olive trees on a bed of lichen and thyme. My head would arch back to the stars above the Moorish wall as those strong, delicate, workmanlike hands of a violinist spread my thighs apart with the merest, impossibly tender touch, and the mouth I've never heard talks to me in a tongue I haven't felt since my second spring. And then, like the never-faltering wonder you are, you would rise up before me, the waters would part, and unlike, very unlike, the rest, never wilting, never failing, move into me, around me, guide me, send me travelling as no man has in fourteen winters, fourteen summers.

O Ben, O Ben, O Ben, Ben, Ben . . .

"Here's my story, Isabella. Like Holland, I changed."

Re-zipped, de-storied, I sat on the steamer trunk by the fountain. Isabella had wedged a cushion between two stone lions. Hanni stood before us, eyes sparkling, poised to recite.

A week after Mama's death, Papa sold the travel business and wrote us two tickets on the *Vulcania* to fight the Fascists in Spain. Mama died on my thirteenth birthday, but as I had been figuring the accounts in the office for over two years, Papa expected he'd find some suitable desk job for me among the Republicans.

Mama had always wanted to tour the Spain of her ancestors. But I don't think guilt played a major role in Papa's choice of destination. Mama was the one who set great stock in death and remembrance. She was the one who collected history books. Papa bought art—well-framed reproductions of Modigliani and Picasso, autographed photos of baseball stars. Papa's vision was forward, always forward. He loved Mama with pride and genuine physical passion. But Mama was dead, her body cremated. Tears had been shed, ashes stored in a discount urn in Queens. The inventory of Halevy Travel now belonged to a Pole named Zenizek. It was Monday, a new week.

I packed ten days' worth of clothing for each of us in two medium-size mahogany-colored dry-cleaning boxes with leather straps. A hand-tooled portfolio held our European maps and railroad timetables. My vision of traveling off to fight for freedom in the parlor car of a regularly scheduled train was not entirely crazy. New York was well insulated from the bitter cold of Europe. The week before we left, the thermometer climbed to 70 degrees for the big Nazi rally at Madison Square Garden, and the Yankees headed off to spring training in St. Pete without signing Joe DiMaggio.

The pain of leaving America struck me only on the morning of our departure, standing with our bags in the shadow of the great hull of the Italian liner at the end of Fifty-second Street. Fifty-second Street itself—not at the Hudson River but in the heart of the heart of the city, the Onyx, the Famous Door, the jazz clubs that Mama and Papa loved, the 78s they brought home, autographed by Joe Venuti, Stuff Smith, Eddie South. And a memory of a river—standing in the middle of the middle of the brand-new George Washington Bridge, the biggest bridge in the world, the three of us spitting down into the Hudson, like Galileo from the leaning tower of Pisa. I had thought of myself as a citizen of maps, and my innocence caught me that much more by surprise. I had never traveled.

"Where's Papa?" Zenizek ran up, out of breath. I pointed to the shipping office. Fifteen minutes later, the two of them returned. Papa hoisted me on his shoulders. Zenizek strapped our luggage on his back. Our plans had changed. The Spanish government had fallen. Franco was in power. Papa was a romantic, but he was not a fool. Two blocks later, we stood in the shadow of the *Queen Mary*. Just after noon, we waved to Zenizek from the tourist-class deck, as we pushed back from the dock and sailed, in front of the *Vulcania,* bound for Cherbourg.

It was a Saturday, February 25, 1939. Bette Davis had just won the Oscar for *Jezebel.*

Because we had booked at the last possible minute, our cabin was cramped, below the lowest of the low. It was equipped with a single bunk—I slept on a fold-out cot—and shared a communal toilet and bathroom with the entertainers. It was there, as I was damping my frizzy hair in the hopes of keeping it down, that one of the long-legged chorus girls told me that Yehudi Menuhin was a passenger and would perform that night for the first-class passengers.

You had to have been deaf and blind in America in the thirties not to have heard of Yehudi, the child prodigy, the chubby little California boy who wowed Elman, Heifetz, and Kreisler himself with a monstrous technique and a fierce concentration. I had seen him play a Paganini caprice at a New Ycar's Day party when I was five—all fireworks and gunpowder. As soon as the last explosion had died away, I rushed over and hugged him so tightly that it was only with the promise that he would teach me a tune that he rescued his violin. We spent the rest of the afternoon together with his beautiful sisters. At bedtime, I told Mama on the spot that Prince Charming could go find himself another bride, I would marry a violinist.

Dressed in the memory of that afternoon, wearing party frock, adult stockings, and patent-leather pumps, I stepped across the chain at five minutes to eight and marched down the corridor to the first-class salon of the *Queen Mary*. I had, of course, sold plenty of first-class tickets in my brief career in the business. But we were a family of travel agents, movers, never passengers. The idea that the restrictions and privileges of class applied to me and Papa was entirely absent from my plans for the evening.

So my struggle against the steward's request that I leave the recital and go back to the tourist side of the ship began as sincerely bewildered innocence. It was only as the whispers rose around me—half-caught half-sentences about my "rudeness," my "hair," my "nose," my "Jewish behavior"—that my resistance turned into refusal. I think the steward would have left well enough alone—the lights were dimming—if I hadn't insisted on maintaining my right to stay by shouting, "Hi, Yehudi, it's me, Hanni!" as my hero walked out onto the stage.

"Perhaps we spoiled you, your mother and I," Papa said a few minutes later, stroking my wild hair while I cried out my anger. "There are rules and regulations in fine print at the bottom of every ticket, yours included."

"I don't like being a passenger," I shouted at him. "I want to go home."

"Another week or so," he said.

"Cooped up in this cabin?" I wailed.

"Here." He handed me a packet of papers. "If you have nothing better to do, read this," and he walked quietly into the corridor.

That was the first time I held the Esau Letter in my hands, the letter I've come to Spain to find. Over the next few years, I read the Letter dozens, hundreds, of times, memorized passages. But that night on the *Queen Mary*, as I sat in the cabin, reading about events five hundred years distant, all I could think was how sad it must be to be my father, to be my travel agent. And hours later, when my godlike Papa returned from the bar leading a flushed Yehudi by the arm for a private midnight recital, it was only the strongest, most supreme joy that overcame my remorse and contrition.

Though we continued to see Yehudi, the sea change in both me and Papa owed more to the triumph of Papa's will. Yehudi had turned into a slimmed-down twenty-one, newly married, with an expectant wife back in California. I had lost a dream husband. No matter. I had fallen desperately in love with my father. And on the fourth day of my trip, on the strength of my father's lesson, I attracted another beau.

The unseasonably sunny weather was perhaps part of the cause for my metamorphosis on board the *Queen Mary*. A change, Holland—not as dramatic, perhaps, as your dramatic growth. A change, after all, is not unexpected in a thirteen-year-old who finds herself bereft of a mother and embarked on the *Queen Mary* in the space of two weeks. Still, sudden emotion and exposure to the sun doesn't turn black hair blond. Brown eyes don't turn blue from tears or from hours of staring at the waves, no matter what the song says. I began to menstruate on board ship, but that wouldn't entirely explain the changes in my features, the rising of the cheekbones, the shortening of the nose. Something happened. That something must have been Papa. Papa's footnotes to the Esau Letter, Papa's lessons about motion. Papa's dreamy-eyed dissertation on travel agents. Papa was preparing me for a new life, a new challenge in our new destination—Germany.

Over the years, and by years Papa meant centuries, the family had developed a theory of survival based more on physics than biology. In the beginning of the universe—and you understand that the seeds of this theory were sown long before Newton and fertilized well before Einstein—all matter was condensed into a single particle. All matter. Everything that might possibly, someday, somewhere, somehow, turn into something—stars, planets, moons, trees, oceans, people, fish, hair, warts, holidays in Tuscany, sleepless nights, falling in love—everything was contained in this single particle. Then something pushed this particle, something split it, something started it moving at an unbelievably fast pace, so fast that the universe continues to expand to this day. Time continues to move forward, people are born, copulate, and die, life goes on.

And you ask yourself, if you are a curious person, who pushed the particle without being pushed himself? Who split this lifeball without herself exploding into hundreds of thousands of millions of pieces? What started the whole ball rolling without losing its balance? Some call it God, some call it the Unmoved Mover.

Our family says it's travel agents, travel agents who move the world.

Of course it's a give-and-take. Sometimes people decide for themselves where and when and how they want to go. Sometimes other people decide for them. Ultimately, they all ask the travel agent, even those who believe they are clever enough to book direct. Ultimately, it is the travel agent who writes the fine print.

"There are going to be a lot of people in motion throughout Europe in the next few years," Papa predicted in the winter of '39. "They are going to need our help." With the fall of the Republic in Spain, the next logical travel hub was Berlin. And by the force of a will that would have been the envy of Hitler had he known of it, in only three days Papa and I acquired an impeccable command of German, as it is spoken by an *echt* Berliner who has been forced—by circumstances unmentioned but undoubtedly to do with the Treaty of Versailles—to live outside his beloved city for a time. My father went from Mr. to Herr, and I from Marjorie Morningstar to Marlene Dietrich.

"Gloria Swanson," Jack said, as he vaulted across the chain

from the first-class deck to tourist during a lifeboat drill. "Gloria Swanson, that's who you look like." He insisted on cinching my life jacket and spent the rest of the afternoon sipping bouillon on the promenade deck with me and Papa, making sure we knew about his brilliant career at Harvard, his brother the Air Force pilot, and how he was off to London to give his father, the U.S. ambassador, a few tips about Britain and appeasement. The next evening, my makeover so successful that no steward approached except to hold my chair, I dined with Jack at the captain's table. I liked Jack, he was a mover. At the very least, he knew all the moves.

"He's got all the makings of a travel agent," I said proudly to Papa after Jack had escorted me back from a flirtatious starlit stroll to the eighth ring of our tourist-class inferno.

"I'm afraid not, Hanni," Papa said, stroking my hair, still marveling over his new, womanly daughter. "He knows how to move people. I wish your Mama could see how lovely you look." I shimmied away from his hand, shy but delighted.

"But Jack needs the company of people," Papa went on. "So too does a travel agent, from time to time, have to be a passenger, to mix, to judge, to consider. But afterward, it's back to the desk, to the phone, to the timetables. Jack is a star. If we do our jobs right, we travel agents are merely the darkness at the center of the universe."

Within four weeks we had set up shop as MittelEuropa Reisebüro on Iranische Strasse in the heart of Berlin. Upstairs, a bedroom and a sitting room, downstairs, the office, with a small alcove for reception, and a large kitchen with an eating nook that doubled at night as a bedroom for our one luxury— Frau Wetzler. An unused basement and dusty attic served to store files, furs, and fugitives, with little thought to their future value. Cozy, efficient.

Even then, six months after the unmistakable signal of Kristallnacht, the Jews of Germany were booking vacations along the Baltic coast, cruises to Reykjavík and the Norwegian fjords.

Until the end of 1941, when the bombing of Pearl Harbor, the German invasion of the Soviet Union, and the Wannsee Conference dealt a serious blow to the travel business, the German government actively encouraged the emigration of German Jews. By moving Jews north, west, south through Italy to Palestine, through Spain and France to Bolivia and Argentina, through the Netherlands to the Caribbean, and from everywhere to the United States and Canada, we were providing a universal service.

We had only two opponents. One was bureaucracy—the eight-page, hopelessly detailed documentation of possessions, from pocket watches to shirt studs. I helped hundreds of families fill in these forms, hired derelicts to stand on line, bribed officials to move our clients up the visa ladder. But our most determined enemy was the Jews themselves, the bullheaded German Jews who wanted to stay and tough it out, the Jews who felt that their exodus would signal the death of German *Kultur*. It took hidden discounts, reduced fares, incentive programs, magicians and Mendelssohn for Papa and me to encourage families to pack, to take their children and grandparents. Twenty thousand Jews left Germany on package cruises in those last few years before travel, as we had known it, became illegal.

Many of these discounts, of course, came out of our pockets, and we had to take on a good deal of government work to make ends meet. Papa joined the Party—there were more than a few secret Jews. I dated appropriate officials whenever appropriate. We consulted with the government to improve the railroad timetables; we passed along the wisdom of centuries on how to move large groups of passengers. We moved by train, by plane, by boat, by car. In the first six months of 1944, we booked over two million individual tickets.

We tried to move more clients westward than eastward. Our unspoken personal defense was rooted in that balance. We kept statistics, in neatly bound ledgers, like good Germans. For the sake of sanity, we couldn't afford to look at them.

Much of our success came through our furniture-moving division. Whenever an officer needed to move house or office—the skeptical aristocrats of the Luftwaffe were particularly helpful—Papa or I would arrange for a few Jewish families, hidden in our warehouses, root cellars, and friendly churches, to be packed in sideboards or piano cases and spirited out of the country. It seemed safer initially for us to make all the arrangements without the participation of either foreign governments or resistance movements.

But one morning—a warm, brilliant 1943 June—a message arrived at Iranische Strasse. A Danish border guard had discovered a sealed boxcar with our stamp—a container of thirty-five ornamental urns, shipped weeks before to Stockholm. I borrowed a driver from a beau in the Gestapo, along with several sticks of dynamite. From one hundred yards away, the stench told me all I needed to know. Thirty-five Jews had either starved or suffocated to death. I had to blow up the boxcar to hide the evidence. I cried for a week.

Papa and I recognized two facts—that we needed help and a change of tactics. Moving large numbers of people was no longer effective. We had to narrow our focus, to move one person in particular, even if assassination was the motion of choice.

So it came to pass, on the night of July 20, 1944, as Papa and I sat numbed by Hitler's voice on the radio, that I first spoke to Zoltan. Hitler was railing, shrieking about an attempted assassination earlier that day that had left him wounded but still firmly in command. I discounted the entire story initially as fabrication, an opportunity to clean out the ranks. But I knew Papa's silence well enough to sense not only that the plot was sincere, but that somewhere along the line, transportation had been provided by MittelEuropa Reisebüro.

There was a knock. Zoltan was ushered in by Frau Wetzler. Papa's face cleared for a moment, a look of relief, perhaps even joy. He flipped off the radio, turned to me to make a quick introduction, and then dropped back into his chair, his face wet, as if tears had blanketed the night like morning dew.

Zoltan was a violinist, another violinist. He was a Jew from Kiev, whether by birth or migration, a staunch Communist, and a musician of such angelic powers that Herbert von Karajan himself arranged his forged papers in order to hire him as concertmaster of the Berliner Staatsoper. As the Reichsquartett, the first chairs of the string section were often called upon to entertain Hitler and his entourage—increasingly so as the war turned and Hitler took refuge in isolation.

I had chartered planes and cars for the Reichsquartett on several occasions, but before that night had seen Zoltan only from afar. He was a striking man with a command, an authority so complete that it created opinion. Not tall but dark, very dark. He looked Russian because I had been told he was Russian. He looked Jewish because I had been told he was Jewish. But if someone had said he was Italian, Greek, Latin, or Moroccan, I think I would have believed that description without hesitation.

"So," Papa said after a moment, looking up at both of us. "There is a train for Saarbrücken departing from Bahnhof Zoo at four A.M." I knew most of the rest, which boxcar would have an empty crate, which guard could be bribed.

"Destination?" I asked Papa, usually only a hope or an intention, but still important.

"Spain?" Papa looked up to Zoltan, who, with only his violin case clutched to his coat, shrugged like a street musician with little money and less choice.

I dressed quickly, took cash, keys, a knife, never a revolver. I was down the shadows of the staircase when Papa called me back.

"Hanni," he said, stroking my hair and smiling. "I want you to go with Zoltan, make certain he is safe."

"To the station, of course."

"To Spain," he said, a command.

"To Spain," I repeated, thinking it was a joke. He handed me a portfolio. My papers.

"Good-bye."

"See you next week," I said.

"To Spain."

"To stay?" I asked.

"If you are so moved." He closed the door. I was all of eighteen.

HOLLAND—HANNI IN LOVE

"The White Rabbit."

"The white what?" Hanni asked. I was staring into the darkness off the west wing of the Villa Gabirol, watching Hanni disappear down the rabbit hole of her flat on Iranische Strasse.

"When I first saw you at the airport," I said, "I thought to myself, that's who she is, the White Rabbit. Alice's White Rabbit."

"One woman's Rabbit is another woman's Alice." Hanni smiled. The lantern light made her chamois skin seem even softer, more elfin. "I can't begin to describe the power of that man—I wondered why Papa had sent me along as chaperon. Which one of us was Rabbit, which one Alice, and what was Wonderland?"

I poured more coffee; Hanni passed around her biscuits. Isabella propped half her hair above one ear, hugged one knee, kept both eyes on Hanni.

It took a few days longer than I'd expected. D-day was two months old, after all, and my railroad timetables were worth more as toilet paper. At Bahnhof Zoo, I was lucky enough to find a boxcar with a roomy Bechstein crate. For the price of the piano, I bribed an aesthetically inclined Nazi, who rented me the entire car, no questions asked, through Wiesbaden and Saarbrücken, Metz and Nancy, out of the Occupied Zone, and down into Vichy. I fed Zoltan kipferln when I could, through a small hole at the bass end of the harp. But once we reached the Rhône valley, I sprung my captive from his music box to taste the irresistible smell of fresh summer away from Germany.

He emptied his pisspot. I had wheeled the door half-open to freshen the car with the scent of the vineyards and the hay. Zoltan stood in the breeze, his clothes a map of Europe, his hair a cratered railway. He stretched his arms to the frame, stretched his fingers, each one moving on its own, playing a ten-part fugue of freedom. I picked his greatcoat from the bottom of the crate, hung it on the hinge to air, and turned back to place his violin on something a little sturdier.

"Stand back," Zoltan said sharply, and didn't so much yank the case from my hands as draw it toward him and fold cross-legged down to the floor of the boxcar in one nervous motion.

The case opened, he lifted the purple velour cover off the violin. The violin itself, a rich matted brown, not too shiny, speckled with age, long and graceful, a Guarneri, I found out later, built more for intimacy than power. Zoltan twisted the pegs, loosened the strings, removed the bridge and tweezed the sound-peg out through an f-hole. Pulling a curved wood-knife from a side compartment, he pried the top off the fiddle to reveal a cheap Swiss clock, three red sticks, and enough wire to inspire a quartet of executions. The bomb was dismantled, the dynamite wrapped in the velour. With greater care, Zoltan skimmed off the old glue from under the top of the fiddle, and asked me to hold the wood while he unscrewed a bottle hidden within his trousers. With the flat of the knife, he spread a fresh coat around the edges, reassembled and clamped the violin, and returned it to its case.

"Thank you," Zoltan said, with the brusque bow of a Russian, turned to the door of the boxcar, and vomited onto the tracks.

This was his story:

The quartet had been invited to play for Hitler at his East Prussian camp in Rastenburg. Mussolini, defeated and in exile, was coming for tea, and his considerate host thought that a little music might ease the pressures of conversation.

Papa arranged the travel documents for the quartet, a chartered plane from Rangsdorf to the Rastenburg airfield. He brought the tickets around to Zoltan's flat on Oranienstrasse on the night of the nineteenth and, with them, the three sticks of dynamite and the alarm clock. With Papa assisting, Zoltan performed a similar operation on the Guarneri, setting the bomb to detonate at five-thirty the next afternoon, when the quartet would be half an hour into their concert, somewhere near the climax of their transcription of the Liebestod from Wagner's *Tristan und Isolde*. Hitler liked to look over the shoulder of the first violin. The plan was foolproof.

They arrived at Rastenburg early in the morning and slept late. They were practicing in the early afternoon when a red-eyed guard burst in and shouted at them, How can you make music while the Führer lies bleeding? Another assassination plot had preempted theirs! Zoltan felt the bomb just above his collarbone and thought about his noble suicide, and how much more painful death would be once the Gestapo impounded their instruments.

But the distress at the camp was general enough, and the musicians' hut distant enough from the center, that Zoltan was able to take his violin and greatcoat to the latrine, and climb out of Rastenburg through the barbed wire without raising an alarm. He was about to dismantle his bomb when a Gestapo officer drove up.

As Zoltan stood, the officer recognized him immediately, and jumped at the chance to transport such a famous passenger all the way back to Berlin. Communications had apparently been cut because of, or perhaps as part of, the assassination attempt, and this officer had heard nothing. So they drove through the afternoon, talking about Strauss and Wagner, Zoltan waiting for the officer to stop for a meal, a crap, anything that would allow him to disengage the bomb. But Gestapo officers are made of sterner stuff, and as five-thirty approached and they were still one hundred miles east of Berlin, Zoltan resorted to prayer.

The bomb did not go off. Six, seven, ten o'clock, still nothing. The officer shook Zoltan's bowhand vigorously and left him at a bar on the corner of Iranische Strasse. He made his way down the block to our flat.

"Without disengaging the bomb beforehand?" I asked Hanni, not quite putting two and two together. Hanni smiled.

"You are a journalist, Holland," Hanni said. "I was a young girl, in love with the greatest violinist in the world. The first sight of Zoltan in Papa's apartment, those eyes—it was only years later that I asked myself that same question. Or why he hadn't dismantled the instrument in the darkness of the crate, or merely thrown it away."

"And the answer?"

"About the bomb? That was the least of my questions. Listen."

I spoke to Zoltan about Papa, about Mama, about myself and New York. He listened, told me of his triumphs, in Moscow, in Leningrad, of Paris in the teens and New York in the twenties. The light of the afternoon faded. After six hours, he took the clamps off the Guarneri and played me folk songs and lullabies, the fullness of the violin soaking into the worm-eaten boards of the boxcar, until my eyes closed and I let him make love to me. It was not the first time, but it was the first time, and it was wonderful.

The train sped up now that I wanted it to slow down. From Montpellier to Sète, to Béziers and Narbonne. Zoltan did nothing but play the violin and make love. Zoltan played everything he could remember—Vivaldi from his student days with Auer, Tchaikovsky from his Russian period, and Bach, Bach from Berlin and Bach from the world. The partitas, the sonatas, the concertos for solo violin, the Concerto for Two Violins, the Triple Concerto, transcriptions of preludes and fugues and piano sonatas. And then the folk songs and lullabies, melodies that watered some half remembrance of bedtime and Mama, tunes both primitive and comforting.

It was then that I found the Esau Letter—Papa had bound it with one of my purple hair ribbons and stuffed it into a side pocket of the portfolio among my papers. I shared pages with Zoltan, stories five hundred years old. Shared history, shared music, souls, bodies in a perfect fit. By the time we reached the Spanish border at Port Bou, I had been moved. As long as Zoltan kept playing the violin, we would win the war, I knew it. My duty was to keep him playing.

I calculated that our best chance at a safe crossing was to approach the border as refugees on foot. At a makeshift camp on the road out of Port Bou, I bought a homespun dress for myself and some sackcloth for Zoltan from a group of French Jews who had been turned back from the frontier that morning. By midafternoon, we stood in a light drizzle at a crooked border hut on the high rocks above Figueras—a gypsy fiddler and his wife, paperless, nationless.

I hadn't counted on an aficionado for a guard. On a slow afternoon, he had all the time in the world to drink brandy and listen to Zoltan play. I knew we wouldn't cross.

"No gypsy ever played like that."

"My friend"—Zoltan smiled with the half-closed eyes of a *gitano*—"there was a time when *only* the gypsies played like that."

"Before my time." The guard smiled back.

"Five hundred years before," Zoltan said, and returned the instrument to his chin.

"Get out!"

"Please, Don Guard," I cried, in an exaggerated Iberian scraping motion. "We must get through to our parents in Rosas."

"Get out!" he said again, and threw open the door. "Go back to Paris, or Vienna, or whatever concert hall you came from. Gypsies, pfah!" and he spit in Zoltan's eye.

Zoltan calmly wiped his face, wiped the rosin from the strings and the parts of the fingerboard and top where it had left a light dusting, placed the violin back in its case, covered it with velour, closed the case, and held the door for me.

"A true *gitano* never held the door for his wife."

"Five hundred years ago," Zoltan said, and stepped down into the rain.

"I have a young son at home who would like that fiddle." The guard opened the door with the toe of his boot. "Perhaps we could come to an arrangement." Zoltan took my arm. We marched back down the path.

Dressed as gypsies, we were unacceptable to the overfed innkeeper of Port Bou. Damp and depressed, we took inadequate shelter beneath an overhanging rock in a fog-shrouded olive grove. We sang songs, talked what little hope we could into the nightfall—a new guard in the morning, a new disguise, sun, perhaps . . .

I fell asleep. I dreamed Beethoven, the Concerto in D, Zoltan and Carnegie Hall. I was dressed all in velvet, our immaculate son on one side, my splendid Papa on the other, in a box, stage left. The broken octaves, the long, rippling arpeggios, the hazelnut-and-sugar melodies, all glided up to us, each one dispatched with a chuff of Zoltan's chin, of his eyes. I gripped our son's hand with pride; he had eyes only for his father. The concerto ended, the audience leapt to its feet. I shuddered awake.

Zoltan was lying on the ground. He had rolled out of our shelter, face up in a puddle of water. His fists were clenched around an imaginary fiddle, an imaginary bow. His lips foamed, the water ran into his eyes, but he couldn't blink. A grating sound, an over-rosined bow pressing too hard on the G-string, rose from some crackling edge of his body. I pulled him in out of the rain, cradled his head in my lap, not knowing whether it was his nightmare or mine that had suddenly seized him by the throat. Words, sounds, came out of his mouth, not Russian, but a garbled kind of Spanish. The rain was a torrent, there was nowhere I could go. I held Zoltan and sheltered myself in a sort of madness until morning. By then he had lost consciousness, the sun had risen. His long fiddler's fingers slowly unwound, and I could read the wrinkled paper in his left hand:

> My dearest Hanni,
>   The inevitable is the inevitable. Violins can stand any-
> thing except rain and heat. I will love you, always.
>
>   Zoltan

In the other hand, an empty vial and a discernible pulse.

It was slow going with Zoltan over one shoulder, his fiddle, our few things and papers over the other. A hundred yards away, a passing farmer helped me drape my burden across his burro and hurried us down to the police barracks. The nearest hospital was over the border in Figueras. As an emergency patient, Zoltan was free to cross the border. I had to stay in France. The guards asked for his papers and took the entire portfolio, Esau Letter, purple ribbon, and all. It was only as they shuffled him down into Spain on a filthy stretcher that I called out for the violin lying on his chest. No one listened. I waited for three days, until I had been told twice he was dead. Without papers, without violin, without Zoltan, I turned my face to Berlin. The Jews were still waiting in their camp, in mourning, singing songs of the destruction of the Temple of Solomon. It was Tisha B'Av, and I was pregnant.

Other women have told me, in the intervening forty-seven years, that they knew, absolutely knew, the moment the sperm found the ovum, or if not then, with the first light of the new day. The Earth felt fresher and brighter, some said, or, in the cases of others, it was as if the air were heavy with thunder and foreboding.

But in a world so suddenly changed, how was I to recognize such ordinary symptoms? I walked north from Port Bou toward Perpignan, then east, into a battlefield, the sounds of the Allies landing on the Mediterranean beaches echoing into the mountains. It wasn't until mid-September, six weeks later, wrapped in the safety of an eiderdown in a chalet hidden by the benign peak of Hornegli in the Bernese Oberland, that I heard a gentle Swiss accent say, *"Dein chlüne cheng werd nöchste Früelig gebore"*— my child would be born at lambing time.

Under the care of Frau Freund and her husband, I stayed warm through the winter, put on weight, and regained my sanity. When they first found me, wandering dazed alongside the tracks of the Montreux–Zweisimmen milk train, I was scratched, bruised, and painfully thin, but moving under the star of the constellation that watches over the innocent and the mad. It was only years later, when I returned to the continent with Leo, that I was able to retrace my probable route with the help of a historical atlas of the war. Somehow, I had lit upon the right combination of trains and barges, footpaths and orchards, to thread the delicate needle between the fleeing Vichy troops and the advancing Americans. If the Freunds had not stopped me, I would have walked through to Berlin by the end of the summer.

Cattle and Hornegli protected the village of Schönried from news of the war. The Freunds, being Swiss, were kind and credulous, lacking all natural curiosity. Before they suspected I'd regained my sanity, I had the presence of mind to tell them I was the American wife of a famous French violinist, who had been caught in the crossfire of advancing troops. Despite the official posture, no one was fundamentally neutral, not even the Swiss, not even the Freunds. Frau Freund had a brother who had made good in Munich. I played it safe.

Why? Why hadn't I given up, given in to the weeks on the road, the certain death of Zoltan, the probable death of Papa? I had watched, even participated, in many of the atrocities the Nazis committed during the first five years of the war. I had lost, it was true, the father of the child I was carrying. But I've met many survivors of the war since, people with stories far more ghastly, who had lost entire families, children, babies. Looked at in a certain light, Zoltan was, after all, only a man I had met on a train.

So what reflex led me to give the right answer to the Freunds? Why did I drink readily of their kindness? Why did I allow them to pamper me, clothe me, why did I look at them with friendly smiles, why did I treat them like my own family? Why did I ultimately run away in the extremis of my eighth month?

You are too young, Isabella, and you, Holland, have been spared the insanity of the pregnant woman. I survived not out of any notion of duty to or love for an unborn child. He was emphatically *not* a child in my womb. A voracious thing-fetus-tadpole, sapping strength, wits, and humor, call him what you like, he was not a child. He was my passenger. I was his travel agent. I set that life into motion, I wrote half the ticket. I survived to carry my passenger to Berlin—whether by first, tourist, or baggage class.

I ate and rested and waited for the snow to begin its spring drip into the valley. I allowed a rich widower-farmer to woo and engage me. On April Fool's Day I stole him blind. By nightfall I had ridden the train past Zurich to the German border.

For ten Swiss francs, I found an eight-year-old boy to ferry me across the Rhine. For another one hundred, a munitions trucker drove me to Donaueschingen and brought me up to date on the Allied advance. The Americans and the British had crossed the Rhine on the west, the Russians were only a few days east of Berlin. For the cost of my overseeing the stewpot, a bargeman, with a cargo of metal scrap bound for Regensburg, carried me down the Danube, past the rock of Sigmaringen, the spire of Ulm, the great abbey of Kelheim, and settled me in the mail car of a train bound for Leipzig.

I slept until I was discovered and hefted from the canvas sacks in Köthen. A night and a day passed until, by accident, I found an empty boxcar headed north and collapsed.

"Wer bist du?" The soldier woke me, I don't know how much later; it could have been a dream.

"Was ist heute?"

"Der erste Mai." He laughed.

"Wo bin ich?"

"In Hell," he said, and burrowed deeper into his shadowy corner to stifle his uncontrollable giggles. The train had stopped. I looked through the door. The sign said Wannsee. Wannsee—where only three years earlier Heydrich and Himmler brewed the Final Solution and turned the world of travel upside down. I had come full circle. I was back in my element. I needed no map to tell me where to go.

I wished the soldier well and slid heavily from the car. As my shoes hit the roadbed, my water broke, thick and red and gelatinous, soaking through my underpants. I left them on the gravel of the tracks. It was a warm May day, and the cool air on my thighs renewed my strength.

My old Berlin had disappeared. I had heard nothing of the bombing in the nine months since I had left, nothing of the constant barrage of the big Russian guns, nothing of the special madness that had kept Hitler fighting past the point of breakage. Only the sound of distant guns convinced me that there was still a war going on. I set my course by smell—there were very few landmarks left standing.

I had my first contraction near Bahnhof Zoo. Fire was everywhere, smoke everywhere else. Corpses missing limbs, corpses missing heads, everywhere horses, half-burned, half-eaten. There was no one about to hear my first cry of surprise. At the second contraction, I winced in disbelief. How could my passenger complain so sharply? But I kept walking. By the time I reached the shambles of the Potsdamer Platz and the billowing smoke of the Reichstag, the contractions were thirty paces apart. I began to sing, the fugue from Bach's Sonata in G Minor for Solo Violin, its constant pulse matching my step, the way it had underscored the click of the wheels as Zoltan and I rode through the Auvergne. Each contraction crunched on the strings with the force of a double-stop, building to a triple-stop, and finally a fully armed four-note chord, stopping me for only the splittest of seconds before wrenching me back to the pulse.

Twenty measures from the end of the fugue, I stood at the head of Iranische Strasse, barely able to walk. The street was paved with the houses of our neighbors, the bodies of soldiers, of old men, old women, young boys wearing hastily scribbled swastikas on their armbands. The police station at the corner was only a doorway and, remarkably, a glass lantern. The Swedish church across the street, where we had hidden so many Jews and other refugees, was a pile of bricks and broken glass. Only our house remained standing.

I had to lean against the doorpost for a moment. The door had disappeared. So had the downstairs walls. I called for Papa, for Frau Wetzler. Nothing. I called again. There was a rustling from upstairs, heavy steps.

Papa! I thought, and shouted, pulling myself heavily up the staircase—a contraction—bits of plaster slipping from under my shoes, the banister falling away with a bang as I reached the landing—another. Bits of wallpaper still clung to the hall, a photograph of my poor dead Mama, dusty but unbroken on its nail—Oh, Mama, help me, I looked in her eyes, willing the pain down, down. The door was closed to our sitting room, and its doorknob came away in my hand as I squeezed it with all the pain of the worst pain so far. Not a moment too soon, I thought, here it comes—Papa! And I opened the door.

I knew he was a Russian from his uniform and his haircut, a slightly dented version of Zoltan's. I was defenseless. There was no time to adapt, no easy Atlantic afternoons to become fluent in Russian entreaty, and all pantomime to explain my condition was redundant. His pants were dropping even as he backed me onto my old, familiar bed. All I could do was think about my passenger and hope there was room for two in the couchette.

I screamed, from the pain, from the fear of the contraction, but he was at me, lifting my skirt, deaf, obviously, from months of shelling and fighting and death, to any human expression. But I screamed also from relief. I knew, before the Russian clawed at my hem, that the passenger had arrived, how completely, I could tell only from the look on the Russian's face, just smelly, bristly inches from mine. There was no way, lying there in the dusty corner, the sound of artillery constant now as the tanks rolled freely into Berlin, that I could hold back any longer. I groaned, a groan of nine months of carting my passenger with the muscles of my legs, the tendons of my back, across Europe, home, home to Berlin. I pushed, I screamed, a Cyrillic scream that finally translated, as the Russian's face jerked back, his lips pulled back from his jaws, his body tried to flee, as my baby, no longer a tadpole, but my great, hairy, toothy boy, reached with his first natal instinct, grabbed the red-veined testicles of the Russian, lifted his head with the upbeat of a born maestro, and sank his precocious teeth—poor, hungry thing—into the Russian's half-cocked penis. Which of us fainted first I never discovered.

HOLLAND—CHACONNE

Isabella's eyes were lowered, the violin case on her lap. I couldn't tell whether she was embarrassed by Hanni's description, tired from the long night, or simply didn't understand.

"When I woke up," Hanni continued, "the Russian and the baby were gone. I was lying in my bed, covered by a clean blanket. Frau Wetzler was stroking my hair. She had arrived in time to deliver the afterbirth, but there had been no sign of either the baby or the soldier. I jumped out of bed, frantic, and ran down to the street. But you can imagine what it was like, the day the Russians liberated Berlin. I followed rumors, sightings, filed official reports in a British DP camp.

"My favorite half-belief was that my son had been traded by the Russian to a British soldier for a carton of Woodbines, and then adopted by a spinster professor of philosophy at Cambridge. Two years later, I slipped into England as a domestic in Leo's house. On my first half-Wednesday, I rode the Underground to Liverpool Street and the train to Cambridge. I walked the mile and a half from the station to the philosophy faculty. I walked from college to college.

"I found the spinster professor's rooms up a narrow staircase in Corpus Christi. Empty. No curtains, no cradle. It could have been Berlin. The porters told me she'd taken a post in the United States. No forwarding address.

"Leo found me, rescued me from the grim confusion of Addenbrookes Hospital, thanked the porters for their attention.

Eventually Leo loved me. Eventually he proposed. His love gave me strength enough to doubt the rumor. Eventually I doubted the birth itself. Because, in our twenty-five years of marriage, longer even than yours, Holland, I was unable to conceive.

"Papa was dead—a knock on the door, a small sound, no time for surprise. There had been a body, a certificate, even a funeral of sorts. I visited his grave once with Frau Wetzler, the day before we were separated. He may have been the only travel agent to be buried among high-ranking Gestapo. He can't have been the only Jew.

"I never went back. That last night, in the shadows of the stairwell on Iranische Strasse, he had given me a message. He had entrusted me with Zoltan and the Esau Letter. With one, I would continue our race, with the other I would continue our history. I had lost both. I had failed him as an agent, I had failed him as a daughter."

"May second?" I asked Hanni.

"May second, yes, nineteen forty-five. If my son were alive, somewhere, he'd be forty-six years old." My age to the day, although I know I was born in Surrey to enormous celebration. "And August second," Hanni added.

"August second?"

"The day I lost Zoltan." A private Granadan thought. The date of my private loss, an emptiness, as strong as any contraction, enough to make me shiver in the Spanish darkness of the early morning. Not enough to make me talk, to tell that story.

"Do you ever wonder," I asked, "very early in the morning, alone and half-awake, whether there are choices we make, have made, that will come around again, and then again? Not whether time will repeat itself, but whether people, things, we have lost or turned against will present themselves to us again? Whether we will have that second chance, that third chance, be stronger, wiser, more capable?"

"There isn't any way of looking at that film, is there?" Hanni pointed at my wheels. I had lost her.

"Which film?" I was stuck in that endless close-up, the face of the Russian soldier on Iranische Strasse. I had forgotten about my wheels, Sandor, Flamenco Halevy, The Lost Tribes.

"Did Sandor ever mention the war?"

"He avoided it, the question." I would have liked Hanni to answer me. Someone. "Before he moved down to Mariposa, he was kept as a semi-indentured servant/semi-houseguest in a bougainvillea-draped cliffhouse on the Costa Brava. His semi-semi-mistress was something to Franco. It embarrassed him in many ways. He was reduced to playing Sarasate party pieces in an ornate gazebo just north of S'Agaró. The more calorific the rondo, the more cholesterol in the glissandi, the higher the tip. His great escape was to the south. I never pushed for further info. I wanted him to play for me. Assumed he'd been in Spain during the Civil War, avoided the question." I'd been embarrassingly derelict on the Sandor shoot. I knew little more about the man than when I had started. I was after a single, live performance, a tape, for purely personal and, I suppose one might unkindly say, reiteratively pornographic reasons.

"So Sandor could be Zoltan!" Hanni's eyes flashed. She screwed the top on her jar of kipferln and stood.

The thought had occurred to me. The ages matched, the virtuosity. Both Zoltan and Sandor were as tall as necessary. I had a momentary something of a something at the black-and-white still of Zoltan/Sandor making love to this eighteen/sixty-five-year-old woman in a boxcar in the south of Vichy/France.

I hooked up the Spinoza to the twenty-five-inch Mitsubishi in Sandor's bedroom. Hanni sat at the foot of the four-poster. I opened a window as the tape began. Over the courtyard, over the far side of the villa, the grey, two-hour announcement of the onset of a new day was just clearing its throat at the horizon. The shadow of the beach was empty, a mile down and away.

An eternity of black silence on the screen, waiting for the

image of Sandor. I fast-forwarded the tape. Nothing. I switched tapes. Flamenco Halevy, Conchita, the military man, me and the owner of the Teatro La Rábida, dancing, my God, dancing. Switch. Ivy's guitar, Roger's voice, Isabella's face looking down at the tabletop of the Santa María. Switch. Three tapes. No Sandor. Had I failed to push Record, inadvertently erased the tape, been unwittingly zapped at Colón by a roving Betaray machine? I knew the answers were No, but what other explanation for a lost fortune?

"Slow down," Hanni soothed from the foot of the bed. "Think. Where have you been? Where could you have left the tape? Dropped it? Has it been in your possession without interruption?"

"Stop being such a travel agent!" I snapped at her common sense.

Then I heard it. Heard, not saw—the screen still dark with the exposed, unenlightened, unforthcome tape. But the sound track—there were the first thick D minors of the Chaconne, regal, dignified, Sandor in caftan. We couldn't see him, but the sound—

"That's it," Hanni said, and when I turned, the music had lifted her off the mattress to a point somewhere just below the ceiling. "Zoltan, Sandor, Zoltan!" I felt her hand feeling into mine, a soft chamois palm. We stood there, staring at the blackness of the screen, each of us seeing something different but undoubtedly the same musician, as chords turned into a line of semiquavers, each one a miracle of precision, yet the entire line an argument, a persuasion with the force of a full novel, fictional notes far more vivid than any dry dissertation. The crystal arpeggios, the crackle of the demisemis, the reprise, the cusp of the modulation into the major—I was holding the hand of a strange woman staring at a failed TV screen, but I was hot, damp, hotter and damper than in the Plaza de Toros two, than in Hampstead fourteen years before. I had soaked through my knickers—the sound even more penetrating and destructive than the night before, when Sandor had been only six warm and human feet in front of me. I was squeezing Hanni's hand, shaking, I couldn't help it, my calves buckling, slipping off my shoes, two hundred measures on the way to a Mach 3 orgasm, when the light through the window caught the tip of a silver bow down below, and my eyes rose from the blank screen, out to the courtyard.

She stood as she had behind the bulletproof glass at Colón, only this time I was above and the glass was air and proof against nothing. Isabella. Isabella, not Sandor, not Zoltan. Although, to be more truthful, it was Isabella *and* Sandor, the pupil having mimicked the teacher so well, not just the style, but the tone, the timbre, the attack, the vibrato, the aura of the musician. A thirteen-year-old girl with a gift of music and ventriloquism so perfect that we had stood fifteen minutes in front of an empty TV screen in the belief that ghosts could play Bach. Hanni, at her lower height, couldn't see. I didn't want to make a move that might interrupt the music, that might distract her, that might break Isabella's magic.

All the same, I was distracted. There are certain taboos that even I tremble at breaking. And I trembled on the brink of trembling. How to turn the heat from my groin to my chest, since, Isabella, I loved you already?

As the Chaconne drew to its final reprise, D minor again, full and strong, Hanni's grip on my hand loosened. She followed my eye and took the step to the window. What power, what strength that girl had, a fortissimo so strong, the last chord as fierce and as loud as the explosion—it could have been the same chord, the same sequence of notes—that destroyed the Santa María.

Isabella looked up. Her bow arm relaxed, then the fiddle, with the smoothness of a sweep-second hand. Her head tossed once, a shiver, the hair back over the shoulder. She smiled. I felt such an emptiness that it was only Hanni's arm pointing, her eyes, unbelieving, threatening to ignite the courtyard, that pulled me up from drowning. I followed the direction of her arm down to Isabella's violin case. There, held tight by the pressure of two auxiliary bows, was a packet of papers, tied in a hair ribbon, faded, frayed, but, even from our height, unmistakably purple.

"Esau."

Tell me a story.

THE ESAU LETTER

A BRIEF INTRODUCTION

In a previous edition of the *Guide,* we printed correspondence with a traveler that we felt bore directly on the question of authenticity. We are reprinting a brief extract in the current edition in the hope of clarifying what we feel to be one of the chief concerns of the questioning traveler.

"Let everyone," the traveler wrote, "confess that there is not in all the world a more beauteous damsel than the Empress of La Mancha, the peerless Dulcinea del Toboso."

While admiring the conviction of the writer, and having no cause to doubt his word, we replied that we were loath to pass judgment without meeting the woman.

"If I were to show her to you," he wrote by return post, "what meat would there be in your confessing a truth so self-evident? The important thing is for you, without seeing her, to believe, confess, affirm, swear, and defend that truth."

Ben

PAPA—25 FEBRUARY 1939

Aboard the *Queen Mary*
25 February 1939

My dearest daughter Hannah,

You are thirteen. You may have thought in the surprise and sorrow of your Mama's death that I had forgotten. I had not. The thirteenth birthday has meant a great deal to Mama's family and mine, which, as you know—if only in a vague sense of felt dinner-table conversations and whispered jokes—are the same family.

It is an ancient principle among the Jews to honor their own at this birthday, which in former times signaled the legal and religious beginning of adulthood and responsibility. Our family has been short on religion, but long on tradition. And in our family, no story has carried on the tradition as strongly as the Esau Letter.

It is a letter, a history, a deathbed testament written by our ancestor, Eliyahu ben Moshe Halevy, to his only son, Eliphaz, 433 years ago. To your Mama, this letter was the sun, the moon, and the stars. To me? Ah, Hanni. Perhaps it is only a father who sees more history in his daughter's eyes than in a few scraps of paper.

You and I are embarking today on an adventure back to the dark continent from whence our ancestors sailed hundreds of years ago. It may strike you as odd that we return while our people are fleeing in ever-increasing numbers. "Our survival is in our motion," Esau writes in his letter. Some read that to mean flight. I read it otherwise, but then, I am a travel agent. Perhaps your eyes will find a third reading that will guide you through the uncertain days ahead.

Your loving Papa

ESAU—A BRIEF RELIGIOUS HISTORY

———

Mayaimi
31 December 1506

My dearest Eliphaz,

When you were small, and I was agile enough to duck, you asked me many questions. Why was I a full head taller than any man in our village? Why did I have a beard when no other man had a single hair on his face? Why was your mother's skin even and dark, while mine was rough and pale? Why was the penis of your uncle smooth like an eel, while mine was rough with the bumps of a lizard?

These are good people that we live among, the Mayaimi. They have shown me only kindness. They have allowed me to show them knowledge. They have accepted me like a brother, and you like a nephew.

But they are not our people.

You have heard me talk, on the warm full moons when the women and children gather with the men on the shore round the council fire, of a land across the water, a land almost as far away as the rising sun. I will not live to see that sun rise again. Listen to my story.

I was born in a land of three tribes. Not the Calusa, the Jeaga, and the Mayaimi of your homeland, but the Catholics, the Muslims, and the Jews. None of these tribes believe in the Fish Spirit. None of them believe in the Deer Spirit. None believe in the Spirit of the Hunt, the Spirit of the Fire, or the spirits of the thousand wonders your playmates and their mothers and their fathers worship. They believe in a single spirit called God, whose breath takes refuge in every thing that lives on land and in the sea, every pebble and every star.

About everything else, they disagree.

Long ago, the Jews were the most powerful. Then came the Muslims, who learned to live with the Jews, most of the time. Then came the Catholics, who hated everybody—the Muslims, the Jews. They even hated some Catholics.

This is my story. Carry it with you.

I was born a Jew in a city called Córdoba on the banks of the river Guadalquivir. My mother and father, their mothers and fathers, and their mothers and fathers were Jews of Córdoba. We traced our family back hundreds of years to one of the wisest Jews since creation, Moses the son of Maimon, called Maimonides, and back before him for thousands of years to the first Jews, a father named Abraham and a mother named Sarah.

My father's family were mapmakers. For generations, the boys followed a tradition. On the Sabbath of his thirteenth birthday, the boy went to the synagogue with the other men of the family, read from the Torah for the first time, and, at sundown, packed a small satchel and floated on a barge downriver to Sevilla, there to board seabound caravels and *gonzalos* of every shape and size, to pass his dangerous early manhood watching, observing, drawing, memorializing bays and inlets, river valleys and mountain ranges, drafts and currents, planets and stars, mapping the peaks and canyons of exotic women, eating forbidden foods in times of need.

The girls of the family stayed at home, grew to a marriageable age, and waited for the maps to arrive. In neat, precise hands, they copied the maps onto parchment, onto scrolls, in charcoal or in gold leaf, depending on the wealth of the customer. As the only clients for maps were shipowners and traders, my father's family became very wealthy. Where other Jews felt lucky to own two sets of clothing, my father's family could change their linen three times a day, 365 days a year, and never wear the same outfit more than four times. Of the five hundred houses of the Judería, they owned two hundred of the finest, decorated in Moorish tile, gold leaf, and imported woods. Of the one hundred streets and alleyways, they owned one third. Fresh flowers filled their windowboxes throughout the year. They traveled, they drew, they did, and they were rewarded.

My mother's family were thinkers and musicians. My father's mother called them the shame of the Jews. My mother's family owned a tavern on the northeast hill, where on Shabbat the most pious men of the barrio gathered for a glass or two of Lágrima Añejo under the pretense of discussing the Mishnah. The tavern was a courtyard, open to the sky, smelling of bougainvillea and roast goat. An arcade of alabaster columns and broken tiles surrounded the courtyard, a puzzle of Moorish stars, sixteen-pointed impossible maps of the sun. A simple fountain defined the center, a shallow stone pool of invisible water, resting on the backs of ten lions. My grandfather told me that the fountain was five hundred years old and the lions even older. He taught me how to melt cooking grease off their manes with the gentle flames of a candle, how to blow the dust from the paws without eroding the ancient nails. He told me the story of the Jew who built the fountain for a nephew of the Caliph of Córdoba, Abd-ar-Rahman III, Protector of the Jews, Beacon of the Umayyads. He told me how the lions stood for the ten lost tribes of Israel, and the invisible pool on their backs the teaching of the prophet Mohammed.

But it was my mother who drew music from the stone, who made the water dance from the spout, made the drops laugh in tiny ripples. I sat at the paws, hiding between two open-jawed heads. I watched her take the breath, I watched her breasts lift high under the coarse wool of her dress, watched them raise the viol up to meet the shaft of the bow. Dry-tongued and open-mouthed as my stone companions, I drank in the most perfect music and wondered when the lions would rise with me on their backs and wander back to Canaan.

My mother was a miracle. A single note from her viol gave the lie to the disputation of a philosopher, the commentary of a rabbi. Starlings hung chirpless in the rafters. The bees in the bougainvillea raised their thoraxes in awe. The fat on the spitted goat caught on the melody and floated above the coals, lest its sizzle disturb the perfection. I could be playing loud, muddy games half a mile down the banks of the Guadalquivir, and a tune from my mother's viol would guide my feet through the narrow alleys back home.

Though her breasts and her arm figure warmly in my memory of that sound, my mother was only the half of it. The viol itself, or rather its silvery strings, were purely and simply possessed. On the day of my mother's birth, her father discovered them, by accident, lying wrapped in a goatskin in a narrow channel under a loose stone beside the fountain. No one knew how old they were, no one knew how long they had lain there. But they fit my mother's viol like the skin on a deer.

There was no explanation.

But let me tell you a story.

ESAU—THE LUTE OF KIMA

Long before the birth of my mother, in the days of the peace-maker Alfonso the Wise, the wife of the barrio apothecary died giving birth to a girl. The baby was born as smooth and as bald as any other child. But by the morning of her naming day, she had grown a full head of thick hair, as golden as late summer on the palmettos. She was named Zehava, "golden" in Hebrew, the holy language of the Jews. Golden and slender, she was admired and coveted by all the families in the barrio on behalf of their unmarried infant sons.

But her father had other suitors in mind for the girl who had replaced his wife in body and spirit. As the date of her maturity drew near, he became increasingly certain that life without Zehava would lose all flavor. To have her nearby, within the walls of Córdoba, would make his thirst all the more grating. The apothecary resolved to visit a distant cousin, a wealthy olive merchant, in the hillside town of Ventas del Carrizal, a full seven days by horseback from Córdoba, with the aim of marrying his daughter to the merchant's son.

Zehava sang good-bye to the Córdoba of her golden youth, to the river Guadalquivir, to the orange trees of the mosque, the garlic and oil of the barrio. They set off eastward—on one side her father, on the other her late mother's sister, the horse-toothed Penina.

On erev Shabbat they arrived at the market town of Alcaudete and shared the evening meal with the rabbi's family. The rabbi had many harsh things to say about the cousin in Ventas del Carrizal, particularly about his lack of piety. His wife was more realistic.

"It is hard to be a Jew these days," she said. "The Nasrids"—for they were the particular Muslims in power—"are less inclined than others to let the Jews of Alcaudete pray at the synagogue. Many find it easier to stay in the hills and pray at home."

"We know what that leads to," said the rabbi. "Prayers get shorter and excuses longer—the cows must be milked, the hay must be stored before the rain, the merchant insists on paying me on Saturday. Lo and behold, you turn around one Shabbat and find yourself behind an ox, while your sons are throwing dice next to the cute little Moorish fountain you built to keep up with the ibn-Mohammeds on the *finca* next door. Before you know it, you are no longer a Jew."

"You are always a Jew," the rabbi's wife said, "before you know it and afterward, too." The rabbi grumbled and poured more wine. The rabbi's wife smiled at the apothecary. "Your cousin's son is tall and handsome."

"As long as he has his health." Penina pinched the virgin Zehava, with the grin of a fifteen-hand mare.

Refreshed by a full day of rest, the three followed a Moorish servant up a narrow road cut into the purple hills to the olive groves of Ventas del Carrizal. As they climbed, the ground grew darker and richer, the trees older and more elemental. The road twisted up

above the clouds, and the heavy-hearted apothecary thought truly
he was carrying his only joy to join her mother in another world.

As evening fell, they came upon the large stone farmhouse of
the apothecary's cousin, a gloomy rock, just shy of the top of a
windy hill. A single light shone from the stables, and the servant
soon established that the cousin and his son were on a ride about
the estate and would return well after the guests were in bed. The
apothecary, golden-haired Zehava, and the horse-toothed Penina
took a quick cold supper——to the grumblings of the servant, who
hadn't counted on extra duty——and were shown to comfortable,
if drafty, rooms at the top of the house.

In the middle of the night, Zehava was awakened by the
sound of hooves and rose from her bed, careful not to disturb the
snoring Penina. In an olive-hued moonlight that made her golden
hair sparkle and light up the courtyard, Zehava watched two men
dismount, one large and irritable, the other the very description
of youthful beauty she had heard from the rabbi's wife. Joseph,
for that was the son's name, turned to the glimmer at the window
and looked up full at Zehava. The light from his perfect smile,
the brilliance of her golden hair, the spring glow of the moon——
the apothecary's trip was a success.

It was customary for the fathers of both bride and groom to
come to a mutual agreement before the first meeting of the young
couple. And so, early the next morning, the apothecary sent
Zehava and her duenna off on a ride through the olive groves in
the care of the Moorish servant. Young Joseph, however, bred
outside the orthodoxy of city Jews, was determined to speak with
the golden-haired beauty he had seen so brilliantly framed the
night before. Once his father and cousin were well into negotia-
tions, he led the quietest gelding from the stable by the forelock
and slid out of the courtyard.

The trail was easy to follow in the deep purple of the olive groves—three fresh tracks, one considerably lighter, one considerably deeper. Joseph rode at a trot up the hill, circling around below the crest, hoping to catch an unnoticed glimpse of his betrothed before displaying himself.

But the glimpse he caught horrified him beyond his darkest imaginings. There, at the top of the hill, half a dozen mountain ponies, topped by Muslim bandits from the neighboring kingdom of Granada, shuffled their hooves in the purple earth. His beloved Zehava lay bound and gagged in front of one bandit, her duenna trussed and flung across the saddle of her own horse like two jars of olive oil. His Muslim servant stood smiling, pocketing his reward from the leader of the bandits. With no thought of the numbers, Joseph charged. But the bandits, whose expertise was stealth, not swordplay, turned on their heels and galloped with their female cargo through the pass to safety, down into the lush green plain of Granada.

At that time, Granada was ruled by a young Muslim prince who loved music more than war and beauty more than justice. He lived high on a hill in the great walled city called the Alhambra, the red fortress of the Moors—two dozen towers surrounding two magnificent palaces, fountains and pools leading into vineyards and gardens, gardens of grapes and flowers stretching to the horizon. His warriors were the bravest on the peninsula, his musicians the most tasteful. His harem, for he had more than one hundred wives, was an inspiration of fantasy. He had, in the course of his tender years, collected women, placed them under his protection, without regard to any classical ideal of beauty but as the God of the Flood chose the animals of the new world— one female of each type. There were, to be sure, strikingly tall and slender brunettes of the sort favored by the Moors. But there were also short girls, fat girls, blind girls, mute girls, girls lacking limbs, girls lacking hair, dwarfs, albinos, jug-eared, horse-toothed, birthmarked, cross-eyed girls with six fingers on each hand, girls with three breasts, webbed toes, mustaches and side-burns, girls of an age and disposition to suit only the most extreme tastes, and as many cross-combinations and permutations as the design of the Alhambra would allow. Mohammed el-Hayzari—Mohammed the Left-Handed, for that was his tragedy—lived within the walls of his fortress. His imagination traveled un-bound.

It was not by accident that the bandits brought the shaken Zehava and her thrashing duenna to the gates of the Alhambra. Spies along the road to Córdoba had sent word to Mohammed's majordomo that a golden-haired Jewish girl was to be found traveling in the direction of Granada. The majordomo dropped a hint, through a zealous lieutenant who was anxious to make an impression on his prince, that this particular feminine type was missing from the harem of the Alhambra. The lieutenant, of course, was instructed to neither cross the pass into Castile nor use the soldiers of Mohammed to bring this girl—for Mo-hammed, aesthete that he was, would marry a girl only if she came to him freely. But this brand of transportation had been effected before, and no more than a nod of the head in a certain tavern was needed to assure deniability.

When news of the girl's arrival reached the perfumed ears of Mohammed, the king rushed from his harem to a hiding place between the marble columns of the Court of the Lions. Zehava was escorted into the courtyard, dignified and composed, sur-rounded by the triumphant majordomo and seven of his best men. The golden hair, the olive moon of a green-eyed face, the lightness and radiance of the girl, moved el-Hayzari beyond the

momentary thrill of a mere collector. He fell in love. Beneath his
beard he uttered a vow to his god, Allah, that should he be
blessed with the love of Zehava, he would abandon his harem
and divide his faith between his god and his wife alone.

No sooner had the prayer left his lips than a wail rose from
the depths of Zehava's soul that sent all the doves of the
Alhambra rising like a column of smoke from a burning field of
cane. She had seen the famous Fountain of the Lions, ten lions
supporting a stone pool. There before her, the ten lost tribes of
the Jews confronted her misery, manes bristling and teeth bared.

"O Israel," she cried, "have you led me through the desert
only to return me to Egypt?" for she could see no other reason
for her seizure and transportation to the sultan of the Alhambra
than a repetition of the biblical story of the enslavement of the
Jews. So powerful, so piercing, was her wail that it drew the lips
back from the gums of the stone lions and left the Muslim guards
weeping, their hands over their ears to protect their delicate
brains. Zehava seized that moment of confusion and leapt into the
fountain, hoping to breathe the leonine waters into her lungs and
find the freedom she had so recently lost.

No one knows if it was Allah who heard Mohammed's
prayer or the God of the Jews, who was not yet ready to receive
Zehava's golden head. But no sooner had the girl jumped than
the transparent waters evaporated. No sooner had her feet left the
ground than she found her thighs and her back supported by the
arms of Mohammed the Left-Handed.

The king said nothing. Nor did he suffer the terrified girl the
look of rattled astonishment that sparked from his eyes. He swept
Zehava from the Court of the Lions before his guards had
regained their feet, and spirited her to a private chamber in the
ornate Tower of the Laurel, high above the ravine of the musical

waters of the river Darro. He dispatched his harem straightaway and called for his majordomo to find a guide to the heart of the heart of his desires.

The resourceful Hussein Baba was, as always, several steps ahead of his master. He had seen in the duenna Penina much more than the body of a cow and the spleen of an ox. She was the key to the manners of her golden-haired charge. If the key could be turned, the door would pivot on its hinge like a weathervane.

Hussein Baba was a modern man. Arguments of faith and reason bored him. Take away the trappings of faith, the mosques and the synagogues, the cathedrals of the barbaric Christians, the names of Allah and Jehovah and Jesus Christ, the rituals, the diets, the wafers and the wines, and all that remained was a single god—Fear. Reason fared no better. Reason was merely another one of the thousands of unpronounceable names of God, and argument merely a way to ignore death. He knew with the certainty that comes of long service that manners were all. Lead the right cow down a flower-strewn path and the rest were sure to follow. Thus he wooed Penina, whose mouth was so well suited to grazing.

Within the year, on a single, windless summer sunset, Sultana Zehava gave Mohammed el-Hayzari three beautiful daughters, born three minutes apart. Kelila was the name of the eldest, Hebrew for the laurel wreath that crowns those who win the race. Kadia was the second—"pitcher," the vessel of water in the desert, wine in the temple. Last to emerge was Kima, whose full head of golden curls, dewy with the liquid of her elder sisters, sparkled like the Pleiades. Three girls, with three Hebrew names. For Mohammed, in the wonder of his love for Zehava, had named his daughters in the language of prophets older than Islam.

Golden-haired Zehava did not survive the sun. To the melody of the river Darro, she died with an infant daughter at each breast, Kima in the arms of the husband she had grown to love with a passion that approached faith. Even the garrulous Penina was struck dumb by the beauty of her passing, and the radiance of the change of fate that had led her from the purple grove of olives to the Tower of the Laurel.

It took a full year to dry the eyes of Mohammed and show him the beauty of his beloved wife in the three gifts she had left him. Kelila flaunted the boldness of the firstborn, pushing aside all obstacles, furniture, sisters, to reach a treasured toy on the far side of the room. Kadia's beauty flowed gently from her mother's green eyes, and sought out the most colorful flowers, the most brilliant gems, for her playthings.

In the legends of the Jews, Kima—the Pleiades, the seven sisters of the sky—is wisdom itself. And behind the gentleness and timidity that allowed her sisters, older only by a matter of minutes, to crawl ahead or win the heavy breast of the wet nurse, shone a thoughtfulness, an intelligence that calculated the future before moving an inch.

On the morning of the first birthday of the princesses, Hussein Baba reminded Mohammed that it was well past the customary time for the court astrologers to prophesy the future of the three precious daughters. Mohammed lifted his left hand in a way that neither forbade nor encouraged his majordomo. But within minutes, he found himself back in the dusty, uninhabited Tower of the Laurel with Penina and the three girls. Three soothsayers stood at the three windows, one for each girl, each bearing his

own charts of the sun, the stars, the planets, each clothed in a
flowing robe, an endless beard, and the scent of rare, fragrant
essences and woods.

All morning, and well into the afternoon, they examined the
infants for moles, dimples, birthmarks, and compared the mark-
ings with their charts. Kelila wailed for the breast, Kadia cried
for the glass beads around the astrologers' necks. But golden-
haired Kima only wrinkled her tiny brow and held her father's
small finger, as if she in her infant wisdom knew the answer and
was merely putting the wise men to the test.

Finally, as the same summer sun cast its last breath into the
Tower of the Laurel, a voice was heard in the room. It seemed
at first to emanate from the mouths of the three astrologers. But
the sweetness of the voice, its gentle timbre, its desolate concern,
told all within that the spirit of their late golden-haired queen was
still among them. "O King, Prince of Granada, Star of the
Alhambra, my Faithful Mohammed," the voice began. "You
are thrice blessed in your loneliness and thrice cursed. You will
need three times the care and three times the luck to see our
daughters through to three fortunate marriages. Let them play now
in the freshness and innocence that fed me as a girl in my beloved
Córdoba. But take care when they reach their thirteenth year.
Entrust their days and their nights to no one but yourself, lest
they be carried off and gain a husband only to lose a father, as
I lost mine."

The voice ceased, the mouths of the wise men shut. Poor
horse-toothed Penina began to bray with the fear of those impure
souls who have some petty misdemeanor to hide from ghosts. But
the left-handed Mohammed smiled for the first time in a year.
For a moment, the sun paused in its accustomed descent and gave
him the additional daylight to carry on.

The girls blossomed under the watchful eye of their mother's duenna. They passed their summers chasing cool shadows on the slopes of the Alhambra, their winters on the warm rocks below Mohammed's Mediterranean castle. Kelila's headstrong courage shaped her into a long-muscled, determined young woman who could outrun the palace guard by the time she turned nine. Kadia embellished the castle at Salobreña with her works of art, her green eyes tracing the unique variation between one flower and its sister, one snowflake and its cousin, onto paper, onto cloth, into olivewood.

But deep seriousness led the youngest princess, Kima, to a silver lute she begged her father buy from a wandering minstrel. Even in her earliest years, when she could play only the simplest children's tunes, the essence of music recognized a kindred spirit and swam to the surface of the strings to meet her fingertips.

And so the years passed.

Mohammed el-Hayzari was examining the rich cane fields of the *vega* one morning from the heights of the Alcazaba when a messenger arrived from the Mediterranean castle of Salobreña. A note from the horse-toothed Penina congratulating him on the birthday of his three daughters lay atop a basket woven with the eight-pointed star of the Moors. Within the basket, on a beach of Mediterranean sand, sat a peach, an apricot, and a nectarine, all dewy and lightly dimpled, firm and tempting in their barely ripened sweetness.

The message was clear. The time Zehava had warned of had arrived. The girls dangled precariously from the orchard of childhood. They had reached marriageable age. The time of surrogate custodians and duennas had passed. Mohammed must himself protect the fruits of his passion. He galloped down to Salobreña with his house guard, twenty of the best. At dawn the next day, the girls bade farewell to their seaside nursery and set saddle with their faithful duenna for the return to the Alhambra.

Mohammed praised the foresight of his wife. Connoisseur that he was, he had never before seen feminine beauty more delicately poised, more primed to burst the skin of innocence. Still, it made his too-fond father's heart ache to watch the tears of Kelila fall on the waves she would race no more, to see Kadia's green eyes moisten for the blue of the sky, the gray of the sea, search for a last glimpse of the changeable line where the two met at the horizon. But none could remain downcast long, as happy Kima, with her lute as companion, sprung lightly astride her horse and, with her instrument bound firmly around her shoulders, strummed a mountain march that set the horses prancing and the guards laughing.

At noontime, with the last view of the sea behind them, the party paused to water their horses at a mountain pool. They were about to remount when a most strange and beautiful sound arose. At first it bore the timbre of a woman's voice, and the left-handed heart of Mohammed, in a state of heightened emotion since receiving the basket of fruit, leapt in the hope of another glimpse of his golden-haired love.

But more miraculous, the melody drifted off the sounding board of the silver lute of Kima, plucked by no finger, hanging, at a distance from its mistress, from the branch of an ancient olive tree. The song was low and mournful, a single melody weaving its spell around a single thread. And though the sound was certainly that of a string vibrating, a human soul seemed just on the edge of making itself manifest, showing its human face, its human mouth, its human voice.

Kelila was the first to break the spell. "Sisters," she said, "can't you see, it's just the breeze that makes the lute of Kima

sing like a woman." And indeed, her sprints with the wind, her
hours of riding on the whims and eddies of the offshore breeze
along the cliffs of Salobreña, made her the likeliest authority on
the mystical properties of air.

"But, sister," Kadia replied, "can't you feel how motionless the day is, how the leaves of the olive trees hang like iron
spurs, as if the sun had tired of its daily ride and the trees had
ceased to grow?" None could question the eye of Kadia.

Kima said nothing but unhooked the lute from the olive tree
and looped the leather strap over her head and beneath the full
length of her golden hair. Her companion played its mournful
music with an uncommon depth and urgency. The strap tugged
at her neck with a force that pulled her past a turn in the road,
out of sight of her father, her sisters, her beloved sea.

Even Mohammed el-Hayzari, whose court enjoyed the services of no fewer than two dozen astrologers, needed a moment to
shake off the spell of the magical lute and mount his horse in
pursuit of his youngest daughter. So hot was his panic that he
nearly rode her down in the middle of the road. For there she
stood, looking down on a small village, no more than twenty or
so buildings. From the center of the hamlet, from a fieldstone
meeting house, a procession of bearded figures wound through the
streets. They were singing, praying. The sound of their dirge, the
very melody of the lute, cried up the hill to Mohammed and his
daughters.

"Ah," cried Penina, grasping the stirrup of Mohammed
more from fatigue than disrespect.

"What is it?" Mohammed shook her off with some impatience. "Speak! Do you understand the meaning of this procession?" When Penina had swallowed enough air—and indeed
her face most resembled the snout of a draft horse when she

struggled to catch her breath——she explained the mystery with a single word:

"Jews!"

Tears poured down the long jaws of Penina of Córdoba. She remembered her long-forgotten Judería, she remembered her friends and family, the familiar songs, the tasty dishes, the Shabbat rituals——the holiest of which she was breaking by traveling on this Shabbat. She remembered her mother and her mother's mother and the religion she had deserted on the far bank of the river Guadalquivir. Penina squinted at the sun and guessed the date——the anniversary of the destruction of the temple of the Jews in the holy city of Jerusalem, twice razed to the ground on the ninth day of the Jewish month of Av. For the song that reached out from the hearts of the Jews to the silver strings of the lute of Kima was the deep lamentation of the holy day Tisha B'Av, the unrelenting "Al Naharot Bavel":

> By the rivers of Babylon,
> Where the waters flowed down,
> And yea we wept,
> When we remembered Zion.

Led by the lute of Kima and the three princesses, the brown-skinned el-Hayzari with his retinue of forty warriors and a single horse-faced duenna, a Muslim river, as richly striped as the Tigris, swirled down the side of the hill, powerless to fight the current of its musical curiosity. And like her sister, the Jewish Euphrates trod its steady course, the three young sons of the schoolteacher at the crest, boys the day before, men on the Ninth of Av, having that day read from the Torah for the first time——as you did yesterday morning, my Eliphaz, my young man, before the assembled braves of the Mayaimi. Those two great rivers met in the valley and spread out into the marshy ground of open-mouthed youthful fascination, as great rivers are inclined to do. The resultant flood, with its deep, searching looks and shy curiosity was, as you may guess, every bit as violent and fertile as the golden delta of Babylon.

The walls had been breached, the inner courtyard defiled, the tabernacle destroyed, the oil spilled, the entire temple razed to the ground. Mohammed sped his party up the next hill, away from the Jews. But he was no match for the elements. The air had carried the music to Kelila, the earth had borne the weight of these earthly princes to Kadia, and the beloved lute of silver and fire had sung sufficient testimony to Kima to remind the princesses that these, and not the dusky suitors of their father's family, were the men they would marry.

Upon his arrival at the Alhambra, Mohammed ordered that the world be moved to his fortress. Within weeks, tropical fish swam in the fountains and Asian bears danced in the garden, all to distract the lively imaginations of his three captive daughters. All was for naught. After twenty days and twenty nights in the Tower of the Laurel, Mohammed was certain his girls would soon follow their mother. Despite the pleadings of Penina, who had been as moved as her young wards by the Tisha B'Av ceremony but was enough of a realist to move on, the princesses sat on three-legged stools and ate nothing but air. Kelila turned her back on nature and faced the wall. Kadia refused all invitations to stroll among the bougainvillea of the Alhambra, in the deep purple of its summer bloom. And the lute hung abandoned, her mistress's ears stoppered from the songs of the birds by a desolation thicker than beeswax. In the shadows of the tower the three young princesses saw nothing but the faces of the three

Jewish bar mitzvah boys, bright-eyed, familiar, full of hope and
the hint of manly beards yet to come. Through the noise of the
wind and the gardeners below their window, they heard nothing
but the mournful refrain of "Al Naharot Bavel," in masculine
voices only recently descended. The old astrologers were sum-
moned, the heavens were examined. But no amount of stargazing
could summon the wisdom of Zehava.

Although Mohammed had charged Penina with the unsleep-
ing vigil of his precious daughters, there were times during the
day, and the night for that matter, when Penina found it
necessary to flee the suffocating trances of the princesses. Besides,
she was a woman, and over the years a certain accommodation
had developed between her and the majordomo, proving not so
much that the Moors are a horse-loving people but that the
mysteries of love are shared equally between the plums and the
prunes.

It was in the course of one of these late-afternoon accommodations, amidst an empty flask and the seeds of half a dozen
pomegranates, that Hussein Baba offered Penina refreshment for
her three charges. The three Jewish boys of Tisha B'Av had
been captured at the Gate of Justice, attempting to enter the
Alhambra disguised as rug merchants. They had immediately
confessed their intention, to woo the daughters of Mohammed,
and at that moment were being fitted for shackles in the Gate of
the Seven Floors.

"Has the king been informed of their capture?" Penina
somewhat carelessly asked Hussein Baba, for though they were
on intimate terms, there was little trust between them.

"Why so curious, my burrita?" Hussein somewhat carelessly answered, knowing full well where the game was leading
since he, after all, was leading the game.

The two lovebirds soon agreed that Hussein Baba would neglect to inform el-Hayzari of the capture of the Jewish boys. The next morning, he would arrange to have them clear the brush from the ravine that led down to the river Darro from the Tower of the Laurel.

It would be misleading to say that the three princesses awoke at dawn to the sound of the lute of Kima, playing solo on its peg. The state of suspension they had lived in for their three weeks in the Tower of the Laurel was neither total consciousness nor total oblivion. But a blush that lit the shadowy tower from the six royal cheeks gave ample evidence that Penina's cure was working remarkably well. Slowly they rose from their stools, slowly they stretched their limbs and floated toward the western window of the tower, where the first heat of the morning lit the russet tiles of the roofs of the Albaicín across the river. The ravine still shivered with the darkness of the night. But the song of the lute, as Kima retrieved it from its forgotten corner and looped it over her golden hair, was echoed by three deep, fully descended voices, naturally mournful in the natural captivity that the Israelites have known for thousands of years.

A single grumbled answer from the sleepy Penina—unaccustomed to being roused from bed so early—told the three how close were their beloveds. And then, what joyous notes poured from the lips of the three beauties, what warmth it gave to the workers! All morning and again after the noon hour, the ravine echoed youthful love and hope, until the sun dropped behind the hill of the Alhambra and the prisoners had to leave their illusions in the garden and return to the Gate of the Seven Floors.

Happy days followed desperate nights, except when Hussein Baba got wind of his master's approach to the precinct of the garden in the ravine. Then he would work the prisoners across the gorge, or amid the sugar cane of the *vega,* or, worse yet for the frantic princesses, keep them chained to the clammy walls of the bottommost of the seven floors of the Gate. Up and down, hope and despair filled the Tower of the Laurel, week upon week, until Penina, ill at ease with bumpy rides of any kind, feared she would expire with the changes in atmospheric pressure.

Only an instinct of self-preservation led Penina to concoct a plan for the elopement of her three charges and their paramours. One noon, during a brief intermission in the song cycle of the sextet, Penina brought the majordomo a small basket of hazelnut tarts, powdered with cane sugar from the plantations of the *vega,* and fashioned in crescents, like the sword of Mohammed, prophet of the Muslims. It was a recipe of Córdoba, one she had learned side by side with her younger sister, and had passed on to her niece Zehava in the happy days before they left the banks of the Guadalquivir to wander amid alien cane. There was a sweetness in the first bite that led one to bite again; a crunch in the second that satisfied the lust of the mouth for eternal motion; a weight, neither too light nor too heavy, that dissolved on its passage down the throat to the vital organs, that left the eater fully, utterly, unquestionably satisfied.

So it was with the second Córdoban mystery that the talented Penina visited upon the amazed Moor—a trick of love so delicate and subtle and yet so entirely cathartic that it left Hussein Baba gasping like a beached tuna. Dry and decommissioned, he could do nothing but lie amid the brush and listen to Penina's plan for escape. At this moment, Mohammed el-Hayzari, king of all Granada, light of the Iberian Moors, on a chance stroll, with a single orderly at hand, happened upon the three Jewish prisoners resting in the shade of the Tower of the Laurel. Fortunately for the two lovebirds, Mohammed never saw them as he marched the three to the Gate of the Seven Floors. For had he understood the extent to which his rule had been compromised, two heads would have rolled into the river Darro with a splash that could be heard halfway to the sierra. Hussein Baba had surrendered his career to the horse-faced duenna. He immediately planned for a mass escape.

It was all Penina could do to keep the squeals of the princesses from alerting their father. For now she informed them of their Jewish heritage and of their mother's dying wish that she see her girls safely married to nice Jewish boys. Only Kima sighed with a breath that spoke of great wisdom. Only she pondered how completely their flight would destroy the soul of their father.

But the determination of her sisters, the argument that her beloved father had kept his own daughters virtual prisoners at the Alhambra, finally silenced Kima's remaining doubts. They packed.

The night was moonless, the escape from the Gate of the Seven Floors not without its dangers and casualty—a single donkey that threatened to bray when it saw the broad-bottomed Hussein Baba approach. The four men stood at the bottom of the Tower of the Laurel, a stone was touched, the signal given. Penina descended, followed by Kelila and Kadia, who were immediately, passionately, albeit silently embraced by the Jewish boys—which ones, it didn't matter, they would sort out choice and temperament at greater leisure.

With her sisters on the ground, it was left to Kima to descend, her lute strapped around her shoulders, her dainty foot perched on the top rung of the ladder. Just then a breeze sprang up. The scent of bougainvillea caused a single note to play on her lute. In those two sensations, everything Muslim that had brought her pleasure, a full and equal half of her soul, drew her back into the Tower. Her sisters pleaded, her suitor entreated, Penina hissed, Hussein Baba threatened. Back and forth that slippered foot appeared, until finally, with a strength neither of her sisters possessed, Kima kicked the ladder to the ground.

By the time the alarm was raised, the party of seven had forded the river Darro, borrowed some horses from a band of wandering musicians, and galloped far enough on their way to the Sierra Pelada that the fastest of Mohammed's warriors were unable to catch them. There, above the town of Ventas del Carrizal, at the farm of their father's father—for by a coincidence that even I find hard to swallow, they were the three sons of the young Joseph, whom the apothecary of Córdoba had hoped to marry to his golden-haired Zehava—they were embraced, fed, married, and then fed again, according to the custom of the Jews. Hussein Baba had no choice but to convert to Judaism and marry the bruised Penina. Though the poor man grew even fatter with the hazelnut tarts that his autumn wife prepared him, he never again enjoyed the second Córdoban mystery that had so compromised him under the walls of the Alhambra.

What of the lute, the lute Mohammed found in the arms of his only remaining Kima, mournfully playing that song of hope and despair "Al Naharot Bavel"? Mohammed's right hand embraced his daughter, praising Allah or Jehovah or whoever might listen that he had spared him one of his treasures. But his left hand, his cursed hand, throttled the silver lute by the neck and flung it into the darkness of the unawakened day, until it lit up the sky like a shooting star. In an instant, that fatal mistake wrought such amazement and contrition upon him that he didn't feel his daughter slip from his arm and fly after the lute until she was halfway down to the ground, halfway up to grasp the soft hand of his beloved golden-haired wife, Zehava.

The band of musicians camping by the river Darro, separated from their horses by Hussein Baba's wedding party, were also awake when the silver star fell with a musical splash just outside their tent. My mother's mother's mother's mother retrieved the lute from the rocks among which it floated, crushed and bent by Mohammed's rage, and carried it back to the fire, where the band quickly determined that its value as molten silver was greater than its value as art.

But try as they might, they could not melt the silver into a smooth liquid. The lute gave up its original shape quite readily but insisted on taking the form of four silver strands of four thicknesses, as if in memory of Zehava and her three daughters, who had finally escaped their own tragic histories at the Alhambra.

It was, of course, those four magical strings that my mother's father removed from their stone case in the courtyard of his tavern. No one knew for certain how long they had lain there, who had hidden them, how they had made the journey to Córdoba. Ten Mohammeds ruled from the Alhambra in the two hundred years before Isabel and her Fernando drove Islam out of Granada. Which of the ten was left-handed? Who were the traveling musicians? What happened to Joseph, and what of the apothecary?

I believe that, left-handed though he might have been, it was Mohammed and not Hussein Baba who effected the escape of the princesses. I believe that his greatest grief was the secret he had kept of his bottomless love for his youngest, his golden-haired daughter, a secret he had kept too long, until she had joined her mother in a red fortress he would never see.

And I believe that there was a magic in the silver of the lute, of the viol, a charm that made one long for the impossible——to gather loved ones, to sing songs of people long dead, to celebrate, conquer, triumph.

And I thank God, the God of Mayaimi and Calusa, of Jerusalem and Mecca, that the strings lie at the bottom of the sea, in the grip of my poor, poor brother, who may finally have learned where the music and the musician part company.

ESAU—MY BAR MITZVAH

The morning my father returned from sea, his leather bags held
enough charts and reckonings to make his fortune thrice over. He
had left Córdoba a boy. He stepped off the half-sprung boat into
the freshwater mud of Córdoba——eight winters frozen, eight
summers baked since he'd smelled it last——a scientific man, a man
of calculation, of reason.

The silver strains of my mother's viol caught him off balance,
one foot in the mud, another still bent over the gunwale. The
noseless ferryman cast off and drifted back into the current,
downriver to Sevilla, oblivious to the scent of music. My father
caught a boot heel in the mud, his brain of mathematics and
observation rocked by the tremolo of the strings. But the melody
grabbed him by the armpits and set him gently upon the solid
bank. It cleared his eye, it freshened his shirt. It patched his
trousers, it rinsed his mouth, it broke his fast. It trimmed his
beard in the latest fashion. Three hundred and twenty-eight
members of the Halevy clan had prepared a banquet on the Calle
de las Flores in honor of my father's return. But the melody
hurried him past the trestles of pickled meats and fried fish, the
baskets of flowers and smiling, dark cousins, and up the broken
cobblestones into the bad part of the barrio, to the Fountain of
the Lions. My father was so driven by the single commandment

of those four strings that no one dared block his way. By dinnertime, my mother's father had given his blessing, by sundown my father had announced his intention to the Calle de las Flores, by moonrise he had carried my mother across the threshold of his father's house, by midnight I'd been conceived. And all the while, the strings traced a song of welcome—to the sailor, to the maps, to the pen that had written eight years across the waters in order, finally, to return to dry land.

My poor father. By tradition, his life's work was done. He had added to the family wealth with his maps of the coastline of northern Africa, his charts of the sandbanks and the seasonal floods of the Nile, his curlicued sketches of the bays and rocks of southern Italy. He had fathered two sons. Enough, certainly, to hope that one would grow up to his own bar mitzvah and sail off to replenish the Halevy family fortune with maps of new seas, new worlds.

But in an instant, the sound of my mother's viol had changed my father into a man who would sooner wish upon a star than calculate its distance from the earth. While he should have been selling maps, he sat at the table of my mother's father, listening to mystical tales spun by wild-eyed uncles and bearded rabbis. While his pen should have been copying the rocky face of the Gulf of Cádiz, it traced the timbre of my mother's viol, drawing spheres and wheels and fanciful whorls, mapping the mystery of the strings of Kima.

He neglected his trade, let his charts of the outer world grow brittle and blow away in the afternoon breeze. He passed his evenings drawing maps of Córdoba for small merchants of the *pueblos,* tiny guides to the shortest route from the Alcázar Gates to the Market; the best plaza to park a wagon when praying at the Mezquita; the shortest route to the tavern that served the

freshest chicken, the strongest *aguardiente*; the secret passage to
the most expensive, the most creative, the most exhausting bordello.

My mother never left her viol. Both Lorenzo the sun and
Catalina the moon would find her either at practice or, with a
goatskin cloth and a polish of olive bark and palm oil, burnishing
the wood, shining the strings, until they produced an absolute
reflection of herself. She found a willing assistant in my brother,
Yehuda, whose arm was as welcome to the instrument as mine—
try as I might—was rejected.

I had a brother, son. A twin brother born within minutes of
my birth. A brother now dead, I am certain of it, dead by the
hand of a Genoese named Colón. But a brother then as alive as
you, as smooth as an eel, with the laugh of a seagull on a windy
day. I loved my brother, protected him in his hairless innocence
from the boys of the Judería, from the barefoot Muslim Mezquita boys, from the wrath of my grandfather Halevy, who spit
twice on the ground when Yehuda passed, after he followed the
path of my mother and learned to play the viol.

It fell upon me—the golden boy, the one to bring back the
golden age to the kingdom of Halevy, the great hairy hope of
the next generation—to sell my father's guides. I labored with
the enthusiasm of a son who adored his father and worshiped his
mother. The farmers loved these guides—those that could read.
For those that could not, I roughed out graphic symbols in place
of my father's Castilian prose.

I also developed a sideline for the New New Christians of
Córdoba. The Old New Christians had fled the city after the
rioting that plagued the year of my fourth birthday. Among these
Old New Christians were some of the great Jewish families of
the city, who had given in to the will of the throne and embraced

Christianity. They were ambitious people who had exchanged not so much gods as manners, in order make a better living in the professions closed to Jews. They tried harder, worked harder than the Old Christians, the ones who had passed directly from their dark prehistoric practices to Christianity without dallying for Judaism. The Old Christians lost business, lost property, lost promotions, lost face, took revenge. For sixteen days my father hid the four of us under a bed until the cries of the wounded and the stench of the burning dissolved in the breeze.

Two years of peace followed between Old Christians and Jews, until ambition reared its two heads, and New New Christians began to appear, eager to make their way in the Gentile world. These were my first clients.

I was a wild success. By the age of seven, I had developed a facility for dead reckoning. My early practice came with finding my way home by the sound of my mother's viol. But later, crowds would gather to watch me—dropped blindfolded anywhere in the precincts of the city—walk the shortest, most direct route to a specified target.

But I owed my juvenile fortune to a secret. These New New Christians were devout Jews. Their obsession with power in the Christian world was matched only by their obsession for devotion in the Jewish. None of them believed in the myths and magic of the Catholics, in a life of kneeling on cold stone in front of a wooden sculpture of a bloody man, of whispering in a language you didn't understand. They were far more pious than the Old New tribe, more pious than many Jews, certainly more than my immediate family.

They spent the morning in the Catedral in public show. They spent the afternoon scurrying to secret meeting places, begging forgiveness of the Jewish God for the hypocrisy of the morning.

They ran a perilous middle course that required absolute secrecy
and terrific stamina. The sixteen days of riots that their predeces-
sors had braved would be the blinking of an eye compared with
the new horrors of the Inquisition should these New New
Christians be discovered engaging in their ancient practices.
More than anything, they needed a navigator. They needed a
guide.

I told them where discreet Jewish services could be provided,
I found them quiet men to make up a minyan of ten qualified
Jews for prayers. I had kosher meat delivered to their homes in
unmarked sacks. Most important, I drew them the shortest route
to their most secret destination, and drew the officers of the
Inquisition the longest. I saved them time. By thirteen, the age,
by rights, when I should sail off to make my fortune, I was
already a wealthy man.

Then came our bar mitzvah.

We were Jews, I told you that before. To the shopkeepers
of the Mercado we were Jews. To the Alcalde in the Town
Hall, to the King of Castile, we were Jews. But to my Halevy
grandparents, the parents of my father, we were a sniff and a
scowl. Jews, hah! Not Jews in their image! Their Jews prayed
in the morning, prayed in the evening, spent one entire day per
week, and many more throughout the year, praying in a synagogue, honoring events that otherwise would be forgotten, in a
language they themselves could not understand.

How could we come close to that image? How could we
change skins into their kind of Jew? Our parents were betrothed
by the string of a viol. Our family was enriched by the sale of
maps drawn for the pleasure trade. For our parents, for me and
Yehuda, God's very existence was a subject of desperate mystery.
Why did we need prayer when there was music, why a syna-

gogue when there was Terra Incognita? How could we follow
custom like lambs when we felt like lions holding the world on
our backs?

It was entirely within their capacity for wonder that my
parents arranged for us to be bar mitzvahed the day after our
thirteenth birthday. They allowed my father's father to teach us
the pronunciation of the necessary Hebrew—although my
mother was incapable of hiding her horror at the monotonous dirge
that accompanied the recitation. They permitted my father's
mother to invite all the Jews of the barrio to hear her grandsons
read from the Torah, and then to celebrate the rite of passage with
a *juerga*. Their only condition was that the ceremony not be held
in the synagogue.

And so it came to pass, in the Hebrew year 5244, on the last
day of the modern year 1483, that my brother and I were
standing before the Fountain of the Lions, reading from the
Torah, when Luis de Santángel forced my conversion.

For years after, Santángel told me later, the rabbis of the
barrio would divide over the question of my conversion. I had
read the week's portion of the Torah, the final passage of
Genesis—the death of Jacob, who wrestled with an angel and
changed his name to Israel. I had performed a *mitzvah*, fulfilled
a commandment, there was no doubt about that. I had just moved
aside to let my brother take up the stylus and wail the death of
David, the great, human King of the Jews, when Santángel, the
treasurer of King Fernando and Queen Isabel, burst into the
courtyard with a dozen armed officers of the Crown.

A whisper rippled around the pillars of the courtyard, more
from recognition of the great man than from fear of what appeared
to be imminent massacre. For Santángel, though few in Córdoba
had seen him, was the most revered, the most mysterious, the

most famous New Christian in Spain. He stood fully as tall, Eliphaz, as any brave among the Mayaimi or the Calusa. His beard was thick and black, with a strong jagged lightning bolt of white whiskers on the left cheek. His open green eyes, topped by a pair of bushy eyebrows eternally raised in seeming surprise, sparkled with life, wit, and secrecy. For a people taught to stoop, here was a man who stood tall in his leather boots. For a people comfortable with wise men and rabbis, here was a warrior and a god. The waters parted as he approached the fountain and the Torah. Here was another set of senses, I thought, that could see through buildings, through people, who could take a dead reckoning and chart the most direct course to a person's soul. It was clear from the moment he entered that he'd come for me.

"Eliyahu ben Moshe Halevy," he said, putting a great gloved hand on my prayer-shawled shoulder. My brother inched back from the fountain into the shadow of my father. "Today you have become a man."

The congregation murmured, several people smiled. The great man was giving his blessing. I knew better. The hand on my shoulder lay insistent, not beneficent—moist and wet, not cool, dry, and welcoming. The hairs tickled my jaw.

"Today you can become a great man. I am here to give you a choice." More murmurs, more smiles. "You have a gift, Eliyahu, whether it is a knack of prophecy or merely a talent for scientific observation, it is a gift that will wither on the vine as long as you remain a Jew."

There it was, the choice, "as long as you remain a Jew." Santángel went on at some length about the possibilities of advancement he was offering to me, the adventures that lay waiting if I accepted his patronage. Not once did he speak the word "Christianity" or "conversion." But by the end of his speech, there wasn't a soul left in the courtyard who didn't understand that I would leave that courtyard a Christian or a corpse.

What could I do? My parents on one side, my grandparents on the other, the congregation was obviously divided, but I couldn't tell how. My eyes were clouded, but my nose was open, and the smells of the bar mitzvah feast filled the courtyard—roast lamb marinated with raisins, chicken massaged with olives, goat stuffed with peppers and glazed with Moroccan figs. There was a music in my ears that no one else seemed to notice, a rumbling in my stomach as enticing as the sound of Kima's silver lute.

Do you remember, Eliphaz, the first time I took you hunting in the scrub pine? How I strapped an old deerskin over your shoulders, draped that silent head over yours, covered you in a smell, a disguise? That is how to hunt deer. It is a lesson I learned in Córdoba.

"I'm hungry," I said. "Let's go."

Santángel scooped a handful of water from the fountain, said a few words in Latin, splashed my face. "You need a new name," he said, "a Christian name for your baptism in Christ."

"Esau," my father's father said. I turned and saw the wrath, the hatred twisting his tongue against his lips. "Esau, that's his name, his new name."

"But, grandfather," Santángel went on, "Esau is a Jewish name, Esau was a Jew."

"And Esau sold his birthright because he was hungry," my grandfather said. " 'Let me swallow, I pray thee,' Esau said to his brother Jacob, 'some of this red, red pottage, for I am faint.' And Jacob said, 'Sell me first thy birthright.' And Esau said, 'Behold, I am at the point to die, and what profit shall the birthright do to me?' And Jacob gave Esau bread and pottage of lentils, and he did eat and drink, and rose up and went on his way. Esau despised his birthright.'' My grandfather looked out over the congregation, over the soldiers. ''No self-respecting Jew would name his son Esau. It's the perfect Catholic name. Tell that to your queen.'' And reaching down inside his throat, my grandfather collected the larger part of his frustration and terror and hatred into a gob of spittle as red and thick as any mess of pottage and, with a mighty effort, baptized the other side of my face.

So I became Esau. Esau Benavides. I had to wait only one week to discover why Santángel had chosen me. My parents were grateful it wasn't longer. For in that week, the Jews turned away, the New Christians turned away. All income from the shop dried up, all patronage at the tavern crossed town. My brother sang alone, the lions stood silent.

Friday evening at sundown, a royal courier knocked on the door. I was forbidden to bring anything with me, neither map nor hat. Only my brother kissed me good-bye. It was the first time I had traveled on Shabbat.

On the eve of the third day, the courier pointed to the castle of Zahara de los Membrillos, the gateway to the Muslim kingdom of Andalusia. Wheeling his horse around, he galloped back the way we had come. I turned my head back to the pass. I fel. calm and clear. Though I had never seen the sea, I knew where to go.

I rode through the night, resting my horse during the day. Cloaked in a skin of invisibility, I passed easily by the Muslim sentries. At noon of my sixth day out of Córdoba, made bold by the smell of salt water, I rode into the Muslim port of Mariposa. The muezzin was calling the faithful to their midday prayers, singing a tune my mother had often played. I thought how delighted she would be by the music of the city, so open and alive after the walls of the Judería. There was no pain in the memory, only the thrill of discovery as the streets emptied before me. My horse found his way to the beach. I was thirteen. I was a man of my family. I was off to the sea.

The sea. We never spoke of the sea, Eliphaz. I wonder—and there are many things I wonder—whether you remember the first time you laid your eyes upon the sea, touched it with the soles of your feet, let it ride up over your hips and dampen your face. You will tell your children to tell their children that your father came from across the sea. That he left a crumbling old world to travel to this fresh new land. That it was the sea that taught him, the sea that carried him, the sea that fed him without ever slaking his desperate thirst—the crackling, bursting, ever-dividing, indivisible sea. The sea that falls like the veil before sleep, that separates history from fantasy, faith from reason, life, perhaps, from death.

For five thousand years, the Jews lived on the other side of the sea. For two months I traveled. When I am dead, you will lead our people into the heart of this new land, to found a new nation. You will turn your back on the sea.

ESAU—THE CAVE

One hour's ride east of Mariposa, my horse dropped dead. I sat on his flanks and looked out at the water. A hot wind blew down from the hills. By the time I stood up, the horse was half-buried.

A stone's throw away, a round wooden hut squatted at the end of a pier, barely six feet above the surf, on stilts draped with barnacles and weed. Smoke rose from a chimney hole, scanned the shore in confusion, and bolted for the sea. I hadn't eaten in three days.

A Moor as dark as burnt cane answered my knock. The gray glow of the smoke hole gave off more light than the embers of the fire. The walls were smothered with blankets and rugs, heat and the smell of coffee. The Moor sat me down along the wall and brought me a cup, strong and sweet, with a wedge of hazelnut cake. Each sip, each bite, accustomed my eyes to the light. By the end of the first cup, I could make out the intricate designs, the star patterns of the carpets. By the end of the second, the stars had broken free of pattern and grouped themselves randomly around the hemisphere of the room. It took me months to unravel the mysteries of these stars. But at that moment, with two cups of strong, sweet coffee, and a hazelnut cake as delicate as any Penina baked for Hussein Baba, I felt more at home than in my

thirteen years in Córdoba. For, Eliphaz, I was sitting at the
center of a map of the universe.

"I will explain." Luis de Santángel, chancellor of the royal
household and comptroller-general of the royal treasury, stood at
the door. His full robes, the streak of white lightning in his dark
beard, the heat on his face and hands, so filled and illuminated
the lintel that I could not tell whether he had entered quietly or
had been crouching patiently within the hut while I drank my
coffee. Two precious candles appeared, pregnant with the wax of
their ancestors. The Moor moved slowly. He twisted away the
star-shaped stone at the center of the hut, the stone that supported
the firebox that cradled the pot of dark, sweet coffee. An iron ring
was revealed, lying heavy and flush with the floor, star-shaped,
rough-hewn as the stone. The Moor grasped the ring with both
hands and pulled up. A panel revealed itself, star-shaped as the
rest, hinged somewhere, on something of mystery. Above the
raised door, the Moor's face smiled in my candle. Below,
shadow, darkness, a staircase.

I followed Santángel. Ten steps, twenty, thirty, fifty, seventy-three steps. Down below the pier, down a stone passage,
impervious to the salt sea, a rocky tunnel pushed and pulled in
a lullaby I learned to trust. Down, down, into the rocky floor
of the beach, Santángel leading the way without a thought to
explanation or weariness. And I followed, thinking, If I could
leave my religion, my family, my river Guadalquivir without so
much as a backward glance, why raise questions now, fifty feet
and more below the sea? My nose told me I was going in the
right direction. My skin was dry and cool.

The staircase ended. Santángel walked forward several
paces—hollow sounds, a pleasant smell of earth and parchment.
He walked around the room, lighting ten thick candles, their

wicks eight feet from the ground, not half the way to the top of the arched ceiling. Niche by niche, the cave brightened. Carvings into the rock, canopies within caverns, honeycombs within snailshells, more elaborate, more Moorish than the Mezquita in Córdoba, than the Hall of the Ambassadors at the Alhambra of Mohammed el-Hayzari. Forty columns supported ten arches, ten arches led to ten corridors. Between the arches, ten leather chairs. And at the center, below the hemisphere of the hall, a freshwater fountain, a pool of stone on the ten stone backs of ten stone lions.

Room by room, the chancellor of the royal household led a thirteen-year-old boy from Córdoba by the shoulder, lighting tall lanterns along the way, guiding him through an underworld maze of mystifying objects. Cases of maps stood next to shrouds of Torahs. Astrolabes shared leather beds with *tefillin*. Notebooks and folios, registers of names and occupations, tax records and Talmudic commentaries rubbed shoulders on shelves that rimmed the walls of the ten tremendous rooms that shone off the central brilliance of the great hall. One room was devoted entirely to garments that could withstand long storage and inclement conditions, another to waterproof bedding.

"I will explain," Santángel said, easing himself into a leather chair in the hall and motioning me to the floor at his feet. "But not too much.

"Within ten years, Esau, the Jews will be expelled from Spain. The crucifix will hang from the ark of the Torah, statues of saints will stand in the niches that once held candlesticks and *tallitot*. Kosher butchers will sell the hindmost portion of a pig. There won't be a Jew or a Judería in all of Aragón, Castile, and Andalusia. The wrath of the Catholic Monarchs Fernando and Isabel will reach its melting point. They will see that the

Jewish *conversos*, the New Christians, are reverting to their old religion. Worse, they will see that those who are refusing baptism are attempting to make Jews of the Christians around them. This will be more than the royal patience can bear. I know. I am the royal patience.

"Some Jews will convert, mostly the rich, whose property otherwise would be confiscated by the Crown. Others will choose expulsion. They will seek out a new homeland. It will not be in Europe. The English and the French hate the Jews more than Their Catholic Majesties. It will not be the African coast. The Muslim world is nervous within itself. It has no desire to swallow three hundred thousand Spanish Jews. The new homeland may be Palestine, if my friend Abravanel has his way.

"I think it will be elsewhere." I followed Santángel's gaze to the ceiling of the great hall. The flames of the candles shone strong and bright without sputtering, yet the shadows of the ceiling refused to stand still. For a moment, I had a sense of floating in a honeycombed bubble, a sense of lightness, of motion.

"We have ten years to find that elsewhere," Santángel continued. "We, Esau—for I am counting on you. You found your way from Castile to Mariposa, from Mariposa to this hut at El Palo. You will find a home for the Jewish people, I am sure of it."

I was not so sure. I was proud that I had found Santángel. But the dead heart of my rotting horse lay on the beach as a challenge, responsible in some measure for guiding me to this dreamworld below the sea.

Santángel rose.

"You understand, of course, Esau, that my responsibilities prohibit frequent visits. Abbas will cook for you. He will bring

occasional messages from me. Meanwhile, read. There is much
to do, and only ten years."

He climbed the staircase. I did not see him again for four
years.

At thirteen, I had not learned to question my heroes. That is
why I feel fortunate to die and leave you this letter. It will
crumble under the weight of questioning. Allow the mysteries of
my story to work their magic, and the letter will last four, five,
six hundred, one thousand years.

For four years I studied. In the morning, Abbas brought
down fire for lighting, water for washing, and bread for breakfast.
I ate half the bread with him, saving the other half for my solitary
midday meal. Then he rose, his robes muffling his ascent up the
seventy-three steps, and I turned to my books.

I read. From the *Annales Francorum* of Eginhard of Fran-
conia I read the story of Yitzhak the Jew, whom the emperor
Charlemagne sent to Harun-ar-Rashid, king of the Persians, and
who returned home with many presents including the great, gray
elephant Abulabaz. I read of the travels of the Radanites, the
Jewish merchants who transported eunuchs, female slaves, boys,
brocade, castor, marten, and swords from France to China.

I read the library of Hasdai ibn-Yusuf ibn-Shaprut, the vizier
of Caliph Abd-ar-Rahman III of Córdoba. I read Sir John
Mandeville's account of the Ten Lost Tribes of Israel, impris-
oned between the mountains of Goth and Magoth by the Cas-
pian Sea. I read the journals of Friar Odoric, *The Voyage of
Johannes de Plano Carpini Unto the Northeast Parts of the
World in the Year of Our Lord 1246,* and the journal of Friar

William de Rubruquis, a Frenchman of the Order of the Minorite Friars.

Most colorful were the journeys of Rabbi Benjamin of Tudela, who traveled to Greece and Persia, to the ruins of Nineveh on the Tigris, to the shining white palace of Caliph Mustanjid al-Abbasi in the city of Baghdad, which stretched for three miles along the banks of the river Euphrates. To Samarkand in the kingdom of Persia, to the forests of Tibet filled with musk. I read of the twenty-eight-day ride to the mountains of Nishapur by the river Gozan.

I read of Benjamin's visit to the pearl divers of el-Katif near Bahrain, of the Duchbins of Ibrig, who worship fire. I read of his forty days' journey across land to China on the Sea of Nikpa, where the hunter-star Orion predominates, and stormy winds prevail.

I read of Benjamin's remarkable eye for trading—cloth for spice, animals for jewels, medicine for food. I read of Benjamin's fascination with a kingdom ruled by a Jew, Rabbi Joseph Amarkala the Levite, who dwelt in harmony with the Kuffur at-Turk, a people who worship the wind and live in the wilderness; who neither eat bread nor drink wine but live on raw meat; who have no noses, but two small holes through which they breathe.

He traveled for trade. But he traveled also for his people. Benjamin of Tudela was seeking, three centuries before I descended below the shore of Mariposa, a homeland for the Jews.

Every day at sunset, Abbas knocked on the hinged panel, fifty feet above, and I joined him upstairs to pray to the east, he to Mecca, I to Jerusalem. We ate our meal in silence. Afterward, he taught me classical Arabic and told me stories of his childhood in Morocco and his life at sea. Once a week I was

permitted to bathe off the far side of the pier, away from the sight
of the beach. Abbas tied a rope around my waist and held the
other end tight while I paddled about in the water. Even after
I had learned to keep myself afloat, Abbas insisted on the rope.
One evening I tried to swim around the pier to catch a glimpse
of sand or tree, to yank Abbas from his station. The Moor stood
firm as a rock. I was happy. I was too important to be allowed
freedom.

And after my lesson, after my weekly bath, I returned to my
cave, put aside my books to turn to my chief delights, my hazelnut
tart, my maps.

I had seen contemporary maps in my father's shop, modern
maps, drawn with the latest techniques, with the most up-to-date
instruments, on the most recent voyages. They were ancient
history compared with the maps of Santángel. My father's maps
were variations on Egyptian maps a thousand years old. They
were trading maps, drawn by merchants, not explorers. They
were homecoming maps, threads tied to lintels, spooled out for the
exploration, reeled in for the return. They were maps drawn by
Europeans, who must always, by temperament, return to their
native land.

Not so with Santángel's collection. His racks held maps of
Arabia fashioned by Arabians, maps of China by the Chinese.
I covered the walls of three rooms with these originals. At the end
of two years, I had combined the mixed contents of Santángel's
map cases into a map of Asia, from Palestine to Cipangu,
complete with chalk annotations, in a variety of seaweed dyes,
referring to the books and journals and diaries and letters in
Santángel's collection. I sent a short note through Abbas.

The reply came in the form of a crate——my first shipment of
new maps.

Where I had been merely astonished by Santángel's maps of Asia, I was struck dumb by the diamonds of Africa. To assemble this new collection, Santángel had done nothing less than form alliances, make personal connections and treaties among the indigenous tribes of the continent. He had traded their storehouses of tribal knowledge for the European sciences of astronomy and cartography. He had worked with them as colleagues, until they became sophisticated information gatherers, draftsmen, and ultimately mapmakers. Most important, Santángel's men had produced charts inaccessible to the European mind, maps that were the morning residue of dreams, the treasure of adventurers following intuition to its birthplace, imagination to the magic chambers of the pyramids, to the source of the Nile.

Every four weeks or so, Abbas brought me a fresh shipment with my breakfast. I chose one of the ten chambers as my Africa room and, with chalk and seaweed, combined these maps, enlarged them in scale, refined them, erased them, made compromises and guesses, followed dream and intuition. And I read. I read the reports of Santángel's African travelers; I read obscure tracts in Latin and Hebrew and Arabic. I read the account of Eldad ben Mahali ben Ezekiel ben Hezekiah ben Aluk ben Abner ben Shemaiah ben Hater ben Hur ben Elkanah ben Hillel ben Tobias ben Pedath ben Ainon ben Naaman ben Taam ben Taami ben Onam ben Gaul ben Shalom ben Caleb ben Omram ben Dumain ben Obadiah ben Abraham ben Joseph ben Moses ben Jacob ben Kappur ben Ariel ben Asher ben Job ben Shallum ben Elihu ben Ahaliab ben Ahisamach ben Hushim ben Dan ben Jacob, who had traveled to Spain from Ethiopia, where he had encountered the other lost tribes of Naphtali, Gad, and Asher on the far side of the river Sambatyon, which rumbles and runs with white water and great noise for six days of the week, but on the seventh day rests until the end of the Sabbath. To save his people, Eldad had flouted the Law. He had risked damnation by crossing the dry bed on the Sabbath. He was my kind of man.

I read and drew, drew and read. I covered the entire wall of my Africa room with a picture of a clump of grapes, heavy with fruit in the north, a single berry dangling in the deep south. The night I drew that final grape I lay down to sleep troubled, certain that I was on the edge of discovery, uncertain of its meaning.

I awoke to voices above, a great commotion. I slid from my bed and crept up the walls of the farthest honeycomb, curling my body into a niche I had previously tested for just such an invasion. I tried to pick apart the sounds. There were three voices that monopolized the discussion; one, I believed, hoped, belonged to Santángel.

The voices went away. Hours passed. My hunger drove me up the steps. I knocked. I waited. I knocked again. I put my shoulder against the panel. Nothing. I pounded on the door. I waited. I returned to my bed. I slept. I woke. I drank fresh water from the still splashing Fountain of the Lions. I slept again. The darkness penetrated my hunger. I could no longer tell whether I was awake or asleep, alive or dead.

But as my imagination grew accustomed to the blackness of the cave, my heart slowed down, I became calm. A moment's concentration lit up the image of Africa in blazing colors. I turned my mind to the continent, to the tapering edge, the arrowhead, the southernmost grape of the bunch. Awake, I saw Africa. Asleep, it hung heavy and purple before my eyes.

Until one sleep, when the grapes tied themselves to a trellis in the courtyard of my mother's father. My father sat at a table, drinking dark, sweet coffee with Abbas. Santángel sat on another stool under the arcade, disputing the philosophy of Maimonides with my mother's father. I crouched at the paws of the lions, peering up at the bare arm of my mother that supported the viol, raising and lowering, heaving and sighing above the shelf of her breasts. She was playing a tune I had never heard, something long and slow, wistful and yet comforting in its regularity. A cool breeze drifted down to me from the strings, yet I felt myself sweat with the effort, the hot desire, to understand from where within the wood, where beneath her skirts, the music was born.

I felt a damp cloth on my brow. Another woman, a younger, copper-colored girl, neither Jewish nor Muslim nor Catholic, squatted beside me. Again and again, she lifted the hem of her garment and, dipping it in the pool of the lions, squeezed it dry against my brow until the drops ran cool down my nose and into my lips. The music ran with the whispers of the men, and the copper girl drew me down, beneath her garment, beneath the lions, beneath the steady bowstroke of my mother.

I awoke. I was certain that the echo of my mother's viol still sounded in a distant room, that the murmurs of men at disputation had only just died away. My eyes ached, and slowly I realized that there was light once again in my cave, too much light for my neglected eyes. Abbas called my name. The shape above me fashioned itself into a torch, a face. I reached out a hand. He lifted me up. I stood at the Fountain of the Lions, the fountain in the cavern. The ten candles were lit. Beneath each candle, in each chair, sat a man.

"Esau." Santángel's voice rang above me, resounded throughout the hall. It had been four years since I had heard another voice in my cavern. I squinted my eyes, felt my swollen tongue in my cheek. It took me a moment to find him, among the ten bearded faces.

"Esau," Santángel repeated. "I have brought some friends; they would like . . ."

But I had forgotten how to wait, how to speak, all the niceties of manners and society. I grabbed the torch from Abbas, rushed up to Santángel, yanked him from his chair, pulled this giant of a man to my Africa room, certain in the discovery of my dream. The men rose as a group and followed, as men must follow a madman.

"Africa!" I yelped, and my dry, caked voice barely broke through the weeks of my hunger, as the meaning of my dream broke before my eyes. "This is Africa." I jumped up and down in front of my masterpiece of chalk and seaweed. "Africa!"

Santángel gently removed his hand from my grip. "Esau, you must be hungry."

But another voice, a high-pitched voice full of kindness, stopped him. "Santángel," it said. "A bunch of grapes. Look what the boy has discovered."

"Yes, yes," I croaked. "Below the grapes. Below the grapes."

"What below the grapes?" Santángel was losing patience with his prize lunatic.

"The sea. The sea!" I shouted.

And that other voice, that high-pitched voice, rose triumphant. "The southern tip of Africa. The sea to the Indies, to Calicut and the Malabar Coast, to the spices of Ceylon and Goa. The boy has discovered the seaward passage to the Indies!" The man came forward, a man about the same age as my father, kind, delicate, gray hints of a beard around a soft face, and put his hand gently on my shoulder. The man smiled, the other men smiled, there was a murmur. And it was then that I remembered my copper girl, and felt that my own garment, below my own grapes, was cold and damp with something more than water from the Fountain of the Lions.

ESAU—COLÓN

Shortly after I was rescued from my two-week hunger, Santángel brought me the news that a Portuguese, Bartholomeu Dias, had rounded the Cape at the bottom of Africa and returned to Lisbon to tell the tale. My discovery had been verified. Santángel was impressed. So were his friends.

Who were these friends?

Luis de Santángel, of course, my patron, born Azarias Ginillo in the town of Calatayud, chancellor of the royal household and comptroller-general of the royal treasury, whose duties included registering the names and salaries of all employees of the royal palace; keeping a detailed inventory of the jewels, arms, clothes, and other contents of Their Catholic Majesties Fernando and Isabel; guarding the financial ledger of all salaries, all gifts, all expenditures paid. He held in his own hands the key to the royal purse and had amassed a considerable fortune as director of the Santángel Mercantile House of Valencia.

Abraham Seneor, supreme judge of the Jews of Castile, confidant of the queen. His son-in-law Meir Melamed. Two of the richest Jews on the peninsula.

Gabriel Sánchez, treasurer-general of Aragón.

The teachers of Talmud and Kabbala, Isaac de León and Isaac Abohab.

Isaac Abravanel, whose appreciation of my map of Africa drew me to him like a son to a father.

Myself.

Zacuto.

Others.

But always ten. Ten men. The Minyan. Enough men to say prayers. Enough to make decisions. Above ground, Mariposa lay in the hands of the king and queen, the Catholics. There were no Jews left in Andalusia. Soon there would be no Jews left in all of Spain. Time was running out.

Only I stayed in the cave, day and night. The others came and went. But always on Shabbat they found their way to my temple. Together we lit candles and prayed before the Fountain of the Lions, reading from our ever-increasing stockpile of Torahs.

They disputed Talmud, argued politics, planned the future course of the Spanish Jews, and pored over my maps. Some argued for Palestine, others for the Congo of Africa. Some urged an eastward trek to the Jewish kingdom of Crangadore on the Malabar Coast.

Others argued out of frustration and bewilderment.

The only man who approached our weekly sessions with composure and faith was my friend and early ally Abravanel. He was the philosopher, a believer in the providence of the Jewish God. He gave me folio after folio of numeric calculations, rows of numbers surrounded by arrows and references, footnotes to the Book of Daniel and the Zohar. Abravanel had established, with a genius that seemed more inspired than rational, that the Messianic Age would arrive in fifteen years, in the year 1503. In 1503, Abravanel told the Minyan, the Jews would have revenge on their enemies. The Jews in the Diaspora, those Jews who had been bullied and driven and scattered to the four corners of the earth, would return to Palestine for the Resurrection and Judgment. From that day forth, all Jews would live in peace in Israel under the Messiah, the Messiah whose rule would extend over all mankind. Half of Abravanel was absolutely convinced that nothing, not even the furious efforts of the Minyan, could forestall the expulsion of the Spanish Jews. The other half came to our meetings.

For three years they argued.

My opinion was never asked. I was grateful. I could concentrate on the facts.

I studied the *portolano* maps of the Mediterranean and learned about ocean currents and prevailing winds. I read the histories of St. Brendan and examined the voyages of the red-bearded Norsemen. Most important, I studied the sky with the astronomer Abraham ben Samuel Zacuto. And that meant release from the cave.

No longer did Abbas slide the firebox aside after our Arabic lesson and send me back down to my cave. Instead, I lay on the pier behind the hut while the sun set over Mariposa, until Zacuto knocked on the door. He walked me through the stars, around the planets. He made me see the pearness of the earth, the attraction of the lodestone, the shape of the universe. I learned how to shoot the sun at noon. I listened as he spoke of the wisdom of the Pleiades, the deception of Orion. We slept on the pier after the lesson, rising at dawn to study the sun, squinting through his copper astrolabe, refining his charts, his tables.

I studied the problem of Colón.

Santángel had met Colón for the first time in 1485, at the Franciscan priory of La Rábida at the mouth of the river Tinto, where the water runs the color of copper. Colón, a Genoese sailor and a politician, had recently arrived, dispirited and hungry, from the Portuguese court of João II, where his proposal to find a western passage to the Indies had evaporated.

Santángel had no personal enthusiasm for a trip to the Orient. Although he adopted an officially neutral position before the Minyan, I sensed that Santángel was partial to the Congo contingent, anxious to see the Iberian Jews carve a homeland out of the crazy, endless equatorial fecundity of the African jungle.

But powerful as Santángel was, he needed a disguise—deer's clothing for his grand hunt. Always on the trail of an energetic ally, he arranged for Colón to meet the monarchs in Córdoba. Santángel needed a captain with a cause, with a belief as strong as his own, but whose outward appearance and manner would disguise Santángel's ulterior motives. Santángel was a *converso*. He prayed beside Isabel as often as possible. She was constantly worried that he might slide back into the religion of his forefathers.

But Colón was a fanatic. Everything he did was as a messenger for God, the Christian God. He had a ready phrase from the Bible, the Christian Bible, to justify, prove, defend every one of his actions and goals. He was purer than Fernando and running at the shoulder of Isabel in the race for Best Catholic in Spain.

Best of all, Colón was a Jew, and didn't even know it.

Santángel did. He had access to the bloodlines of every animal that ate and shat within the confines of Castile and Aragón. Beneath the patina of Catholic fanaticism, Colón possessed, Santángel believed, a Jewish soul. Here was the man to seduce the royal seal from the royal hands, to transport the Spanish Jews—and, most important, all their worldly goods— to a newfound land. Here was a Moses, born a Jew, raised a

Catholic, ready to return to his people and lead the Israelites out of Egypt to their new homeland.

When Colón met Isabel in Córdoba, Santángel and the Minyan had not yet determined the destination of the Israelites. Santángel persuaded Isabel to hesitate, to set up a commission, to keep Colón on a long leash.

The leash was long enough for Colón to return to Lisbon and glean the news of the Dias discovery. The discovery of the seaward passage beneath the tip of Africa to the Indies snuffed out Colón's Portuguese dream.

"Why would the Portuguese need a westward passage," Santángel asked me one starry evening when he, Zacuto, and I lay on the platform behind the hut with cups of dark, sweet coffee, "when an eastward passage lay open below the tip of Africa?"

"And with all that land across the ocean to the west, hiding Europe from China," I agreed.

I don't know what I would have said if Santángel had let me continue. But the slackened jaw, the wide eyes, were enough to stop me in mid-sentence.

"All that land?" he finally asked. "What land?" I looked to Zacuto for support, but his eyes were focused westward. What support could he have given me? The words had sprung immaculate from my lips, unfathered by thought. I knew I was right, knew that there was a vast continent west of Europe and east of the Orient. But how could I explain what I didn't understand?

"I don't know." I finally apologized to Santángel. "I don't know why I spoke. But I know it's true. There is land there. A lot of land."

"Zacuto!" Santángel drew the astronomer around. "You tell us. Is there land west of Europe and east of the Indies?"

A warm breeze stirred the waves around the piles of the pier. Inside the hut, Abbas hummed a tune about sand mountains and sailing ships. Zacuto raised himself up on his elbows and let a slight smile draw a slit in his dark beard. "Either there is land, Don Luis, or there is one hell of a lot of water."

The conversation moved on to provisions and sail size. But for the rest of the evening, I felt the gaze from the mild eyes of Zacuto, a curiosity mixed with a new respect. I felt dizzy, discomfort somewhere between throat and stomach, my equilibrium lost between intuition and knowledge.

I dreamed that night, for the second time, of my copper-colored girl.

Two years passed, two years of constant study with Zacuto and Abbas, of frequent congregations of the Minyan, of occasional visits from Santángel. But not a word of the mysterious Colón. Until one cool morning in the autumn of 1490, a retinue of the chancellor's guards appeared at the door of the hut with a string of horses and an extra set of clothes in my size. Colón was back in Spain, at the priory of La Rábida. I was going to meet him, and possibly the queen. I washed. I changed. I mounted the horse. I had been in the cave for seven years.

It was a different Andalusia I crossed. An Andalusia without Jews, it was true. But the brilliance of the sky after so many days in candlelight, the vastness of the real earth after the fine lines of my chalk drawings. It was impossible to share Santángel's concerns, his obsessions. For five days, over the mountains of the Serranía de Ronda, through the marshes of the Coto Doñana, I reveled in my freedom from darkness and secrecy and Judaism. I rejoiced in my conversion.

The priory of La Rábida was set at the edge of a rise, through a broad park of fir trees and sand. On one side, scrub trees and

berry bushes stuttered down to the banks of the river Tinto. On
the other, the land dropped off to a wide sand beach and the
ocean.

We approached the priory at the hour for evening prayers.
Santángel met me at the gates and thought it better to delay my
arrival past vespers, rather than display my absolute ignorance of
the form and ceremony of the Catholics. While he chatted with
the captain of the guards, I wandered down the dunes to the shore
of the ocean.

We had ridden all day, and though the sun was sinking, I
was eager for an encounter with this new sea. Stripping off my
clothes, I dove without rope or barrel or hesitation into the waves.

The ocean was warm with the current of the river Tinto,
warmer than I had expected. As free as I had felt under the
Andalusian sun, I felt freer over the vast ocean deep. I dove till
I touched bottom. I swam out farther and dove even deeper. I
held my breath for what seemed like hours, picked up rocks and
shells and bits of overwashed wood. I lifted myself up as high as
I could above the surface, and then floated for minutes with my
nostrils barely out of the water. I turned eastward to the shore,
northward toward England, southward toward Africa, westward
toward a land I knew was somewhere, if only I were a strong
enough swimmer.

As I turned back from the west, I saw a figure on the beach,
a young girl, already stripped naked, wading out into the water
as if to greet me. I was far enough away, and my boy's head
bobbed close enough to the waves, that I remained invisible to
the girl. But young as she was, she was enough of a large-
breasted, dark-nippled girl that even water and dusk couldn't hide
her sex from my eyes. She waded, she swam. What she felt
when the final wave was crested and she floated into my trough,

gray-eyed and unstartled, I could not tell you. I was twenty years old, son, and had known only the copper-colored girl of my dreams.

Who was responsible? I for being the boy? She for being the girl? The waves for hiding me? The waves for enticing her? The waves for their backward, forward, ever-bobbing motion, revealing me to the chest when she was close enough to see, revealing her to me when she was still too far to hold? The fading light for making all judgment of distance irrelevant until she swam into my touch with the gray of her eyes, the perfect corks of her nipples? The tow for drawing us in and in? The sand for netting our single starfish? The ocean for its undrawn loneliness, stoppering all conversation unbegun? The earth for its revolution? The moon for its tides? The stars for their luminescence? The universe for its motion?

We lay on our sides in the sand, too close, too weak to look into faces. My body was curled like Africa, her breasts above my shoulders, my face in her belly. Her knees were drawn up, thighs warm against my chest. We lay there, nudged gently into slumber, gently, by the waves. When I awoke, the moon had risen, and she was six feet away. The groove on the beach where the water had slowly separated us, grew shallower, fainter with each wave. I was still curled like Africa, she lay still on her side. But I saw her gray eyes, north of her belly, wide, inviting, familiar, dreamlike, lost. In the moonlight, her skin was copper.

Then she disappeared.

I returned to the priory, naked, shivering, unwilling to say a word either to Santángel or Father Juan, whom I had met in the cave of Mariposa. I asked the cook for a cup of soup and a bottle of sherry. Up in my room, I wrapped myself in a horse blanket and stood by the window, the moon shining full through the glass.

There was a knock on the door. I told the cook to enter and put the soup on the table. I squinted through the moonlight for traces of my girl, even at the height of the priory over the beach. I turned to my soup. There was a man. Not a cook by the cut of his garments and the light in his eye.

He set the tray, with its soup, sherry, candle, and tankards, on the table by my bed. I said nothing, so deep in my confusion that I could only hope he would leave quickly and not think me entirely insane.

"Don't mind if I take a drop of your sherry, do you?" he asked, pouring himself a generous dose. "You are Esau." I thought he smiled. I smiled back. He raised his glass. "They call me Colón."

Hardly the intimidating monster I had imagined, chased from the courts of Spain and Portugal. Shorter than I, heavier, more pockmarked, more chinned. He was more Abravanel than Santángel, more kind companion than daunting teacher.

"I think," I said, then stopped to control my mouth, still caked with salt and sand and saliva. "I think that I have discovered something."

"Sit." Colón took a glass to the window. I pulled my blanket tighter around my shoulders and sat to my soup. It was hot. Colón refilled his glass, poured me a drink from the bottle, and returned to the window. "Now," he said, "your discovery?"

I told him about the ocean at sunset, about the girl, the spiral Mediterranean of her hair on the surface, the broad shoulders, the peninsular weight of her breasts below the water, the stiff, salt corks of her nipples, the gray sea eyes. The very telling painted a memory more vivid than the encounter.

All the while, Colón's voice, his Abravanel voice, encouraged without urging, led me closer to a discovery that I was certain was just over the next wave. Suddenly, the complete map flashed in front of me, as if I had drawn it on the wall of my room.

"Africa," I said. "I was Africa."

I dropped my blanket and took my chalks from my bag. Naked as on the beach, I scrawled for half an hour on the whitewashed walls of my cell, while Colón held the candle.

"Here am I, Africa," I said, tracing the drawing with my finger, "all curled up, my back the north coast, my head and shoulders the bulge to the west, my buttocks Arabia, my toes pointing south to the seaward passage to the Indies."

"I know." Colón spat on the floor. "I was in Lisbon when Dias returned."

"And here's the girl." I swallowed. "First, as we were when . . ." and I drew her in the waning moments of our first passion, as we lay curled up in one another on the beach. There were her feet, just below mine; her knees by my chest; my head, the bulge of west Africa, in her belly. Her large, tropical breasts rested warm on my back.

And then I moved her, as the water parted us, so that the gap between us, between Africa and her body, revealed her neck, her face, her hopeful, inviting, lost gray eyes.

Finally, I drew Europe above my Africa, and filled in the bits that matched above the girl's body. No longer were we girl and boy, momentary passion, the heat of creation, but two mature continents, pulled, pushed, cooled, drifted apart by time.

This was my answer, the ultimate map of my seven-year apprenticeship under Santángel. The girl was the new continent that no one, not the Portuguese, not the Africans, not the Arabians, not the Chinese, had imagined. This was the land that blocked the westward passage to the Indies, the land I had guessed at that warm evening on the pier above the cave. But what a land! A land that once, long ago, Europe and Africa had clung to in deep, prehistoric heat. The mate that once upon a time fit the Old World, the Known World. The wife, the mother, the daughter that had gone away, run away, floated away. The Unknown, the Terra Incognita, the Promised Land, the only Canaan left for a new Moses to find, to found a new people.

"This is where we must go!" I shouted at Colón. "Here is the continent we must find!"

Slowly, Colón turned to me, the candle casting shadows past his chin, his nose, up to the crown of his head. A smile drove across one cheek.

"I remember," he said, "I remember what it was like the first time. The earth moved."

I felt a chill. He didn't understand.

"Then I grew up." Colón opened the door, and the draft hit me full force. "Spices. Gold. The Indies. Everything else is sentiment and illusion."

"Columbus was a Jew?"

"Oh, Holland, don't disappoint me!" Half the pages of the Esau Letter remained in my lap, half were scattered on the floor beside my armchair. Hanni and Isabella lay on their stomachs on Sandor's bed, elbows on the duvet, chins on palms, a pair of teenagers.

"You can't be serious."

"It has nothing to do with being serious." Hanni stood up and shuffled through the unread pages of the Esau Letter. "The most you'll hear Spanish officials admit is that Columbus's father was a converted Jew, which, technically speaking, makes Columbus no Jew at all. But, ah, here it is!" She handed me a page marked "Bibliography." "This is just a partial list of the critical articles that the family has written over the centuries."

"Your family?"

"Who else would bother? Columbus, Esau, the whole Discovery of America—look at how many countries have reinterpreted the story to suit their own purposes."

"Spain, Italy, the U.S.," I guessed partially.

"Portugal," Hanni continued, "Denmark, Iceland, Ireland, Colombia, of course, and the rest of South and Central America while we're at it. Even the Japanese have a theory."

"Columbus was on his way to Japan," I added.

"To what Marco Polo called Cipangu."

"And your family?"

"The Jewish question, at least, was solved at the end of the last century by a cousin on my Mama's side—a chemist at the University of Oklahoma—through analysis of ink and handwriting. He found a number of short notes written in Hebrew, from Columbus to his son Diego, and published a monograph with an interpretation of Columbus's signature that proved him to be a practising Jew at the time of his voyage to the New World."

"But Columbus has always been painted as a rabid Catholic," I said, "always quoting the Apocrypha, calculating the distance to the Indies with measurements from the New Testament."

"And as the greatest sailor the world has ever known."

"Exactly."

"Two facts about Columbus, trumpeted by all the modern historians?" Hanni smiled and crawled back onto the bed.

"Yes?"

"All the modern methods at their disposal, navigational, historical, forensic?"

"I suppose."

"If the second—Columbus the Greatest Sailor, et cetera, et cetera—was shown to be not only false but ridiculous, wouldn't you be inclined to doubt the first?"

"Columbus the Catholic?"

"And replace it with Columbus the Jew?"

"Are there any other options?" I looked over at Isabella, wondering how much of this she was catching.

"Certainly." Hanni sat up and crossed her legs. "To forget about Columbus, for one."

"And concentrate on Esau?" I smiled.

"Are you sure you aren't Jewish?" Hanni stretched her arms above her head, in pleasure, I thought.

"It's a little difficult," I said. "Whenever I see the name Esau, I think of Alan Bennett as the Anglican vicar in *Beyond the Fringe*. 'But my brother Esau is an Hairy Man . . .' "

" 'But I am a Smooth Man.' Leo and I saw him in Edinburgh in '61. Wonderful!"

"So you understand why I have difficulty taking the story seriously."

"The story, or Esau, or Alan Bennett?"

"All three I suppose." The bed looked awfully inviting. I had just hit the wall of fatigue and ached for a pillow to cushion my fall.

"Holland, sit up!" My eyes, always a giveaway. Hanni ran down the steps to the courtyard and returned with the jar of kipferln. "Open," she said, and popped two in my mouth. I chewed through my irritation.

"Now don't answer and just listen to me for a moment, Holland. You are a documentary filmmaker. You keep your eyes open, your ear to the ground for subjects, histories, stories, things, things that might keep a couple of million people awake on a Monday night. I'm not asking you to accept the Esau Letter with the same unquestioning spirit that I and thousands before me have. I'm asking you only to ponder the answer to the following question:

"Here we are, you, I, this child, on the last day of the four hundred and ninety-ninth year since the Columbus expedition to the New World, since the Expulsion of the Jews, somehow thrown together, somehow finding, after a disappearance of almost fifty years, in the villa of a man who may be the incarnation of the thieving corpse, a missing letter, the missing history of that discovery. If my kipferln are not enough to keep you awake, then certainly that miraculous coincidence must jolt you into consciousness."

"What did you put in those kipferln?" I was awake, but more from the irritation of being lectured on my profession.

"What did *I* put in the kipferln?" Hanni laughed. "Read."

ESAU—LA RÁBIDA

The rule at La Rábida was poverty and abstinence. Our cowls were threadbare, our belts thread itself. Our beds were boards until the boards wore out, and then we lay on straw until our nocturnal restlessness ground the chaff into the cold stone. Our daily meal was soup, our soup thinner than water. On the rare day when a farmer brought us a chicken, it was more gristle than skin, more bone than gristle. We ate it undercooked. I had tasted sherry for the last time.

The few books at the priory were Bibles, with the accent on the New Testament of the Christians. Where Jews were mentioned in the text, colorful illuminations left no doubt as to the dim view Catholics took of the people they accused of killing their God, Jesus. One Bible pictured a dark-haired Cain drinking the blood of his blond brother, Abel. Another showed a group of Jewish moneylenders nailing Jesus onto the Cross. Another clothed a snake, the original Satan, in the skullcap of a rabbi.

The few other books the priory possessed were little better. Jews raping Christian women, Jews drinking the blood of Christian children, Jews converting to Christianity to rise to power and rule the world for the Jews. Books of hatred and pornography, by Franciscans, Dominicans, even Thomas Aquinas, the Aristotle of the Christians, which only proves, Eliphaz, that stupid people have no monopoly on stupidity.

I never felt more Jewish than when I read these books. And make no mistake, I devoured them. I was so hungry for knowledge of any sort, for novelty, that I made letters out of the clouds and read them frontward in Spanish and backward in Hebrew. Cloaked in my Franciscan cowl, surrounded by books that mocked and attacked my ancestors, I felt safe in a foreign country, safer even than when I sat at the feet of my mother in the courtyard of the lions.

I loved the stories of the old men in my grandfather's tavern, the biblical stories of Cain and Abel, Jacob and Esau, Joseph and the Coat of Many Colors; Ham, Shem, and Japheth; Joshua, Judith, and Job. I loved the lute of Kima, the endless nights of Scheherazade, the songs of the troubadours. But whenever the subject turned to Law, the Law of the Jews, the rituals, the prohibitions, whenever the old men of the tavern or the ponderous Talmudists of my cavernous Minyan chewed over the do's and the don'ts of the Jews, whenever lively talk would give way to unthought, to mumbled prayer, I would walk, run, lose myself in the alleys of Córdoba or the secret passageways of the cave, until a thumb and forefinger homed in on my ear and dragged me back.

In my cowl, I didn't have to be a Jew. I didn't have to feel bad about not saying prayers, about not keeping the Sabbath holy. I could mumble the litany of the Catholics as easily as I could tie my belt and pull on my sandals. I felt as safe as I do hunting with you, tracking deer, the freshly skinned hide of a buck draped on my shoulders. No guilt, only the good hunger of a cold, clear morning.

My few free moments were spent on the beach, searching for

my broad-shouldered mermaid. Nights tumbled by with desperate, unsatisfied dreams. I was bursting with knowledge, more swollen by the day. I longed for my cave.

Two more years were to pass before I saw Santángel again. The Inquisition had not yet reached our little corner of Spain, but elsewhere it was raging out of control. Stories of confiscations, water tortures, hot pincers, execution by fire, ran into our priory weekly, often sung with glee by my fellow friars. The Catholic Church was intent on financing the war against the Muslims with the funds of backsliding New Christians. Abraham Seneor and his son-in-law Meir Melamed, respected members of the Minyan, had become pet projects of the queen. Despite their generous donations, Isabel finally put her lien on their souls. They were baptized.

Even the Santángel empire was in imminent peril. Already rumors had percolated up through the grinds of the Inquisition that Santángel had been dressed by the court in the variegated *sambenito* of a practicing Jew. I knew he was running the delicate ridge, currying favor with Their Catholic Majesties, and planning for Colón's trip to the Indies. For it had been clear to me, since our arrival at La Rábida, that Santángel had chosen Colón to lead the expedition for a homeland.

I thought it was a big mistake. After our first conversation, Colón and I spoke very little during his infrequent visits to La Rábida. Friar Juan even let me know, in a most politic, thoughtful way, that I would do better to avoid contact with Colón's little boy Diego, a boarder at the priory. Colón had gambled his entire career on there being nothing but open sea between the Canaries and Cipangu. I was a nuisance.

But amiability was not my goal. I stopped arguing because it was clear that Colón wanted neither what Santángel wanted (a homeland for the Jews) nor what I wanted (satisfaction). Colón wanted spices, gold, the Indies. But he knew neither the mystery of the spice nor the beauty of the gold nor where the Indies might be. And let me tell you, Eliphaz, there is nothing more pointless than drawing a map for a man who doesn't have the slightest idea where he's going. You might as well give him a blank sheet of paper and a kick in the pants.

Also, I believed that the first voyage of exploration was in the offing. The Muslims had retreated to Granada and were making their last stand in the towers of the Alhambra, where Kima wept at the flight of her sisters. The Umayyads had withstood a siege for several months, but no one believed that the day was far off when Fernando and Isabel would control Castile, León, Aragón, and Granada. Isabel had assured Santángel that once the war was over, the peace dividend would fall to Colón's expedition.

He had not counted on the Grand Inquisitor. Tomás de Torquemada, whose hooded eyes had sent thousands of New Christians to their deaths, spent just as much time at the side of the queen. When Santángel told me he was the conscience of the queen, he was admitting only half the story. The queen's soul was hardly Terra Incognita. And Santángel's flag did not fly alone on its shores.

On January 2, 1492, the Muslim siege ended. On January 6, the Feast of Epiphany, when the Three Kings of the Orient first saw the innocent baby that was to cause so much pain and suffering in the world, the last king of the Muslims handed over the keys to the city. Fernando and Isabel rode into the Alhambra.

That afternoon, as a hundred cooks prepared a great feast of celebration outside the Palace of the Abencerrajes, Santángel led the king on a tour through the gardens of the Generalife, gardens in which he had passed countless days as ambassador for Castile to the Moors. The subject, as always, was the king's pocketbook, emptied past the point of promises by the long siege of Granada. The two men were resting in the shade of a large cypress when the queen approached, with Torquemada at her side. "My dear," the queen murmured to her spouse in tones as placid as the river Darro, "I would like to make an announcement at the banquet this evening."

Torquemada cast his bushy eyebrows across the two monarchs to his opponent. The king nodded to Santángel, who hurried off in search of a horse. He didn't have to stay to hear the words "Expulsion of the Jews." He only needed to reach Isaac Abravanel and Abraham Seneor before dinner.

Fortunately, both men were in residence at the elaborate tents they had erected in Santa Fe during the prolonged siege. In a matter of moments they dressed and mounted. By sunset, Santángel had arranged an audience with the king and the queen in the Courtyard of the Lions. While Abravanel spoke with the queen, pleading the long history of the Jewish people on the Iberian peninsula, antedating the Moors, the Visigoths, the Romans, Seneor placed three bags of ten thousand ducats apiece in front of King Fernando and promised much more if he would revoke the planned Expulsion. It was a piece of theater that had played with great success many nights before. Listening from the shadows of the hundred columns, Santángel fully expected another standing ovation.

But his antagonist was also in the theater, and his lines proved stronger. "Judas Iscariot sold his master for thirty pieces of

silver,'' Torquemada cried, in a gravelly voice that sounded like
Death himself. ''Your Majesties would sell Him afresh for
thirty thousand: here He is,'' and he held a magnificent jeweled
crucifix above his head that could easily have fetched the price in
the gem bazaars of Mariposa. ''Take Him away. Take Him
away and barter Him!'' With that, he threw the crucifix into
the Fountain of the Lions—the same fountain into which the
golden-haired Zehava had so unsuccessfully dived—and stormed
from the court.

If Fernando had been the oak seat and the mahogany back of
the throne, he would have pawned the cross for another thirty
thousand then and there and given the Jews another five years
remission. But he was merely the cushion and the tassels. He was
so compromised in front of the queen, in front of these sophisticated Jews and his friend and adviser Santángel, that he could
do nothing but suggest that the announcement of the Expulsion
be delayed a few months, lest it dilute the glory of the conquest
of Granada.

The queen acquiesced. The monarchs prepared to go in to
dinner. But Santángel was not finished. He handed a document
to Their Majesties for their signatures.

Why on earth would Their Catholic Majesties sign such a
document when they had refused Colón for seven years?

''Timing,'' Santángel told me, ''the secret to all negotiation.
It had been a long day. They were hungry.''

And that is how Colón received the royal charter for his
voyage of discovery, the likes of which had never been seen
before. He was to be named Admiral of the Ocean Sea. He was
to retain one-tenth of whatever he discovered. He could invest
directly in the voyage and reap the resulting benefits. And his

heirs would continue as governors and viceroys of any new lands he discovered.

In Santángel's language, this translated into royal approval to outfit as many boats as he could, to transport the Jews of Spain to a new home. Colón was merely a cover. Santángel had agreed to lend Fernando and Isabel over one million maravedis, the Crown's entire investment. Abravanel and Seneor would bankroll Colón's ten percent. Colón would set sail immediately, establish an initial colony by the end of the summer, and ready a second expedition by the beginning of 1493 to transport the three hundred thousand Jews of Spain.

This at least was the story that Santángel brought to me on the beach of La Rábida, one miserable twilight at the end of January, when loneliness and the Franciscan diet had blinded me to the import of Santángel's plan.

"I am sorry, Don Luis," I said to him, staring down at my big toe, tracing a crescent moon in the wet sand. "Colón will not find the Indies. You will be throwing away a fortune."

"Look at me!" he shouted. His nose was no more than a foot from mine, his eyes shining with the last of the day's light. "I have thrown far more than a million maravedis after gambles that matter less."

I looked down at my toe. In the beginning, there was a boy and a girl . . .

"Ten years ago, Colón decided he wanted to sail west to the Indies. Why? Because no one had done it. No matter that a seaward passage south of the African continent is closer, easier, quicker. That challenge became Colón."

"But there is land in the way, Don Luis!"

"Shh, shhh!" Again the pat on my shoulder. "Colón told

me about your cosmic orgasm, your pet theory of the male
continent of Europe and Africa and the prehistoric female continent drifting apart.'' I shrugged his hand from my shoulder and
began marching up the beach to the priory. There is nothing
worse than being mocked for your first love.

''I believe you, Esau!'' Santángel shouted after me. I
stopped. ''Why do you think that I have risked one million
maravedis?'' I turned. I walked back down to him.

''You are as obsessed as Colón, my boy.'' He laid his hand,
more kindly now, on my skinny shoulder, a lesson from Abravanel. ''But *you* are obsessed with knowledge, with an unfillable
desire to know, to learn. You search out new experience, feast
greedily on new books, new maps, new ideas. You are always
ready to listen, because you are always ready to change your
mind. You draw exquisitely, Esau, because you know how to
erase.

''I am a New Christian, Esau. But I am also an Old Jew.
I am a rationalist, but I am also a believer. I believe that
everything on earth and in the heavens can be explained by
physical law and reason. But there are too many questions and
too little time for me to demand a logical proof for each one. So
I have cultivated the faith of a gambler.

''I have cultivated you, Esau, because there are things that
you have discovered that I know are true. I have watched you
work for nearly ten years, in the silence of the cave at El Palo,
in the poverty of the priory of La Rábida, and I have never once
had cause to doubt the results of your investigations. I am perhaps
not as perfectly ready to gamble my life away on your dreams.
But time presses. I throw the dice.''

''Thank you, Don Luis,'' I stammered and knelt on the

sand to ask forgiveness of this great man I had so completely misunderstood. He pulled me up short.

"Listen to me, Esau, there is no time. There is a shipowner in Palos, six miles up the road. His name is Pinzón, Martín Alonso Pinzón. He will provide two of the three caravels for the voyage. You will sail with him as navigator. Wait for him, he will contact you."

Six months later, Abbas knocked on my door. I hadn't seen him in the two years since I'd left El Palo.

"Three presents, Esau," he said in a whisper. He handed me a brass astrolabe and a book of navigational tables. "From Zacuto. He says he wishes he were going."

"What's the third, Abbas?" I looked around for a wandering friar and slipped the gifts into the sleeves of my cloak.

"Bad news, Esau. I've been to Córdoba. They're gone."

"All of them?"

"What's left of your grandfather's tavern is a warehouse of olive oil."

"My family?"

Abbas shrugged.

The next night, while I was trying to raise myself from the deep water of a dream, two pairs of hands grabbed me and bundled me into an empty barrel, along with Zacuto's gifts. I cried out. A voice told me to hush—I believe it was Santángel's. I was loaded onto a horsecart and bumped the six miles to the port of Palos. Through a chink in a barrel staff I saw three ships at anchor in the river Tinto. The Santángel voice gave orders to handle me with care. The other voice, a sturdy big-bearded man, kissed a woman good-bye, and then a girl, long-haired, broad-shouldered, could it be? I was hoisted up and onto a rowboat,

out and into the hold. As the sun rose, I felt the wood of the
ship creak into motion under the wood of my barrel, heard the
sounds of a crew, sounds I had only imagined before, a crew at
sea.

And faintly, very faintly, the sounds of a viol, mixed with the
voices of hundreds, perhaps thousands, of Jews singing "Al
Naharot Bavel," "By the Rivers of Babylon." It was Tisha
B'Av, in the Hebrew year 5252—August 2, 1492. I was
twenty-one years old.

ESAU—ADRIFT

Spacious enough that I could stand at the center, wide enough that I could lie on the bottom in a not-too-uncomfortable curl. None of my prisons had prepared me for ten weeks in a barrel. Abbas, my warden of Mariposa, brought me a meal once a day, waited patiently while I disposed of my previous one. I lacked nothing. I lacked everything.

I had seen and heard enough my final night on shore to scribble a rough sketch. I was on a boat, one of three; three boats were planned for Colón's expedition; I was on Colón's expedition. That much was easy. My imagination could draw more precise hypotheses. I was on Pinzón's boat; that was Pinzón kissing the woman and girl good-bye; the girl I made love to on the beach of La Rábida was Pinzón's daughter.

But my guesswork came up short against the hundreds of questions that remained. Why was I taken at night in such secrecy? Why the barrel? Was I the only member of the crew barrel-bound? What were the voices I heard in lamentation the night of our sailing? Why the sound of my mother's viol? With so many questions, bound and blinded, could I possibly be the navigator?

We sailed for ten days, dropped anchor for two weeks, sailed again for a few days, dropped anchor, began again in earnest.

From time to time I heard voices close by, other barrels, other men. Abbas said nothing and held a knife to my throat when I threatened to speak.

At night, I wrapped my body at the base of the barrel, my head oriented in the direction of the ship's motion, secure in the knowledge that Colón's expedition was headed west. I curled into Africa and dreamed clear, precise, wonderful dreams of Pinzón's daughter on the beach.

Two weeks out, Abbas spoke to me for the first time.

"A question from the captain."

"Who's the captain?" I asked.

"He wants to know how long."

"How long what?"

"Till we reach land."

"Let me up on deck."

"Impossible."

"Then let me sleep."

I dreamed my dream. As always, I came to her unsuspecting in the surf, our hips drawn together by the motion of the waves, entwining her, arms, legs, fingers in hair, entering her, floating, if possible, the lightest millimeter above the spray, pulled by the tide onto the gentle sand. Then the drifting into a first dream-sleep, me curled, Africa head in her lap, her surrounding breasts on my back, above—mystery. Then the second dream-sleep, somehow dividing, drifted apart, eyes opening. But this time, instead of meeting her gray storm-eyes, instead of letting my dream move the girl to her wonted bittersweet disappearance, I grabbed the half-consciousness, took control of that half-sleep of my dream. Gently, I reached forward from the coast of Africa, stretching my fingers fanlike across the sand, trying to touch any part of my dream-love, how far, how far?

My palm brushed her knee. Close, my elbow still bent. But a knee, after all, even her divinely mysterious, lightly muscled Amazonian knee, is only a tertiary landing place, a momentary stop in the search for a homeland, and far too far south of the latitude we were sailing. And so I pulled my arm up, rotating clockwise from my shoulder, the needle of a compass. I wiggled my fingers, stretched, strained, knowing what I would find if only closer, tempted, maddened by the equatorial humidity that teased my fingertips, tickled them with the suggestion of fertile, pungent, adolescent hair, finally relaxing my fingers, bending my elbow to relieve the strain, and discovering, of course, with a heat that ran through my arm and to the prehistoric heart of the Congo, that my palm fit perfectly, wonderfully, beneath one warm, tropical breast.

I noted the position of my arm, then relinquished control, and fell into a deep, perfect sleep.

"He wants to know." Abbas brought me an extra cup of water with my salt beef the next day.

"Let me up on deck."

"Impossible."

"Then let me sleep."

"Again?"

This dream, I wasted no time in vain explorations but reached directly for the large, dangling fruit, made my quick observations on the change in the angle of my elbow, and then passed the few remaining moments of control in thumb-aided evaluation of the lovely moles and ridges of the ocean-side of her breast.

The next day Abbas brought no water.

"Let me have some water."

"Not until you tell him."

"How far did the ship travel yesterday, Abbas?"

"That is known only to the admiral."

"Colón."

"Yes." My first piece of solid information.

"Let me up on deck."

"Impossible."

"Then let me sleep."

"He says enough with sleeping."

"One more night, Abbas, tell him one more night. And if you bring me the information, how far we traveled yesterday, and how far we travel today, I will tell Pinzón down to the mile how much farther."

"How do you know it is Pinzón?" Abbas was lost.

"Let me up on deck."

"Sleep tight." Abbas dropped the lid back on my cask.

I came to my dream later than usual. We were close, my elbow was well bent, though try as I might, I could not raise my head to a position of greater appreciation. But this time, whether from thirst or curiosity, I let my hand slide down to tease the hard, salty nipple, and was surprised to find a drop, two drops, a whole rainfall of drops along the sand in that mysterious gulf between her breasts and her unreachable vagina. I drew my hand, cupped and damp, back to my mouth and sucked furiously on my palms and my fingers until I woke myself in a frenzy. My lips were wet, my mouth tasted strongly—no imagination—strongly and sweetly of milk.

Abbas brought me the information. I made a quick calculation, with a double portion of salt beef and water.

"If we continue to sail at this speed, Abbas, three more days."

"Three more days!" Abbas smiled broadly. "The captain will be pleased."

"Let me up on deck."

"Impossible."

It must have been shortly after midnight on the twelfth night of October when a thunderstorm of angry voices shook me awake. The sound of hatchet meeting wood mixed with a curse of frustration. The top flew off my cask. I rubbed my eyes and looked up. A torch lit the ceiling of the hold and below the torch three faces, unshaven, angry, and then terrified, as if the sight of me was the last thing they had expected. Screams, bootsteps, other screams, echoes, then silence and darkness as before.

I stood up warily, hesitant, wanting to look, afraid. Gripping the rim, I bent my elbows, pulled myself up, with none of the ease of dreams, none of the warmth, only pain in unused shoulders and aching back. I peered over the top. A grayish light oozed through the planks of the deck, between the slats above the waterline, the sound of water lightly urging the boat forward. As the minutes passed, the shadows moved, lightened into four other pale faces, peering out in terror and in wonder.

With great effort, I drew myself up to sit on the lip of the barrel. There must have been a hundred casks in the hold, hogsheads as big as tree stumps, double hogsheads as big as a blacksmith's, all lashed together with hemp. Mine stood in the middle of the field. The only exit was a stoop-shouldered duck walk from the top of one cask to another.

At the foot of the ladder leading up to the deck, I joined my four ghostly comrades. Silently, we squinted, as pale and tentative as moles sniffing the gray air, reaching out paws to touch, confirm. Yes, this was a nose, these eyes, ears, hair, the familiar necessities. And yes, something different, something more, something felt, something less. Jews, all of us.

Up the ladder, through the hatch leading onto the deck, there was only the creaking of wood, the soft rush of fresh air. I signaled to my friends that I would ascend first, and they gladly gave way, ready to crawl back to their barrels at the first sound of danger.

On deck, Eliphaz. If ever there was a moment as fine and soul-strengthening as my first sight of the sea it was this, when my feet first touched the deck of a seagoing ship in the midst of a warm, calm ocean. I breathed, once, twice, three times. I felt——to the bottom of my feet and the ends of my hair——air, water, the smell of rotting wood and nighttime fill my lungs, my bowels, channel the life I had missed, my many weeks in the hold. The gray light disappeared. The boat rocked gently up and down. In the privacy of utter darkness, I rode a single plank over the surf, with the supreme weightlessness of the crest of a wave. I reached my arms out to the side. Zacuto's astrolabe and book of charts fell out of my sleeves and clattered to the deck. No matter. The wind at my back filled the Franciscan cowl I still wore into a pair of angelic wings. An invisible hand pulled aside the curtain of a thick cloud, and at once all was bathed in the brilliant wash of a full moon.

Ranged before me stood twenty-five men. With a single breath, they stepped back to the rail, all eyes fixed on me as if on a ghost. One knelt. Suddenly they all knelt, crossed themselves, prayed, gasped, bowed their heads. A sound came from above, piercing the mumbling of the heads below. Tied to the foremast was a man. Another sound cried out above me. On the mainmast, silhouetted against the sails, the heavy square sheets shining against the clouds, another man. Halfway up each of the three masts was a man, standing in the same position as I was, feet down, arms stretched out to the side. But while I was free, these men were bound.

The men on the hempen crosses were *conversos* of a type all too familiar to a boy who had spent two years in a priory. And the men before me, cowering in the clarity of moonlight, were twenty-five mutineers, terrified that, thirty days past their last sight of land, they were just forty waves away from the edge of the earth. Quickly, I grabbed a knife from a kneeling sailor, climbed the rigging to the foremast and freed Abbas—for it was he, gasping for breath, the weight of his body pressing down on his chest. I eased him down to the deck, where he lay unmolested, the sailors still frozen in horror. Climbing up the mast at the stern, I reached a pair of broad shoulders.

"Captain Pinzón?" I whispered, unable to speak fully after ten weeks in the barrel. The man raised his beard from his chest, and I looked into the gray eyes of the father of my drifted love.

"My son!" He smiled. No words of gratitude could have matched that perfect expression of my hopes. I wanted to sit with him, high above the waves, pester him with questions. What was she like as a young girl? Does she sing? Does she walk on the beach at dusk with her eyes toward the west? How soon can she join me in the new world?

But there was another man hanging from the mainmast.

"Good morning, Admiral Colón," I rasped.

"Esau, where the hell did you come from?"

"Now do you believe me, Admiral?"

"Believe you what?"

"Land. Between Spain and China."

"Get out of here and leave me alone." My back was turned to the bow, but I knew what Colón would see in a matter of moments.

"Surely you don't want to stay up here?"

"What makes you think you know what I want?" A real martyr, our admiral. No doubt about it, a Jew.

"You want to go down in history."

"Leave me alone."

"As the Great Discoverer."

"Spices. Gold. The Indies. I told you before. Everything else is sentiment and illusion."

"As the Savior of the Jews."

"You and Santángel," he said, struggling against the ropes. "There is a saying in Spain, do you know it? 'In three cases has water flowed in vain—the water of the river into the sea, the water in wine, and the water at a Jew's baptism.' "

"So you are one of us," I said, smiling. But this man, this Colón, was reaching down inside himself for a Catholic answer. For if truth be told, I was right and Santángel was wrong. Colón was a nation unto himself, a nation so angry, so confused, so thoroughly pleased with itself, that, crucified as he was, his sole rebuttal was a gob of spittle to baptize the cheek my grandfather had missed.

The men looked up from twenty feet below, confusion, wonder, terror, such a mixture of mysteries and symbols peculiar to the Catholic religion, my dear son, that it would take me ten letters to try to unravel what these poor men saw in my two minutes on deck. But for me, after ten weeks in a barrel, what a feeling of control, power beyond the manipulation of my own dreams, the admiral beside me, the crew below, the sparkling nighttime sea.

I wiped my face with my sleeve, then turned and pointed. The crew peered as one through the gray-eyed dawn. There on the horizon, lit clearly, superbly, unmistakably, a success beyond my map of Africa. Not a breast, but an island nonetheless—a drop, life-giving soul food. I licked my thirsty lips and discovered salt spray. I swallowed, and my cracked, deserted voice box moistened with the dreamy taste of her sweet, sweet milk.

"Land," I shouted. "Land Ho!"

ESAU—FLORIDA

When I woke from my dream, the taste of milk was still fresh on my lips, a woman's breast only a bent elbow from my nose. I was lying on my back at full length, on the most comfortable straw mattress this side of my Córdoban childhood. There was no face attached to the breasts, no body below the hips, the artist had merely fashioned the obvious around the nipples of two knots in a plank of the ceiling. I turned my head. Hundreds of other knots winked back at me, similarly adorned. Abbas, standing guard, smiled.

I sat up on the bunk, careful of my head, and swung down to my friend. I pointed to my mouth, asking to speak and drink all in the same pantomime. He handed me a gourd. I tasted. Fresh water. I drank. Not the brackish liquid of ten weeks at sea, but fresh, clear water. I emptied the gourd as Pinzón entered the cabin.

He stood for a moment, huge in the frame of the door, a man clearly designed for a voyage of discovery, for great things. His chest dwarfed the slender Abbas. His head almost brushed the ceiling. His graying hair, still in the thick of youth, spoke of energy and wisdom. His hooded gray eyes were filled with a thirst, demanding knowledge from a world too small to answer all his questions. His voice rang, not in the insinuating, argumentative tenor of Colón, but with the rich basso profundo of a man.

"My son!" he said again, and let the echo fill the cabin with its unambiguous message of delight and gratitude.

"Captain Pinzón," I began. He put his finger to his lips.

"There will be plenty of time for you to speak, Esau," he said, closing the door gently behind him. "But first, taste this," and he held out a dull orange root to me, freshly picked and still shining. I needed no further invitation. I bit and swallowed, barely chewing. The root tasted of dirt and water and home.

"The first fruits of the new world"—Pinzón smiled—"rightfully belong to you.

"Now," he continued, as I wiped my mouth with the sleeve of my cowl, "I suppose you deserve an explanation." I nodded, still chewing. He sat on a bench opposite, motioned Abbas to guard the door. "I am afraid I can explain very little about the expedition. Until you were brought to me, the night of our departure from Palos, I knew only that I owed my ships, my family, my life, to the generosity of Don Luis de Santángel. I would follow any design of his without a murmur, even if it led to the depths of the Ocean Sea.

"I had heard of Colón, had met him at the occasional Mass in Palos and the infrequent visits I made with my daughter to La Rábida. He was a fanatic, without a doubt, too converted, too full of miracles and prophecy to lead an armed expedition to the slave coast or a merchant ship to Genoa. He was strong enough only for the impossible. I have known dozens of men like him. The dockyards of Cádiz, Lisbon, Mariposa, Valencia, are full of shipless captains ready to sail west to the Indies, south around Africa, or east through some imagined channel into the Arabian Sea. Don Luis came to me and said, 'Don Martín, I need you to be the brain of an expedition whose heart beats in the breast of a crazy man.' I was skeptical. But Don Luis asked. I requisitioned the ships, hired the crews, even in the face of the rumor that we were sailing beyond the edge of the world.

"In those last moments before the Expulsion, my days were already full with renting carracks to transport the thousands of Jews pouring into Palos. It was only seventy-two hours before our own sailing that Don Luis instructed me to package you and the nine others in barrels, and make certain you were on board before midnight on the day of the Expulsion."

"Pardon me, Don Martín," I croaked, "but what expulsion are you talking about?"

Pinzón laughed, started to go on, paused, laughed again, stopped laughing. He looked at me, troubled, gray eyes.

"Were you so cloistered in that monastery, poor Esau, that you heard nothing of the Expulsion of the Jews?" Silence. "Esau, my poor Esau." He shook his head. "Your patience has been abused. Fourteen ninety-two was a busy year. Shortly after the turn of the calendar, Their Most Catholic Majesties finally conquered Granada."

"That much I know," I said, "and that they agreed to Colón's expedition."

"They did, in theory." Pinzón nodded. "But the contract was not signed until April, two weeks after their signatures appeared on the Order of Expulsion. The Jews of Aragón and Castile had until the end of July to sell their belongings and take only what they could carry out of the country. All of them."

All of them, I thought. The Jews of Córdoba, my parents, my brother. I looked at Abbas. He had tried to tell me at La Rábida. How could he?

"Don Luis rode to Palos to assist me. You were the easiest;

we knew where to find you. The other nine came from all over Spain, handpicked by Santángel."

"Handpicked for what?" I asked.

"Esau, sit down," Pinzón said. I was standing above him. I sat back on the bunk. I unclenched my fists and laid my palms flat on my knees. "Esau," he began again, history lesson over, time to move on, "I have just returned from the most beautiful beach I have seen in all my fifty years of sailing, more beautiful than the Azores, than the Canaries, than the Cyclades of Greece. The natives, the fruit, the streams, are warmer, purer, sweeter than any I've known in Europe. Your people will thrive here, multiply, be a great people once more."

"My people?" I asked.

"The Jews." I had almost forgotten. "Did you never hear of the Minyan?" Of course I had heard of the Minyan—the Minyan that held its disputations and religious observances in my bedroom, in my study, in my living room, in my wonderful cave in Mariposa.

"Ten Jews made up the Minyan in Spain, Esau," Pinzón said. "It will take ten Jews to make up the Minyan in a new homeland." I had been handpicked. It will take ten Jews. In a new homeland. For weeks my ears had heard only wood against wood, seawater against wood. I had to pass Pinzón's words from my lips to my ears several times until the sense became clear.

I was not just a navigator, as Santángel had told me. I had been picked by my benefactor, handpicked, along with nine other Jews of Spain, to sail with Colón and Pinzón, to lay the foundations for a new Temple of Solomon, a new Garden of Eden. The four ghosts who climbed from their barrels in the moonlight were my fellow Jews. Five others remained hidden in

barrels in the hold of Colón's boat, the *Santa María,* their
presence known only to Pinzón, Abbas, and an ordinary sailor,
who kept them fed as Abbas did us.

"Tonight, Esau"—Pinzón lowered his voice—"Abbas
will row you and your friends to the *Santa María,* and finally
all ten ashore. I guarantee that the rest of the crew will be dead
drunk."

I hated to disappoint a man I so revered. But Santángel had
named me navigator.

"Captain Pinzón," I said, "I believe we have found only
an island."

"Yes?"

"A small one."

"Colón believes it to be one of the islands of Cipangu."

"With all due respect, Don Martín"—I blushed—
"Colón has been spending too much time with Marco Polo and
not enough with his charts."

"So?"

"Could you imagine a homeland for the Jews the size of
Zahara de los Membrillos?"

Pinzón sighed. "What do you recommend, Esau?"

I opted for more wandering, urging Pinzón all the time to sail
north-by-northwest to the womanly peninsula we both knew so
well. In so doing, I doomed all ten of us Jews to a few more
barrel-bound weeks at sea.

You see, Eliphaz, the crew of Pinzón's boat, the *Pinta,* the
mutinous crew that I had faced down to save the lives of Colón,
Pinzón, and my watchdog, Abbas, still wondered whether I was
flesh or other. My four skinny friends had never climbed the
ladder, had never materialized beyond the vague homunculi that
the mutineers had imagined when they smashed open our hogs-

head havens in search of weapons. Pinzón, in his wisdom, thought it best to keep it that way. Five phantoms held far more power at sea than five unexplained Jews.

So back to our barrels we went, the five of us. And the next morning, when the crew had regained their sobriety, we weighed anchor.

Colón wanted to sail to the southwest, the vaginal southwest, a maddening choice of destination for a breast-mad young man. Certain as I was, even in my barrel, that we were no more than two days' sail from my dream peninsula, I would nonetheless have supported the plan with enthusiasm. But an unforeseen fever drove the crew mad and, for a time, interrupted my search for a homeland and Colón's for the Indies.

Gold. Gold. There were three captains and ninety-six sailors aboard the three ships, all infected. Against ten barrel-bound Jews. The odds were not good. So we bounced from island to island, small to large to small, sending out landing parties, finding just enough of the shiny stuff to keep us going, enough to keep us from the real work of the expedition.

One afternoon the ships changed course and turned eastward, back in the direction of the Old World. When Abbas brought my dinner that night I insisted on speaking with Pinzón.

"Don Martín," I said, when we were safely inside his cabin, "you must seize control of the expedition and head north immediately. There is a peninsula of a large continent there. It is the source of all goodness, all life on this hemisphere. You must drop our Minyan there. Two days' journey, that is all." Pinzón looked at me in amazement. The six weeks had worn worse on him.

"With all due respect, Esau," he finally whispered, "you are out of your mind. I can no more control Colón among the savages and the waves than I could in the port of Palos, where I had friends, family, and ammunition. You saw how he was, the night of the mutiny. He'd sooner be crucified than give up command."

"Don Martín," I continued. "You have seen where the desire for gold has led the king and queen of Spain. The Jews were their final mine. They booted them from the country and seized their possessions. If this expedition turns into a single-minded search for gold . . ."

"I can do nothing," Pinzón whispered and dropped to the bench. I looked to Abbas. He was looking at me. I put my hand on Pinzón's shoulder, as Abravanel had his on mine. I felt great love for this man who had kidnapped me, whose life I had saved, whose daughter filled my dreams. But it was time for the son to act.

"In that case, Don Martín, with all due respect, please remain in your cabin. I must take control of the ship. Abbas, open the barrels."

The night watch put up no resistance when I appeared on deck with my four wraiths. North was the course I gave. North was the course called down to the helmsman below deck. As we came about, I heard a whisper in the wind from off the port side of the *Santa María*—a loose rope, a coded message, a new world bird, my mother's viol? My heart was my lodestone, locked to its magnetic pole, feeling its way across the strait. There was no turning back. I was sure of my direction. I left to others the how.

After an hour's pursuit, the *Santa María* and the smaller *Niña* gave up the chase. I hadn't expected Colón to alter course and follow mine. At best, I hoped for a meeting away from the sight of his latest El Dorado, a chance to whisper the name

Santángel in his ear, a chance to steer him, move him to the right course.

Eliphaz, my son. As we approached the coast two dawns later, the sun at our shoulders lighting the waves as they broke along the reefs, flocks of long-legged birds shimmering in circular clouds overhead, and Don Martín, up from his cabin for the first time, rested, with the gleam of moral righteousness in his eye and his hand, steady and heavy, on my shoulder once more, my lodestone of a heart near to bursting, pulling us forward, forward, that extra foot over the waves, I saw Home—for the Jews, perhaps; for the five of us, certainly; for myself, without a doubt.

I left Abbas with a map for Santángel and a copy for my teacher, Zacuto. The rest of the crew stood at the rail as we lowered a boat.

"I will try to send Colón," Pinzón said, "with his five Jews."

I felt unsure—with only a bar mitzvah education and the little I picked up from the Minyan—what it meant to leave Jews six through ten in Colón-bound barrels, how shaky a community I would be building with only five male Jews. I could only feel my way to action, no more blind now, at the helm of an unfamiliar vessel, than I was in my cave, my cell, or my barrel.

"I will try, Esau," he said. "I will try, at least, to send your brother."

My brother. My brother. All at once, Eliphaz, the sound of the viol overwhelmed me. That was the music I heard as we left shore in Palos. My mother's viol, passed on to my brother, Yehuda, to make new music in the New World. Pinzón spoke as if I knew the plan all along. I blessed Santángel silently and showed no emotion.

"Better yet"—I spoke quickly to relieve him of the need to fulfill my dreams of reunion—"tell Santángel that you succeeded."

"I will bring New Christians next trip. Women." My mind moved from Yehuda to long hair, broad shoulders, gray eyes.

"I owe you much, Don Martín. I should like to name this new land after you."

"No, no, Esau, much better a saint . . ." He caught himself. "Or at least a woman."

The first man, whom the Jews call Adam, was given absolute authority to name the beasts and the plants of Paradise. I carried with me, in my barrel, in my Franciscan cowl, twenty-one years of a language, and an unusual way of seeing things that was at once part of me and outside of me. What that power was, that drew me from Córdoba to Mariposa, from Mariposa to the beach of La Rábida, from Palos across the ever-changing maze of the Ocean Sea, was a force that not even the Mayaimi have named. I love your mother, Eliphaz, as I love my own life. But a man always carries with him his first love. And if that love moves him, guides him, becomes the land that nourishes him, baptizes him, redefines him, well—any attempt at forgetting would be immoral.

"You have a daughter, Don Martín?"

He looked at me, another gray-eyed question. I looked out at the shore. The four Jews were perched in the boat, a week's supplies lashed to the bottom.

"A daughter? You mean Florida?"

New York, New York
1 October 1919

My dear Son,

In the latest fair copy I was able to examine, belonging to Zebulon Whiteman of Edom County, Missouri, dated 1882, the story of the discovery of the mainland of the North American Continent and the naming of the peninsula of Florida constitute the final words of the Last Will and Testament of Esau Benavides, born Eliyahu ben Moshe Halevy, my great-great - great - great - great - great - great - great - great - great-great-great-great-great-great-great-grandfather.

In adapting the copy of 1882, which was itself taken directly from the 1763 translation of the original and certified authentic by the Franciscan missionary Bartolomeo de las Camas, I have merely attempted to impose a fluidity onto the literal translation from the Spanish, with the goal of persuading an American publisher to broadcast to a wider public the true history of our proud family, which is the true history of our country.

In the course of my studies of this remarkable document, I had occasion to visit most of the reputable booksellers of Judaica up and down the East Coast of the United States. Many of them provided valuable material on the history of the Jews in Spain and elsewhere prior to the Expulsion. None of them, however, was able to lay his hands on documents relating to the further history of Esau, his son Eliphaz, or any of his

offspring and succeeding generations. Similarly unsuccessful
were my communications with the few identifiable descendants. The history of the Mayaimi merged with that of the
Seminoles. The subsequent removal of the Seminoles in the
1830s by the Gentiles into larger reservations in the Oklahoma
Territory destroyed the requisite curiosity of origins. Only *my*
direct ancestors have taken Esau's advice to heart—in motion
there is survival.

But as I was nearing the end of my work, one of my many
inquiries finally bore fruit. I was visited one day by a decrepit
bookdealer who claimed to have run a business in Sephardic
Judaica out of his tenement on Essex Street in New York City
for over thirty-five years, although God knows I have walked
the length of Essex Street dozens of times without hearing its
name. He boasted that he possessed several documents, in
Spanish and in English, that might pertain to the history of
Esau Benavides. Upon further inquiry, and a personal visit on
my part to his attic, I discovered merely that he had recently
received a letter from a Mrs. Albin Barker in Olive Hill, Kentucky, offering for sale several ancient pieces of paper she had
discovered stored in a clay jug at the narrow end of a bat cave
behind her truck farm. She could read nothing on the paper—
she believed in her confusion that the symbols were Egyptian
hieroglyphs—except for a large scrawl at the top of the first
page: YSWA.

I paid the dealer five dollars for the woman's address. For an
extra five, the documents were mine. Written on vellum and
dated 1653, these must be fragments from one of the earliest
copies made of the original letter. They could even be part of
the Spanish copy from which the translation of 1763 was taken.

I am a ham-handed translator of Spanish, and, with the
scant information that exists on the Native Americans of
Florida, the whole is therefore sketchy, full of gaps, mysterious
at times, and at others unbelievable.

Nevertheless, there is no doubt in my mind that these are the last pages of the Will and Testament of Esau Benavides. With the fondness of a father, I have rushed to finish my translation in time for your bar mitzvah.

Happy birthday,
Papa

"This is absurd," I said.

"You should see what other boys get as bar mitzvah presents." Hanni was leaning back against the headboard, snugly surrounded by half a dozen pillows, eyes half-closed. "My Papa was a very lucky young man."

Isabella still lay chin on hands, giving no sign of either boredom or understanding. The pile of paper I had read was spread around the armchair like a pinochle fan. There was one more sheaf to go, bound in its own purple ribbon.

"Did your grandfather honestly expect any publisher to believe that a Jew named Esau discovered America?"

"Why shouldn't a publisher believe? There is the proof, in front of your nose."

"This?" I whispered. "This copy of a copy of a translation of a copy of who knows how many other copies? Maybe if you could find the original . . ."

"The original?" Hanni finally opened her eyes. "Would you expect a double-breasted publisher, smoking a Montecristo at a mahogany desk high above Union Square to read a cardboard box full of tree bark in the original Castilian?"

"You mean you've seen the original?"

"Have you seen five-hundred-year-old tree bark?" Hanni smiled back. "My grandfather would have been laughed out of every waiting room in Manhattan if he had claimed to be carrying the original."

"But you have no other way to prove the authenticity of the letter!" I felt I was explaining the alphabet to a summer intern. Hanni's face dropped. Not as if I had finally twigged her to the

crucial weakness of her obsession. More as if she had come to
the realization that it was I who had failed to qualify for the
summer job.

"Look at your own work, your documentaries. Are any of
your viewers demanding to see the original?"

"No," I said, "but they believe in the process of making
copies of a film."

"I mean the original scene, before you put it on film, with
your subject walking in his garden, or sitting in her chair, full
body, not a tightly framed soft-focus close-up. Does your audience have to be there in order to believe you? Do they have to
walk with the astronauts before they believe that man really
stood on the moon and not on some highly sophisticated TV
set? Would anything less than being Neil Armstrong satisfy
them? Would anything less than being Esau satisfy you?"

"That's ridiculous!" I said, what I always say when I can't
think of a good retort. She did have a point. I never could trust
a camera crew.

"Holland," she said, with remarkable equanimity, "I think it
is worth realizing that, put between two leather-bound covers,
televised on any public broadcast system, preached from any
pulpit, religious or otherwise, just about anything will be believed by most people."

"Then you admit this is all a fiction?" I smiled triumphantly.

"Of course not," she said. "We were merely discussing the
need for what you called 'authenticity.' Now stand up!" Isabella was on her feet in an instant, Hanni a moment later. My
legs had fallen asleep. "Let your head drop, chin on chest, roll
it slowly to one side, then the other. Head up, raise your hands
slowly above your head . . ."

"Hanni, what are you doing?" I asked. My watch said 5.45.

"In America we call it the seventh-inning stretch."

The storm swept away the last of my companions. The Minyan was down to one. One Jew, one God, one Florida. I hate to say I was happy, but I am a monogamist at heart.

"All Jews dead?" I asked Hanni.

"Yes."

"Except Esau?"

"Of course."

"Very convenient. Kill off all your witnesses with Hurricane Jehovah. Very *Moby Dick*.

"Moby Dick was a whale."

"It's still deus ex machina. Automatic and unsatisfying."

"It's what happened," Hanni said. "I thought you were the stickler for authenticity. Do you want Esau to give Queequeg CPR just to satisfy your literary tastes?"

I turned back to the letter.

I was hungry. Hungrier than I'd been in the cave, hungrier than during the hundreds of pointless fasts I'd endured as a Jew and a friar. Hungrier than I'd been since my bar mitzvah. Along with my friends went my food. And among the many books that Santángel left me, among the many lessons that Abbas and Zacuto taught me, those on "How to Catch a Fish" or "How

to Make a Fire from a *Stone*" or "How to Tell the Edible
Mushroom from the One That Will Turn Your Tongue Black
and Choke You to Death" were conspicuously absent.

I had cowered on the same small square of sand since our
arrival. It had brought only misfortune. I turned my back to the
beach and walked inland. Half an hour later I was at the shore,
another shore. Another island? Could my dream have been so
misaligned that what I had thought was solid breast was merely
another lactic mirage? In the distance, beneath the afternoon sun,
more land rose from the haze, a mile, perhaps half a mile, away.
More broad-leaved trees, more sand. I was on a reef, maybe only
an accident of the storm. I turned to the north and began walking.
I hadn't gone far when I heard the first *pahk*. I stopped in my

"There's a gap here," I said.
"There always is. Keep reading."

beyond the huts came another *pahk* and then a loud grunt, as
if a small crowd of people had been slapped on the

"Hanni!" I complained.
"I was beginning to like you, Holland," she said, shifting on
the pillows. "Don't be such a whiny little girl."

I couldn't tell whether it was ceremony or entertainment, war
or game. There was a ball. There was a stick. Can you
remember, Eliphaz, the first time I took you out to the Ball
Game, the wonder, the mystery, the feeling that the intricate
rules and rituals were only steps in a path toward losing yourself
in the rhythm of the game. That was how I felt, son, lying on
my stomach in the sand, peering between the stilts of the hut, the
backs of two braves only a few feet

a crack, as the stick hit the ball, the sound of sap bursting in fire, of a spear shattering against the shoulder of a twelve-pointed buck, of breaking bones, of my grandmother quartering a chicken against the sharp edge of the Fountain of the Lions. I jumped up and ran, knowing that the ball might clear the roof of the hut, watching it white against the blue of the sky, then coming down, down, so wrapped up in the game that I gave no thought to whether to hide or to catch, but held my palms up, wanting desperately to be part of the game.

When I opened my eyes, my hands were full. And two braves stood before me, mouths open, terror and gratitude both mixed

on their shoulders into the midst

the Calusa beaten, gathered up their

then, that I opened my hands and found, staring up at me—I know you will find it hard to believe that your people were once so cruel—the rounded, ball-shaped, sun-bleached skull of a baby

I looked up from the page. Hanni was beaming, munching away at a kipferln.

"Do you want a translation?"

"A paper bag would help."

"Anthropologists have dug up hundreds of these skulls in burial grounds all over the South, scarred and dented from repeated blows. They've condemned the aboriginal American for murdering defective infants, unwanted babies, et cetera."

"Esau's description is rather horrifying," I said.

"But think for a moment—what if these babies had died of natural causes, miscarriages, stillbirths, prehistoric Sudden Infant Death Syndrome? What if the holiest use you could make of your child's remains was in your holiest ritual?"

"A ball game was a holy ritual?"

"Have you ever been to a baseball game?"

"No," I had to admit.

"Keep reading," she said. "It gets easier."

I was brought onto the platform of one hut, larger than the rest. The braves, Eliphaz, set me down in front of their father, another Santángel, another Pinzón. I understood by their gestures that they were giving the chief a step-by-step reenactment of how I had risen out of the reeds, the savior of the game against the Calusa. The whole tribe had gathered around, only about thirty people then. You notice that, fifteen years later, people who have never seen me still stare. The excitement of the Mayaimi the first time they saw me was almost enough to drown out the voices of your uncles.

Then silence fell as they turned to me. I was expected to explain how I happened to fall from the sky to catch the skull at the end of the game, two braves out, every base occupied by a grinning Calusa, the winning run standing stick in hand before the lodge. I mimed as best I could the voyage across the water, the storm, the disappearance of my fellow Jews.

A brave entered the hut. A fish smelling of smoke and pine stared glassy-eyed from a bed of palm leaves. Bowing low, he laid it on the ground in front of the chief and drew a sharpened fishbone from his loincloth. With a practiced hand he cut one slice and handed it to the chief. Your grandfather picked up the long, thin strip of flesh and held it to the light of the door. With a snort, he threw the strip out the door, grabbed the fish knife, and knocked the brave to the ground. It was the first time I saw the terrible anger of your grandfather. And his terrible concentration. He took a full minute to cut my slice, another full minute for his own. Placing each piece upon a round wheel of cassava bread, he held a third piece to the light, so I could admire his artistry. I never again saw a man slice fish so thin.

In that orange glow, through that translucent piece of smoked salmon, I first saw your mother.

She is a woman of great faith, your mother. This evening she brought me a broth of wild fowl, boiled in water from the forbidden Fountain of Everlasting Life. I never tasted finer, not here, not home in Córdoba; my hunger will survive till the last. But my faith is from the Old World, and I believe only that these New World waters will be my last meal.

Your mother has poured water on my wound. She has dabbed at the pus oozing from my eye with a remnant of my Franciscan cowl dipped in the water of the forbidden Fountain. It gives me comfort, the copper-colored girl dipping her hem, cooling my wound. I can hear my mother's viol, a happy melody, no lamentations.

My eyes grow heavy. I look for sleep, for dreams. This wound will not heal. When I am dead, pour water on your anger toward Straight Arrow as you would on a smoldering fire. His name belies his accuracy, but many of us travel by names that seek to hide rather than reveal. His arm threw the ball, his fingers shaped its progress. And yes, perhaps his fingers did move to his mouth and place his spittle upon its seams. But who among us is wise enough to trace the sudden jumps and swerves of a fast ball back to the arm that threw it? Who among us can swear to the God of the Stars that it was not the fault of my own eye to catch what was meant for my bat? Was it my punishment for converting the Mayaimi and the Calusa and the Jeaga from the gruesome human skull to a ball of jay feathers and deerhide? A child's skull would have fractured harmlessly against my cheek.

Feel no anger against the Calusa. Do not allow my death to

become a cause of war. My greatest success was their conversion from the Ball Game of War to the Ball Game of Peace.

Feel no grief for me. I have had a greater fortune than any man since Noah. I have walked upon a great beautiful continent, I have known passion, I have sired a son. I have stood, bat in hand with three men on base, and hit the ball out of the village.

Bury me in the warm beach of the Mayaimi, on the coast of my Florida. Let me lie in the heat of her breast until the continents drift back together.

You are now the only Jew in this new world. What does that mean, you ask me, to be a Jew? I was sent here by Santángel to preserve the Jews. The Expulsion struck the ears of the Minyan in tragic tones, as the funeral dirge of culture, as the death of a rich era of Jewish achievement in Spain. I heard a different chorus. I heard the wailing from the boats as we sailed down the river Tinto from Palos. The tragedy of the Expulsion was the tragedy of three hundred thousand unique voices, each with its own wonderful human melody.

There are those who would argue, since your copper-colored mother is not Jewish, that you are not a Jew. Those others live thousands of miles away. You are one-half my child, and entirely my son. Today the Mayaimi say you are one of them. Tomorrow you will be different. You are a Jew.

You will have children, they will be different. They will grow beside their Mayaimi sisters, they will play ball with their Mayaimi brothers, but ultimately they will become free agents. They will be welcome among any tribe as long as they can still hit the long ball. Then they will be asked to leave, to move, against their will. They will be different. They will be great— but a great, different, new people.

You will have to guide them. You will have to take control

of the motion of your people. I, too, began to feel my way alone at the age of thirteen. I had to reinvent, I had to disguise. I had to wear the cloak of a Franciscan, the skin of a deer. I had no rabbi to guide me. By being Esau, I have been a Jew. By being Eliyahu, I have been a Jew. By being a friar, a sailor, a castaway, a Mayaimi, I have been a Jew.

As the wife of the rabbi of Alcaudete said to the apothecary of Córdoba, the grandfather of the lute-loving Kima—you are always a Jew.

Now it is time for you to be Eliphaz.

Games not war, deerhide not skulls. When in doubt, eat, but avoid shellfish. And when they pitch you high and inside, as they will, move. My destiny is secure in your survival. Your survival is assured only in your motion.

> Your loving father,
> Esau

HOLLAND—SANTA ISABEL LA REAL

Ben, Ben, Ben,
 What don't I believe?
 Let me rephrase that.
 You have always been the Beacon of Reason, Ben, the Master of Aeronautics, the Grand Invigilator of Steam, Electric, and Internal Combustion Engines. To me, Ben, to me. That's what you've been to me.
 Is it really possible that you are different? With other people, other women?
 This woman Hanni, your client. Her trip to Spain, for the sole purpose of finding the Esau Letter. Esau, Columbus, Mayaimi Beach, baseball, Jews, Jews, and more Jews, for Christ's sake! You can't believe it, can you, Ben? You don't believe it. Say it.
 I knew it.
 You are in cahoots with Sandor, with Zoltan, aren't you, Ben? You knew he had the Letter. You arranged for him to leave it with a student. You undoubtedly booked Isabella in the seat next to Hanni's on British Armadan Flight 802—Delayed Due to Weather at Destination—reckoning that natural curiosity would effect the transfer six miles above ground. You only wanted to elongate the mystery, pull the taffy of a nice comfortable trip for a crazy old lady from Miami, give her a little flutter before the happy ending, and then send her home minus the largest possible commission a travel agent can squeeze.

You just didn't count on the Strike.

"Accidents can happen," Hanni said to me when I ran this thesis by her, back in the fresh air of the courtyard. Hanni stirred the water of the fountain with a little finger. "Look at what happened to Esau and the spitball. Look at what happened to Esau and the Red Men."

"The Red Men?"

"The Mayaimi. Later on, Eliphaz and his descendants began to call themselves the Red Men, after the translation of the biblical name for the descendants of the biblical Esau—the Edomites."

"But the Edomites were the Romans, weren't they?"

"According to whom?"

"And Esau was only named Esau through the accident of conversion," I argued.

"You see?" Hanni grinned. "Another accident. If travel agents could plan everything, all train travel would be westward, all Germans cultivated, all Russians perfect gentlemen, and all passengers would reach their final destination with passport and wallet intact."

She ran her fingers through the stone manes of the lions of the fountain. It was almost six A.M. Only a few stars were left in the sky.

"I'm going to try ringing Ben," I said, to no one in particular, "and the airport. Perhaps they've reopened." I retrieved my handbag from beneath a woven pillow. "Give me your ticket, Hanni, and I'll check for you, too."

Hanni walked over to the steamer trunk. Isabella's violin case sat next to Hanni's bag, though Isabella had disappeared inside the house. I found Hanni's coupon.

"You're travelling on to Sosua?"

She looked up at me, those cornflower eyes. "That was my original plan."

"You should look up some friends of mine." I searched my bag for my notebook. "They were very helpful—I don't know

if you ever saw my documentary 'Sosua: Dominican Kibbutz'?"

"Ah," she said, "that was yours? I have a friend, a boy who
once rented a room from me in London, just after Leo died. He
called me, it must have been last year, the year before, told me
it was on TV. A nice boy, about your age."

You must know the story, Ben. One of the two good stories
to come out of the Dominican Republic—Sosua and baseball—or so said the Dominican taxi driver who shepherded me
down to the Plaza de Toros in New York for Hook's Floating
Fiddle Recital.

"We had a dictator, lady, in the Dominican," he said, "by
the name of General Rafael Leonidas Trujillo, who for thirty-
one years pissed off everybody and everything, including your
President Roosevelt, before they got him in 1961."

I told him Roosevelt was certainly not *my* president.

"Back in those days, lady, you're too young to remember,
and me too, but I heard the story. Back in those days, 1937, '38,
the Jews were a very unpopular people in the world. Hitler
wanted to get them out of Germany, but nobody wanted to
take them. Nobody except Trujillo. He said to Hitler, 'Go
ahead, Adolf, gimme a hundred, two hundred thousand of
them Jews. I'll give them a piece of land for farming, they can
make cheese, sausage, write some books. Marry some of our
pretty Dominican ladies and put some brains into our banana-
heads.'

"Trujillo, he liked to talk big. He also had bad press, on
account of accidentally murdering fifteen thousand Haitians a
few years earlier. But it's a good story, lady, a good thing we
Dominicans did. Still some Jews down there now."

I later discovered, when I flew down to Sosua for Rest,
Relaxation, and Research, that fewer than seven hundred refugees landed in the D.R., and most of those either stayed in
Santo Domingo or migrated to the States after the war. But a
few Jews remained, letting cabanas to the Germans and Austri-

ans who had infiltrated the coast. Enough Jews, at least, for a fifty-two-minute film that played abysmally on TV but made a small killing in the home video market.

"There was a group of Swiss Jews that made it to Sosua, wasn't there?" Hanni asked, leaning back against the fountain. "And another party from Bayonne? We booked their passage, Papa and I, on a boat hauling scrap iron to Lisbon, then over to Puerto Plata."

"We? You mean MittelEuropa?"

"Not the furniture-moving division, this time," Hanni said.

"You're flying over for a reunion?"

"Of sorts," she said. "I'm doing a favour for Benjamin, in return for my Spanish excursion." She told me the deal. Oh, Ben. Don't you think I deserve at least a Bank Holiday weekend in Upper Slaughter for my end of the steamer trunk?

"Ask Benjamin a question, Holland," Hanni called over to me as I walked across the courtyard to the kitchen telephone. "Ask him if I can ship his trunk as freight."

"And fly directly back to Miami?"

"And stay here."

"But you have the Esau Letter."

"Yes," she said, and turned back to stroking the lion's mane.

I tried your Mariposa office. I tried the airport. No success. Through the doorway back out to the courtyard, I could see the shadowed form of Isabella, sitting against a pillar of the far arcade, wrapped in a shawl from Sandor's bed, violin case now on knees, knees pulled up to chest, neck arched, eyes, those grey eyes, to the sky.

"You want to stay to see Sandor." I returned the ticket to Hanni. "Zoltan."

"I'm curious," she said. "Very curious. But that's not it." Hanni let her hand slip from the stone of the lion and walked slowly over to the alabaster pillar next to me. "You've had bad dreams, Holland, strange dreams, the night you grew, other times, maybe?"

"Yes."

"You asked me before, about second chances, about whether I thought our old mistakes came around to us a second time."

"I didn't think you'd heard me."

"There are things that I have done, always wanting to do good, to follow the lessons of Papa, things more horrible than you could ever imagine. Things so simply evil that I have bricked them up behind my dreams and nightmares. I have been more or less successful. The dangerous side effect is that I am no longer certain about what has actually happened in large chunks of my life." Hanni fingered the veins in the alabaster, her voice in a half-whisper that smoothed the gravel edges into a childlike bedtime murmur of pebbles in a stream.

"The story I told you, about my reentry into Berlin. There's another story that does battle with it in my memory. In that second story, I am picked up in a two-seater by Albert Speer, the architect of the Third Reich, and flown into Hitler's bunker to try to persuade the Führer to surrender and save the remaining fragments of Berlin and Germany."

"Do you think that's true?" I wanted to cajole her back upstairs into Sandor's bed. She must have been exhausted.

"No." She looked at me abruptly. "I don't. Now that I've found the Esau Letter, my memory has regrouped itself around an old certainty, the old certainty that I've had to doubt for many years to preserve my sanity. I had a son, Holland. In Berlin. I gave birth in Berlin, a boy."

"You told me," I said. "The Russian."

"Maybe not the Russian," she smiled, "but the boy—no question. Will you help me?"

"Call Ben?" I asked.

"To find him. Will you help me find my son?" I sat Hanni back down on her steamer trunk. I fed her a kipferln. I put my arm around her.

"We should find Ben." There was a Mariposa address—on

the beach at El Palo—below your telephone number on the back of the ticket jacket. "I'll call the Hotel Mayor, ask them to send up a taxi. We'll drive to his office—it can't be far. He gave you good advice last time. On the Esau Letter."

"You think so?" Hanni leaned against me. Where was the strength that walked her across Europe, that brought her to Spain, hair soft against my cheek?

"*Mira.*" The voice floated across the courtyard. Isabella's arm was raised, pointing to the sky above our heads. I helped Hanni up. We walked over to the girl. I crouched down to follow her finger into the sky. The stars. The first light of day was dimming their luster, but the west was still dark enough for the constellations. The Plough, Orion's Belt. And away and to the right, the Seven Sisters.

> " '*Canst thou bind the sweet influences of Pleiades,*
> *Or loose the bands of Orion?*' "

I looked down at Isabella. This was the same quiet Spanish girl I had gazed at for the past three hours. But the voice, the language?

> " '*Canst thou bind the sweet influences of Pleiades,*
> *Or loose the bands of Orion?*' "

She handed me a book, and turned it to the proper page. I squinted in the shadows—a bilingual Bible, Job 38:31, Queen Isabella on one side, King James on the other.

"You've learned some English?" I asked her. She smiled. I flipped back to the inside cover, in all innocence, if there is such a thing.

I saw the words. I read again. Again.

" 'El Convento Santa Isabel la Real, Granada'?" Granada. Granada. Isabella's smile vanished. I must have looked as if I had just come out of a barrel after fourteen years at sea.

"No, Señora, no send me back."

"Is it the Convent Santa Isabel, on a hill, above the Albai-cín?"

"No send me back." She began to cry, standing with the violin case tight against her chest. The chord that I had heard in the Santa María, the violin chord came at me. Faintly at first, but growing louder. Not now, I prayed, quiet, not now!

"How old are you, Isabella?" I grasped for the words, *"¿Cuántos años tienes?"* The chord louder, please, no planes.

"No, Señora, please!"

"The Mother Superior? *¿Cómo se llama? ¿La Superiora . . . ?"* I stammered for the word—the face I could see clearly, stern and skeptical—but it would never have been heard over the roar of the jet engines going which way? They flew above, across, inland, out to sea. Not now. Not now, when I need silence, focus, answers.

"Isabella!" I grabbed her arm, took her chin in my other hand, and lifted her face up so the hair fell back and I could look straight into eyes as grey as the morning mist. Were they mine? Were they Hook's? I wanted to speak, I wanted to shout. I wanted to make her smile, I wanted to say something maternal, to find the twenty-five words that would end in her forgiveness. I wanted to ask enough, to ask fourteen years of questions, to be absolutely, absolutely sure.

But all I saw was grey fear, cold fear, panic. And only afterwards, unable to run after her, out the gate, down the road, did I realize that the sound of the violin, the terrible chord, rang from the violin in the case pressed between our two bodies. The violin, the wood, the strings, knew, beyond all need for proof, that I was Isabella's mother.

ITINERARY THREE

VILLA GABIROL

LA SUBIDA

EL PALO

LA ROSA NÁUTICA

AEROPUERTO

Over the years, in my personal search for the Perfect Sound, I have made several recordings of scales, both diatonic and chromatic, in an attempt to condense the sum total of my many years of string playing into the individual notes that are the atomic particles of all music.

Time being what it is, my experience is finite and the result necessarily imperfect. The act of recording poses its own problems of hiss, click, and vibration. The act of listening, changing as it does from hall to hall, from room to room, from ear to ear, further complicates the quest, editing out vast possibilities from the enormous repertoire implied by my scales.

No longer a scale of Western chromatics, or Eastern quarter-tones, or all-encompassing glissandi whose compass is still limited by physics and anatomy—the Perfect Sound will capture the disembodied moment of infinite possibility.

The moment between the upswing of the bow and the down. The moment of the touching of the string. The moment between the climax and the eruption, the wide-eyed stare shared by sperm and egg before the inevitable. The moment before birth, the unborn baby still undistanced. It will be a moment carrying thought and potential in all their musical brilliance, before life disappoints and diminishes. It will be a triumph over Time, Motion, and Beauty.

Remember—"How do you get to Carnegie Hall?" is a question as much of motion as of ambition.

—Sandor, *In Search of the Lost Chord, A Brief Guide,* p. 269

A NOTE FROM A READER

A distinguished traveler, the Khalsoum Professor of Ethnomusicology and Comparative Literature, writes:

Dear Ben,

   When I was a young man, there was no music that pleased me, that excited my sense of sound, of taste, of smell, of vision, of passion, as completely as that of flamenco. I sought out the pure, the rough. I traveled with the gypsies of Spain and North Africa. I ate with them, traded stories, shared cold skies and hard ground. I joined the chastened company of Cervantes, who learned "there is no gypsy girl twelve years old who does not know more than a Spanish lady of twenty-five."

   As the dabble of youth turned into the study of a lifetime, I was honored with invitations to flamenco *juergas,* solely as an aficionado, but certainly thanks to my familiarity with the gypsy music of Spain and elsewhere. While the purpose of the *juerga* is to trade repertoire, performance, and anecdote, the ancestry of flamenco often squeezes its callused rump into the firelight and demands its share of wine and debate.

   The dust is blown from the familiar genealogies—that flamenco was brought to Spain by the gypsies in the fifteenth century; that flamenco grew out of the Arabic music of the Moors. Each camp has its worthy share of intellectual knights and emotional squires.

   It was on a recent trip to Córdoba, however, that a tour

guide (one of those free-lance linguists who ruminate just inside the portico of the Mezquita) pulled me into just such a discussion. We had crossed the ocean of marble and alabaster columns of the mosque of Abd-ar-Rahman II, circumnavigated the pungent Basilica of Charles V, and were standing in the echo chamber of the *mihrab* of Caliph Hakam, when the wail of a *saeta*, the flamenco call to the Virgin, filtered through the stone lattice of the outer wall.

"There is a little-known fact about flamenco, Señor," he said, pulling me into the shadow, "that is familiar to all knowledgeable Spaniards but shared with very few outsiders. As you seem to be a man of some considerable acquaintance with flamenco and skepticism about the state of the world, I would like to invite you into our community."

I followed him out of the Mezquita and through the alleys of the Judería to a cup of Moroccan coffee at the low, dark tables of the Bar Abulafia. I expected little more revealing than where an Anglo tourist might find flamenco danced in the altogether.

"The fact is, Señor," he continued, "that the true flamenco, the Cante Jondo, is of neither Islamic nor gypsy parentage, but is the bastard grandson of the passionate sadness of the Spanish Jews."

I sipped my coffee, a delaying tactic I employ when my leg feels heavily pulled.

"You may not believe tonight," he continued. "You will believe tomorrow."

He opened with the etymology of Cante Jondo—not Deep Song, as I had always believed, Song of the Roots, of the Earth. Rather, Cante "Yom Tov," Song for the Good Day—Holiday, in Hebrew. The *saeta*, the flamenco verses to the Virgin we heard through the lattice of the Mezquita, was born from the womb of the Kol Nidre, the Aramaic song of lamentation sung on Yom Kippur, the Day of Atonement. In the Kol Nidre, the *conversos*, the Jews forced to convert by the Inquisition, sang to Yahweh, the God of the Israelites. They begged him to wipe them dry of their spurious baptism, and renew their Covenant with the God of their fathers. The remorse, the sense of shame, heated by the full-lipped fire of the Sephardic tune, became the trademarks of the *saeta*. The guttural *"Ayyyy"* to Yahweh became the rough *gitano* *"Ayyyy"* to the Virgin. The wail of the Jews, cornered in their house of worship by the gangsters of the Inquisition, became the wail of the gypsies, cornered in a cave in Granada, a town dump outside Columbus, a council flat in Manchester.

That evening, I sought out a little-known flamenco *tablao*, in the shadow of the yellow lights off the Avenida del Generalísimo. Garbage muffled the sounds of the street. A heavy-skirted mother squatted on the doorstep, nursing her child with one arm, grabbing for my pants leg with the other. The gypsies inside the tavern sang five notes and whined for money. I refused to pay, and the lights went out. On the walk home, I digested the message. I was stopped three times by the Guardia Civil, and had my pocket picked in the vestibule of my hotel. Was it always this way? Had I never noticed?

I know little but flamenco, I live for nothing but flamenco. Never again will I listen to flamenco. If not for tenure, I would die.

HANNI—HAPPINESS

Ach, Benjamin,

What to make of it?

There were weekend train excursions in the 1980s—mostly in the United States, where the population has a fat man's hunger for that confused fiction called mystery—during which a seemingly innocent passenger was stabbed, shot, or garrotted in the wee hours of Friday night. The remaining passengers, some of them paid actors—like the poor corpse, presumably—some of them paying guests, passed the rest of the weekend attempting to solve the murder. Meals and naps were taken as directed by an unseen artistic hand. By Sunday night, the mystery was solved, willy-nilly.

It is now Tuesday, December 31, 1991. Sunday night is decades off. Do I have to wait until the end of the week, or just the end of the year?

After Holland ran off in pursuit of Isabella, I sat on your albatross and munched through half a dozen kipferln, a gray-blue early morning pick-me-up. I've always accepted the bottomlessness of my bottomless jar of kipferln as an act of faith. I've never questioned how Penina's tarts passed down to Esau's family, how Esau carried them from Córdoba to Mariposa, from Mariposa to La Rábida, from La Rábida to Florida, how they survived the storm that swallowed his four companions, how they survived the next five hundred years. When Papa stowed them in my portfolio with the Esau Letter, I never asked whether my thousands of cousins each had his own personal supply, or whether I alone bore the self-reproducing manna for the bottomless family hunger. I never sat up with strong coffee, camera at hand, watching the jar for the miracle of mitosis. I never asked whether the key was cookie or container. I never tired of the taste of hazelnut and butter and sugar.

Until this morning. In the silence that followed storytime.

I wandered through Sandor's villa looking for clues, the unremembered details that might re-create my passage with Zoltan, that might tell me with the clarity of dawn that Zoltan and Sandor were one and the same. Nothing. No photographs, no awards. No letters, no music. None of his recordings bore his picture. The only books seemed carved into the stone— Spanish, Hebrew, Arabic, old, words unread, pages uncut.

I grazed through the handwritten manuscript on his desk— *In Search of the Lost Chord, A Brief Guide.* A book of aphorisms more than techniques, more Gibran than Flesch, a lot of disembodied hoodoo about the Perfect Sound, the Perfect Player, the Perfect Ear. Not my Zoltan at all. The Zoltan of the apple scent of the Auvergne was a man who gloried in impulse. He was a Zoltan who could touch a measure of a Beethoven sonata fifty-seven different ways and fall in love with each like an underfed teenager. His desire for knowledge was a desire for experience, not ideas. His desire for happiness was the full peasant downbow of a Hungarian folk song, the meaty slap of thigh against thigh on the planks of a German boxcar. If Sandor was Zoltan, he was Zoltan grown old, dried, and wrinkled in the Andalusian sun. Almost eighty.

Wishful thinking, Benjamin. Is that the reward of old age? Where is the promise of Wisdom, of my ancestress Kima? Shot full of holes by K'sil the Fool?

"Good morning, Señora." Señor Carranque looked unnervingly fresh. His feathered hat still clung to his bear-oiled head. But somewhere, somehow, he had exchanged the baggy suit for a fresh pair of slacks, a clean shirt, and a sleeveless plaid sweater-vest. I confirmed my own impossibly dry and independent scalp and thought, Of course, the rest of the world is civilized, the rest of the world books a hotel room, shower and breakfast included.

"How did you know where to find me?"

"There are not that many taxis in Mariposa. I have already warned the Junta Andalucía that they will have a riot on their hands when the Americans arrive next summer." I looked out the window through the front gate, at a fender and a tailpipe that could very well have belonged to the chariot that rescued us a few hours before.

"I don't think I paid him last night," I began. Carranque held up his hand.

"All transfers included."

"A travel agent!"

"Answers later, breakfast first."

"But the taxi?"

"Will wait."

"I can make . . ."

"You've had too much coffee, Señora, if you'll pardon my saying so. If you wouldn't mind boiling some water, I have an infusion." Carranque pulled a golden cloth pouch from the pocket of his sweater-vest. "Maté de Avellana. I serve it to my clients in Cuzco. For the altitude."

"We are only a few hundred feet above the Mediterranean, Señor."

"Don't you expect to be flying today?"

We took our maté out to the fountain. Through the smoke hole of a sky above us, a few puffs of clouds had burned red with the dawn. Far down the hill, the kerosene engine of a motocyclette droned toward us, away, unseen.

"You should have left the trunk at Maraquita's."

I said nothing, sipped on the drink, bitter, late autumn, dead leaves and smoke. Isabella had disappeared down a rabbit hole.

Holland had run after. Your trunk, Benjamin, could have been left, happily, snugly, safely at Cristóbal Colón.

"I only meant that Maraquita's clientele is made up of a trustworthy sort of person."

"Is that what you are, Señor Carranque," I asked, "a trustworthy sort of person?" He frowned, a little pout of modesty. "I took those letters, you know, the ones you left at the flamenco."

"I expected you would."

"I haven't read them yet."

"Ah. That I did not expect."

"But I did find the Esau Letter."

"And you read that?" I nodded. "Another surprise."

"There is a young girl, a student of Sandor's most likely, very pretty, thirteen years old, long, dark hair, eyes . . ." I sipped on my maté, missing my Isabella and my Holland. "She had the Esau Letter in her violin case, wrapped in an ancient purple hair ribbon."

"That much I know," he said. "What I did not expect was that you would read the Esau Letter first. Before my letters, that is." I stared hard at Carranque. His nonchalance woke me more completely than the maté.

"How could you possibly know?"

He held up a palm. "My questions first. Did you enjoy the Esau Letter?"

"More maté," I grumbled. He stood to pour, inclined from the waist, the telltale of the better class of travel agent.

"Señora Hanni." He sat next to me on your steamer trunk. "Much of what seems cloudy would be blazingly clear if only the sun were higher in the sky."

"But as it's not . . ."

"Patience." He put his hand on my arm. "You were about to tell me. The Esau Letter. Was it as you remembered?"

I stood and moved away. I set my teacup on the lip of the

fountain and looked past the surface into the reflection of the blushing clouds. I dipped my hands in the water, cold through the knuckles, pressed the backs of my wrists to my eyes, looked at myself, wrinkled, rippled, wrinkled.

"No, not the same." He waited for more. I waited. He waited—he could edit out the pauses later. "I hadn't remembered the old Esau," I said. "The young one, yes. The bar mitzvah boy, the Esau of the cave, of the barrel. Especially the Esau of the beach, the Esau discovering Florida once, twice. I had remembered the Letter"—and I turned back to Carranque, looking up at me with encouragement, his hat tilted back the merest inch from his clear hairline—"as a story. I had forgotten it as a letter. I had forgotten it was a letter to a son. I had forgotten the son."

"Eliphaz."

"The son." I didn't need to tell Carranque the story of my son. I was too far sunk in need to wonder anymore at the source of his deep knowledge.

"Here." Carranque offered me my bag, Zoltan's leather portfolio bursting out the top, holding the unread letters. "Would you like to read them, or would you prefer to listen." I preferred. "I am going to help you find your son."

"You know where he is?"

"You said 'listen.' I will help you, Señora. But these letters may help you more." I sat back on your trunk.

"Do you remember the story your mother used to tell, the story of Kima?" Carranque asked.

Of course I did. But for a moment, so close to my so-long-lost Esau Letter, I could not figure out which Kima he meant—the lute-playing triplet of Mohammed, or the social-worker daughter of Maimonides.

"Maimonides' Kima," Carranque added, shaking my memory briefly to attention. "You remember how the poor girl's husband, Joseph ibn-Shimon, wrote to his father-in-law complaining of his wife's infertility." I nodded. "And you also remember how Maimonides responded, scolding Joseph for his own lack of faith?" I nodded again. Carranque opened the portfolio and held up half a dozen pages.

"A loose translation from the Arabic":

My Most Revered Teacher, Moses ben Maimon:
Listen, please listen!
We are of one tongue and one mind. Yet you attack the friend who came to rest his soul in the inviting shade of your love. You attack the friend who opened his heart to your intellect and his mind to your faith.
Listen, please listen!
I, it is I, Joseph, who speak. And you must speak too. You must, if you have words, refute me.
In days not long gone by, Kima, your favorite daughter, captured my heart. I wooed her according to the law of faith and the *Halakha* of Mount Sinai. I gave her friendship money as the price of courtship. I wrote her a poem of the thousand names of love. I presented myself as her bridegroom. I invited her into the tent of joy. I did not force her, I did not press her. My love won her love. My soul embraced her soul.
But under the canopy of the perfect marital sky, she turned her affections to other friends. She became an adulteress. The sky grew dark. She found no failing in me, yet she left me. She stole out of my tent and covered her face, her lovely face, her lovely voice.
You did not scold your daughter for her insolence. You did not reproach her for abandoning her duty. To the contrary—you encouraged her, you spurred her on! O noble teacher, that was not right. Restore the wife to the man—he will pray for you, for your long life. And he will pray for her, and for her honor.
Blessed is the man who restores lost goods. Thrice blessed is he who restores a beautiful woman, the husband's crown. I stand here, awaiting her return.

The truest of your devoted servants, whose desire is to look upon your honor's countenance and embrace your feet in the dust:

Joseph ben Judah ben Shimon

"I didn't catch anything about infertility," I said. "Only infidelity."

"Infidelity? You are certain?" Carranque turned his neck to me, his elbows on his knees, working the papers between thumbs and forefingers.

"Infertility?"

"Infidelity."

"That seems pretty clear."

"Shh." He stopped me. I forgot. No questions. Not even those phrased as statements. "Maimonides' reply:"

Ayyy Joseph,

Hear, O sages, my words. Come closer. Cup your wrinkled hands behind your downy ears. Settle a dispute between me and my favorite son, and, if I have erred, then testify against me.

I married Kima, my child, to K'sil. But he regarded the girl, reared in the sphere of faith, as tainted with sin because she covered her face. As soon as she fell into his clutches and, to his disgrace, stood before him in her nakedness, the spirit of jealousy came over him. He began to despise his wife. He deprived her of food, clothing, a place to live. He lied about her, told fabulous tales, brought her ill fame. He burned her bridal gifts in the fires of jealousy.

His goal was to make her disreputable in my eyes. Thus the husband said to me: "Your daughter became adulterous under the marital sky. Oh, look upon her shame and avenge her sin and adultery, and compel her to return to her husband, for he will pray for you and her."

You sages, you know the man and the way he speaks. He lies in wait for the opportune moment, for just the right occasion to undermine a reputation with a grand phrase or two. He is known to be a man whose lips can be read many different ways. But she, Kima, my child, is immaculate. No hands have ever touched her. It is impossible for her to break her troth to the lord of her marriage.

O my son, my K'sil, your thoughts are a perplexed people, none of which shows reflection. But you, and you alone, are the master of your people. Listen and learn. You are ill-advised to cast suspicion of immorality on any wife, especially your own. Take care, lest your lips bring your mouth to the brink of ruin.

Listen to me, my son. Here is your wife, take her and go. Do not let your tongue lead your flesh to sinful ways. My lips announce only truth. You may seek and sift, you will find nothing false or twisted. If you are wise, then you are so for yourself, to understand and to teach.

Forgo all pride. Do as I advise. I will lead you to the path of wisdom. Honor intelligence as a father and wisdom as a sister.

Moses ben Maimon

"Adultery!" I jumped.

"And immorality," Carranque added.

"And immorality."

"Strong words."

"Strong words," I agreed, wanting him to get to his point, "for the time and place, I imagine."

"Because he's talking about a human being."

"His daughter."

"The wife of his favorite pupil." Carranque put his glasses away and squeezed the bridge of his nose. "And adultery is a grave crime."

"For that time and place," I repeated, not wanting to offend a man I had met, after all, in a whorehouse.

"Do you think it is possible, Señora Hanni"—he raised his hand from his face into a sky-pointing lecturer's pose—"for there to be other adulteries—adulteries other than those of the body?" I had been up all night. I didn't have the slightest idea what he was talking about.

"Could you give me a hint?"

"Adulteries of religion—a woman is unfaithful to her God."

Sarah painting the town with Baal? Miriam and the Golden Calf? "A *conversa*, for instance?"

"For instance"—he nodded—"adulteries of ideas—a man forsakes a longtime belief for the latest theory that shakes its formula in his face."

"But adultery?" I protested. "An open mind is hardly an open marriage."

"Listen to this story: A young man travels a great distance in search of a renowned teacher. Like all young men, like all men, by nature, he has the desire to know. Word has spread throughout the Mediterranean that in Egypt lives a teacher of tremendous wisdom, a man who possesses a secret of extraordinary power.

" 'Teach me the secret,' the young man begs. But the teacher insists that he first study the Torah, learn the written law from front to back, from back to front. That he saturate his very soul with Faith. And the young man does.

" 'Teach me the secret,' the young man repeats, some time later. But the teacher insists that his pupil first study Talmud, the oral law, ask questions, peer around every corner, underneath every carpet of every question. And the young man does.

" 'Teach me the secret.' The teacher insists that the pupil first study the philosophy of the Greeks, the astronomy of the Arabs, the medicine of the doctors of Spain. He insists that the young man learn to apply the scrutiny of Reason to the Heavens and the Earth. Not only to the works of Science, but to the works of Scripture.

"The more the young man studies, the more confused he becomes. He is fascinated by the movement of the stars, the study of navigation, the physics of creation. Too fascinated, in fact, to move. The teacher has given him two powerful tools, Faith and Reason. He doesn't know which one to pick up first. Wisdom loses its virgin, Grail-like glow. Bewildered, he becomes . . ."

"Angry," I said.

"Angry," Carranque repeated. "He uses words of passion— 'adultery,' 'immorality,' 'infidelity.' He accuses the teacher of desertion."

"And the teacher responds with anger."

"In part," Carranque said. "But the teacher is, after all, the teacher. He knows there is something missing—the spectacles that will show his student that they speak of one and the same thing. What is missing is the translation that will demonstrate that the six days of creation are compatible with the Big Bang of physics, that Faith and Reason are inextricably linked in any apprehension of Wisdom. What is missing is a guide that will interpret, sift, coddle, lead the pupil through his confusion.

"The teacher sends an angry letter, then sits down to write a thoughtful book." Carranque paused to sip his maté, now ice-cold.

"*A Guide for the Perplexed?*" I asked.

"Exactly."

"The pupil is Joseph and the teacher Maimonides?" I asked.

"And the year is 1190 of the Common Era." He smiled.

"But what about Kima?"

Carranque laughed and put his cup carefully down on the lip of the fountain. "I speak only of Kima."

"I mean Kima the daughter of the teacher, the daughter of Maimonides, my great-great-great-whatever." Could Joseph have been as confused and angry as I was?

"My dear Hanni." Carranque lifted me by the hand from the steamer trunk and pointed up to the brightening, starless sky. "There is your Kima."

"I don't understand."

"A parable, a symbol. Kima was the scientific wisdom

Maimonides had given his pupil. Joseph, far away in Aleppo, had difficulty reconciling this newfound mistress with his faith in a God-created universe."

"His newfound mistress?"

"Kima was a daughter, a wife, a mother, a constellation, but only in story. As useful and beautiful an image as the six days of creation, and just as metaphoric."

"My Kima, Mama's Kima, is just a metaphor?" I was afraid to look down from the sky. If Kima didn't exist, if Kima had lost face, breasts, and womb, then what about her son, what about Mama, and me, and my son? I willed, I willed a miracle, I willed the appearance of seven stars on the blue morning sky.

"Then why"—I turned on Carranque with a ferocity that scared the hat from his head—"did the Alcalde de Córdoba send Mama an invitation to return? Why did he write to her as a descendant of Maimonides?"

"There are many people who believe exactly what they read," Carranque said. "It's a reasonable mistake."

I have never believed in God, Benjamin. But in those few minutes, those few words of the Peruvian travel agent, I was shaken as hard from a belief I never knew I held so strongly, shaken as hard as any Lubavitcher who eats pork and lives.

"Think of yourself as the young pupil, Hanni."

"But I know nothing about Torah or Talmud or Orthodoxy," I said. "I barely know my name in Hebrew. Even if I were an observant Jew, you forget, I am a woman. Who would teach me?"

"My dear Hanni," Carranque said, folding the letters back into the portfolio and threading the lace through the eyehole. "Even in the English language, debates do not survive the centuries over an unfaithful wife or an errant husband. Judaism, Christianity, Islam, survive because of metaphor, because of story. They survive because wise men are able to recognize parables, arguments, theories, intangible lessons, in the tales of these warm scriptural actors."

Just as I had achieved certainty, just as I had smelled the warm baby smell of connection, of the knowledge that my son, my gift to the line of Kima, was nearby, the sky of doubt was bearing down, the ground of confusion opening, the great wings of metaphor were flapping in my face, talons open and clawing. Carranque caught me.

"I am here to lead you to another guide."

"Benjamin?"

"The taxi's waiting."

HOLLAND—REMEMBER, REMEMBER

Dear Ben,

I almost doubt. I almost believe that I lay down to sleep on the Naugahyde benches of Colón and dreamed until, through, past, this stumbling, heel-wrenching, wheel-snagging chase down the crumbling alley below the Villa Gabirol.

La Subida. The name on the still-shadowed alley sign. The Rise. Yet, I drop. I fall. I read from right to left. Neither steps nor street, neither inhabited nor deserted. No lights, no glass, knotted clotheslines, many cats, the smell of human droppings, the sound of flies. And far below, every wave of her long-maned head drifting her farther away—Isabella, my daughter, Isabella.

Here is the story:

I occupied the larger part of the autumn and winter of 1977–78 in the company of our mutual friend, Hook. During the day, he worked for me, or more specifically, worked in my office on assignment from our American affiliate. Between the hours of six P.M. and midnight, between the days of Monday and Saturday, between the months of October and February, he pitched tent in my front parlour. Dinner, drinks, and Sandor were the programme. No furtive kisses, no subterranean exploration. Nothing, nothing, nothing.

So you can imagine my surprise when, one frozen February Monday, I walked into my GP on suspicion of the flu and walked out with the news I was pregnant.

I drove at unsafe speed to the Cromwell Hospital, where, one year before, as a still-married woman, I had been diagnosed as irretrievably infertile. This was the rosy-fingered dawn of British obstetrics, the Moon Shot Morning of In Vitro Fertilization, when the obstetricians of the Realm rose to the invigorating strains of "Mrs. Brown, You've Got a Test-Tube Daughter." Though British dentistry, surgery, oncology, and gastroenterology were the laughingstock of the Third World, the Cromwell boasted a baker's dozen of the finest Tube and Womb men in the Universe. I marched into Obstetrics, past a sputtering duty-nurse, and into the first hi-tech examining room. Three bearded doctors turned around.

"Three months," said the first.

"Fifteen weeks from conception," said the second.

"Where did you buy that jumpsuit?" asked the third.

"John Lewis," I said.

"Fourteen weeks, then." All protest was useless.

"Fertility is a strange and wonderful thing," the first called. I was already in the lift.

Fucked by a cliché, I thought. Because you have to understand, Ben, I had last slept with a man, I had last had sexual intercourse with a man—my ex-husband, to be precise—on September 1, 1977, over five months earlier. And I had never— to the envy of my friends, and the shame of my adolescence— never, ever menstruated.

But I could still do simple maths. One hour later, parked across the street from my house, I calculated back fourteen weeks. Early November. I rummaged for last year's *Economist* diary, still note-pocked and rubber-banded in the silty bottom of my shoulder bag. November 8th, a Tuesday, my first day back at work—a form of penetration, but not a satisfactory explanation. November 7th, a recital at St. John's Smith Square with Liaden. The sixth a blank. November 5th.

Remember, remember, the fifth of November. Certainly you, a cosmopolitan Yank, must know the rhyme. Guy Fawkes

Day. Gunpowder and Roman Catholics, a seventeenth-century plot to blow up Parliament, a twentieth-century celebration for shopkeeper, yuppie, and skinhead, a chance to forget the C. of E. and go Druid around a bonfire.

I stared out the driver's window of my Volvo, past the withered grass and blasted plane trees of the Heath, through the dull February afternoon, to that November Saturday. Hook rang my doorbell—must have rung my doorbell—at six o'-clock. I cooked him dinner, God remembers what. We talked, we always talked, most probably we talked about my inescapable return to the Beeb. We had just settled down in the front parlour for our evening ritual of Sambuca and Sandor when I noticed a crowd gathering on the far side of my window, on the far side of the street. I insisted, far too strongly, that we delay custom, that Hook join me and experience our quaint British bonfire, touch a happy moment of childhood.

A crowd of small huddles were scattered about the meadow, greeting acquaintances at a visibility of ten feet. The sulphur light of the streetlamps, the weak pub lanterns of Jack Straw's Castle at the top of the rise, travelled only to the frontiers of the camp. At the center, in vague silhouette, a ten-foot pile of broken doors, bits of shed, scrap lumber, claw-fingered branches, and a growing boneyard of hand-stitched effigies of Guy Fawkes squatted at the junction of the random bicycle paths that stumbled out of the wood. Each new committee brought its own Guy—pillowcases stuffed with newspaper, burlap sacks filled with woodchips, charcoaled and rouged grimaces, amateur, crude victims—as English as Christmas Panto and Cumberland Sauce.

The stroke of ten from the bell at Ivor Heath rang its instructions. We became coherent. We became a circle. As the numbers grew, we stepped back from the center to accommodate. I held Hook's long fingers with my left hand, the fatty paw of a schoolboy with my right. At the farthest arc, the circle broke, and a figure emerged from the wood bearing a flaming torch.

The torch shone through the warm breath of the man, shone over the scattered limbs of the Guys, spread-eagled, upside-down, twisted, on the pyre. We all breathed in. Silence.

With a whup, all was ablaze, the flames fifteen, twenty feet above the highest Guy. The pop of sap, the roar of burnt autumn air. Otherwise, not a sound, not a movement, no rustle of trees, no traffic behind, no whispers around, nothing but the heat of the fire and the two hands. Hook shifted. I shook him to be still, never questioning the orthodoxy of our British ritual. His shifting continued. The schoolboy's family muttered in a way only the English can, and frankly, I agreed with them.

Hook disappeared. One moment there—the next, the hand of my Pakistani greengrocer. I stayed for another moment, and then another. It could well have been half an hour before I crossed back over the far side, to find Hook drinking in the dark, curtains drawn, an A-minor scale of Sandor.

I said nothing. I curled my feet up under me on the sofa. For the first time, the music lulled me into a daze—or perhaps merely fortified the light hypnosis of the bonfire—to a point where I was conscious of sound, yet as paralyzed as in my deepest sleep. As always, the music stirred a cauldron between my thighs, this time with even greater force and heat. From the driver's seat of my Volvo, three months later, I could almost convince myself that Hook had scaled the sofa and made delicate, yet effective, love to me that night. But as I looked out the window to the Heath, the ashes of Guy Fawkes Day three-months blown from Primrose Hill to Golders Green, I could almost convince myself that one, and perhaps more, of those faceless, poorly stitched De Chirico Guys had floated on fire and smoke across the road, through a keyhole, into my parlour. Almost.

It was nearly five o'clock of that February afternoon when I climbed out of the Volvo and into a hot, but not too hot, bath in preparation for a serious chat with our friend Hook. My perfect new body gave up few clues, not even the merest hint of the active volcano ruminating beneath the surface. The unsought, the unhoped, was too new to frighten, excite, upset, affect. I pulled on a blouse and a pair of woollen trousers with no need to adjust belt or buttons. I brewed a pot of rose-hip tea.

At 6.01 I panicked. At 6.05 I began to cry. At seven o'clock I phoned the police, at eight, the hospitals, at nine, the morgues. From ten P.M. until the seven A.M. sunrise I sat by the phone and listened to the ticking of the kitchen clock and the entire repertoire of the possibilities of time. By noon, it was clear that Hook had disappeared.

When I ran to Liaden in Granada two days later, I was as lost as on the morning after my divorce. I needed guidance, someone to explain the children business, the love business, to me. The thought of abortion never crossed my mind, but neither did the thought of carrying the pregnancy to term. Physically, I was walking, flinging my arms about, feeding myself. Emotionally, I was in traction.

The Beeb was relieved by my sabbatical and resisted any explanation. The police likewise. The gentle winter, the easy Granadine life, built a fence around my belly. My perfect body became perfectly pregnant. I read Elizabeth Bowen, Lorca in translation, a secondhand copy of Washington Irving's *Tales of the Alhambra* rescued from a kitchen cupboard. I walked whole days away, through the alleys of the Albaicín, up the hill of the Alhambra. I purchased a secondhand guitar. Sammy L., after a day out working the tourist trade, brought home cheese and fruit, lamb and shellfish. I cooked, we ate—sometimes together, more often not.

I didn't twig, until it was too late for action, that I too was part of the tourist trade, and that Sammy L. had quite subtly assumed the job of tour guide and was leading me to a gentle Andalusian birth. Our lives ran on such independent planes, in different time zones that twisted into only the most occasional intersection. There was a morning coffee on the tiny Plaza of

San Miguel de Bajo. There was the evening at La Bulería. And there was the business at the Carmen de San Francisco.

It was August, close to the end. I was large, very large, and very hot. I walked only to the shops and only in the first hours of morning or after the sun had cast the Albaicín in shadows. I passed entire days under an electric fan, decorating my fantasies with floral advertisements from magazines and catalogues. My Hampstead dressing room could be wallpapered and draped for my tiny new friend. The guest room, without alteration, would delight the most discriminating au pair, should I return to a Beeb that seemed the height of tedium at the moment. Career anxieties had been pushed into the same crowded corner that now held my stomach, bladder, and intestines—acting up, now and again, but small and lethargic in comparison with the impatient baby.

At eleven that morning, Sammy L. drove me to my final examination with the midwife at the Convento Santa Isabel. I stepped like a queen from the air-conditioned comfort of his Renault 4 into the gentle shadows of the arcades of the convent, secure in Sammy L.'s promise to wait. Sor Juana reached gently inside me, assured me that, large as I was, my cervix was well effaced—she would see me within the week, it would be an easy delivery. I walked out past the crumbling murals and looked up at the green-shuttered balconies of the maternity cloister—quiet, peaceful, my midsummer hotel.

There was a message at the gate. Apologies from Sammy L.—an emergency. An invitation to dinner—ten P.M., the Carmen de San Francisco, a tourist, a client he wanted me to meet. Fine. I was in no rush to go home. The fastest route, in fact, was not by Sammy L.'s taxi, which had to run the circumference of the ancient Moorish fortifications, but downhill, down steps, down alleys. One of the sisters guided my belly home through the maze, on her way to teach geography at the boys' school on the Sacromonte, past the caves of the gypsies. I invited her in for a cup of tea. She begged off, with a blessing I understood only much later: "You are truly a vessel sent from God."

I slept much of the afternoon and evening. I had been spared the morning sickness, varicose veins, constipation, and moodiness that Liaden had reported in pregnancies past. My only symptoms were growth and fatigue.

At sunset, I bathed carefully, dressed in a local cotton tent, and rang for a taxi. It was fully dark as we drove up the hill of the Alhambra, up the narrow Cuesta de Gomerez, the gift shops and guitar garages shuttered against the night. Groups of fives and sevens strolled through the Alameda, past the Puerta de las Granadas, the battlements of the Alhambra illuminated for midsummer assignations. A regiment of German schoolchildren sat under a plane tree—Eurorock on a boombox.

The taxi dropped me at the purple keep of the Hotel Alhambra Palace. From the entrance of the hotel, the city dropped away into the precinct of the Catholic God, the domes and spires of Santo Domingo, the Catedral, the Capilla Real, the ornate restaurants of the archbishop and his minions. The heights were reserved for Moorish nostalgia and unreconstructed skepticism. I had been lunched at the Carmen de San Francisco on several occasions by admirers who struck up conversations in the Patio de Lindaraja of the Alhambra. University professors, begranted artists, jacket-and-tie bohemians who climbed the hill on the backs of their patron saints, Lorca and de Falla. I would listen attentively, ask questions designed to flatter. In return, food, company. These were the dark days, Ben, before success.

The Carmen was tucked one hundred yards down a narrow-walled alley. The parking guard at the hotel stared without embarrassment—I thought of asking him to walk me but couldn't think of the Spanish words to make the request legitimate. The lanterns that gripped the walls of the alley lit the jagged shards of glass along the top of the private edge and dropped insignificant puddles into the darkness on the public side—no protection from gypsies and muggers, real or imagined. Small light, high drama—Sammy L.'s typical Spain. I was frightened, excited. My journalistic curiosity hadn't entirely run down the plughole of my placenta. Sammy L. never spoke of individual clients, only genus and specie. This might be my only opportunity to observe him in action. Once the baby was born, I'd fly back to England, the opportunity would be lost.

The Carmen de San Francisco showed only a small wooden door onto the alley. Inside, a vineyard of candlelit rooms draped the side of the hill into the lights of downtown Granada. The client was waiting for me at a windowside table.

"You are exquisite," he said, by way of introduction, staring deep into my belly.

"I am due this week," I explained. You never know how much you need to explain to men. He looked up into my face for the first time. Kind eyes, a small moustache, long fingers stroking, hiding a weak chin, a wedding band. An American. I had dined with worse.

We were sitting at a table for four, but there were no jackets, wraps, purses, or disarranged cutlery to indicate any other companions. I had expected Sammy L., had expected, perhaps, a wife, a girlfriend, that I was making up a four, not a three, certainly not a two. He offered the pertinent details— forty-eight years old, married, for the second time, a photo of a Subaru, a golden retriever. He was a professor of Medical Ethics attached to a minor hospital outside New York. He ordered a bottle of Sanz while we waited, drank it alone. And when it was clear that Sammy L. had failed to join us, ordered a meal for himself, a simple consommé for me.

We ate in silence, his choice, I assumed. My thoughts revolved so completely around my active center that there was little room, at the time, for annoyance at Sammy L.'s desertion.

The American was pleasant enough, didn't slurp or belch. The meal would be over soon, he would deposit me in a taxi. I would be in bed by midnight.

"Sammy L. told you about my wife?" The American wiped the thin corners of his moustache with an edge of linen.

"Sammy L. told me absolutely nothing," I answered, hoping that he was one of those Americans who can't drink coffee after noon.

"A year ago this month, my wife and I were on vacation, right here, at the Alhambra Palace. She was in her eighth month, but the doctor told her it was okay to travel. We took it easy—taxis, siestas."

"I'm very sorry," I said, guessing at the rest, wanting to break off the line of conversation immediately.

"I miss her very much." He called for the bill.

"Your first wife?"

"My second, and current. She's fine, fine." He patted my hand. "Thanks for the concern." We waited. He paid. We stood, walked to the door. "She'll never know your joy, that's all."

Outside the air was fresher, the sky darker. From behind the wall, the rinsing of dishes in the kitchen, the opening theme from *Dallas*. The American seemed in cheerful spirits, in spite of his confession, and suggested a walk through the lamplit gardens of the Alhambra. I had asked Sammy L. once, without success, to drive me up to the fortress at night, to see the moon over the trellised walls—the moon that figured so large in the folktales Washington Irving had collected during the summer he passed in the governor's apartment above the Patio de la Reja. I wanted, before I left Granada, to see the moon in the alabaster fountain, where the teenage virgin Jacinta was given the magical silver lute by the phantom of the Princess Zorahayda.

The Lute of Zorahayda. The Lute of Kima. Ben, that story of Esau's—it's in the Irving collection. Irving leaves out the

Jews, as far as I can remember, but otherwise tells much the same story. Could Irving be a descendant of Esau? Could Esau be a descendant of Irving? Did both men retell ancient folktales or create history?

I took the American's arm to guide him along the northern wall to the Torre de las Infantas, where Zorahayda last saw her sisters flee down the ravine with their Catholic—according to Irving—Catholic cavaliers. We leaned over the narrow parapet, gazing out to the Sacromonte, where the gypsy caves were beginning to glow with the tourist trade.

"You're very nice to come out like this." The American turned to me. I smiled with a raise of the eyebrows and pointed out the small palace of the Generalife, across a tiny bridge.

Suddenly the American was trying to kiss me, reaching up with one long-fingered hand for my chin, reaching down with the other to caress my belly.

"Please," I said, pushing him gently away. "Your wife—" The most effective tranquillizer I know.

"I thought Sammy L. told you," he said, immediately disengaging.

"Told me what?" And where was Sammy L., after all?

"Oh, please!" I could see he was embarrassed in his academic way.

"I think"—I tried to put it kindly—"we have both been taken for a ride." But I wondered what Sammy L. had told the American about me, my physical, my emotional state. I began to walk along the parapet away from the tower, but the path was blocked by a wheelbarrow and a ribbon barrier—"Junta Andalucía."

"Holland!" His voice. I turned. It was August in Granada, but the call, the single name—September, the Heath, Hook. But where Hook's voice had warmed me back across the road into my house and mystery, the American's call struck only icy dread into my belly—the reverse, the opposite, the evil.

He reached, I recoiled, both of us kicked, but I had to do the running. Under the ribbon, sliding down loose gravel and ancient bricks to the grass channel ten feet below. A hole in the wall barely large enough for my belly. Down, steeper than this Subida, if less fragrant, not stopping to look around until I reached the dirt path through the ravine and across the Darro. This time, no ancestors of Esau, no itinerant musicians to pick me up, melt me down, and carry me back to Córdoba.

Half an hour, an hour, ten minutes later, Sor Margarita answered my ringing. I was shaking, crying. Yet I had my handbag, I had my shoes. I was unscratched, unbruised, as if some unseen hand—Mohammed el-Hayzari, Kima, Zorahayda?—had picked me up and tossed me gently, with love and regret, from the ramparts of the Alhambra to the river Darro.

I was led to a bed, undressed, and bathed. Sor Juana closed the door gently and gave me her hand.

"When did your contractions begin?" I hadn't noticed. "It will be soon," she said. "Try to get some rest."

The room was filled with portraits of female saints. I felt strong, protected, impervious to all men. Jesus, it seemed, was even barred from the room, the bare crucifix on the wall protected only by a philosophical Virgin. The walls were cool stone, bare of whitewash, clean, not sanitized. The low ceiling was comforting, the single shuttered window peaceful. A young novice sat by the door saying her rosary. Every bead or so, she glanced quickly up at me.

"Are you praying for me?" I asked.

"For your baby."

I closed my eyes and thought of my sister's phone number. Three days in the convent, I thought. Enough time for her to wire me the plane fare back to England. I could leave Spain without having to see Sammy L.

"Can you tell me one thing?"

I opened my eyes. I had forgotten the novice. She stood and approached my bed.

"I shouldn't be bothering you, Señora, but I don't under-stand," she said.

"What is it?" She looked down at the floor.

"I know that the Bible, the Old Testament of the Jews, tells that the Pharaoh of Egypt decreed that all male Jews be killed at birth. I know that the mother of Moses gave up her son into the care of another woman in order to save his life. That was in Egypt, thousands of years ago. There are no such laws in Spain today. I cannot imagine that your country requires such practices."

I reached a hand gently up to hers. "What is your name?"

"María." She blushed.

"María," I said, lifting her chin, "I don't have the slightest idea what you are talking about."

She looked up, pleased, I thought, but surprised. In a mo-ment she was at the window, spreading apart the slats of the shutters the merest crack.

"Those two men," she whispered, "in the cloister." I swung my legs over the side of the bed and waddled over to the window. The light was bad, a few bare bulbs hanging under the arcade, but there was no doubt. Sammy L. and the American, talking quietly. I took María by the shoulders.

"What do you know about those men?"

"I only know that your husband told Sor Juana that you were giving over the child to an American professor, that you were unable to care for the child, that you did not even want to see the child when it was born, but let it have a good, new life with a loving family."

I feel more panic now, Ben, searching for Isabella in the early dawn, than I did that desperate night in the Convento Santa Isabel. I think the barefoot run down the ravine and up the Albaicín had callused me to whatever pain the night could possibly muster. Sor Juana walked in on the two of us. Once I had told her that Sammy L. was neither husband nor father but merely storyteller par excellence, she was in total solidarity with her large, fertile sister.

I never discovered what happened to the men. Isabella was born at dawn, a full head of golden curls, eyes already searching, clear and open, grey as the Ocean Sea. I named her after the patron saint of the convent. We stayed on for three months, my daughter and I, in a beautiful corner room with a painting of Santa Isabel on the ceiling and the music of a fountain through the window. We were fed, fussed over, petted, spoiled. I arrived back in England on Guy Fawkes Day, a year after.

Alone.

Why lie to you, Ben? Forget about the three months. I gave her up. I left her. As fast as this older, independent Isabella is running from me, I ran faster. Not three months later, not after an Eden of baby clothes and breast-feeding. That night, the moment she was born.

The reason? Sammy L.'s fiction was not entirely unattractive. Below, in the cloister, stood a plausible ending to my Andalusian folktale, a needy man to solve my ambivalence. I hesitated.

I was willing to leave her—I didn't deserve to keep her. The moment of doubt was the moment she was no longer mine.

The truth? Have you ever felt as if your entire body were being ripped apart, not in the proverbial two neat halves, but in jagged shreds, flesh, bone, hanging, stinging, pain so engulfing that you don't know which part of your body that tiny devil is going to leap from? The noise of pain, as strong as the violin, as strong as the jet fighters that smashed the windows of the Santa María, tearing an "*Ayyyy*" from deeper circles than the deepest flamenco has ever plumbed? The lies you will tell under torture, the curses you will sing, the loves you will disavow, the nods, the yeses, the papers you will sign?

At the moment of birth, the moment of decision, something in me retreated, something got small.

The truth? Three years later, when my biological statistic

writ itself large and I went actively in search of a babymaker, I found only limp members and Zen aphorisms. My letters to Hook, my letters to the Convento Santa Isabel la Real went unanswered, were returned.

The truth? I never wrote.

The truth? Why not ask Hook?

La Subida is relentless, Ben, the greater the light, the more horrible the stench.

The truth? I have become wildly successful. Why capture Isabella? Why catch my heel? Why Carnegie Hall?

HANNI—RITUAL EYE-OPENING

Benjamin,

Inside the Bar El Palo, ritual eye-opening. Coffee, *aguardiente,* men. Outside, the sun fully awake, the last Lorenzo of an old year. A cruise boat, one hundred yards of beach, maybe two miles of Mediterranean away, steaming west into the port of Mariposa. One hour until your office opens.

Señor Carranque had taken a table outside, in a sunny corner of the terrace, where the elements had burned a hole in the reeds of the canopy. Hot chocolate, a basket of *churros.* Our taxi driver sat at the next table, smoking his way through a thin box of Schimmelpfennigs and pouring liberal doses of cheap sherry into a bowl of coffee.

Past the far wall of the landward side of the café, occasional Mariposa-bound traffic blew along the coast road. An offshore breeze chilled my exhaustion. I was desperate to hunt. I was desperate to sleep.

"¡Periódicos! ¡Periódicos!" A gray-stubbled, gray-suited old man scraped across the concrete of the patio. Strips of lottery tickets hung like a *tallis* around his shoulders. Under one arm, the local rags—*Mariposa Ayer, Mariposa Hoy, Mariposa Mañana.* He stood in front of me, shading the sun, his mouth a black *O,* the blue wool vest beneath his jacket a crumb-pocked journal of breakfasts yesterday, today, and tomorrow. The taxi driver took a copy of *Hoy.*

"Could you ask him," I mumbled to Señor Carranque, "if there's any news about the airport strike?"

"My dear Señora." Carranque smiled. "Last night's news will not be published for two days, perhaps three. You may enjoy staying awake all night, but in Spain, journalists like to sleep."

"Then how am I to learn about the strike?"

"You are seriously interested?"

"I'm looking for clues."

"Forty-five minutes," Carranque said. "Ben's office will open. You will find all the clues you want." I stood up, irritated, ready to buy my own paper, make my own investigations.

"Oi, lady! You want to know about the strike?" It was a language I recognized—English, as spoken by an educated Londoner determined to acquire the common touch. I sat down.

"You're surprised by my accent," the taxi driver continued. "You didn't blink at Maraquita's last night."

"You're the taxi driver from the airport?"

"And the cavalry to the Villa Gabirol."

"I was about to ask."

"Of course you were." The taxi driver snickered. He was a tall boy, fifty, even fifty-five, but a boy nonetheless, well over six feet—hair white, grown long; beard cropped, gone gray—a well-built boy with an earring, a collarless shirt, and a nasty attitude.

"What about the airplanes?" I asked.

"Airplanes? What airplanes?" I was about to answer when he burst out laughing, looking to the lottery man for support. I turned to my aide, but Carranque was communing with chocolate and *churro*.

"You saw a bit of traffic last night." The taxi driver stopped laughing, began to pour himself another sherry, thought better of it. "Low-flying, possibly military. But it's a long time since you stayed up late spotting aircraft, if I've got my history down right."

I nodded. History down right?

"I've been in Mariposa off and on for well over twenty years. This is the Outbound and the Inbound of the Mediterranean, the Arrival and Departure Lounge between Europe and Africa, the New World and the Old. Our planes fly out, their planes fly in. Sometimes it's the other way around. No one complains, unless they miss their flight."

"Or their windows shatter," I added.

"The bar? The Santa María?" The taxi driver laughed. "He won't complain."

"Who won't complain?"

"Who?" The driver slapped the newspaper on the table. "Carranque, how long have you been leading the Señora on?" I turned to Señor Carranque as well. As a guide, he was leaving much to be desired. As a gentleman—everything.

"Señora Hanni, you have my deepest apologies for the tone of this conversation. You will soon understand that there is little I can do."

"Carranque knows I need half a gill of argument to prime the morning pump," the driver sighed. "More in winter when the tourists drop off."

I stood up. It looked a good ten minutes across the half mile of beach to your office.

"It isn't worth it," the driver said. "He won't open the door until nine sharp."

"Benjamin is there now?" I asked.

"No, no," he laughed, "the gatekeeper, the majordomo, Abbas."

Abbas? Bar El Palo. The beach. The location was familiar, a few miles east of Mariposa Antigua. What was now only ten minutes by taxi could have been an hour by horse in Esau's time. From my distance, the building Carranque had indicated could easily have been on a pier.

The headquarters of Santángel's Minyan. Esau's cave. Your office.

"Abbas is a common Muslim name," the driver continued. "Means Pops, as in Father, or Dad, or Old Man. Don't let it distract you. Coincidence is the poor man's Miracle."

Nevertheless, I turned to your *Guide,* p. 303:

LA ROSA NÁUTICA

One of our readers writes:

"La Rosa Náutica is properly approached on foot by a narrow pier leading from the parking lot on the beach of El Palo, approximately 4 km (2.5 miles) east of town. (There is also a small landing for private boats on the seaward side.) The building is constructed in the octagonal shape of its namesake, the Compass Rose, with the pier providing the traditional extra length of the Due North leg. A circular bar, reputed to feature the widest selection of Spanish brandies in the country, fills the middle of the restaurant. A spiral staircase at the bull's-eye leads down to the subterranean kitchen, a structure that dates from at least the end of 1491, when, legend reports, Columbus huddled with ten advisers to plan his final assault on the purse of Ferdinand and Isabella."

The structure has been owned continuously since the early fifteenth century by the Santángel family, originally of Calatayud in Aragón. Though of Jewish origin, the Ginillo family moved from their ancestral town—Qalat al-Yahud, meaning Castle of the Jews—to Valencia, converted to Christianity, and changed their name to Santángel at the time of the Disputation of Tortosa. This did not prevent one of the family from conspiring in the assassination of the inquisitor Pedro de Arbués, and paying for his treachery at the stake.

The present owner, Luis de Santángel, is named after the famous comptroller-general of Ferdinand and Isabella, the man who lent 1,140,000 maravedis to Columbus's historic expedition of 1492. It was at La Rosa Náutica that Santángel assembled the team of navigators, cartographers, and scholars that advised Columbus. And it was to Santángel that Columbus first wrote with news of discovery. In recognition of his value to the Crowns of Castile and Aragón, Santángel received a coveted *limpieza de sangre* from Ferdinand, asserting that his blood was clean of any Jewish taint. Consequently, the Santángel family weathered the storms of the Inquisition, the reign of the Bourbons, the occupation of Napoleon, the Monarchy, the Republic, the Generalísimo, and landed in the late twentieth century in an ideal position to capitalize on the global fascination with travel.

"She's read the Esau Letter." Carranque interrupted my study with an offhand nod to the taxi driver. It seemed to me that everyone had read it. I walked around to the driver's table and sat at the edge of a sun-warmed chair. I disliked the man intensely; my letters were being pawed by strangers. But I was waking up.

"What do you really want to know?" There was an edge of cruelty in the taxi driver's question. But it was impossible that Carranque had relayed the story of my lost son to this man—I had been with both of them for the past hour.

"My friend," Carranque said, "is not a great believer."

"You've got me wrong there, *my* friend. I believe. I believe in Esau and Columbus and Pinzón and especially"—the taxi driver crooned toward Carranque—"I believe in Señorita Florida."

"But not in—"

"Allow me to tell the lady what I don't believe." Señor Carranque raised a palm in surrender. The driver poured sherry and coffee into his bowl. "I'm happy to buy the story that a Jew from Córdoba named Esau Halevy was the first European to set foot on the North American continent. Why not? I've heard barmier. But you're asking me to believe that a group of wealthy and otherwise educated Jews and *conversos* would pour the combined contents of their combined mattresses into the visions of a hairy little boy, on the off chance he would find a piece of real estate suitable for the relocation of three hundred thousand Jews?"

"But certainly"—Carranque dipped another *churro*—"Esau's success belies your skepticism."

"Success? How many Spanish Jews found their way to the New World? Ten. Ten boys like Esau, who could barely yodel their way through a bar mitzvah. And how many of them survived? Now, consider this—how many priests found their way, how many inquisitors? How many secret Jews were converted into New World bonfires over the next couple of hundred years? Thousands! Success?"

"Your explanation?" I asked.

"Failure. Simple, dismal, complete. Esau may have been a navigational Einstein and a regular Babe Ruth with a cane stalk. But at the end of the day, the only skin he saved was his own."

"What of the success of the Expulsion?" Carranque asked. The driver was momentarily silenced.

"Success for the Catholics?" I ventured.

"Certainly not, Señora." Now it was Carranque who laughed. "The Expulsion of the Jews was an unmitigated disaster for the Catholics. For a brief time, Their Catholic Majesties feasted on the properties and treasures left behind by the running Jews. But after a very short while they awoke to the truth that their best and their brightest had fled. Gone were their merchants, their statesmen, their doctors, their artisans and their artists, their poets, their musicians, their singers, and their leatherworkers. Without its Jews, Spain dried up into the shriveled olive it is today."

"So the success?"

"Was the success of the Jews—the Jews who fled to Morocco, to Italy, to Greece, to Turkey, to the Netherlands. They spread their art and learning across the Mediterranean,

through the Strait of Gibraltar and northward into Europe.
They made a virtue of exile, found their greatest reward in
exile, found their humanity, their lost identity, in exile."

" 'Your survival is in your motion,' " I quoted Esau.

"Exactly." Carranque smiled. I smiled back, pupil to
teacher.

"Waaaauuugh!" The taxi driver hit the top of his table with
two large, flat palms. "You're beginning to sound like a couple
of Jews thanking God for Auschwitz because it gave them the
State of Israel."

"I've never been to Israel," I answered simply, unwilling to
relinquish my allegiance to Carranque.

"That's not the point," the driver said.

"But I have been to the Holocaust."

"And I was in Berlin when the Wall came down," he coun-
tered.

"Picking up shards to sell to the tourist trade," Carranque
jabbed.

"Give me some credit, Carranque. Those shards I sold came
from a ruined Moorish watchtower a mile up the road."

"Having been to the Holocaust," I pressed on, "I don't
thank anyone for the smallest part of it—not for Zoltan, not for
my son, not for the life I have made since the Russians liberated
Berlin. I may be the only Jew in Miami Beach who doesn't
thank anyone for the State of Israel or talk twice a day about
moving to Jerusalem. But then I'm one of the few who don't
have full-blown Alzheimer's."

"You are not alone, Señora," Carranque said, and signaled
for another pot of chocolate. "As a travel agent, some of my
biggest commissions come from bar mitzvah charters to the
Wailing Wall, singles weekends at Masada, honeymoons on the
shores of Caesarea. But between you and me, I book more Jews
to Rio and the Galápagos."

"Listen to me, Hanni." For the first time I felt frightened by
the gaze of the taxi driver. "I've worked the moving business

for almost twenty years. I've seen how Ben operates. Back in '80, I watched him charter fishing boats out of Bac Lieu and Dong Hoi, moving Vietnamese to Singapore and Hong Kong. When Castro opened the prisons and mental hospitals, I saw how quickly Ben could spread the word to every pleasure-boat owner from the Mouth of the Rat to the Tip of the Tit. When the Democratic Germans could not bear to cut short their Hungarian hols in '89, Ben cobbled together hundreds of coaches and trains for a free side trip, transfers included, into Bavaria."

I laughed, as deeply and insincerely as the driver had only minutes before. I didn't know what to believe, Benjamin. That you could do all that?

"Last night's airplanes—who do you think supplies them, who do you think moves them?"

"Whose airplanes?"

"French airplanes, Russian airplanes, bought by Iraq, by Libya; U.S. airplanes bought by Saudi and Israel. Theirs, ours. Conversion only costs a fresh coat of paint."

"You're talking about armies, about nations!" I shouted. Carranque looked down at his cup. The roadworkers walked out of the bar and slipped their fluorescent vests back over their heads.

"Nations bicker, armies fight," the taxi driver explained with a tension that I mistook only briefly for patience. "By nature they are stick-in-the-mud, static lumps of clay and plastic. They are dedicated to borders, to creating, maintaining, protecting, enforcing borders. I am talking about motion," the driver said, "something neither nations nor armies desire nor understand. Motion, pure and simple. I haven't even mentioned what the PLO owes Ben for the Beirut-to-Tunis run, or Israel owes him for forty jetloads of Ethiopian Jews."

"Owes Ben?"

"Your a-gent"—with a working-class stress on "gent," just to lay claim to both sides of the tracks—"believes he sits above the fray, consulting, doling out advice, guidance, on motion. Motion with consequence, he will admit. But motion without motive."

"And you work for Benjamin?" I asked.

"I didn't say that."

"But you know quite a bit about his methods." He smiled and drained his cup. "Answer me this." I stood and walked over to your steamer trunk, parked in the shade by the door to the café. "If Benjamin is such a mover of nations and armies, why would he bother with me?"

In inarticulate answer, a barely controlled blue panel van flew off the coast road and shot gravel from the parking lot into the far side of your trunk. Three faded hippies fell out of the front seat, stomped across the terrace, and swallowed a table whole.

"Jimi?" asked the skinny one.

"Yep," answered the leader, a bright-looking man, older than his haircut.

"Janis?" asked the third, pulling a guitar out of a multi-labeled case.

"Yep." The leader turned and called for a pot of coffee.

"Who?"

"Yep."

"Stones?"

"Not really."

"Beatles?"

"Certainly not."

"Doors?"

"In spirit, yes, but Morrison's a baritone, a tough call."

"Moody Blues?"

"With all that orchestration?"

"Iron Butterfly?"

"Even more pretentious."

"Cream?"

"Especially the drum tattoo at the top of 'White Room.'"

"Jethro Tull?"

"Jethro Tull . . ." The leader mused for a moment, then turned to us. "Let's ask the taxi driver."

"I was waiting to be consulted." The driver yawned. *"Dígame."*

"¿Quién es más flamenco?" the guitarist asked. "Which rock groups are the true heirs to the flamenco tradition?"

"Do you want the truth," the driver asked, "or are you just trying to separate the screamers from the sophisticates?"

"Wha-haay!" The leader nodded. "A real aficionado!"

"I just asked about Jethro Tull," the skinny one mumbled.

"To begin at the beginning," the taxi driver began. "True flamenco thrives only under fascism—the Spanish Jews before the Expulsion, the gypsies up to the death of Franco, American rock through Watergate. Forget about anything after that."

"What about punk under Thatcher?"

"Latvian protest songs?"

"Oum Khalsoum?"

"Tania María?"

"Black Stalin?"

"Swedish C&W?"

"That Japanese salsa orchestra," the skinny one asked, "what's its name?"

"Like Jethro Tull," the driver stood, "they have elements of flamenco in performance."

"A deep-felt tragic weltanschauung sort of a thing?" The skinny one walked over to the driver.

"Let me give you an example." The driver took the guitar, propped one booted foot on a chair, wedged his cigarette between the strings up by the tuning pegs, and began to pick a slow series of arpeggios.

I felt invaded. What about Benjamin? The army band was playing martial tunes.

"Of course," said the guitarist in admiration, "Led Zeppelin."

" 'Stairway to Heaven,' " said the skinny one.

"Get my pipes, Vim," the leader commanded. The skinny one, being Vim, rushed back to the van and returned with a case holding a soprano and an alto recorder. Placing both of them in his mouth, the leader, one Roger, began to play a lyrical descant above the guitar chords.

"Ahh, mi Perú," Señor Carranque sighed and explained, "The pipes of the Quechua, the pipes of the Inca."

"Better than that, Carranque," the driver said, "try singing Kol Nidre over this."

"Kol Nidre," I asked, "as if it were Yom Kippur?"

"Just try it," the driver insisted, "not the sanitized Ashkenazic way, but old style, the way the Sephardim, the Spanish Jews, used to sing."

And Carranque sang—the long *"Ayyyy"* that precedes the atonement of the Kol Nidre, in a Sephardic tune that was Greek to my ears and sounded so much more like one of Flamenco Halevy's Greatest Hits that I was honestly not surprised when the Laurel-and-Hardy guitar and vocal duo of Halevys emerged from the bar of the café and joined forces.

There I was, Benjamin. The taxi driver plucking a mildly pleasant tune on the guitar—something I'm sure I heard in Sonny's record collection, or on the radio in my Mini over the years—the Halevy guitarist improvising, Roger tootling a mildly pleasant Incan harmony on two recorders, and Señor Carranque and the portly Spaniard singing Kol Nidre three months after Yom Kippur.

What was the lesson? That Led Zeppelin was more flamenco than the Beatles? That the Incas sang Kol Nidre? Or was it simply the nursery school trick that "Row, Row, Row Your Boat" can be sung at the same time as "Twinkle, Twinkle, Little Star," and no one gets lost? There were eight of us on the patio. The beach was empty. What was I doing? And where were my girls, my nighttime daughters?

"We're just jamming." The taxi driver winked over to me.

"Jamming"—Sonny's word when he improvised violin solos above the rock and jazz records he played on Leo's cabinet stereo in the green room. Weekends mostly, but occasionally during the week, when I thought he was expected at work or at school or at whatever mysterious project he'd come to London to complete, I'd return from the shops or from visiting friends to find him playing at medium volume, the classical violin strangely at home with the wild sounds of his electric playmates. The sound was inescapable, humming through the walls, even at the farthest reaches of the house. It was not unpleasant. It was company. At times, it caught me unawares, and I had to sit down at the kitchen table and cry for all the wanderers—Leo, my son, myself.

So when the sound of a violin crept up on me with the gentlest of nudges, jamming along with the rest of the impromptu terrace orchestra, I was surprised only that it was 1991 and that I was in Spain. The sound, for it was the same sound, was the same green-room violin, the same apple-orchard Bach. I turned, knowing who it would be—the girl, the long-haired Isabella. She sat on the step of the open side door of the band's blue van, as beautiful and composed as when she played in the early dawn of Sandor's courtyard. The music—the second movement of the Bach Double Violin Concerto.

"It all fits," I murmured. The taxi driver smiled.

"Of course. Gypsy flamenco, Jewish lament, baroque church music, all from a single source."

"Zoltan," I whispered.

"Zoltan, Sandor." The driver smirked. "Let's not give the old fart too much credit. He's overstated it in that treatise of his—all music emanating from an original vibration. There's plenty of stuff—good stuff, at that—that would grind all this into gazpacho."

"What he means to say, Señora"—Carranque took a break

and let the flamenco singer take a verse—"is that the flamenco song to the Virgin, the *saeta*, was born from the Jewish lament of endless travel."

"There you go again, Carranque." The driver put down his guitar, as the music carried on without him. "Taking credit for the Jews."

"What about Eric Clapton?" Vim called over to the driver.

"Of course," the driver shouted back, "especially 'Layla.' "

"You know—the flamenco mordent?" Roger took the pipes out of his mouth for a moment. "Da-la-da-la-da-da-daaah."

"Also written by the Jews." Carranque nodded.

" 'Layla'?" The driver looked truly surprised.

"*Alf Layla Wa Layla*," Carranque said. "*A Thousand and One Nights*, also known as *Arabian Nights*. At least one third of the tales, a good year's worth of nights, belonged to the Jews."

"Give it a rest." The driver scowled.

"And," Carranque added, "the final editor was a Jew who lived in the time of . . ."

"Maimonides?" the driver groaned.

"Of course."

The flamenco singer raised his hand and shifted from Kol Nidre into an Iberian-tinged verse of, presumably, Led Zeppelin:

> *There's a feeling I get when I look to the west*
> *And my spirit is crying for leaving.*
> *In my thoughts I have seen rings of smoke through the trees,*
> *And the voices of those who stand looking.*

Esau, I thought. Esau, looking to the west, the spirit of the expelled Jews, the smoke of the Mayaimi, the voice of Florida, of Santángel, crying for leaving. Had they all read the Esau Letter, all these men, none of them still young, all of them Esaus, all of them more or less hairy? Had all these men read my Esau, been carrying my letter around with them in their male code, this rock-and-roll sema-meta-phore?

Through the smoke of sun, hair, and music, another shape approached, with the trudge of a Sisyphean traveler struggling to catch a train through a rush-hour crowd, a departing caravan across deep sand, dragging wheels behind her.

"Holland!" Vim was the first to call.

"Vim!" she gasped as she set her wheels on the terrace.

"Señora!" The mustachioed boy with Isabella stood and smiled at her with a width of patio between them. Holland's mouth snapped.

"Stay away from that girl!"

"Holland!" I called to her.

"Hanni." She turned to me with a look that I first thought was relief but that paled into something outside the dictionary of expression as the taxi driver raised his cheek from the guitar, turned in his chair, and gave her a full-toothed grin.

"Holland!"

And from her mouth came a cry that was more flamenco than Led Zeppelin, Flamenco Halevy, or J. S. Bach.

HOLLAND—SANTÁNGEL

Oh Ben,

They fled, of course they fled. Not only Sammy L., who retreated back to his taxi more gracefully than the others, always facing me, always grinning through beard and moustache, even his feet, his boots, toeing and heeling, backing over the sand, laughing at me, more infuriating in that he had deliberately placed himself a patio's-width away in the bare-assed confidence that he could, being a man, always outflee consequences. But the rest of the pricks—Roger, Ivy, Fredo, of course, but even Vim, who would have won the thank-you of his Cantabrigian dreams had he the sophistication to don shining armour and stand up for me against the pack. They fled because they knew. They fled because they were ignorant. They fled because none of them had lived with emptiness and were damned if they would face it first thing on a Spanish winter morning.

Hanni stayed. Hanni sat with me at the bar drinking hot chocolate, matching my Fundadors—no Carlos of any number here—cup for shot. Not since the honeymoon mornings with Foss have I resorted to liquor so early in the day—but to see the devil again after so many years and miles, so close to the daughter he snatched from me . . .

I couldn't tell Hanni. I could barely tell myself. I felt certain you'd have the answer, Ben. An answer.

Would you have fled?

"Señora. Señorita." A tall black man stood in the doorway, backlit by the morning beach. I found my legs and stood.

Abbas led our minicaravan across the sand, Hanni's steamer trunk riding on one of his shoulders, the other arm encircling Spinoza, tapes, and wheels. The wind had cleared the beach of morning clouds. At the yacht club, farther to the east, three boys in pastel-sashed wet suits were jousting with surfboards. I shivered—my run, my rest, my brandy, the anticipation of seeing you, the knowledge, once I set foot on the pier, that your office and La Rosa Náutica were one and the same.

The restaurant was empty and unlit, except for a grey, floating glow that seeped through the windows from all the petals of the compass rose. The tables were set for luncheon, but no clang of cutlery or shouted orders of preparation came from the kitchen below. Silence, and the smell of espresso.

Two steaming demitasses sat on the counter of the bar. I left Hanni with Abbas and made a beeline for the coffee. The Fundadors had been a miscalculation. I had cheated on Carlos and was paying with Kabbalistic penance. The Moroccan coffee was strong and sweet. A few fishnets drifted from my eyes. For a moment I felt a clear equilibrium. Perhaps Hassan the Palestinian academic was right, all those years ago in Paris at the Battle of Trocadéro. It takes a balanced mixture of Catholic brandy, Jewish pastry, and Islamic coffee to achieve intestinal harmony.

"Is this yours?" Hanni stood just behind me. I turned. Laid open on the maître d's lectern was another copy, neither mine nor Hanni's, of your *Guide*. I told Hanni I had written a favourable review of La Rosa Náutica. She told me she had read it, only half an hour earlier.

I wrote that review last night, Ben, chez Conchita.

"Read this," Hanni commanded.

EVENTS OF NOTE

Tuesday, 31 December 1991

Teatro La Rábida: *¡Adiós, Colón!* (shows at 20.00, 22.15, 00.30, 02.45) Plaza La Rábida 10, tel: Mariposa 19 59.

Plaza de Toros: Joey and the Arimatheans (21.30) res: Mariposa 33 35.

Carnegie Hall: Sandor (23.30) res: 46 65 13. The final concert of the universally acclaimed violin virtuoso who put Mariposa on the map. The maestro writes:

> As you well know, I have been seeking, ever since the end of the War, the Perfect Sound. I have been searching for a way to produce a sound that glances off the history of the listener and refracts into images of music heard and unheard throughout the listener's lifetime.
>
> In my childhood, in Peru and elsewhere, I was happy to study scales, impossible arpeggios in tenths, happy to tackle the minor challenges of the knotty bits of repertoire. I was happy to struggle for greatness, by playing great pieces in imitation of great men. But after the horrors of the War, I recognized that if perfection were to be reached, it must cleanse itself of Man. It must cleanse itself of virtuosi. The cults that surrounded Heifetz and Horowitz were nothing more than pagan fertility rituals. The Beatles telecast of the Ed Sullivan Show was no less horrifying than the Nuremberg Rallies. As far as I was concerned, Hitler was just another Paganini.
>
> I stopped giving concerts. I tried recording. I needn't tell my most devoted followers how recording only concentrates the heat of the artist, leaving sound still full of the imperfections of imagined bodies and faces.
>
> Recently, the solution became clear to me—to achieve the Perfect Sound, the artist himself must dis-

appear, without a murmur. He must capture the entirety of music in that split of a split moment before bow touches metal, breath crosses mouthpiece, hammer kisses string. That moment becomes the seed of ultimate creation, the infini-second before the Big Bang, when all possibility is stored up in a single invisible, unobservable point. It is a moment of silence, pure and antiseptic. It's a moment easily destroyed by the infection of the artist's personality. To play the Perfect Sound, I must disappear.

At midnight tonight, I turn eighty years old. I have been rehearsing—if that is the word—for this anniversary concert for a more personal reason than the Perfect Sound. I will not disappear in order to play the Perfect Sound. I will play the Perfect Sound in order to disappear. I am tired of wandering. I no longer want to be twenty.

"The Wandering Jew," Hanni whispered. She knew as much as I had learned in my late-night lecture at the Santa María, and perhaps an extra stanza or two.

Of all the magical drafts I'd been served in the previous twenty-four hours, Benjamin, this was the most difficult to swallow. Sandor, my Sandor, Zoltan, her Zoltan, the Wandering Jew? After all, if the story was to be believed, the Wandering Jew was a Christian myth, an anti-Semitic morality tale cooked up to show, one, how the Jews hocked their collective spittle on Jesus, and, two, that before the Boy on the Cross would set his bloody feet back on Earth, the Jews, Wandering and otherwise engaged, would have to convert to Christianity.

"But it can't all happen spontaneously," Hanni argued with your *Guide*. "You need someone, something, to set the concert in motion, to introduce Zoltan, to sell the tickets, a Grand Promoter—" And she stopped. I saw teeth clicking into gears within the chaos of her grey hair. "Benjamin," she said, smiling at the *Guide* on the lectern. "That's where Benjamin fits in. He's diversified with the knack of a modern Esau. He's added to his business of guidebooks and bookings. Expanded from the business of Motion to ProMotion. And without a word to us, his best clients."

"I will explain." Deep, masculine. You, I hoped at first, with the thrill of walking into a celebrity interview. But the tall Spaniard at the door, whose left hand guided Isabella gently by the elbow to our side of the circular bar while his right cradled a cut-glass snifter, was the proprietor of La Rosa Náutica.

"Señor Santángel," I said with a second chill, a recognition that carried with it a hundred unformed questions.

"I was hoping it would not be long before we met again, Señorita." The voice beneath the greying goatee was strong, soothing, not altogether trustworthy. Isabella stood at his side, holding her violin case with both hands, her eyes locked on the sawdust at her feet, her cheeks glowing with the light through the windows, through rope nets and glass orbs.

"We want to see Benjamin. Immediately!" Hanni's first command would not have been mine but would do for starters.

"Abbas!" Santángel spoke, and Abbas disappeared behind the bar with my camera and Hanni's trunk, descending, presumably to raise you from your office. I swallowed the last of my coffee.

"Leave the trunk," Hanni called.

"Señora Hanni." Santángel soothed and ignored. "Perhaps I can answer some of your questions."

"Where is he, downstairs?" Hanni moved towards the bar.

"If you would like to see Ben, nothing could be easier."

"Who are you?" she barked at him. Santángel turned his gaze to me. I turned it right back. It was time that the staff of La Rosa Náutica made their own introductions.

"They call me Santángel." He smiled. "You recognize the name?"

"You work for Benjamin?"

"You might say that."

"With Señor Carranque?"

"Who?" My turn.

"I know Señor Carranque quite well."

"And that man, the taxi driver?"

"Sammy L." I hissed. Santángel laughed. An all-too-familiar laugh.

"Are these your questions?" he asked.

"Why?" Hanni snapped back. "Do we run out at twenty?"

"No, no, ask away," he said. "Only I'd much rather give you more substantial information. Questions like these you could ask in many other, less . . ."—he searched for the proper word in his snifter. "Let me just say that La Rosa Náutica, and myself as its proprietor, were hoping to answer more fundamental, fulfilling questions."

"Such as?"

"Señorita Holland," he scolded lightly, "you can't have it both ways."

"What about the strike?" Hanni asked.

"Good question"—Santángel set his glass on the bar—"but not really what you want to know."

"I want to know whether Benjamin can get me a flight out of this confusion right now, this morning."

"I thought you wanted to find your son."

Hanni stopped breathing. The dusty haze froze in midair.

"Then you must know my question," I whispered, looking at Isabella's downcast eyes.

"If I might make a recommendation." Santángel stepped away from the bar. "Yesterday afternoon, Señorita Holland, when you were lunching here with Señor Sandor, I expressed the hope that I might entertain you, at some convenient time in the future, with a modest exhibit I am preparing for the celebration of the five hundredth anniversary of the Expulsion of the Jews. I feel, in fact, I am certain, that both you ladies will find many answers in the presentation."

"You have the film here?" I asked.

"It is not exactly a film." Santángel placed the tips of his fingers together. He knew he had caught me with my question.

"I don't have time for pictures," Hanni said.

"Not pictures, Señora—letters."

"I've come to see Benjamin. I don't have time for your demonstration."

"I prefer to call it a Disputation." Santángel spoke to Hanni but kept his eyes on me.

"You heard me, young man." Hanni, the imperious airport harridan.

"All is prepared downstairs," he said.

"I don't care where . . ."

"In the Cave of Esau." Another jab to the gut. Hanni had to pause. "Señora Hanni," he continued gently, "surely I do not have to remind you of my estimable ancestor and his role in the survival of your family."

Santángel led the way. Behind him Isabella, then Hanni, then me. Ten steps, twenty, thirty, fifty, seventy-three steps. Down below the pier, down a stone passage impervious to the salt sea, a rocky tunnel pushed and pulled in Esau's favourite lullaby. Down, down into the rocky floor of the beach. My nipples stiffened under my jumpsuit—I wished Abbas had left me my Issey Miyake jacket—my entire body told me that I was going in the right direction.

The staircase ended. Santángel walked forward several paces in the dark—hollow sounds, a pleasant smell of earth, parchment, and water. In the light of the torch, I saw my camera. Santángel touched my arm with a long finger, and I stopped, at attention behind my trusty Spinoza. He led Hanni to her steamer trunk, Isabella to a third point with her violin. The three of us in a triangle, a spooky parlour game.

Santángel walked away and made a tour of the room, lighting ten thick candles, their wicks eight feet from the ground, not half the way to the top of the arched ceiling. Niche by niche, the cave brightened. Carvings into the rock, canopies within caverns, honeycombs within snailshells, more elaborate, more Moorish than the Mezquita of Córdoba, than the Hall of the Ambassadors at the Alhambra. Forty columns supported ten arches, ten arches led to ten corridors. Between the arches, ten leather chairs. And at the center, at the center of our triangle, below the hemisphere of the hall, a freshwater fountain, a pool of stone on the ten stone backs of ten stone lions. The Cave of Esau.

I was utterly confused.

I had not expected the truth, or at least the description of the Esau Letter to be so immediately confirmed, or confirmable. For all I knew, the Letter could have been written earlier in the week by a writer standing at the spot where I now stood. I felt—and feeling is ultimately the most one can ask for after a night without sleep, a three-mile jog, and two shots of Fundador matched by two of café Maroc—that perhaps, as Hanni had tried to tell me, authenticity was not the point. That the date of the authorship of the Esau Letter was less relevant to the demonstration, or Disputation, of Santángel than our very presence. It was not that Esau had once stood on the spot we now stood, but that we were standing in his place—three of us—even if my daughter, my Isabella, refused to acknowledge my presence.

Somewhere, above, around, I began to hear the sound. In the chairs, the ten chairs that ringed the cavern, ten men— Santángel, Roger and The Lost Tribes, the flamenco troupe from La Rábida, others. A new Minyan. For what, Ben? A new voyage of discovery? The murmur grew louder, the murmuring of men, the sound of jets, the violin, a gently rocking continuo, slow, but not too slow, a seabound second movement 12/8 that I knew, Hanni knew, Isabella knew so well.

And across from me, across from my daughter, the slouching, sneering laugh of the devil himself, Sammy L.

With that, there was no more light. Only the all-encompassing, all-defining, all-knowing Music. And I began to see.

HANNI—THE CAVE OF JACOB

Benjamin,

When I awoke, or came to, or gathered my lost senses about me, I found myself wandering down a rocky concourse toward a distant light. I ran my fingertips along a dark forest of glass cases, the leather spines of tall books, velvet covers, parchment—seeing, without needing to see, the library Santángel had built for Esau. The tunnel ended. I stood in a large circular room. Above me, the ceiling tapered up into a long, thin chimney—an impossible bottle of Chianti reserved for the tourist trade. From the opening at the top, the sky, enough light somehow reflected to show that the walls of the cave were covered with writing.

Not a map of Africa, Benjamin. Not Esau's map. But a letter, yet another letter, from another survivor.

31 December 1550

My dear daughter,

Once upon a time, far across the ocean, in the land of the Conquistadors who drove your mother from the House of the Chosen Women, there lived a boy named Eliyahu, who changed his name to Esau and left his brother standing in the middle of his bar mitzvah. This brother's name was Yehuda, a boy born merely minutes, seconds, after his beloved Esau, a boy left behind to carry the burden of his parents' love and the shadow of the departed Esau's name.

The name of Esau was the name of a dark god, the name of a son who turned from his father, a brother who turned from his brother. A hairy man. When Esau left, Yehuda became Jacob, Jacob the smooth-skinned brother of Esau.

That boy, my daughter, was I.

I am past surprise, Benjamin, past thought, past wondering how writing met wall. I stand in the Cave of Esau. I read the Letter of Jacob. Unknown, undiscovered, unperturbed.

Within a year, I became an orphan of the Inquisition.

Through the gaps in the letter, where the sea has overrun the chimney of light fifty feet above and selectively edited Jacob's prose, I can see the charred ruins of the tavern in Córdoba, the fountain still bubbling, a young boy sitting in tears.

In time, I inherited the estate of my parents.

I can see a violin and a bow lying on the stone floor to one side of Jacob. On the other, half-cradled by her son, Jacob's dying mother. Jacob touches his lips to her bloody hands, where the soldiers of the Crown cut off fingers that once held a bow, fingers that once held a violin.

It was as Jacob, eight years later, that I left Spain. It was as Jacob, the night we sailed from Spain, that I awoke, curled up next to my mother's viol on the bottom of a double hogshead. The instrument, snug in its case, played to me, played by itself, unbowed. Far from trying to dampen the strings, to keep it from disclosing my hiding place, I listened carefully for its message.

Boards creak close to my ears, distant splashes, I can smell old wine and olives. Esau in his barrel, Jacob in his. Far away, music, a violin, a viol, Jacob, Zoltan.

It sang to me, my viol. It sang to me a wordless song of my brother, a message that my brother, my long-departed, long-converted brother, Esau, was nearby, sailing, somewhere in our fleet. I fell asleep to the melody, happy in the thought that as long as the viol continued to play, as long as my brother was nearby, I would survive.

When I awoke, all was silent. The viol kept its own counsel over many weeks at sea, until the morning before I was freed, when once again it sang the presence of my brother. By nightfall and landfall, truth had replaced hope. He was not among us, my brother Eliyahu, my brother Esau. I was beached with a small group of men for whom I had neither sympathy nor patience. By morning, I was gone.

By the grace of my viol, I made friends with the native population at every step. I was fed, clothed, and above all, transported across the island. My questions, the answers I received, led me southward, back onto the water with native sailors, who asked no other payment than five minutes of melody. I landed on the coast of this great continent and followed the beckonings of my remarkable instrument inland, sometimes resting among the welcoming locals, sometimes traveling, for months at a time, out of sight of all mankind.

Until I reached Cuzco. The year was 1497. It would be thirty-five more years until Pizarro and his Conquistadors set foot in the Temple of the Sun.

I walked into the imperial city with the dawn, from the eastern forests of Antisuyu. It was the longest day of the year. The streets of Cuzco were empty. I wandered freely, past the beauty, the musical perfection, of the enormous stone walls, the lacy aqueducts, the temples and the houses of the city. I was ragged but clean, thin but not malnourished. My viol was safe and unrotted in a case of hardwood lined with moss.

I walk with Jacob, Benjamin, as I never could with Esau, into downtown Cuzco, into the center of the web. The sun rises in the plaza. Ten thousand Incas murmur morning prayers, stand on ten thousand feet, shake ten thousand ankles in the air. At their center, motionless, stands a man, a demigod, on a platform raised on the shoulders of twenty motionless priests. Jacob draws nearer. Other litters, carried by other priests, and on them, the mummified bodies of whom? Gods, children, mothers-in-law?

As I entered the plaza of the Coricancha, the Temple of the Sun, a sound, a music filled the skies above the prayers. My viol raised its voice from within its case, unbowed, unplayed, a miracle it hadn't performed since the day Colón deposited me on the beach of Hispaniola.

All ankle-waving stopped. On one foot, the crowd pivoted. I walked the aisle. Hands gripped my thighs, and I was hoisted level to the Inca. I held my viol, still playing in its case, an offering. The Inca held out his arm, the little finger of his bow arm, and touched the case. The music stopped. The crowd stood motionless, hardly daring to breathe. I smiled. He smiled.

"Inca Huayna Capac." He turned the little finger to his chest.

"Yacov." I held the case in one arm and turned my own little finger upon myself.

"Huaca?" he asked. I nodded. It was a close enough approximation.

But with that nod, the people of Cuzco fell on their faces on the cobbled streets of the plaza. "Huaca," the Inca word for God. I had my brother, and his choice of names, to thank for my career.

I became a high priest of the Incas. My viol was installed in the Temple of the Sun and named Huarneri, the living incarnation of Music. I had arrived at the beginning of the most holy festival of Inti Raymi. For the next five days, I joined the thousands and carried Huarneri in the procession to the fortress of Sacsahuamán.

There I feasted alongside the hundreds of other priests with their hundreds of other huacas. On the seventh day, I was asked to assist in the festival of the capacochas.

My aclla was a thirteen-year-old girl from the great lake Titicaca in the Collasuyu to the south. The fame of her extraordinary beauty had preceded her, and the plaza before the Temple of the Sun was filled to bursting with admiring humanity. In all my seventy-nine years, my beautiful daughter, I have seen only one other girl to compare with my aclla.

I hear music. Jacob, in his Inca vestments, with his violin beneath his chin, plays a familiar tune, the tune of departure from the Old World, the tune of arrival at Cuzco. "By the Rivers of Babylon." A dirge in Andalusia, perhaps. But in the thin, siesta air of Cuzco, a lullaby to weigh down the eyelids of the young *aclla*.

The priests lowered my sleeping aclla into the dry cistern. I was told to keep playing. I waited to see them raise her up again, reborn, resurrected. Instead, they replaced the stone.

I played on, well into the night, alone in the plaza. My only comfort was the belief that, as long as I played, she would sleep, and as long as she slept, she would never know the panic, the suffocation of being buried alive, a gift to the Sun.

Oh, Benjamin, is it possible? The Lute of Kima, accessory to murder, and such a terrible, terrifying murder at that?

For thirty-five years, I guarded my Huarneri, living among the virgins, among the acllas and the mamaconas, the most beautiful women in the empire. For thirty-five years, I served the Inca, first Huayna Capac, and when he died, Huáscar Inca. For thirty-five years, I did not touch a woman. I did not touch my viol. I made a wide berth around cisterns and I was content.

When the pox broke out, scarring the faces of half of Cuzco, killing Huayna Capac and a third of the town in a single month, I knew that the Spaniards had landed on the continent. It was only a matter of time before they reached Cuzco. I dreaded their arrival. But I had not forgotten my brother.

"You wish to join your people?" Huáscar Inca asked me in his wisdom.

"I too have a brother," I said. His face turned pale with sadness. His brother Atahualpa had turned traitor and run north to the Spaniards.

"There is a city," the Inca continued, "six days' march north of Cuzco, high on the mountains over the Urubamba River. Machu Picchu was once a place of great beauty. It is now a city of silence. Go, take your Huarneri. From there you may observe. From there you may make your decision."

It is dawn in the forest. I walk with an older Jacob from the dense forest to an open gate, the vast terraced city of stone houses and thatched roofs, high jungle and high peaks, the guardian tower of Huayna Picchu before us. Utter silence, except for the roar of the Urubamba far below.

For one hundred days, I explored the ruins of Machu Picchu with a herd of llamas. I moved as softly as I could, listening for sounds of an army of Spaniards, or an army of Atahualpa's Incas. I slept lightly, I lit no fires.

When one hundred days had passed, I could bear the silence no longer. I restrung my bow with hair from my animal friends. I picked up my viol, strings shining as brightly as on the nights my mother played in her father's tavern. I walked at dawn to the Inti-Huatana, the Hitching-Post of the Sun, and gazed out as the snow up the valley caught the first rays of the longest day of the year. After thirty-five years of silence, the strings were still in tune, alive and vibrant with the soul of my ancestral aunt— Kima.

For six days I played, from dawn till dusk, dawn till dusk. On the seventh day, as the sun rose, in that invisible moment as my bow touched the string, the sound of voices came to me from the south. A woman's voice. The voice of many women.

Not one woman. Not one voice. But a river, a flood, led by one distant beauty, drawn by the tune.

The Virgins of the Sun, one hundred of them, had heard the music of my viol six days' march to the south and had followed it, invisible to the guards of Atahualpa and the Spaniard Pizarro, who had overrun the city of Cuzco and murdered my friend, my Inca Huáscar. One hundred acllas and mamaconas. As young as ten, as old as fifty-seven. One viol. Mine. One man. Me.

For five years, the Chosen Women lived with me in the city they called Machu Picchu, weaving and brewing, planting corn and coca. I did nothing but play my viol, from dawn to dusk. But they had come too late. The European diseases had swept down from the north into their virgin bodies. After five years, only one woman remained to keep me company—the midwife to the wives of the Inca, the mamacona they called Pachamama, the Earth Mother.

I can see the wedding, Benjamin, the wedding of Jacob and Pachamama. A wedding, Benjamin, according to the laws of Moses. Jacob holds the gourd for Pachamama to drink, Pachamama pours *chicha* into the mouth of Jacob. Jacob takes the empty gourd, holds it briefly up to the admiring rays of the setting sun, places it beneath his foot, and smashes it with one echoing thump. Mazel tov.

After fifty years of virginity and obedience, your mother gave of herself, so that we might continue a people. We had a girl. We have a girl. Three of us. For all we know, we are all we know.

And now I am on my way out. Your mother gave of herself, thirteen years ago, so that our people might live. And now she wants to sacrifice you, the thirteen-year-old fruit of our two worlds, in the Inca belief that such a sacrifice will make me live forever. Are our people so important, my daughter? Are they worth your sacrifice? I can neither persuade nor dissuade. But your mother sits beside you as you write down my words. She listens as you write down my words.

There, next to the altar stone, the open cistern, the weakened old man Jacob, his wife, and the young girl. I know these people. I know these questions.

I have reached the age of seventy-nine, my daughter, well past the allotment for Jews and Incas. There is a legend, not among my people, but among other Spaniards, Catholics like Pizarro, about a man called the Wandering Jew. It is said that he lives forever, that he cannot die. That on the dusk of his eightieth birthday the years drop off him like mist from Huayna Picchu into the roaring Urubamba and he becomes a healthy youth of twenty once again.

I was a young girl once, Benjamin, kneeling at the deathbed of my mother. I was a young woman once, kneeling in the rain with my dying lover. Was I worth the sacrifice?

I am a musician. My brother, he was the wanderer. Find him, my daughter. You are young, you are of my blood. Take my viol and find my brother. Take my viol, it will play for you. It will lead the way.

Lead the way—down from the hand of Pachamama, ready to let her daughter down into the uncertain magic of the cistern. Down from the trusting eyes of the daughter, the tired Western eyes of the father, tired of wandering, but so in love with his daughter he would turn twenty all over again just to watch one last sunrise on her sleeping face. Down from the sun to the viol, the music playing, once more, unbidden and unbowed.

I can see, Benjamin, down the terraces of Machu Picchu, past the Temple of the Three Windows, I can see people— Incas and Spaniards of a bygone age. I can see down the terraces, past the Temple of the Condor, past the houses of the *acllas* and the *mamaconas*, now, nearly five hundred years later, bare of thatching, ruined, the grass well manicured to encourage immortality. Down the terraces, down toward the Urubamba, people, people, the throng of Jacob's family, my uncle's family, multiply and divide, branches of a family tree, names and dates resting in the short grass at their feet, shoes and costumes of the multitude increasingly modern with the drop in altitude, coachload after coachload of tourists in period dress, daytrippers from Cuzco, overnighters from Lima, all those thousands of inbred cousins of mine, filling up, clogging up the hillside, until, at the banks of the river, standing, as if posing for a portrait, on the final three terraces, like the final three grapes of the bunch of Esau's Africa, stand a Father, a Son, a Granddaughter.

And I call to these words, these imaginings on the high chalky walls—"Zoltan! Sonny! Isabella!" I know these people, these faces, these children of Jacob. And my knowledge, the sound of my discovery, ricochets through the tunnels of the subterranean cavern and comes back to me in the no-longer-proper but desperate tones of My Lady Journalist—"Sandor! Hook! Isabella!"

A long night of echoes and reverberations, of resonances and overtones.

And you—Benjamin, Ben, ben.

You and Sonny and Hook. My son.

Our family—as strong and secure as the continents, as miraculous as the lute of Kima, the discovery of Florida, the meeting of three women on a dark winter's night.

I dreamed this night would come, Benjamin. One long night ago, I curled up beneath the protection of a clump of olives and dreamed that your father would one day stand on the stage of Carnegie Hall, that we would be there, with him, together, palm against palm, applauding, palm in palm.

I am crying, Benjamin. At last, at the end of sixty-five years of nights, my body is melting into a tired, gray woman. Where are the palms to support me? Where are the stone lions to lift me up. I cry for myself, my son, my self.

My tears fall short of the stone floor.

Your steamer trunk stands open at my feet beneath the
Letter of Jacob. The steamer trunk I've been schlepping
around Mariposa all night for you, for you, as only a mother
would for a son, open for the first time. A peach, an apricot, a
nectarine, wet with the dew of my tears. Three pieces of fruit,
all supported by a beach of Mediterranean sand. We have
ripened, the three of us women—the message as clear as when
horse-toothed Penina sent her fruit basket to Mohammed el-
Hayzari.

But to the side of the nectarine, in case I failed to get the
message, a letter. Oh, Benjamin.

Dear Mother,

Is any other revelation necessary? Do I have to bend down,
read on, pick up the paper, dropped when? In the time of Esau,
in the time of Jacob's daughter, in the brief time while I read
and tried to understand?

I call to you, my son. I want so badly, so badly, to see you,
to touch your hair, to beg your forgiveness for all those lost
years. The Urubamba roars, the music of the violin grows
louder, the voice of Zoltan, the voice of Jacob, a voice, voices
call from mountaintops and boxcars, "Turn around, Hanni
Halevy, turn around"—and I feel you there, Benjamin, my
son, as surely as Orpheus felt the breath of Eurydice on his
shoulder, and I reach behind me. Take my hand in yours, my
hand!

"All along I think Ben meant for us to come to this pass,"
Holland murmurs. She has found me. The light in the room
has turned yellow. I am no longer standing before the Jacob
Letter, before your trunk, but before ten silent men, at the base
of the Fountain of the Lions.

"All along, I think Ben meant for us to choose ourselves, for
ourselves, to see or not to see. Santángel, Carranque, Sammy

L., Roger and the boys—this Nouveau Minyan has nothing to do with our ability to choose."

Ten chairs, ten men. Ten men, all with mothers.

"Esau's story is compelling," Holland whispers in my ear, "the torture of Jacob's mother horrifying, the dilemma of Pachamama has a prehistoric power. But ultimately, I care more about you and Isabella. Whether or not you are my mother-in-law or Isabella my daughter, whether or not we share a history and tradition that spans thousands of years—the answers matter less than the prospect of passing a few brief decades together. Think, Hanni." Her voice more urgent. "Don't make the mistake of Esau and let the real Florida get away."

The flesh of her hand, a second time, the way it felt just hours before, in the cool dawn of Zoltan's villa as we stood listening to the perfect music of my granddaughter Isabella. Isabella, standing near, still apart. Now, looking up at her mother, smiling for the first time, understanding, a virgin of the sun.

What shall I do?

Let me tell you a story.

Do you remember, Benjamin, those months, after Leo died, when you, alias Sonny, rented the green room downstairs. The cereal and eggs sunnyside-up for your American breakfasts, the short drives in my Mini to Karl Marx's grave in Highgate Cemetery, the late-summer concerts by the lily pond at Kenwood House. The autumn evenings in the front parlor by the gas fire, listening to Zoltan's—your father's—Tchaikovsky on Leo's—my dead husband's—phonograph. And the plans I had for the spring—day trips to St. Alban's and Bath, a small *Macbeth* at the Young Vic. All for the days you made impossible when you disappeared.

Would those days have been different if I'd known you were my son?

Let me tell you a story.

Leo had an uncle, a man who ran a thriving family business

before the war, selling kiddush cups and menorahs to the wealthy Jews of Berlin from a spacious store in the lobby of the Hotel Bristol. He sold the store for next to nothing after Kristallnacht and moved with his wife and daughter to a small apartment in Amsterdam. After the Nazis overran the Netherlands, the family went into hiding, much as Anne Frank's family did. And, as with the Franks, the uncle's warren was eventually discovered and the family shipped to Birkenau, where the daughter was shuttled off to the labor camp at Goleszow, presumably to perish, and the wife immediately gassed.

When the Red Army liberated Birkenau, Leo's uncle made his way south to Odessa, and then by boat to Marseilles and England. Leo set him up with a flat in Golders Green and a stall in Portobello Road, where he sold *tchatchkes* and gave consultations on silver for a small percentage. Every year or so, he would put on his one good suit and trudge down to this town council or that community center for a meeting of Displaced Persons, less in the hope, especially as the years wore on, that he might meet some friend or distant relative from Berlin or Amsterdam, than in the strength it gave him to see that his loss was shared by others.

In 1969, some society or other booked the Hippodrome, a large white backdrop to the cherry-red bus depot of the Golders Green Underground station. As always, Leo's uncle put on his suit and stopped at Bloom's Delicatessen for a brisket sandwich and an orange squash, nodding to the owner, to the librarian on his lunch break, to a young woman, not so young anymore, whom he recognized from the morning Underground platform, to Mr. Schay, a collector of silver Judaica.

He hurried off after his sandwich. At the door of the Hippodrome, he was met by a friend who claimed to have found someone who knew Leo's uncle from Birkenau. The reunion was made. And when a few tears had been shed and the usual information had been exchanged, the man inquired after the health of the uncle's daughter. The uncle cursed the man, enraged by his lack of sensitivity. But rage turned to bewilderment as he noticed the look of surprise on the man's face. The man hurried off, demanding that Leo's uncle remain where he was. In a minute, he returned with a woman. Your daughter, the man said.

There stood the daughter who had been taken to the labor camp at Goleszow, who had not died but had been rescued from a frozen boxcar by the famous Oscar Schindler. There stood a young woman, not so young anymore, the woman who had shared a train platform at the Golders Green Underground with Leo's uncle, the woman he had nodded at for twenty-five years.

Would seeing your face, Benjamin, would putting my arms around your shoulders, mean more after a lifetime than clutching the tattered covers of your *Guide* to my chest. You were smarter than Leo's cousin. In your few months in the green room, we were able to live together, free of guilt, obligation, history.

If happiness is knowledge, knowledge of one's origins, then let my origins begin now. Forget about Zoltan, forget about Esau, forget about this vague hodgepodge of a people called the Jews. Maybe some people live in a world where link to tradition, devotion to a cause, where binding Aristotle to Moses, Reason to Faith, where following a packet of letters and a cave painting, are the road to happiness. My priority is to the living. If that makes me shallow in the eyes of the Carranques, the Santángels, the Sammy L.s, the Maimonideses, if that makes me shallow in your eyes, Benjamin—tough.

I start now, with this woman, with this child. Whether they are flesh of my flesh, blood of my blood—I couldn't care less.

The truth, Benjamin?

I haven't eaten a kipferln in hours, is that it? I am free at last to make a choice, unguided by butter, sugar, hazelnut, and memory.

The truth, Benjamin?

As your mother, I've got to say you missed a good bet with My Lady Journalist.

The truth, Benjamin?

I know Esau better than I know you. Look at the freedom Esau had to build his own ball team from scratch.

I left you once, Benjamin, I can leave you again.

The truth?

The seats are empty, the Minyan has disappeared. The door at the top of the stairway stands open, a faint shaft of light. I look around. Holland without her camera. Isabella without her violin. All our possessions—gone. Only we remain.

The truth?

Can a woman forget her baby, or disown the child of her womb? Though she might forget, I never could forget you.

The truth, Benjamin?

Esau said it best—we are all Jews. Our survival is in our motion.

Mama

HOLLAND—¡ADIÓS, COLÓN!

Dear Ben,

I found Conchita near where I'd first met her, standing before the copy of her family landscape, the mural on the back wall of the tiled Ladies' of the Aeropuerto Cristóbal Colón. She was tying an apron around the waist of the subdued sack of her waitress costume as she pondered the mosaic—far less provocative than in the black dagger of her striker's uniform. She was, I think, waiting for me.

"*¿Qué lindo, no?*"

The smouldering ruin on the hill, the seascape, with its three caravels, the backs of faceless women waving handkerchiefs from the dock, the few dull shacks falling into the river, were no more beautiful than the night before. A strong odor of ammonia made the blue of the ocean less dull and the crosses on the sails more garishly red.

What had changed was beneath the tiles. Beneath the tiles were barrels. Beneath the barrels, boys. Beneath the dress of the broad-shouldered, grey-eyed girl onshore, the secrets of navigation. But the ruin? A monastery? A mosque? A synagogue?

"Was it revenge for my desertion?" Conchita and I turned away from the mural. Hanni stood at the sinks, talking to the mirror, talking to us. "What do you think, Holland? Was this enormous puzzle, this guided tour—were they all in on it— Carranque, Santángel, Sammy L., Gershon Mundel and his light-fingered wife? Was this all just the pastime of a jaded travel agent with nothing better to do than torture his mother?"

"His mother?" I said. I took the brush from her hands and tried to put some order into her hair. "What about me? The rest of you were born into this crazy story. But Ben picked me, me to be the mother of his child. Why England, why the BBC? I'm not even Jewish, I'm . . ."

"A *shiksa* goddess"—Hanni turned to my unreflected face— "like Esau's Florida, like his copper-coloured girl. Like Jacob's Pachamama."

When did you choose me, Ben? Before I grew? Afterwards? Was the choice made in Berlin, in Surrey, *in utero*? Or was it merely some grand coincidence of bonfire and Bach?

"Why couldn't Ben have met us at the airport?" Hanni restored her hairbrush to her bag. "Before the strike?"

I'd asked myself the same question. Why not, Ben? After all you've made in commissions, why couldn't you have plumped for a leisurely five-course meal with three wines, and told us the whole convoluted story in straightforward, genealogical English?

"My dear Señorita." Conchita finished tying her apron. "A travel agent cannot indulge in direct revelation. He can only guide the client with bits of art—entertainment, trickery, parable, pictures in a cave—into a certain understanding. He must make the client believe that all choices are hers alone, all her experiences one of a kind."

For all the news of strikes and jet fighters in the *Herald Tribune*, I could have dreamed away the night on the Naugahyde benches of Colón. I have crossed the waterless rivers of Mariposa, I have danced the *bulería* with Conchita on the stage of the Cine La Rábida. Yet I remain nothing more than a departing passenger.

I turned back to the mural. Three women.

If our paths cross, Ben, in some distant concert hall or

out-of-the-way airport, I will be tempted to ask you a few questions. I reckon you may have a few of your own. For now, the women on shore are pocketing their handkerchiefs. We have a plane to catch.

Holland

ISABELLA—FULL-ARM VIBRATO

Mother, Grandmother:

Let me tell you a story. It is a story I was born knowing. It is a story I have told myself every bedtime as long as I can remember.

When Naomi arrived at the airport, she turned to Ruth to kiss her good-bye. But Ruth refused to leave.

"Do not ask me to go away. You are my White Rabbit. Wherever you go, whichever hole you jump down, whichever door you open, I will follow. And wherever you sleep, if you ever sleep, whether it is in a condo in Miami or an airport bench in Frankfurt, that's where I will sleep. Where you die, will I die and be buried. For only death will take you away from me. I was not born of your people, but you are my people. And though you were born of your people, you are mine. What we are, we will be together."

And Naomi nodded and turned to the gate.

But there was another standing by.

And Ruth turned to the girl with the downcast eyes and said, "Will you come with your grandmother and me?"

And the girl said nothing, but kept her hands in the pockets of her jacket, where the fingers of her bow hand folded and unfolded the letter that told her who she was and who she would be. And the girl looked down at the floor and thought of the other floors she knew so well, from hours and years of staring herself into another place, a place outside the sound of Mass and dry women's voices.

And Ruth reached out her hand until she almost touched the girl's chin and repeated, "Will you come with your grandmother and me?"

And the girl still said nothing, but squeezed the folded paper in her pocket, and looked down at her feet, and thought of the thousands of mornings she had hoped, in the revery of lacing and knotting, that she would sit at the edge of another bed that very same evening, and feel the gentle tug of her mother's hands release her feet from the hard-soled shoes and toss them away forever.

And Ruth stood back, and her shoulders dropped, and her chin sank to her breast, and she began to speak so low that the girl could at first hear only the melody of the voice. But gradually the words of the mouth became the words of the paper—

> My dear daughter,
>   This letter is hardly an ark of bulrushes, but it may, as you grow older and desire to know, bring you some small comfort.
>   You have a mother. A mother who carried you for nine months. A mother who gave birth to you. A mother who left you for reasons that are a mystery to her, like so many other mysteries in her life.
>   Know this, my daughter—a time will come. It may not be while you are still too young to read this letter, it may not be before you are old enough to hate me for my desertion. But a time will come when I will come for you. And there will be an end to mysteries.

And the girl said nothing, but slowly drew her hand from her pocket with the paper she had folded and unfolded since before she could remember. And she raised her hand up, and her eyes to her hand, and she opened her fist, and the paper scattered like fairy dust upon the floor of the terminal, like the notes of a minuet she would never again repeat. And her mother reached out and filled her empty palm with her own.

And as the plane flew smoothly through the afternoon sky, its shadow chased curly-horned sheep and gray-bearded goats up and down over mountains and valleys. And as the plane flew smoothly into the night, the shadow slipped into the sea and swam deep to play with the whales and the porpoises and the sea monsters of fairy tales.

And Ruth's daughter curled up, with her feet on the lap of Naomi, and her head in the lap of Ruth. And as she closed her eyes, as the murmurings of the stories of the women grew sweet and warm like a full-arm vibrato on the G-string, she reached up with one hand to the generous breast of her mother, her elbow crooked into third position, poised for the first note— perhaps the second movement of the Bach Double Violin Concerto in D Minor, perhaps a favorite tune of an Alhambran princess—and fell into the peace of a first sleep, in the happy knowledge that every breath drew her closer to her new world.

Also available from Vintage Contemporari

. . . .

Where I'm Calling From
by Raymond Carver

The summation of a triumphant career from "one of the great short story writers of our time—of any time" *(Philadelphia Inquirer)*.

0-679-72231-9/$12.00

Wildlife
by Richard Ford

Set in Great Falls, Montana, an absorbing novel of a family tested to the breaking point.

"Ford brings the early Hemingway to mind. Not many writers can survive the comparison. Ford can. *Wildlife* has a look of permanence about it." —*Newsweek*

0-679-73447-3/$9.00

Bright Lights, Big City
by Jay McInerney

Living in Manhattan as if he owned it, a young man tries to outstrip the approach of dawn with nothing but his wit, good will and controlled substances.

"A dazzling debut, smart, heartfelt, and very, very funny." —Tobias Wolff

0-394-72641-3/$9.00

Mama Day
by Gloria Naylor

This magical tale of a Georgia sea island centers around a powerful and loving matriarch who can call up lightning storms and see secrets in her dreams.

"This is a wonderful novel, full of spirit and sass and wisdom." —*Washington Post*

0-679-72181-9/$10.00

Anywhere But Here
by Mona Simpson

An extraordinary novel that is at once a portrait of a mother and daughter and a brilliant exploration of the perennial urge to keep moving.

"Mona Simpson takes on—and reinvents—many of America's essential myths... stunning." —*The New York Times*

0-679-73738-3/$11.00

. . . .